YOUNG'UN

By

HERBERT BEST

New York

THE MACMILLAN COMPANY

1944

A WARTIME BOOK

THIS COMPLETE EDITION IS PRODUCED
IN FULL COMPLIANCE WITH THE GOVERN-
MENT'S REGULATIONS FOR CONSERVING
PAPER AND OTHER ESSENTIAL MATERIALS

PRINTED IN THE UNITED STATES OF AMERICA
BY H. WOLFF, NEW YORK

YOUNG'UN

CHAPTER ONE

THE great brown oxen, rough-coated still from winter, halted in the snow-covered wheel ruts before the trading store and continued to blow four jets of steam into the cold air. Old Man Post laid long-barreled flintlock rifle, hunting bag and powderhorn across the sled. He shouldered a crackling bundle of hides and pelts and ducked beneath the lintel log to dump his load on the broad pinewood counter.

The trader, a short fat, shave-faced man, greasy down the front of his tow apron, loosed the rawhide tie, and spread out the stiff pelts. Grunting disparagingly, he swept a good half of them aside.

Zeph Post looked on, angered but helpless. It hadn't always been this-a-way, being treated like an Injun. Time was when Zeph Post knowed the best trapping grounds from the Falls right up to Canady. And time was when folks knowed he knowed. Clear on down to Albany, most anywhere he cared to turn in, there had been a bottle and a "Help-yourself-Zeph." It had been "How's Injuns up your way, Zeph?" and "Still wearing your scalp I see, same's ever!" And folks wanting first pick of his fine pelts, and mighty glad to pay, even in hard money.

Old Man Post made another trip to the sled and came back with a sewn birch-bark drum of maple sugar. The trader put his nose to the contents, prodded with his finger. "Soft as mush. Liable to sour on me."

Couldn't help but be soft, sugaring off early and hasty so's to catch the last snow to ease the sled runners. But 'twasn't nowise liable to sour. Or not more 'n any other.

Old Man Post bowed his head to the low lintel and returned with two loads of potash. What with felling and burning and washing out the ash and boiling off the water, and cutting more wood for the boiling, it had cost a deal of labor. And splitting and shaping the staves and coopering the kegs had taken more time than running a line of traps.

The trader drove in the top of a keg, and ran some of the potash between his fingers. "It's dirty, see?" he challenged. "How often I got to tell you settlers to keep the smoke out of your boiling? Ain't no sale for this stuff, hardly."

Then in more kindly tones, "Come for your spring vittlin'? Help yourself." And raised a flap in the counter for the old man to come behind.

Old Man Post rumbled behind his beard like a dog afraid to bark outright. Settler! He wa'n't no settler. Course he'd bided overlong in one camp, what with having a poorly wife and raising young'uns. But just as soon as they could fend for themselves, Zeph Post would be quit of ploughing and hoeing and . . . and sugaring and ashing for fat-bellied traders. Most any day now. Eldest was sixteen and Dan'l and Young'un wa'n't so far behind. *Settler!* Why, he'd scouted through this land, trapped and hunted over it, kept tight aholt of his scalp, seen these very Falls before there'd been a sawmill on the river or a fat-bellied trader in the whole countryside.

He looked over the contents of the sawn lumber shelving, scarce heeding the prices the trader called out for the better pelts, or the squeak of his slate pencil. The Posts would need to go careful on their victualing this year. Credit on pelts and deer hides and sugar and potash wouldn't stretch far, the way the trader had mispriced them. But salt he must have; the old kind that would stand the damp of the hill clouds, not the newfangled stuff all ground to a flour. He rolled a keg towards the door. A few nails would be mighty handy to save boring and pegging. And a new earthenware crock to take the place of the one Ma had broke last time she was took with her falling spells. Seemed like she was took more frequent these last seasons. Then two flints for the rifle, seeing he owed Gunsmith back home at Cold Brook.

He had to pass by a canister of best Edinburgh powder and content himself with a cheaper kind. A few yards of bright patterned

2

store cloth to put Ma in good heart again, though it'd be mighty costly. Two-three of the new steel traps that would earn their price in a season. And a loaf of sugar would be kind of nice after naught but tree-sugar, and souring at that, all winter.

But the trader caught his eye. "No sugar. And hang those traps back on the peg. Don't know as I'd ought to let you take all the rest that's here either."

That was the way things were, these days. But he'd have himself a couple shots of hard liquor from the pelt he'd held out; more than a couple, though there'd be the feed for the oxen to come out of the pelt too.

If it took courage to draw down to the Falls to trade and be cheated, it took the same to start on the slow haul home with only the half of what was needed. Old Man Post paced stride by slow stride ahead of his lumbering oxen, wondering what he'd done wrong. For a whiles he'd traded with a neighbor, Sim Higgins, who claimed that with his horse-team and wagon he could draw further south and sell dearer and buy cheaper than at the Falls. But it hadn't seemed to work out that-a-way, and now he owed Sim too much to trade with him any longer.

'Twas relief to draw uphill from the river and all those houses. To hear the chaw-chawing of the big gang saws still to no more than the grunting of wild beasts.

* * *

A day later he'd drawn back as far as Fort Ann. The Fort little now but rotted wooden ruins, but the settlement of a handful of wooden houses prospering, with farms strung out north and south along the road. A coach overtook him, spattering him with churned-up mud and snow. The coach drew up to change horses, then overtook him again, with more splatterings. Zeph Post could mind the time there had been no coach and no road. He could recall the soldiers building the first stockade. And back of that when the place was no more than swamp and forest at the northern end of the Long Portage. Just a natural trail between the Hudson River, in the south, where Fort Edward stood now, and this Wood Creek here, running into Lake Champlain. Mighty dangerous the portage was, those days, a loaded man being forced to keep to the easy trail, and being in no shape to defend himself. And now there were coaches with blue-coated officers bound for Whitehall and their military posts up north, and city folk in broadcloth with females in ribbons and laces. Seemed like the tide had swept on, and left Zeph Post stranded.

Reluctantly the oxen swung off to the rougher road leading to Cold Brook and the hills. Zeph Post had seen no sense to wasting part of the pelt's price on feed instead of liquor. An old hunter didn't need to fill his belly three times a day every day like other folks. But oxen were like settlers in more ways than one. So he'd need to lead on even slower than usual to ease the beasts. Dan'l would look sullen angered if Peter 'n' Paul reached home all tuckered out, and Young'un would cast her arms about their necks like she was going to weep. They'd more feeling for dumb beasts than they had for their own pa, seemed as if.

Fast, with oxen, meant almighty slow, and slow meant shuffling along the pace of an old squaw under a berry basket. He'd ought to've learned the oxen to Gee and Haw to his voice, so he could bestride the sled and crack a long blacksnake whip. But with Young'un to walk ahead up and down the furrows, he'd never gotten around to it. He'd admit, right now, to a sight of things he'd ought to've done and hadn't. But doing what he hadn't ought to've done had caused the most harm. That and staying on in this countryside, like a trout in a pool when the summer drought sucks the water from the streams.

He averted his eyes from the pile of bark, sawdust and trimmings beside the road, and picked a way for the oxen through and around the ice and mud in the hollow. There wasn't enough water coming down from the hills yet for the mill to be turning, or the hatches would be drawn, and he'd have been forced by the water to draw out and around a good quarter mile. He had led the soldiers here to the little island so they could post a picket. Then 'twas a fort, the soldiers scaring and shooting all the game for miles around. And now for years a sawmill.

It was like that all around. The Wings with their Queensbury Grant settling what was now the Falls; the settlers at Kingsbury where he'd stopped over for the night; and Major Skene who fought well against the French and redskins but turned Tory later, starting

4

his grant over by the Lake. They called it Whitehall now, not Skenesborough, and Major Skene had been drove out to Canady; but the settlers had stayed on.

A man that wasn't a settler, nor minded to be one, should have took warning. But Zeph Post had waited on, and fit agin Burgoyne and his men all the way from Wood Creek to Saratogy. It was after the victory there, his mouth still ringed black from blowing down the muzzle of his rifle, that he'd looked up and seed a thin pale slip of a girl most like Eldest was now. Being in his right senses he'd lit out and put fifty miles south of him before he'd stopped for as much as a drink of water from a stream.

Next thaw-out he was back again, with his pelts, breaking his fool neck to find her. Afraid to ask, and not so much as knowing her name. And there she was, throwing corn to her Auntie's hens, and no more than spitting distance from where he'd first laid eyes upon her. He used more talk on her than would serve a hunter a full year, but it hadn't availed. She wouldn't look at the best of his pelts, nor consent to run thumbnail along it, nor hear talk of a Preacher, without he took land and settled himself.

Her talk of settling scared the sense back into him just in time. That night he pulled a trader out in his bare skin, excepting for his nightcap that looked mighty comical, and made him write down credit for the pelts. It wasn't till he was two days north, and breathing free again, that his shoulders felt kind of light, and he remembered he'd brought back no more stores than he took down. He made out all right, despite; Zeph Post could always make out in the north woods.

Five years later he'd trailed south again. And there she was, still awaiting him, knowing right well he'd come. And he knowed he was beat. They'd made shift around Saratogy for the best part of a year, then he remembered the ledge up overlooking Champlain Lake, where he'd scouted General Burgoyne's boats down below the cliff and the French before that. To suit Ma's scairt notions he could call it a farm, roll up a cabin; and trap and shoot for all their needs. But from the first, Ma had seen different. One year 'twas clearing and breaking sod for a garden patch. Next year 'twas the same, only for a corn patch. Then Ma taking poorly. What pelts he'd got he'd

5

had to trade for a cow for fresh milk. That called for a lean-to barn, and more clearing for pasture, and cutting and haying for winter feed, and hoeing more corn. 'Twas Ma's own hard money she'd treasured that went to buy a plough team. Looked like it would be a saving, but the two horses meant more clearing for more pasture, more ploughing, and more feed to set by for the long winter. And stopping home to feed and to melt ice and snow to water them, when he'd ought to've been laying his trap lines and hunting.

Then Eldest was born and Ma stayed poorly quite a whiles. And Dan'l and Young'un followed in the years, and Ma took worse with her falling spells. And the team was too old to work, being old from the start off. The Posts was nigh to've starved, digging and hoeing for a season, till they altered two young bull calves and had them broke to pulling. And there was Zeph Post, still caught by the paws in a trap, without the courage to break loose account of the way it would pain.

*   *   *

Long slender rifle on his left arm, he shuffled ahead of the plodding oxen, the light-loaded sled sliding easily on its thick oak runners, save when it jerked down into a frozen wheel-rut. Wheel-ruts right here in Welsh Hollow. Showed what things was coming to. And clearings beginning to stretch right across the width of this rich bottom land. Forest of thick pine and bare gray beech would begin to close in comfortingly on the track for eighty rod or so. Then another white snow-covered clearing and another cabin and log-built barn, the ground trampled dark by cattle. A man hadn't room to think, not with so many folks crowding him in.

Three hours, with yoke and pole and sled creaking behind him to the slow nodding of the oxen. A steep downward slope where he stopped to cut a stake and lash it sprag-fashion to the runners, so that the sled should not over-run the oxen. The bare gray granite face of High Rock overhanging the trail on the right, and on the left, trashy short-needle pine and more rocks. Ahead a swamp, hard frozen. Here were no cabins, no clearings; the tightness lifted from about the man's head, he could think again.

There had come to be more folks than the country could hold, he could see that now. So, 'stead of being able to live on what the

Good Lord had provided in lake and stream and forest, they had to fell, and draw rocks, burn and wash potash, to plough and everlastingly to hoe.

'Twarn't the first time it had happened, neither. The Book told how Adam had lived in a countryside mighty like these woods had been with their deer and bear and squirrel and coon for meat, and nuts and acorns and beechmast for bread if a man was so inclined. And fish so many you could noose them with a rawhide string, and roots if you was sick and knowed which was the cure.

Adam had sinned and been throwed out to dig and toil just like any settler. Zeph Post couldn't call to mind where he'd angered the Lord. Not for certain sure. Like as not 'twas that time he shot the Injun squaw through the rump as she bent to wash. He'd thought 'twas a deer in the failing light as his rifle swung up. But afore he pressed the trigger he'd suspicioned otherwise. She'd pitched into the Lake and not come up again. Maybe 'twas that. Or again maybe 'twas his leaving the bound girl at Albany, knowing she was in the family way. But he'd been mighty young at the time, so 'twa'n't right the Lord should hold it agin him so, keeping him to delving and toiling.

A wolf paused at the margin of the woods, one foreleg crooked like a dog's, but faded from sight before Old Man Post could step aside from the path of the oxen and raise his rifle. A good ten rod away, and not worth the waste of powder and ball for a poor spring pelt. Like to be the last wolf of the season, and maybe crippled or old, waiting for easy meat. The most of them would be trailing north, and folks would be loosing their geese and hens most any day now.

The hog wallow in the track just south of Cold Brook settlement felt solid to moccasins and gun butt, the heavy oxen toiled across with scarce a splaying of their hoofs. A scraping rumble as the sled runners drew across a rough wooden bridge over the frozen brook. Voices and a smell of cooking from the tavern on the right. Old Man Post's stomach gave a squirm, but he averted his eyes. A'ready he'd chalked up back of the ordinary door more than he could pay. On the left Gunsmith's shop with its waterwheel to turn the heavy stone for grinding gun barrels. The wheel was frozen still, and the light tapping on the anvil sounded like Gam Reed was forging lock parts.

7

Old Man Post smoothed a finger along his firearm. It was a Gam Reed gun, and they didn't come any better. He'd admire to have it all paid for before time came to take it back for reboring and to have the rifling drawn out fresh. But it still threw mighty sure.

Four-five more houses, the older ones rolled up of popple logs, the newer ones faced with sawn lumber drawn up from Kane's saw-mill outside Fort Ann. Most every one had a barn behind, a farrowing pen for the old sow, and suchlike. Zigzag fences of split rail bordered the rutted road, and back of that, reaching up to the bare trees of the hillside woodlots, tree roots had been drawn into line fences, or walls had been built of field stone, according which was the nearest to hand, roots or stone, and most cumbered the ploughlands.

Old Man Post turned from the spectacle and began the slow creaking haul up a winding hill. Folks had no call to huddle together like a litter of hairless mice. There was land enough for all at the start off, and still was land if folks would go find it. Far enough off so there was no need to fence so much as a rod. No call to huddle.

Over the brow of the hill the climb eased off. Two more farms. Maybe it all come of shooting off the redskins and making the country woman-safe. Men and their women would keep a-coming and keep a-coming now, with nothing to hinder them. Civilization had given the white man powder and ball, and the surest shooting rifle the world would ever know, and axes and good skinning knives. But Civilization hadn't stopped there, it had gone on and was still going on, undoing all the good it had done by taking away the land which the rifle had won from the Injuns, the French, and the British, and giving it over to settlers. To huddling settlers. Redskins, he could see it now, had done no harm. They'd knowed what the land was rightly for.

An icebound ford across a smaller stream. Then, leaving the rutted trail, a haul inch by inch up ice-crusted treacherous rock face. At the top he halted while the oxen blew their four jets of steaming breath into the chill air, their sides sucking in and blowing out like the bellows of Gunsmith's forge.

Below, the summer's water all stood white and silent. Under the gray sky not a bird nor beast broke the snowbound peace of the hills. From here Old Man Post could see across the top of the

8

T-shaped valley, over Cold Brook hidden in the hollow, to High Rock and far beyond, without setting sight on fence or clearing or house. No trace of humankind except his own sled tracks of four days ago, coming out of the black tunnel in the hemlocks; a tunnel he had cut for himself nigh on twenty year back. Another hundred rod and he'd be through the woods and into his own clearing. He shuffled on, the oxen following.

But on the verge of his cleared land a faint troubling odor hung between the bare gray trunks of the beech trees. His stride lengthened. He thumbed back the flint of his rifle, finger on trigger to deaden the click of cocking. Though the creak of yoke and sled behind would deaden it.

Stale woodsmoke and something beside. Like when he and another of Rogers' Rangers had come too late to warn a homestead. The Injuns had come and gone, but . . . But there were no Injuns now.

A stretch of white snow, with a black hole in its whiteness. Not clear black, as Old Man Post strode nearer, but gray in the middle where the cabin and barn had stood end to end. Gray ashes, a black ring where fire had melted the snow, then white.

* * *

He just stood, did Old Man Post, till the oxen came up with him and halted. And nudged him forward a pace to say they was ready to be unyoked, watered and fed. Old Man Post just stumbled forward and stood again, looking.

He must have thought the young'uns was gone too. Till they came out, still frighted, from the forest. Old Man Post questioned Eldest, but she couldn't do aught but weep. And the little girl just held tight ahold of him awhile and said nothing. The boy Dan'l, stocky and kind of sullen in his grief, told what little there was to tell.

As soon as their pa had drawn out of sight, four days agone, Ma had taken with one of her spells, crying and angry both to once. And drove the children out from underfoot. So the three young'uns took the handaxe to cut a hole in the ice of the lake, and went·a-fishing. Before first dusk they had scrambled back up the trail, hoping their ma might be a mite better. Seeing a glow, they hurried. But when they came out from among the trees there was little left but embers.

They had huddled together, there in the last of the chilly sunset, asking one another what had happened, and what were they going to do now. Before it grew too dark Dan'l cut them a shelter of hemlock boughs for windbreak, and another pile for bed. Eldest drew an ember from the ashes, kindled herself a fire in front of the windbreak, and broiled a mess of fish.

Eldest had wanted Young'un to run for a neighbor. But Dan'l said there was naught ary neighbor could do now, so they'd best wait for their pa.

That was all Dan'l had to tell of the happening; except that of course they kept the fire going back there in the woods in front of their windbreak, and they'd visited the trap line and emptied the sap buckets like their pa had said to do. Sap wa'n't running too good.

Old Man Post listened to his son, but didn't say aught. Just unslung his powder horn and hunting bag like they had grown too heavy for his shoulders, and hung them over the muzzle of his rifle. He made as if to unyoke the oxen. But their stall had been in the barn, and there was no house, no barn, no lean-to asher, no stall. Nothing.

Old Man Post just stood, like he didn't know what to do. He said to the little girl, "No call to bite your fingernails, Young'un," and she smiled up at him, because for once she hadn't been biting them. He looked almighty tired, more shrunk in on himself than ever, his beard grizzled and yellow against the whiter snow. He stood for a middling while, not taking his eyes off the ashes that had been his wife and home.

Then he sighed, slung on his bag and horn again, shifted the rifle to the crook of his left arm, and turned about. Dan'l made to follow. But his pa said, "Stay there, son."

And Old Man Post just walked off northward into the forest.

CHAPTER TWO

EVEN small fish weigh a-plenty if there's plenty of 'em. Eph Birdsell, spread-eagled across the face of a steep slope overhanging Lake Champlain, knew it for a fact. He dug one moccasined toe between two rocks that felt as though they might stay put, twisted the other foot back of an exposed root, dug his knife into the soft thawing soil above, and so set free one hand to reach down and haul up his strings of fish.

He hadn't calculated on the bright spring sun sucking the frost out of the ground this-a-way. The fresh smell of earth beneath his nose, the drip-drip of water and musical gurgle of a stream did not concern him so much as a sapling cedar which drew out by the root almost before he set hand to it. He should have walked around by the old deer trail, he told himself. The cedar dislodged a rock big as his head, which rolled past his shoulder, bounced once or twice on the way down, and plunged through the ice floe a good hundred and fifty feet below.

But another complicated spiderlike movement brought him to the top. After a short crawl he was free to stand upright, to wriggle his aching toes and fingers, and brush dirt from his short silky beard and the collar of his patched deerskin shirt. Come to think of it, he hadn't ought to've chanced a broken leg or neck, not while the cow was so near to calving and still penned up for the winter. Might be a week or more before a neighbor passed that way and heard her bawl for water.

Still and all it was good to stretch and look across the headwater of the lake and the deep wooded valley, to the dark pine-covered hills opposite. And to feel that it still lay in you to finish whate'er you set hand to; even if 'twas no more than a climb that you'd no call to've started. And then to force your way through a belt of trees and undergrowth to pass judgment on a farm that opened to view.

Scarce a rod of sound fencing, though 'twould have taken Old Man Post no more than a morning's hewing and splitting to have his haystacks railed off. Come a hard winter and the deer would fatten and his own beasts starve. It would have saved him labor to draw the hay up nearer the house and make one good stack, instead of those small piles moldering here and there about the pasture.

Striding up the gentle slope Eph could see more things amiss. It seemed like Old Man Post had only cleared where the trees were smallest and easiest cut, and that meant where the soil was poor and least worth the labor. And it didn't look like he'd pulled a stump in all these years, but just ploughed around. Old Man Post had no ambition, no ambition a-tall.

A narrow strip of fall ploughing was greasy underfoot with the heat of the sun, but still hard froze beneath. A wooden plough, broken and left to rot in a furrow, showed further shiftlessness that was angering to a good farmer. For it should have been drawn home to be patched during the long winter.

Still and all, Eph reproved himself, when a man was a next-neighbor you'd no call to pass judgment on his shortcomings. It would be more fitten to leave the old man a mess of fish, and in such way that he wouldn't take offence.

The upper pasture was still brown with winter. If it was Eph's he'd take and burn it over, soon as 'twas dried out. And what he would set thought and hand to, first and last, would be the saving of steps. All winter Old Man Post drew water from the upper spring for his family and the three beasts, and when the spring froze he had to chip out ice and carry it in to thaw. Now if the farm was Eph's, he'd set right to, and dig him a well in that likely hollow he could remember, near the house. Deep enough so that there'd be no freezing up, and scarce five rod from the beasts' stalls.

He'd dig him a well he would, right there, and line it with good field stone, and steyn a three-foot curbing around the top, account of the young'uns. A few more paces, over the brow of the upper pasture, and his eyes would light on the very spot. The northern limit of the clearing came into view. The tall trees on the little spur that

protected the building from the cold western winds. But no house.
No building.

Eph broke into a run, the string of fish flapping against his side.

*   *   *

An end of rawhide string, that had been a washing line, still
hung from a scorched butternut sapling Old Man Post had planted
handy to the kitchen door, but which had never prospered to give
shade or nuts. All that the other end of the string had once been
tied to was now an uneven pile of ashes. Foot marks, small ones, led
in among the flaky grayness. Maybe a next-neighbor could still help.

Eph let out a yell. "Zeph Post! Zeph Post! Anyone to home?"
Though of course there was no home left for Old Man Post to be to.

Dan'l Post came out of the bare woods so silent-like he might
have been his own ghost. But he was carrying a thin wooden pelt-
stretcher, and was working wood ash into a squirrel skin with the
back of a knife. Ghosts wa'n't like to cure squirrel pelts, and there'd
been the tracks in the ashes besides. Back of Dan'l, Eph could see
now, was a kind of shelter and what looked to be Eldest and Young'un
among the tree trunks. And at one end of the small shelter, sure
enough, the brown rumps of the two oxen. 'Twas God's Mercy. Best
yoke in the whole countryside.

"Ma's dead. Burned. And three hens and the old rooster," Dan'l
summed up the tragedy. "Pa's gone."

Eph separated two of his four strings of fish and hung them to
a tree. He'd a right to do that, being next-neighbor. Not that the
young'uns looked to lack for food. There were small skewerfuls of
meat, maybe squirrel, drying over a slow fire, and Eldest sitting on
the sled was opening and cleaning fish for smoking or salting. Hurrying her hands on account the thaw.

He'd be a figure of fun down in the Settlement, and Phebe Callender would come nigh to taunting his ears off with talk of a young
cockerel that thought he was a broody-hen. But he'd make the offer:

"I'd take it neighborly if you was to come under my roof till your
Pa's back and raises him another house."

But Dan'l, who was mighty sensible for his age, said no. "Pa didn't
. . . don't hold with taking help, Eph. Pa'll be back afore fall. We
c'n make out someways."

Eldest kind of nodded, without so much as glancing up from her task, to show she agreed with Dan'l. Young'un, Viney was her real name, hooked down Eph's two strings of fish with a crotched stick, being too short to reach. She didn't speak her thanks, but her eyes wrinkled a mite at the corners, and her mouth turned up like ox horns. Eph turned away feeling right noble to have made the child happy that-a-way and with no more than a string or two of fish.

That put him in mind of what he'd do with the rest of his catch. The thaw looked to have set in, and fish wouldn't keep. As he strode along the trail he wondered if there was anyone in need on account of death or sickness, but couldn't call any to mind. Next best was to give the fish to Gam Reed, the gunsmith. He was mighty indebted to Aunt Mary and Uncle Gam for one thing and another, ever since he was little. But Aunt Mary would chaw his head off if he said so. He never knowed whether he was really scairt of her, a little white-haired woman like that, or only making believe, to rile her. But he'd leave the fish in Gunsmith's shop, so Uncle Gam could carry them in.

Eph swung down from the Posts' sled trail through the hemlock grove, over the steep rock face, and onto the rutted road. Swung off to his barn to see Molly had fresh water, and wasn't in need of aught else. And dropped down the hill to the settlement of Cold Brook.

* * *

One of the two big doors of Gunsmith's forge was propped open for the first time this year. Inside, Gam Reed was bending his white beard over the bench, shaping-up bullet molds. Cicero Ditch had perched himself on an upturned keg, his short legs in their knitted stockings and cobbled shoes scarce reaching the ground, his hands folded in his tavern-keeper's apron, for he was always one to feel the chill. Cicero was explaining his idea why a twist-bored barrel just naturally had to throw straighter than a straight-cut. There were others: Sol Broadmoor, blocking up half one side of the room with his bulk; Sim Higgins, small as Cicero and bandy-legged beside, shuffling his feet and nigh to doing a dance, impatient for Cicero to get finished so he could explain better. After that they would both appeal to Sol, and Sol would ask Gunsmith, and Gunsmith would say he didn't hardly cal'late to know the why of it.

14

The argument wasn't new, but had been said over and over all winter, and most winters before. Eph didn't wait for it to finish. He handed a string of fish to Sol Broadmoor's young'un and said to carry it in to Mis' Reed. Then told his news.

Nobody wanted to break in on that tale. There'd been naught happen all winter long, and even Sim Higgins stopped shuffling his feet, slewed his head sideways, and tried to get the whole of the happenings, so he could tell it again down to Fort Ann.

"I cal'late maybe 'twas the wood chimney, and a dry lug-pole to set it off." Eph tried to account for the happening. "Old Man Post never got around to tearing down the old chimney and setting up one of clay and field stone, like he ought."

He left them debating if might be 'twas the falling sickness was responsible for the fire and for Mis' Post not getting out to loose the hens and rooster. Next they'd be on to why Old Man Post had lit out, and when he'd be back, and shouldn't maybe something be done for the young'uns. They'd have it all turned this way and that before they went home to their dinners.

Just across the way was the Tavern, and in the Tavern was Phebe Callender, hired girl. Only two days back Phebe had nigh to've chewed his ear off, account of his saying something about Albany, the town she was reared at, and told him to get from under foot in the kitchen, the same as if he was Mis' Ditch's old black spaniel dog. Or worse. He'd tell her how he come clost to having him a family only this morning, the eldest sixteen, old as Phebe herself mighty near. She wasn't like to believe him at first. But he'd tell it so she'd laugh, and 'twas a laugh clear as a distant sheep bell, and worth the trouble of drawing out. Her laugh over, she'd see him for what he was, a man who could afford a wife and a family both. So she'd have her mind made up when he got around to asking her. He wa'n't minded to ask her and be refused. Not when he'd got a tidy little farm, and folks willing to buy the chairs he made, right down to Fort Ann and beyond. Nossir!

He swung round by the stable yard, avoiding the ordinary and those who might be there, and came in by the kitchen. And there was Hepziba Ditch, busied with a bowl and a stirring spoon.

"Cicero's across at the Forge, as always. Times I feel like a widow woman." Her hands didn't slow their mixing, but her eyes caught Eph's. "Times I wish I was."

"Seed him there." Hepziba made him talk short and gruff, never knowing what she had in mind, or hoping what she said was just her way of talk. And he wasn't the only one. Even when, like now, she wasn't wearing her silk, her clothes sot so close they looked to be her own pelt, and set you to wondering where you'd start to skin her. "Seed him there." Not having aught else to say he said it again.

"And Phebe's taken her shawl to run down to Sol Broadmoor's to get the loan of a dozen eggs. You must have seen her." Hepziba's eyes took on a smile. "Nobody to home but me."

Hepziba Ditch's words was worse than the clothes she made pretence to cover herself with. There was too much you could guess at, or thought you could. Some folk said that was the way folk talked and dressed in the cities, though the worst that even the women could tell of Hepziba was that 'twas mighty strange the way coach folks stopped off at Cicero's little tavern, when they could have drove on to Fort Edward and been real comfortable. If her lips wa'n't so red, and didn't part that way, half smiling . . . Eph felt he'd got to say something.

"Just dropped in, Ma'am, to see could I skin . . . could I leave these fish. For Cicero," he amended hastily. "Tell Phebe old Mis' Post is burned to the ground, and the hens and rooster. And . . . I got chores, Ma'am, and I'd best get along."

He was out in the yard before he remembered he'd kept no fish for himself; and up the road a good ways before he recollected he'd spoke of old Mis' Post being burned to the ground, which wa'n't quite the sense of it. But he was sure glad to get clear of that talk of skinning and what it might have led him to say. Phebe claimed there was no harm to Hepziba Ditch. Maybe no harm, but a sight of flusteration.

* * *

That noontide there was a deal of talk in the settlement and beyond. Mouths that hadn't opened at table for a twelvemonth save to let in knife or spoon, must have busied themselves with more than just victuals. Widow Wilson came running to the Tavern, and was surprised to learn that the Post young'uns were still alive, and

Grandma Truttle brought along old Killsure, her rifle, to fight off the Injuns. By the time they had the rifle away from her, and got her quieted down, there must have been a round dozen, including children, who had stopped on their way up to the Post place.

Sol Broadmoor was the last to arrive at the Tavern. He drove up with his team and a wagon, ready to draw down any bodies for burying, if the need was. He was mighty strong, and always willing to help those in need, but not as quick in the mind as some. When they explained to him again there was no corpse he left his soap and razors across at Gunsmith's, and offered to draw up any children and women that was minded his way.

Not wanting to be outdone, Hepziba called to Black Sam to hitch in and bring the light wagon. Those that didn't fit in to sleds and wagons set off cross-lots down through Mosquito Hollow.

By rights, those on foot should have got there first, but the boys and dogs treed a coon, and the men with rifles followed a bear trail a ways till they lost it. When they arrived at the Post place, Hepziba Ditch and her wagonful were standing around the ashes, and Sol was just drawing out of the woods, having made his women passengers walk most of the way. Sol was right careful of his team, and of all dumb animals. But women was different to his way of thinking.

Eldest Post, whose name was Deborah, was saying to Mis' Ditch, "Best ask Dan'l, Ma'am. He's took aholt since Pa lit out."

Dan'l and Young'un came scrambling out of the hole in the ground that served for root cellar. They had been lifting turnips and cabbages to eke out the hay for the oxen, the two oxen watching to see they did it right. Dan'l brought along an armful of roots, and dropped them beside a chopping block. Time being food or hunger to the Posts, he rubbed the dirt off the roots with his hands as he spoke.

"You heard most all of it, Ma'am. Ma's burned. Pa's gone for a-whiles."

"It was very wrong of him." Mis' Ditch could have said nothing and said better.

Dan'l took up the axe and began to chop the roots into clean pink-yellow slices. Young'un chewed one to see 'twas fitten cattle feed, then held out slices to the oxen. Peter and Paul lipped the turnip

17

delicately, then ate. Folk took their eyes off Dan'l and Hepziba, and watched the oxen like they'd never seen oxen eat before.

The afternoon sun shone warmly on the protected northwest corner of the pasture. You could most hear the gummy popple buds bursting out on the trees, and the grass underfoot was turning from brown to green as you watched. Or seemed as if.

"We've come to take your ma," Hepziba was still aiming to do good. "So's we can give the remains a Christian burial."

Dan'l continued to chop. Then, "Ain't rightly sure which is Ma. Not yet."

The oxen seemed disposed to lumber down into the root cellar. Young'un called to them with a soft whistle. Their heads went up, and she whistled again. Gently but irresistibly they shouldered through the small crowd towards the chopping block. She fed them another slice each, for reward, and stood between them and Dan'l's axe.

Hepziba Ditch had thought of another reason. "You must let me do as I think best, Dan'l. And besides, I'm an old friend of your ma's."

"Hain't never heard tell." Dan'l wasn't angered, but telling the simple truth. They were still mazed, the three Post young'uns, not answering greetings from other young'uns, and looking right at them unseeing, as though the sorrow that compassed them was one of the hill clouds that wrapped their farm from view. Menfolk and some womenfolk looked like they wished they hadn't come.

But Grandma Truttle, who still suspicioned Injuns behind every bush, wasn't minded to leave the young'uns to be tomahawked nor captivated by the savages.

"Let Miriam Post lay, Hepziba. She'll come to no more harm. 'Tis the living we'd ought to cherish." Grandma Truttle stretched out two kindly old bird-claw hands towards Eldest. "Come bide with me, childer, and welcome. Set all ye've a mind to take on the sled, and I'll help ye yoke in. I ain't forgot how. I've a setting hen, early though 'tis in the year, and two kitty cats, and . . ."

"Nossir, Ma'am," Dan'l was firm. "Pa wouldn't hold with leaving the land to go back to sumac and popple. Thank ye, Mis' Truttle. No."

What had set Grandma Truttle in mind of her cats was the Post cat, that a dog had chased up a tree. Now the dog caught wind of the fish drying beside the shelter. Eldest called warning, Young'un lifted a stunted turnip in her left hand. The crowd shifted weight to its left feet, to a man, to the smallest small boy. Viney let fly, caught the dog neatly in the ribs. The dog yelped with surprise and made off. The crowd breathed, "Ah," and settled back onto both feet.

By now the men were for taking Dan'l's answer as right and reasonable. They'd made note of the hay and roots and cabbages and potatoes, and there was the fish and what Dan'l trapped. Some day soon Old Man Post would come back, or the young'uns tire of toil and loneliness; one or other, small matter which. Sol Broadmoor swung his team and wagon, and some boys and men went along after, up the trail through the woods.

But the womenfolk stayed on. Womenfolk fight hardest when, if they was menfolk, they'd know they was licked. Widow Wilson had her an idea, an idea which wasn't rightly charity, unless to herself. Having buried her husband less'n a year after she got him, she'd been put to a sight of scheming the last seven years. A woman with a man has got two chances to be right, hers and his; and a man to blame when she's wrong. But a lone widow woman is like she's got only one foot to stand on and has to be careful where she sets it down.

Widow Wilson picked her way through the mud that folks had churned up out the soft-thawed meadow, and laid a hand on Eldest's arm. Then she made a "Teehee" noise to tell folks what she was going to say was comic-like and they weren't to take offence. She'd used it a lot of late, that sound, as her tongue got sharper. A misspent kindness like showing a pig the sticking-knife and making believe 'twould be all in play.

"Now, Deborah dear, there's no call to feel you'll be beholden if you come with me, teehee. You'll earn your keep, I'll warrant."

Yes, a girl going on seventeen as Eldest was, good and strong and willing, would be worth the little she'd eat, and a new dress each springtide. Couldn't be the Posts were used to eating much either, the way their pa had raised them. Looked to be a good thing for Widow Wilson, for the next two-three year maybe.

"But if Hepziba wants you to help around the Tavern,"—it wouldn't serve for the Widow to tangle traces with Taverner's wife, seeing she lent a hand, times, at the Tavern,—"why, I'll take Viney and teach her cooking and needlework. And Dan'l shall do my chores to even."

The young'uns, scairt at the thought of being parted, drew closer together for company. Dan'l stopped chopping, and said, polite but firm, "I got me my own chores, Ma'am."

Hepziba Ditch tried to take Eldest's hand, with a "Come, Deborah dear, we must go." But Eldest slipped 'twixt the two oxen.

Widow Wilson made a grab for Viney, but Viney stepped behind Dan'l. Dan'l, small for his age but square-set, was kind of weighing the axe·in his hand. Hepziba and the Widow drew back right smart.

Hepziba called to Cicero to take the axe away from Dan'l because boys that age was liable to cut theirselves. Cicero didn't seem to hear. And what other men were left started off down the hill talking loudly so they shouldn't hear.

Hepziba stamped her foot. Cicero just stood there, holding the horses' heads and smiling. A dog went to sniffing among the ashes. Dan'l, his knuckles white on the axe-helve, was saying over and over, "Pa said to stay. Pa said to stay."

Something was all set to happen, the size of it. Viney took a glance at the dog, who was maybe looking for part of her ma, and lifted a turnip. Maybe she didn't take aim, or maybe she did. That turnip came as near to flattening Mis' Ditch's nose as hide comes to flesh. Before the next throw caught the dog square on the rump, Hepziba and the Widow were climbing the wheels of the wagon, and calling to Cicero to whip up.

Cicero waited for others to climb in the back, then led around up the slope. His wife and the Widow had their legs covered again, and were talking about "ungrateful children" before he swung up to the driving seat and took up the reins.

Cicero could hold to a joke the way some horses hold to a pill long after you think 'tis swallowed and gone. And it ain't always as funny as he thinks when he blows it out. But he'd got as much courage as, parceled out, would serve a whole regiment. He stopped the wagon up the trail where its nearside wheels were 'most on the edge of a fifty-foot drop. And he dropped the reins and slapped his knees, and crowed the silly way he had.

"Fair's fair, Hepzi!" He kind of yawped the words between laughs. As he slapped the reins on the horses' rumps, Mis' Ditch looked around. Dan'l was back to chopping the turnips again, as though naught had happened.

"Not a shift of clothing to their backs. Nor a tool, but the one axe. No roof against the rain nor shelter against the heat or cold. Not a mouthful of food stored up, except for the cabbages and roots." The way she spoke, it was as though each was a separate triumph for Mis' Ditch herself, to humble the ungrateful Post childer. "Two weeks at least, and they'll come running to beg a crust or a crumb. You mark my words, Jessie Wilson!"

CHAPTER THREE

IT WAS pleasant to set the forge to glowing while the morning was still gray and cold. To throw off coat, to roll up sleeves, and tie on the heavy cowskin apron with its rawhide thongs. To carry out chips and shavings that daily gathered ankle-deep beside the bench and set them to burning outside the wide open doors. To glance up the road, and down the road at the breakfast smoke still pluming up from neighbors' chimneys. Then to cast eye over the snapped trace chains, the broken wooden ploughs, and all the rest of the gear lying about the doorway inside and out, and plan what job to start the new day with.

Gamaliel Reed gave another few strokes to the big bellows while he considered. It was mostly a question of who was in the sorest need. Hebron Miller could make shift with rope or twisted rawhide instead of the chains. Sol Broadmoor ought to have made himself a new ox yoke last winter. But seeing he hadn't, he'd be able to draw no stumps until the makeshift splice he'd made in the old one was strengthened someways. Six bolts and a plate each side, forged to the curve, would answer best. Gunsmith drew a long iron rod from among the beams overhead and set an end to heat in the forge.

Twice a year he had to drop his proper trade of gunsmithing, and patch and makeshift out of plain neighborly duty. Between whiles he had to take an hour off here and a day off there for shoeing. The first Thursday in the month, and sometimes more often, the journeyman blacksmith came up from Fort Ann and borrowed the use of forge and anvil. But no sooner had he loaded his tools on sled or wagon and started back home, than most every beast in the countryside seemed to start casting old shoes, or going lame on new ones. That was the way of things; no use to complain.

Gunsmith judged the iron to be hot, and swung it from forge to anvil. Tapped it with the light hammer, rapidly as a woodpecker drumming on a hollow pine, turning it the while. Then laid it on the upturned chisel of the anvil and cut off. He thrust the bar back into the forge. The tongs seemed to have slipped into his hand without his reaching for them. With them he picked the cut-off end from the floor, and dropped it into the hole in the anvil, mushroomed out the end with another woodpecker's drumming, and as it cooled, tapped it up from its hole, catching it neatly in the air with his calloused palm, and laid it on the bench.

Without pause he reached for the bar again, started on another bolt. That was the way life ought to be, he felt. Good metal to work with, and old tools coming smoothly to hand, knowing their craft as well as the craftsman did. When the job was done you'd fixed it so a man could haul or plough and grow more food for himself and others. Or made a rifle so the childer could have meat, or be saved from wolf or bear. And earned yourself food too, and the goodwill of your neighbors, though all you'd done was to ply your craft the best you knew how. Not all folks were so lucky.

There was Preacher now. His trade was with folks, and maybe with the Lord too in a sense. Scarce through with his apprenticeship, was Preacher, and not yet able to judge which way the grain lay in people, and which ran true and which was flawed. You'd ought to be sorry for Preacher and try to help, and not get riled with him for his lack of understanding. Take last night now.

* * *

Late it was, so late that Mary and Gunsmith were sitting close in to the fire, getting the last good of it before covering it over with ashes till morning. Gunsmith, hearing a shout, had hurried out with the candle lantern. When Preacher swung off his old gray, his knees collapsed, and Gunsmith had to drop the lantern and grab him. For all his twenty-five years and six feet of gangling height he hadn't weighed more than a well-filled sack of beans.

It was due to the buryings of course. Folk who died in the winter—and old people were mighty unaccommodating that way—were kept in the lean-to asher, and then in the cellar for coldness, until the frost heaved out of the ground and graves were easier dug. Then Preacher got called in an almighty hurry, and all ways to once, till he was worn thin and fretful as a hound that's swallowed porcupine quills.

Mary had taken one look at his dark set eyes and the lank lock of hair straying down over his white clean-shaven face with the blue veins on each temple. Then peeled his wet coat off him and set him in the big chair almost atop the embers of the open fire. Before he'd a chance to say what brought him, she'd set a hot bowl of squirrel meat stew between his chilled hands, and was standing beside to see he ate it. For a little white-haired woman she could be mighty menacing.

Gunsmith went out to lead the gray round to the barn. He rubbed the caked mud off legs and belly, and fed and watered him. Then fussed over his old Congress awhile so she wouldn't be jealous and take to kicking the stall.

When he got back, Preacher was feeling strong enough to argue. 'Twas Mary's hot spiced cider he was drinking, a drink that'd 'most set a coonskin cap to stealing corn. He was saying he'd climb to the little room above and sleep on the pallet bed for the night. And insisting. But Mary wouldn't look at his lips when he spoke, and being she was stone-deaf, 'twas as good as shutting her ears.

She let him finish his talk and just told him. "You'll sleep next to Gamaliel. You'll have need of his warmth towards morning, Phineas Jones, being you're all tuckered out."

Then Mary went off with the betty-lamp swinging on its chain and casting her shadow up the steep steps. Gunsmith had a task taking off Preacher's boots and breeches and getting him to bed. What with the dark, and Mary's spiced cider, it was easiest to pick Preacher from the chair and carry him across to the bed, and then go back and ash-over the fire. There was more trouble getting into bed, to keep Preacher from climbing out. Could have been some hours later that Gunsmith felt chill. Preacher was sitting stock upright, the covers all drawn around him.

"You killed her! Then burned the house to hide your crime!" Preacher's voice was pulpit-solemn. "Zephaniah Post, I come to call you to account! The deep waters shall not hide you nor the dark woods afford you refuge."

That was mighty fine talk, Gunsmith would allow; but this time

24

of night a mite out of place. Preacher was still talking when Gunsmith set a couple of fingers in the neck of his shirt and drew him down, the covers with him.

Come this morning they had it out, Gunsmith proving that Old Man Post was innocent as Preacher himself. Then Preacher said 'twas a Christian duty to see that all was left of old Mis' Post should be brought down and buried. Gunsmith didn't see it that way. That was for the Post childer to judge, he allowed.

Over breakfast Preacher was still insisting. "You talk like a heathen, Gamaliel Reed. If you refuse your help, I will go around to your neighbors, and make the necessary arrangements." And, his long face sulky looking as a boy's, he picked his teeth and was gone.

* * *

It would have done young Phineas Jones a sight of good to be set to work in a forge for a morning, Preacher or no Preacher. To learn him patience and the real nature of things. To take him down a peg, and show him that all his windy words weren't worth so much as one blow of the bellows.

Gunsmith jerked down a thick sheet of iron from among the beams and, sight-measuring Sol Broadmoor's ox yoke, started to chisel off two side plates. He was still mighty mad with Phineas Jones when Simpkin Higgins came spraddling along, looking as though the forge, and all Cold Brook for that matter, belonged to him.

"Morning, Gam." Simpkin Higgins hitched himself on to the workbench, and began to finger the set of wood chisels hanging in their rack. "First come, first served, so I'll be obliged if you'll start and fix my shovel." One of his little bandy legs kicked out and pointed to it. "Don't cal'late I ought to pay nothing, seeing you straightened it once afore, and it ain't stayed straight."

Gunsmith punched the last of six holes in a side plate, marked the second plate with a center punch so the holes should correspond, and set the second plate on the forge. He didn't need to look at the shovel. He'd wondered already what tarnation fool had driven a loaded wagon across a light shovel, well nigh ruining it. He felt his temper rising, what with Preacher and now Simpkin telling him what he ought to do and what he oughtn't. Preacher was safe away. If Simpkin would slip out too, or at least sit there silent till Gunsmith

25

could kind of simmer himself off with work. Boring the six holes in the seasoned wood of the ox yoke would work the devil out of anyone.

"How much d'you cal'late to be paid for all this?" Simpkin swung a foot to indicate the jobs waiting on the earthen floor.

"Haunch of deer meat, half a load of hay for Congress, or the loan of a plough and team to turn my garden patch next fall, and half a dozen 'Thankee Gam's' paid right down on the nail." Gunsmith wondered if his words made sense; they'd seemed no more than sounds when they came out, his mind being set on taking Simpkin Higgins' straggly little beard between the tongs, and dropping him outside in the brook.

Simpkin cocked his head, doubting maybe. "And what pays for the iron?"

Gunsmith combed his long beard with the big gnarled fingers of his left hand. Mary had begged him not to, now his beard was white. But he had to think, and that was the easiest way to make the thoughts come. If he could think of the ledger, now, he might be able to forget Simpkin Higgins. A big leather-bound book it was, showing every smoothbore, rifle, and pistol that had ever borne the stamp, *G. Reed.* It told the exact description, the price, how it had tested out in Mary's hands, and who had ordered it made. When the bloomery over on Furnace Mountain wanted money for the iron they mined and smelted and bloomed and rough-forged under their water-driven triphammers, Mary would look through the ledger. Then she'd write two-three notes and send down by the coach, reminding folks that hadn't paid for five years or more. Mostly then they paid.

Mary would set aside as much money as was needed for victualling, and the like, and have Hank Bloodgood, the coach driver, hand the rest of the coin to someone he knowed was passing the bloomery. 'Twas right businesslike, with the big ledger and all. And that was what paid for the iron for the repairs on the floor here.

Simpkin Higgins' head tilted sideways yet more, as though he were straining to hear. Some said 'twas trying to listen to the voice of his conscience. But none claimed that Simpkin's conscience had ever spoke up so he'd heard it. Mostly it meant Simpkin was figuring on skinning somebody to a trade.

Simpkin's head came back to the normal, his heels stopped drumming. "Gam, I'm minded to let you into a secret. A secret that'll make you rich. Now what d'you say to that?"

Gam didn't say anything. He was still trying not to speak, still trying to keep his big hands on his work, and not stretch them towards Simpkin Higgins.

"What say, Gam, you and me joins partners?"

Gam didn't really hear, though it might have been Sim's words that gave him the start of an idea. Simpkin wa'n't such a bad little feller, like as not. Just plumb idle. So idle he had to cheat and trick to feed his wife and himself. Now if someone was to learn him how to work real hard, if only for part of a morning . . . Gunsmith strode over to the big doors, swung them shut with a bang, dropped the bar in its sockets.

Simpkin Higgins slid off the bench, looked hastily from housedoor to window, and back to the bar on the big double doors.

"Now, Gam, I'm only aiming to profit you. Don't seem you make as much on your guns as you'd ought to. Now if I was to handle the money end . . ."

He shrank back as Gunsmith approached. But all Gunsmith did was to place an auger in his hands. Sim turned it over this way and that, puzzled but relieved.

"The way I see it, Gam, we go fifty-fifty, for there'd be the hire of my team and wagon and my own keep as I go around selling what you make. And o' course I'll collect all that's owing to ye already, and maybe charge you less than fifty-fifty on that. I hain't exactly figured out . . ."

But Gunsmith's plan was of the present, not the distant future. His hand closed over Simpkin's collar, urged the man not gently across to Sol Broadmoor's ox yoke, pressed him down to his knees so he could see the six punch marks where holes had to be drilled for the bolts.

Sim set the auger point to the first mark, and began to turn. Likely it seemed the safest thing to do for the moment.

Simpkin Higgins might be able to talk without working, but it didn't seem he could work without talking. Even though the pod-auger began to take hold and to turn with greater difficulty. The first hole brought the sweat to his face, and the start of a blister, but still he talked on.

He drew a sad picture of himself out on the roads in heat and cold while Gunsmith stayed comfortably at his forge; and offered to take only forty cents on the dollar, for a start off. He said he'd take only thirty, though he and his wife and team would be like to starve. Maybe 'twas the blisters making him sorry for himself, but there was a shake to his voice when he offered to take only twenty. And still Gunsmith said nothing, didn't so much as change the beat of his hammer, or the swing of iron from forge to anvil and back again.

Then Simpkin Higgins made his mistake. Guns would sell better with false graining added, and more brass-work ornament on the stock, he suggested. And what extra work went into that could be saved on locks and barrels. Just so long as a barrel didn't burst before 'twas paid for.

Gunsmith's hammer missed a beat.

Maybe, Sim suggested, Gunsmith made his locks and barrels too good. Once they were sold there was scarce enough profit on their repair.

Gunsmith ruined a good bolt, struck it flatter than a mouse beneath a wagon wheel, and flung the hammer from him. Three strides and he plucked the bar from the doorway, kicked open the doors. Sim shot under his arm, and was out on the road before the hinges had ceased to creak. Maybe 'twas as well. Sim could not see, and 'twa'n't a thing you could rightly explain, what good workmanship meant to a craftsman. A gunsmith now, he had to cherish his reputation same as a girl, almost. Maybe more so, seeing that what a girl had to mind wasn't spread out all the way from Albany to Ticonderoga.

Gunsmith took a last glance at Simpkin, spraddling away down the road on his bandy legs as though a swarm of Cicero's bees had lit on him, and went back to his forge. Anger had left him. He felt peaceful and purged like after a blood-letting. Shamefacedly he picked up the flattened bolt and set it back in the forge. While it heated he went out into the road to recover the auger from where Simpkin had dropped it, and came back and lifted the yoke onto the bench. Why, the poor little feller hadn't knowed how to bore a straight hole in wood, and he'd wanted to go partners! Gunsmith touched up the edge of the auger with a file. Why, Sim wasn't even fit to be a 'prentice!

* * *

Simpkin's botched work was made good, and the yoke plated and bolted so 'twould last for another season, when Preacher came plunging in. He was so angry-looking that Gunsmith was glad for a beard to hide his chuckle.

"You talk like a heathen, Gamaliel Reed." The end of his breakfast-table argument came bursting out long after, like a hangfire from damp powder. "Mind you, I don't blame this boy, Daniel, so much as his neighbors, who should know better."

Plain to see that Preacher had got nowhere in his talk with Cicero and Sol and Eph Birdsell and the rest.

"But I shall insist, yes, insist, that his mother's remains be taken up and interred in a suitable spot, with proper Christian rites." Preacher pointed a lean pulpit forefinger. "And that you come with me and help."

Saying naught, Gunsmith hung up his apron, raked ash over the forge, and reached down coat and old coonskin cap. Maybe he could help, at that. Preacher wa'n't in no state of mind to be let go alone. Gunsmith opened a drawer in the workbench and took out a powder horn. Spit new it was, so it would serve for what he had in mind. He slung it on his shoulder and led the way across the road and down through the Tavern yard.

Cold Brook still roared with the wet draining out of the thawed ground. But the smell of earth, the budding of trees and the freshening green of those pasture lands which lay along a southern slope, all showed that winter was taking a running leap into summer.

Often as not it happened that way, up in these hills. Then all the way to harvest, a man would find himself one jump behind, ploughing when he should be sowing, dragging when he should be hoeing.

But Preacher couldn't be expected to understand that. And anyways he was too weary to think, too weary to talk for once, stumbling over sloping meadowland which had been pocked by the cattle's hoofs, and slithering on sodden bottom land. When he and Gunsmith came to a stream, not Cold Brook, but the one that joined the brook from Mosquito Hollow, water a good foot deep swirled over the stones. Gunsmith cut Preacher a staff so he could feel his steppings under the gray-white slather, though but for his pride 'twould have been easier and quicker to carry him across.

They found Dan'l Post squatting on his heels to hammer a trenail into a new oaken plough with the back of his axe. The tall thin girl, Eldest, was holding up the pole, and Viney, whom they called Young'un, was shouldering the cross-piece at the end of the handle. Chips and bark all around showed how Dan'l had shaped the body of the plough out of a living crotch. The two big brown oxen, yoked, but waiting for the yoke to be hitched to the pole, slowly chewed their cuds in the warm spring sunshine, and looked to be offering neighborly advice.

Gunsmith stepped up to admire the plough, for it was a clean workmanlike job of hewing. But Preacher started right in, just as soon as he had his breath from the climb.

"You have done wrong, Daniel, grievous wrong! Yet the wrong may still be amended. And the Creator in His Mercy will . . ."

Preacher stopped. For Dan'l, sitting back on his heels, didn't look aught but surprised and dumbfounded. Except kind of hurt.

Dan'l, short and square, and the squarer seeming for his creased up buckskins and squatting like a toad, peered upwards. Preacher, tall and thin in his close-buttoned homespun, stood over him, peering down. Gunsmith, Eldest and Young'un just watched and said naught.

Then Preacher must have realized that his words were harder than were called for. This time he loaded a lighter charge. Wouldn't Daniel, he asked, like to run along to his neighbors, his good and kindly neighbors, and beg their help to carry all that was mortal of his mother to a more suitable resting place? And Preacher promised that in a month's time he would come again and say a few words over . . .

"Nossir, Mist' Jones!" Dan'l still seemed bewildered, but his tone was firm as it had been with the womenfolk. "Nossir!"

Then it was Preacher's turn to look puzzled and maybe hurt. He was no more than trying to show Dan'l his duty, and hadn't counted on so flat a refusal.

Dan'l must have seen he'd hurt Preacher's feelings. "It's this way, Preacher, Mist' Jones. Cain't move Ma, not till Pa gits back and says to. But if you're minded to view the remains, Eldest will show ye. Cal'late to be able to spare her awhiles."

Gunsmith took Eldest's place holding up the draft pole of the plough, while the girl, slender and almost stately despite her patched and outgrown homespun, led Preacher up the hill. She moved to a tall maple on the edge of the forest, unhitched a long rawhide cord, and lowered a basket from a crotch overhead. When the basket rested on the ground, still brown with last fall's leaves, Preacher's hat came off, and two heads, Preacher's black as a crow, and Eldest's yellow as ripe corn, bent reverently over, nearly touching.

Gunsmith hoped Preacher would see that as much love could go into the weaving of a bushel basket, as in paying for a polished pine coffin with best wrought handles and a silver nameplate. And if Preacher would see that a basket slung high in a tree wasn't disrespectful, but only the safest place common sense could devise . . . But looked to be that Preacher was saying a few words of consolation to Eldest, and giving her the loan of his fine linen handkercher so she would enjoy her weeping more. Why . . . tarnation . . . looked to be that Preacher had some sense after all!

* * *

Dan'l tapped in the last whittled trenail, chopped off the head, and smoothed it with his knife. "There! She'll hold awhiles." And stood up.

Gunsmith unslung the powder horn. "Don't happen your pa drawed up more salt in his spring vittling than you're liable to use? Seems I could do with a horn full."

Dan'l looked pleased, and led the way to a windbreak shelter that wasn't even so much as a hunter's shack; just a throw-together of boughs. Yet it was dry and roughly comfortable, with bunks of hemlock, the soft tips uppermost. Worthless pelts from the late season trapping were laced together with sinew as a curtain for the doorway. At one end was an ox stall, at the other a clay hearth for use in bad weather, and all swept clean with a tied bundle of twigs. The sled served for both table and workbench.

Dan'l reached under a bunk and hauled out a sack of coarse curing salt. He filled Gunsmith's horn with the crystals.

"You're welcome to all you need, Mist' Reed, before the porcupines thieves it all. 'Tain't likely I'll get around to coopering me meat kegs for salting down, much before fall. Nor the three of us won't eat as much as five used to do."

So the boy was already planning ahead to next winter. Not really counting on Old Man Post, for all his talk of "Till Pa gets back." Gunsmith glanced around at the strings of smoked fish on peeled withes, at the dried venison hanging from the roof. He'd admire to know how Dan'l had killed his deer without a gun, and how the youngsters had managed to set by so much already.

"You're making out mighty good, Dan'l. Seems as if."

"Aim to skin me some popple, soon as the sap is riz good. When ploughing and hoeing's ended, and haying ain't yit, we'll start to roll us up a cabin and lean-to. Peter and Paul can summer here," he nodded towards the make-shift stalls, "but 'tain't nowise fit for their wintering."

It seemed the boy had it all figured out. This was good news. Mary would be as pleased as he was.

"Somewheres in the ashes there'd ought to be your Pa's broadaxe, drawknife, frow and suchlike. If you'll bring them down to the forge some evening I ain't busy, we'll put the temper back, and helve them. Don't do no harm to be forehanded."

Dan'l agreed. Just as soon as the ploughing was done he would be around. And mighty grateful.

Gunsmith considered. So far the trick of borrowing salt that he didn't need had served its purpose. But there was much the Posts must stand in want of beyond just tools. "Seeing you loaned me the salt, Dan'l, how'd it be if I was to draw you up a few bags of corn or suchlike in return? I've more than my needs."

But the boy's mouth tightened, as Gunsmith had feared it might. "Nossir, Mist' Reed. A horn of salt don't measure up to all that corn. And Pa didn't say to git to borrowing."

There was naught to do but return to the oxen, where Young'un was waiting and telling Peter and Paul just what they were to do, and just how well she expected them to do it. While Gunsmith held up the pole, she backed the oxen, flicking them on one nose and then the other with a finger, till the ring of the yoke slipped over the pole. Then Dan'l threw his weight sideways on the handle, so the point would run clear of rocks and turf, and the two Posts and two oxen paced slowly and earnestly down towards this year's corn patch.

Gunsmith stood watching. Arrived at the ploughland, Young'un walked ahead of Peter and Paul, while Dan'l clung to the kicking cross handle that needed a grown man's weight to steady it. Together the four of them broke their first furrow; a fair furrow, not overly straight by reason of the stumps that Old Man Post had never got around to drawing, but right for sun and drainage. A good start.

But where would they find seed? Their own, saved out of last year's crop, was all burned up. Dan'l had refused Gunsmith's offer. And assuming they had seed, there'd be the sowing, and then weeks of hard hoeing till the corn stood high and strong enough to fight for itself. And even then the work would only be started. There'd be fencing if Dan'l wanted to lay by hay for the winter, and cutting and carrying the hay, and a garden for their own foodstuffs. Harvest would call for the full strength of all three children. And as Dan'l said, there was a cabin and lean-to needed.

Six months they'd have for it all. Six months before the hard winter would set in once more. A task it was for a grown man and a brave woman. But the way Dan'l had set his hand to the day's work and his mind to the work of the morrow, it looked like the Posts might win out yet. If the season favored.

Gunsmith watched the slow-stepping oxen and the eager young'uns increase in size as they came up the field. Saw the boy throw all his weight on the plough handle to clear its point from the soil, then swing the handle sideways so the clumsy log could make the turn and start on the next furrow.

If the Posts could find food to keep up health and strength for their labors. If the season favored them. If they could come by seed corn, and beans, squash and cabbage and other seed . . .

Gunsmith's fingers combed his long beard in troubled puzzlement. There were a sight too many "ifs."

CHAPTER FOUR

CAT skittered ahead up the trail, his white paws dabbing at things he pretended were hiding under the dry leaves. Young'un chased after, with three steps and a prance, three steps and a prance, just as she'd dreamed last night. 'Twas the whippoorwill step, the only step that could be danced to whippoorwill music. So it was right useful to know, being there were no fiddles, and no barn raisings up here in the woods. And nobody for partner. If it hadn't been for the squirrel-skin bag she carried, she could have risen to her toes on the final note of "will" and done a wing-flap with both arms. She'd try it sometime if she ever found herself going anywhere with empty hands. Which wa'n't nowise likely. Not while Dan'l and Eldest had breath to call.

Dan'l was bowed beneath the farm, and trying to act like he was Pa, so nothing would suit Eldest but she'd got to be Ma. And go Ma one better, for Ma wouldn't have needed the salt ground fine. 'Twould have been enough to crack it small with the back of the axe. Eldest was getting pernickety. Which was why Young'un was off up the trail with a squirrel skin of salt, and hunting for a smooth worn rock, and a water-rounded stone to grind with. Cat had come along, part for company, and part because Cat was growing mighty wild since the house was burned. He'd be the better for a little play and cosseting, would Cat.

The leaves were kindly to Young'un's bare feet after day-by-day trudging over the ploughland. She picked up an acorn between her big toe and the next, to find how long she could carry it that way. Then changed her mind and tried with a kick and a spreading of the toes to throw the acorn at Cat. The acorn missed, but Cat plunged for it with his front paws scuffing up the leaves, as though it were a mouse.

34

'Twas good to be free to run and jump if so minded, after the long slow walking in front of Peter and Paul. At the thought, Young'un stooped to sweep Cat into her arms, and, short locks bouncing to her stride, raced up the trail as though howling Injuns were waving tomahawks behind. Then stopped to put Cat down, and to laugh within herself for the plain joy of having arms and legs that felt so happy.

A break in the gray trunked beeches to the right of the trail showed a patch of green stemmed popple. That was where Pa, liking the rich dark mold, had cleared him a potato patch years back. None but Pa would have toiled to clear and plant where the first-growth trees on all sides would shut out the sun. Even now, with the forest not yet in full summer leaf, the popple had to reach up, tall and spindly, towards the light.

Poor Pa. He belonged in the woods, not in the cleared farmlands. Knowed every sound and sign, and could call beasts and birds so they'd call back to him, or sing. Young'un twittered to a watching squirrel, and got him to scolding, but Pa would have had him nigh dropping out the tree with rage. Pa said there was nothing like a good political argument with a squirrel. Didn't matter which side you took, the squirrel could still outcuss you. But there! It wasn't fair to wish Pa back again. He was like to be a sight happier in Canady or wherever he was at.

Poor Ma, down in the burying lot back of the Settlement. The neighbors were right, Young'un could see that, when they came for her. And the things the Preacher had said then, and later over the grave, had been nice as nice. Most everyone had wept to think so noble a woman as Ma had gone from the earth. And it was good to be told she was so certain sure of the Everlasting Life. Still and all it was hard to know she was gone for good; Young'un had been down to the burying ground since, to talk to Ma and tell her how well things were going, so Ma shouldn't feel lonesome.

Young'un slipped on down, down into the slight hollow, that would make good cleared land one day. Ahead was the big oak that must have growed up sole alone after a fire, and so gotten the start on other trees. Not shaped like a straight up forest tree, but spreading wide as it was tall. The leaves and sparse undergrowth were shiny wet with honeydew. Young'un plucked a handful of leaves, and licked them. Sweet they were, just like honey the only time she'd tasted it. Some said bees made it in the tree. You could hear them buzzing high off up. Others thought 'twas that food in the Good Book that came down from heaven. God didn't drop it except on this oak, that she'd noticed. Maybe He favored it for being so big and beautiful. 'Twould be nice to grow big and beautiful, and be special-favored.

She scooped up Cat again, for he'd been stopping in the road to mew soundlessly that he wanted a ride. The clump of chestnuts was fully leafed-out already. It looked as though they might bear well this year. There'd been no spiny burrs with shiny dark brown nuts inside last year. Or only two-three, though she and Dan'l had barefooted over most every fallen leaf to feel for them. It was seldom that chestnut trees set in a clump this way. Might be the Injuns had cleared land for a garden patch, and left it for the squirrels to seed down with nuts later. Nearly every foot of the forest had a story, and mostly it was of a fight of tree against tree. Popples and birches spreading a thousand thousand seeds for every nut that hickories and chestnuts and beeches could drop. Squirrels aided the nuts by carrying them off and planting them, but squirrels mostly ate the beech mast instead of hoarding. So beeches, to make up, spread their roots far and wide, and from each root sprang up more shoots to make trees. Pines, hemlocks and the like had their own way of war. They waited till the other trees had shed their leaves each fall, then crowded in on them. Like Injuns attacking while the settlers slept. Come to think, it was mighty like the wars between French and Injuns and British and Continentals, each with their own ways of fighting like Pa used to tell. But the trees were still fighting, and always would.

The roar of the waterfall came up to her as she left the trail and slithered down the steep banks of Mosquito Hollow. There'd be smooth rock a-plenty beside the stream, with convenient small basins scooped out and washed clean by the winter's floods. It was hot, the sun glancing down from overhead through the break in trees, and the trees penning the warm damp air as though 'twas too lazy and contented, listening to the murmuring waters, to leap out and away.

Young'un set Cat down, and found a pot-hole stone rounder and smoother than a playball. But it was wet from the water, and she had to set it aside in the sun to dry. Scarlet-headed sumach, growing among the scorched dead trees, came down almost to the rock she sat on. Five years ago a fire had come nigh to burning out Eph Birdsell, but the wind, changing, had driven it roaring down to the stream, just at this point. Some said Sim Higgins had set the fire out of spite, but Pa said 'twas more like to've been set by a seegar thrown down from the coach. Pa misliked the newfangled coaches as bitter as some misliked Sim Higgins.

When you part closed your eyes, the sumach flowers still might be flames. But when you opened them wide, there were bees darting in and out of the flames. She watched them. Earlier in the day the hind legs of the bees would have yellow balls on them, but now their legs were clean and black, for the bees were busy gathering something else. Honey belike. If they flew north, they'd be making for a bee tree. She'd tell Dan'l, for he'd find a way to trail them to their tree. And come fall, they could drop the tree and take the honey. A good bee tree was worth a mint of money.

But the bees all flew south, to the hollowed logs that Mist' Ditch kept in a row behind the Tavern. Young'un remembered the time one of the bees had gotten into Meeting and stung her ma when Ma batted at it. Taverner had given her a sup of honey to take away the hurt, after Meeting. And Young'un had been let to suck the spoon. Sweetest tasting ever. If she was rich, she thought dreamily, she'd eat nothing else.

It was hot sitting hunkered down on the bare rock, grinding the clear icelike crystals of salt into a fine white flour, pounding and rubbing, rubbing and pounding. Young'un stopped, shed her airless doeskin shirt, flicked a drop of sweat from the top of her nose, so that it should not drop into the salt; and bare from head to hip, finished her task.

By then her white skin was glistening damp with the heat. She stood up and glanced around her. A big eagle floated across the narrow strip of sky above. Cat and a chipmunk were watching each other from opposite sides of the stream. Young'un loosed the hide string threaded through the top of her dusty doeskin pants, let them drop and stepped clear of their stiff folds. The water would be ice-cold, it always was, seeping out from under great rocks, shadowed by overhanging trees, and scarce seeing the light o' day except just here. But it was whiter than cream where it poured down over the ledge above, and clear brown speckled with gold in the deep still pool, with every twig and rock showing through. Tempting, it was.

If she were so minded, she'd plunge in. If so minded, do no more than wash hands and face and feet. She stood on the brink, toes curled to grip the edge, enjoying the will-I won't-I, and the feeling that not even Eldest, maybe not God himself, could come between her and what in the end she decided to do.

A pity Pa wasn't here. 'Twas he had taught them all to swim, taking them down to the Lake and throwing them in, time after time, till they could. Ma was in a taking when she heard. But Pa said that some day settlers would set the forest afire, and the only safety would lie in the water.

Young'un swung her arms and dived. Opened her eyes under water to grasp at a small fish, a trout belike. But had to come up to gasp for breath that the cold had choked out of her. The sun felt good again as she climbed up onto her rock, rubbed her hair and her skin to clean herself, dived again, and stretched out to dry.

Cat, driven off by the splashing, came back from among the sumachs, stalking to the edge of the water. He watched a pine cone rocking in the ripples, reached down and patted it delicately to shore. Then looked back at Young'un to see had she admired his boldness. Young'un gathered him up, and hugged him to her, for the soft feel of his fur on her bare stomach. Did Cat's fur feel as joysome to him on the other end, she wondered? She patted her own wet locks, but they didn't feel the same at all, either on the outside or on the head end. She gave her head a shake to help the drying. Cat sprang from her shoulder, and stopped safely out of arm's reach, to wash every last separate sprinkle of water from his coat. Mortally offended, he was. Young'un laughed.

Then swiftly she felt sad. For it was a day when sorrow and laughter started off in opposite directions, only to meet, unexpected, like squirrels chasing each other around a tree bole. And there was a sort of happiness lurking in the sorrow, and when you laughed there was a kind of choke deep inside you. Maybe 'twas no more than the sun stroking on bare skin, the roar of the waterfall, and knowing that the ploughing was ended for the year. Or maybe—'twas a solemn thought—she was a growed woman today.

Ma once said, "If aught happens to me, Viney, you'll need to act like a growed woman. There's no pith to Deborah. She takes after her pa." And Young'un had promised. But how did you know when you were grown up, or did you wait till other growed folks told you? When she was quite little, she'd believed that girls' hair grew longer than boys, and women's hair longer still. But of course she saw how silly that was. Freckles were a surer sign, for when did you see a growed-up with freckles, or a young'un without? Viney gave her body a careful search, but it was all pink-white, where she could see it, from the chill water and warm sun. Except for an old axe-scar still showing on one knee, and new bramble scratches around the ankles. Stooping over the darkest part of the pool she tried to see the reflection of her face; but the water wouldn't stay still enough, account of the waterfall. Anyways, real freckles didn't come this early in the year, and the tag end of last year's freckles wouldn't hardly count.

Eldest was sixteen rising seventeen. Two years ago, or it might be three, she'd taken to going off like she was hiding a secret, and wouldn't tell. Taller she was, string-bean tall, but she hadn't the heft to her that Young'un had now. Nor she couldn't split rails nor hoe corn the way Young'un could. Times Young'un could outdo Dan'l even, or near to.

Young'un flexed her biceps the way Dan'l did. Admiring them. Thighs, calves and forearms were good and hard too, when she pinched them right. She tried her breasts. They were hard; but not like muscles, they wouldn't tighten and loosen at will. And that reminded her. Growed women's breasts were bigger, like Ma's; but Young'un's were most like Eldest's already. And they'd grow, like a heifer calf's bag did. When a heifer was ready to calve, they grew still more. Leading a heifer to the bull, and growed up folks getting married in front of Preacher, were someways alike. But neither Ma nor Eldest could see that, or made pretence they couldn't.

She caught Cat up to her breasts, rubbed him against them for the tickly feel. Then set him down again in haste. Growed women didn't sit bare-skinned on rocks idling away the livelong day. Young'un

39

jumped to her feet and grabbed up her clothes. And the squirrel-skin bag that had lain under them, to protect it from chance damping, flipped away into the pool. By the time she had it out she was wet again; not that it mattered, the day being hot. But the bag, that needed to be special dry for the salt, was sopping.

A few minutes ago Young'un would have pelted back up the trail for another bag, or poured the salt in the sleeve of her shirt. But that wasn't fitting now, since her discovery. Growed women went visiting, when in need, and borrowed the loan of, say, a wooden bowl, to carry salt. She slid into her clothes, called Cat to follow, and fought a way through the sumach and berry tangle beyond.

"Just took a fancy to go visitin'," she would tell Eldest. And Eldest would know right off that she was a woman now, and maybe call her Viney instead of Young'un. Then she'd go down to Dan'l in the lower pasture and say "Took a fancy to go visitin'," and his brows would draw together and he'd be mad as hornets. Not understanding, being only a boy.

She would have liked to take the road, and follow it plumb through the middle of the settlement. Some day she'd do just that, brave as though going to Meeting. This time she'd make shift to slip into the Tavern yard unseen and have word with Phebe Callender, who wasn't above seventeen years for all she was hired girl. And Phebe would lend the bowl when she heard how bad it was needed for the salt.

She kept downhill, cross-lots, getting a scare from someone's strayed sow who charged out from a berry bush where she had her sucklings, and stopped to pass a few words with Taverner's old sway-backed mare who had been freed from work since before she could remember. The geese out back of the Tavern drove Cat up an apple tree and she had to climb after and then carry him. The bees in four log hives were working their fool heads off, in and out and in and out. Seven other hives looked to be empty. Pa said Cicero cherished his pesky little insects more than most folks did their livestock. She'd like to tell him how sorry she was those seven hives had been winter-killed, only he wasn't around. No more was Phebe. Only Mis' Ditch making talk with some strangers in the ordinary.

Young'un looked up the road and down, before coming out of the Tavern yard, then scuttled across the ruts. She would liefer wade Cold Brook in a snow storm. But one day she'd stand spang in the middle of the road, before Meeting, gowned in homespun of her own spinning and maybe weaving, too. She'd be tall, and thin, and delicate seeming, and exchange greetings and talk of ailments with other women. It shouldn't be hard to have ailments once you learned the way of it.

Gunsmith's shop sounded perilous with the splashing of the waterwheel outside, and the groaning and creaking of timbers within. But when Cat was past the doorway, he saw it was safe, and with Young'un comforting him sheathed his claws. There was Phebe, sitting in the corner in the littlest prettiest armed chair that anyone had ever set eyes on. Gunsmith, with careful strokes of a plane, was deepening the groove in a rifle stock for the barrel to set in. Phebe gave a nod of welcome and turned her eyes back on Eph Birdsell. Nobody was saying a word, which was mighty pleasant.

It wasn't clear, at first sight, what Eph was fixing to do. He had something like a small table before him, with a stick of wood spinning across the top. What made it spin was a cord passing around a pulley wheel on the table, and running to one of the big slow-moving wheels of the machinery beyond. He laid a long-handled chisel to the spinning stick, and shaves of sweet smelling wood curled off as easy as if the wood was no harder than winter butter.

Young'un moved up closer to watch. Eph set her gently aside "If that cord breaks, as it's liable to," he cautioned, "it licks out to cut worser'n a teamster's whip."

Eph's stick was whittling down finer and finer, with rings cut in and ridges left on, like the rungs of Phebe's chair. That's what he was making, another chair. You could depend on it. That big wheel splashing outside, the big oak beam turning and groaning and groaning, all to shape up this pindling little stick. Kind of pernickety. A man ought to do more with his strength in farming season, or there'd be hungry bellies come fall and freeze-up.

Thinking of hunger reminded Young'un to ask, "Don't happen you could lend me the loan of a wooden bowl, Phebe? Just a small one."

41

Phebe said, "Why yes. We'll go get one." She looked a mite surprised, not knowing how Young'un was growed up today.

Then Eph grunted, "Save your steps—we got a bowl here, good as," and picked up a chunk of wood that hadn't so much as a hollow to it to show what he meant. He pressed the cord sideways off the fast spinning pulley, pulled out the spindle he'd been shaping, and set the block in its place. He slid back the cord on to the pulley, gave the block of wood a spin with his hand to get it started, and laid the chisel end against it so the bark began to fly.

Mary, who was Gunsmith's wife, came in with a rifle on each shoulder. When she set them in their racks, they were taller than she was. She hung up powder horn and bag, and leather apron, slipped off her leather sleeves. She caught sight of Young'un, gave her a real tender smile, stroked Cat in passing, and went on up the three steps into the house. Young'un couldn't help but like her, stroking Cat that way. Most folks wouldn't have thought to make Cat welcome, but have patted Young'un's hair instead, all clean as dandelion silk from bathing.

The log chunk was shaping up, bark off, and spinning the smoother for being rounded. Eph lifted the chisel and beckoned, "Give Phebe the cat and take aholt of this."

Putting his hands over Young'un's, Eph showed how to steady the chisel against a rest and bring the hollowed point lightly against the spinning block. Eph's hands were real broad farmer's hands, that just swallowed hers from sight. Big as Dan'l's were fixing to be, not like Pa's, long and thin.

"Kind of fun!" she told Eph round past her left ear, not daring to take her eyes off the bite of wood unreeling from the chisel like twine from a ball.

Eph swung the handle a mite to leave a thin bead of wood for ornament on the smooth surface. "Gunsmith learned me, when I was a young'un."

Phebe spoke up, her voice sharp against the roar and rumble. "Eph's getting up in years now, Viney, beard kind of sparse, and teeth and hair . . ."

Young'un missed the rest. For the chisel dug sharply into the wood, and 'most jerked the handle from their combined grip. She hadn't stirred a finger. 'Twas Eph's hands had slipped. The pretty new beading was all torn off, too.

"No call to give heed to Phebe Callender." Eph examined the scoop-shaped end of the chisel. "She just sets there to aggravate."

It was right strange talk of Phebe's. For it was plain to see that Eph's beard was black and thick, and long for a young man's, as much as half a hand's span from his chin. And he looked to have all his hair and teeth.

Eph worked over the outside of the block to leave another beading. Then slid the cord off the pulley, and refixed the block with a screw in the bottom, to leave the other end free for cutting. He didn't ask Young'un's help to scoop out the inside of the bowl, though, and 'twas plain he was angered at Phebe's talk.

Phebe just sat there, soothing Cat so he was purring to rattle his hind teeth. Whenever Eph looked her way, she set a smile on her lips that was just shaped to aggravate him. 'Twas a wonder Eph bore it. If Young'un did that to Dan'l, he'd backhand her across the mouth, or give her a clout on the behind, whichever came handiest. And he'd have the right of it. She'd do the same to Dan'l, even if she had to run for it after.

Gunsmith was bending close over the bench, till it seemed his long white beard would get caught. Young'un drew near to watch. Gunsmith kept laying a rifle barrel along its groove in the stock, taking it off, shaving down the wood just the barest possible and trying the barrel again. "Got to have it just so, or the best barrel ain't no better than the worst," he explained. "Pin her tight here, and loose there, and she'll throw all ways come Sunday."

Young'un's fingers itched to help. There couldn't be a nobler craft than forging barrels and filing locks and whittling down stocks and forming them together into muskets and rifles. With high up officers and rich merchants writing to say 'Please Viney Post to make me a pair of pistols, seeing I've a duel to fight' and such like. And she, Young'un, would make the best pistols and rifles, and maybe cannon too, if they weren't too difficult. There'd be a sight of tools to learn to handle. But if Gunsmith would take her as 'prentice, just as soon as Dan'l had the farm . . .

But no, 'Twouldn't do. Not if she aimed to be a woman. Men

43

were for smithing and the like, just as sure as oxen were for ploughing. 'Twas the fitten way of things. And that 'minded her to see
could she draw Phebe aside where she could talk secrets about
growing up.

With her silences and with her words, Phebe was still taunting
Eph Birdsell. Could it be he was afeared of her? Why, he could
lift her up as a ma cat lifts her kitten. It seemed almost as though
that was what Phebe wanted. Aggravating Eph Birdsell till he'd
reach down, grab her up and dust her off with one of those big hands
of his.

"Do seem a man of all your years and experience ought to've
benefited from them." Phebe was scolding, "Building a chair so small
there's none but me or Mary can sit betwixt the arms."

The bowl was shaped, and Eph had laid aside the tool, and with
two handfuls of shavings held against it was burnishing inside and
out as it whirled around. He could spare his eyes from the work,
and turned them on Phebe. "Measured it so's you could have a place
to rest, and nobody else."

"Oh," said Phebe, and stopped stroking Cat, who'd got to sucking his tongue and smirking.

"Don't seem I can do without you." And Eph had picked up
Phebe's aggravating smile, and spread it clear across his face, beard
and all.

"Oh!" said Phebe once more, and her face was hot as though
she'd been baking bread.

"You're kind of like the itch, Phebe, the way you rile." Eph
looked back to the bowl. "Ain't much to the itch itself. But I get a
heap of satisfaction scratching where it itches."

Phebe shot from the chair so fast that Young'un had to catch
Cat in mid-air. Phebe Callender was out the door and running across
the road like Mis' Ditch had called her.

Eph unscrewed the bowl, carried it across to the bench, and began
to saw the spare off the bottom. There wasn't so much as a trace
of smile on his face.

"Now, Eph, 'tis your fault this time." Gunsmith sounded right
sorrowful. "You and Phebe acting bear and bear-dog this-a-way.
There's not a mite of sense to it."

Eph didn't say anything. He sawed the waste wood off the bowl, let the bowl fall to the floor, and handed the waste to Young'un. Then, seeming to recollect, picked up the bowl and gave her that, as he'd intended.

So the bowl must be really hers, Young'un's. It wasn't fitten for men to have bowls and suchlike, they were woman's gear. Young'un hadn't purposed to, but found herself hugging Eph, Cat, bowl and all. And so he shouldn't feel too bad, she hugged Gunsmith too. They stopped looking grim, the two of them. But she must get back, fast as she could run, scoop up the salt, and show the bowl to Eldest and Dan'l. The first thing she'd ever handled that was truly hers, sole alone.

As Young'un bounded out through the door, she heard Gunsmith's voice, "Don't do no harm to pleasure 'em, once in a whiles, Eph. Fourteen years old or forty, they're all women."

CHAPTER FIVE

"You're a man full growed, Eph Birdsell, and for the last time I'm warning you. If you don't choose yourself a woman, a woman will choose you." Gunsmith's little white-haired wife hooked powder horn and bullet bag off the peg in the workshop. "Seems like I've mothered you overlong; it's high time a younger woman took on the chore."

Then Gunsmith swung a hot gun barrel from forge to anvil, tapped home the cold iron core, and the welding hammers began again.

When two more inches of the tube had been welded, Gunsmith knocked out the core, and swung the barrel back to the glowing charcoal.

Leaning his heavy sledge hammer on the anvil, Eph looked around at Mary and grinned aggravatingly through his short black beard.

"If a man aims to live and die a bachelor, he'd best go hide him in a cave," Mary's whispering voice was strangely sweet for a woman deaf these thirty years and more. "He's plumb crazy if he sets new shingles to his roof, the way you've done, hollows himself an eaves trough, fixes himself a rain-water barrel, keeps a load of firewood under cover and handy, and even plants a laylock by his door. For where there's a home there's just bound to be a woman. And it don't serve none for the man to struggle."

Mary reached down from the rack the rifle she was to test this morning. She folded some greased linen patches into the box in the side of the rifle butt and snapped-to the brass lid. Her gray eyes twinkled with satisfaction as she considered a new menace.

"There's plenty widows and women of sensible age, forty year and up, will marry a good farm like yours." She slid her head through the loop of her leather apron, pulled on deerskin sleeves over her faded workaday homespun, and halted at the door for a final shot. "Yessir, Ephraim Birdsell! They'll marry the farm, and plumb shut their eyes to the pesky man that owns it."

She had a feeling of satisfaction as she turned away. For Eph had stopped grinning. He was stubborn as Den Birdsell, his father, had been, but maybe she had him seeing sense at last. Crossing the bridge, she admired, as she couldn't help but admire, the little settlement of Cold Brook. Small it was, with all the friendliness that went with smallness. Of course, here as elsewhere, womenfolk would quarrel, and menfolk come to fist-fighting over a boundary or straying beasts. But then someone would fall sick, or a cow die, and neighbor must needs turn to neighbor to give the aid a neighbor should.

Mary swung off the road to skirt the deep mire that lay there from thaw most all the ways to freezeup. Too deep for horse and wagon. Even the coach turned out, swaying perilously up the steep bank and back again on to the road where it was harder. A hog lifted himself with a sucking sound out of the wallow; then, pretending fright, fled through a flock of hissing geese. Cornfields and grazing lay beyond. And back of that, on the rising slope of the thick forested hills, stretched land that was cleared, but not yet stumped. And beyond that the woodlots. Each winter the forest was driven back by axe and fire, to make way for grazing and corn. Each spring, when the trees leafed out, the forest seemed to thrust in again. A tide of green it was, that ebbed and flowed, but always receded.

The wild beasts had their tides, too. A hard winter and rabbits would strip the bark off the apple trees, deer come down to steal hay and frosted fruit and vegetables. There would be fresh wolf tracks in the snow around the barn. Bears hungry and ill-tempered would interfere with the spring boiling up in the sugar bush, and try to burst a way into the Tavern outhouse where Cicero wintered his bees.

But 'twas five year or more since Mary had killed her last bear, though of course they still roamed the woods. The tide of beasts, like the tide of forest, was drawing slowly back. You could tell that from the guns that were ordered. Time was, a bore big as that of a

47

musket was favored. Nowadays half-ounce balls were thought too heavy; and since there was no wear-out to G. Reed rifles, the old ones were being sent back for new squirrel barrels to be fitted. Like the one across the bend of her arm, that would scarce take the tip of her little finger down the muzzle.

Not a new weapon, and scarce one that was repaired, would leave the G. Reed workshop without Mary Reed had proved it, sighted it, and found no fault. From an eighty-rod rifle so heavy that Gam had to carry it for her to the testing ground, to little brass-barreled pocket pistols made to some rich merchant's special order, firearms were all one to Mary Reed. She had never fought a duel—she smiled at the thought—but she still had a hankering to show how G. Reed dueling weapons should be handled. 'Twas a slight upon good gunsmiths the way duelists missed each other at twenty paces and less.

Mary balanced across a stream on a tree trunk that Gam had felled and smoothed for her. Under the bare gray granite face of High Rock she looked over her marks, pieces of soft pine trunk, two feet high and a foot wide, cloven down the middle to leave a yellow-white surface. On each was painted a black X, and in and around this were bullet holes which she stuffed with grass so they could be distinguished from new holes. Around the standing marks, like the dead on a battlefield, lay the marks of other years, riddled and splintered until they would no longer stand; some no more than mossy hummocks. There had been a year or more the rock face had served, with a pot of charcoal and linseed paint to daub out the silver bullet splashes. A time Gam had wanted to set up a heavy iron butt nearer the forge, and a shelter for Mary to shoot from. But the cleft pine logs were simpler, and down in the flats here was space for all ranges, and no danger from flying bullets.

Mary paced back five rod, set rifle butt to ground, and swinging round the powder horn measured the small charge into the narrow muzzle. She set greased linen patch on top, seated bullet on patch, drove it flush with her clenched fist, and tapped the butt of the rifle to ground to pack down the powder. With one clean drive of the slender ramrod she seated the patched bullet on the powder charge, bounced the ramrod once to make sure all was tight, slid ramrod back into its thimbles beneath the barrel, and brought the rifle to the horizontal. 'Twas simple and unthinking after all these years as putting spoon to mouth. Yet there was still pleasure to the handling of a G. Reed stock and barrel. She could tell one in the dark, just by the heft and balance. Her right thumb flipped up the frizzen while her right fingers shook the fine priming powder into the pan. She let down the frizzen, took a glance at the flint as she drew it back, the polished maple butt sliding into the curve of her shoulder. The sights rose up and rested on the center of the black X as her finger took the slight pressure of the trigger. A puff of smoke, and a push against her shoulder. The trigger, she noted, had a good short travel, and didn't stick or scrape. Gam would spend hours over his locks, hardening, stoning, polishing, after most folks would say they were already perfect.

A glance at the target. The ball had hit just about right. Reloading as she went, Mary moved back to the twenty-rod mark, and lay down on the smooth topped outcrop of granite, which Providence had placed just right. And the Sherman girls, twins they were, appeared from nowhere with their cow. And the taller boy, that the young'uns called Stumpy, came swinging down the road on his crutch. Mary rested the rifle muzzle on a block of wood, fired, reloaded, and fired again. Then the young'uns came scrambling up the rock, and begging could they shoot, just the once. She could read their lips asking it, as she pricked out the frizzen hole and reloaded.

But they were good children and lay down beside her without pestering, as she stood up to load and lay down to fire. The Sherman twins, with their eager brown eyes peering up towards the mark and their thin knobbly legs stretched out behind, were arguing could they see the flight of the ball through the air, and why not. Bartholomew, whom it was hard not to call Stumpy the way the others did, was waiting to show his new crutch, all polished knobs and ornament like the spindles on a chair. Eph Birdsell must have turned it on the lathe, just to pleasure the boy. Eph ought to have young'uns of his own. So ought Phebe Callender. Good barrel and good stock, as you might say, wasted for want of being brought together.

As she finished her shooting Mary's thoughts went on. She walked back to the mark and found the bullets had struck in a nice clean group no more than the width of her palm. Which was good for so light a ball; light balls being flighty. And she let the children clean the priming hole, load, and fire, once each.

If Eph and Phebe hadn't got the sense themselves . . . still hesitating she watched the young'uns search out what flattened balls they could find, and run back to give her the lead for remolding.

* * *

And then, of all people, came Eph Birdsell, cantering his young horse, with a rumble, over the bridge, and laughing, as the roan made pretence to pitch him into the slough. Eph wasn't much more than a colt himself, the way he acted. Man and horse crazed by sunlight and their own youth and strength. A right purty sight.

Catching sight of Mary he tossed his hat in the air and caught it again. He called something, but Mary could not see his words. He rode off south.

"Ain't no such girl or woman." Stumpy was certain sure. "Not in Fort Ann. Not in the Falls even."

"'Aim to get me a cook that ain't never argued, nor like to!' That's what he said," one of the twins reported. "Eph ain't aimin' to get him a wife, is he, Aunt Mary?"

"High time he did!" Mary let slip the words. "Now hiper along and tend to your cow. And you, Bartholomew, you run ahead to the Tavern and tell Hepziba I'd be grateful for the loan of Phebe Callender. Say . . . Say I'm minded to make another batch of candles, if the day don't turn too warm."

She was back in the forge and cleaning the gun barrel when she saw Gam turn his head. Viney Post, it was, had come in, though at first sight she might have been any of the young'uns. With her hair tied back with a sinew she looked to be a boy, even by the way she stood there by the door. Hatless she was, and garbed in old wrinkled deerskin, and snub nosed and freckled as they all were at that age. She held out a wooden bowl.

"Eldest says I've no right to it without I earn it some ways." She said Eldest's words first so there would be no mistake. "Eph was just riding off as I passed and likely he didn't hear my holler."

Gam laid down the draw-knife he was using and took the bowl. Then handed it back. "'Tis the bowl Eph turned for you and for no one else. There's both Phebe Callender and me for witness that 'twas a free and unconditional gift. Now run home and tell your Eldest those very words."

Mary was dallying over the gun barrel before going back into the house to write down in the ledger how the rifle had proved. Gam had a patience with childer that he'd ought to show to Sim Higgins and to others that riled him. And mighty solemn he was over a little'un or a young'un that had a trouble to tell. But this time it didn't avail.

"Eldest says that 'twas only believing it was a loan made her borrow it these two months. When I told her it was a gift she said for me not to bring it within her sight again."

"Nor Eph ain't like to take back what he's given. So we're kind of cotched between the two of 'em." Gunsmith passed his fingers through his white beard, and for once Mary was too interested to tell him not to. "Seems there's only one way out, to please the both of them. We've got to figure out how you can work and earn that bowl."

Then Stumpy came pounding in on his crutch and hollered. "Miss Ditch says to say, 'You're welcome, and good riddance to a baggage.' Them's her very words. And she told Phebe to finish packing her box now, so Mis' Ditch could see what went into it. And . . ."

"No call to shout, Bartholomew. Spare your breath and I can still see what you say." Mary spoke sharper than she purposed, for the boy had done no more than Hepziba's bidding when he gave his message.

Stumpy had caught sight of the Post young'un, and the two were eyeing each other sideways, like strange dogs. Those in the settlement were mostly that way with those that lived out beyond; and the Posts, at such times as they came down to Meeting, held close together, not speaking.

He might have stayed to torment the girl, might Stumpy, only for what he had seen and heard at the Tavern. He swung about on his crutch, and before Mary could think to warn him not to, off he went to spread the tidings of Hepziba and her hired girl.

Naught ailed Bartholomew, only his shriveled leg. But that was enough to turn him into a talebearer and a troublemaker. It was always that way. A man like Sol Broadmoor, or Gam here, could

51

afford to be good-natured most of the while. But take Stumpy or Sim Higgins, or even little Cicero Ditch in a way, and their tongues and their cunning ways were always making trouble for those less handicapped than themselves. With women 'twas different. A little woman could always get her own way, and others to help her too, when a big woman like Hepziba had to fight and struggle. But that was the way of the world, and no use to try to change it.

Mary Reed set her rifle in the rack, drew off sleeves and apron and went into the house.

* * *

Before Mary had the kettle of tallow fat properly hot and the bars to support the dipping rods ranged across two chair backs the door burst open. Phebe Callender's eyes were red from weeping, and she was still close to tears.

A little thing she was, but high bosomed and prideful. She'd a waist slim as the wrist of a Kentucky rifle, that a young man's hands should just naturally reach for, whether he intended or no. And Eph Birdsell, it seemed to Mary, was young enough and man enough.

"Hepziba been plaguing you again?"

Phebe gulped. "It's worse than that, Aunt Mary. She's bade me pack my trunk and leave by the next coach. And I haven't the coach fare nor . . ."

Nor anywhere to go, of course; Phebe being an orphan from down Albany way. Mary let the girl's story trickle out piecemeal as she measured wicks, tying two to each dipping rod. In the days when Phebe used to come across to the forge for a sight of Eph Birdsell, Hepziba Ditch had called her an idle good-for-nothing, and boxed her ears a-plenty. After the quarrel between Phebe and Eph, Phebe had stayed home in the Tavern, scarce setting foot outside for two whole months. And that seemed to make Hepziba mighty suspicious, being what she was.

Then there had been that trouble when some coach folks had tried to kiss Phebe and she'd thrown a mugful of cider over their fine linen stocks. Hepziba, who wouldn't have found a kiss or two amiss, had called the girl a sight of names, but Cicero had come out from behind the bar and stood up for her. He couldn't have done more harm if he'd tried. For a week Phebe had tried to avoid meet-

52

ing Cicero without Hepziba was there, till Hepziba was sure her suspicions were right and the girl had something to conceal. "And 'tis no fault, Aunt Mary, of my own," Phebe claimed.

"Can't rightly blame no one else," Mary's tone was noncommittal. "Hepziba hires a girl that don't amount to more than a skinned cat, and in six months' time, through no fault of Hepziba, the skinned cat turns into a mighty purty woman."

"You think I'm purty, Aunt Mary?" Phebe sounded surprised.

"Ask Eph. He's marrying you. I ain't." Mary dipped another stick of wicks in the big iron kettle and set it to harden on the bars. The candles were still only rushlight thickness.

Phebe's eyes opened. "But Eph don't intend . . . he's so aggravatin' . . . he . . ."

No more had a young fellow named Gamaliel Reed, Mary said. Hadn't no idea of marrying. Womenfolk was too hampering when you aimed to build the best rifles ever was. And little Mary McIntosh had had no more sense to her flighty head than to outsmart him at the Thanksgiving turkey shoot and humble his pride. Too chicken-brained she was even to borrow a G. Reed rifle to do it with too. Just had it all planned out that if she won the shoot, she'd have her man and her turkey both. "Little women sure make the biggest addle-pates when they set their minds to it."

"But how did you come to get . . . how did Uncle Gam come to change his mind, Aunt Mary?" Phebe's stick of wicks hung in mid-air, dripping tallow on the clean scrubbed floor.

"Took a deal of contriving to get that young Gamaliel up in the woods, and hook the trigger over a hemlock snag and shoot myself in the leg where 'twould hurt, but not harm. And then he was like t'have run for help instead of doing as I was minded." A slow blush accompanied Mary Reed's reminiscent smile. "Gam's been more partial to limbs since. Mine anyways."

Phebe laughed, perhaps the first time in two months, as Mary had intended she should. She dipped four more sticks of candles, her eyes narrowed in thought. "I'd be heart-willing, if so be we can borrow a gun and you can show me how."

It was Mary's turn to smile. "It don't serve to spin flax on a wool wheel. Gam and Eph Birdsell's different natured. Gam was afeard of women, though I didn't know till after. Now Eph . . . we'd best study up on him."

Eph's parents had died, the both in one winter, when he was five going on six. It was all Gam could do to bring little Eph back to live at the forge, and then only by promising that some day he would return to the farm and cabin his pa had made. Young Eph had been handy and willing enough, learning to handle every tool that was within his heft. Whenever he turned up missing he'd be found at the farm, looking at the gaps in the shingled roof, and the rotting fences, like he was fit to weep. Till Gam had to get together two-three tools and go up and show him how to set things straight.

But time and again he was back at the cabin, patching here and replacing a timber there. It was clear, Mary said, what was in his heart all along.

" 'Tis the farm he's wedded to, I know that." Phebe's plaint was a wail of despair.

"Same as Gam was wedded to his rifles. But a woman's kind of useful to have around. Gam ain't throwed me out yet."

It was seven years now since Eph had moved back to the old place, and in all that while till Phebe came along he'd scarce glanced at maid or married woman. But menfolk were like butternuts; the harder to crack, the sweeter the meat . . .

"There's been times I'd as lief crack Eph Birdsell as marry him!" Phebe was getting her spirit back. "Telling me to my face I'm like the itch!"

"That being the way you were acting to draw his notice, he'd a right to the belief." Mary was firmly judicial. " 'Twas as foolish as me outsmarting Gam at the turkey shoot."

Gunsmith's wife thrust back her chair. The dipping was over. The candles, still hanging limp from their sticks, were carried down into the cellar to harden. Poor looking dips they were, owing to the weather, but they had served their purpose.

"I'm half-minded to be sorry for Eph Birdsell," Mary let the cellar flap fall shut with a bang. "Riding off blithesome to Fort Ann without a thought for the trouble that's in store for him."

"Then you've a notion how . . ."

54

"I've a notion Gam's going over with you to fetch your trunk. You'll stay here till I can send word to Preacher."

"Preach . . . !" Phebe couldn't even finish the word. It implied too much.

"Land sakes, girl, Eph wouldn't nowise hear of an unmarried woman living on that precious farm of his!" chuckled Mary. "If you want Eph Birdsell you'll just have to marry him, for all his faults."

"All his faults! But Aunt Mary, he hasn't hardly got a one," Phebe flashed out in his defense.

"There, there!" Mary patted her arm. "I don't cal'late he's any worser than Gam." She raised her voice. "Gam! Gamaliel Reed! I want you should bring over Phebe's trunk."

CHAPTER SIX

GUNSMITH hadn't so much as kindled his forge next morning and planned his day's tasks, when there in the wide doorway stood Widow Wilson. All dressed up, was Jessie Wilson, in the velvet she had worn at Seth Wilson's burying seven year ago. But today the velvet had scarlet ribbons at the neck and ribbons on each sleeve. And the widow was plumper and smiling.

"Mary's away, Jessie." Gunsmith shredded tinder into a musket pan, shook a pinch of priming powder among it, let down the frizzen and snapped the flint. A puff of smoke, and Gunsmith began to blow gently on the smoldering tinder.

"If I'd but risen betimes, Gamaliel, I could have stepped across to the Tavern and borrowed you an ember." The Widow practised an arch smile. "But there! I'm such a little slugabed!"

Gunsmith set the glowing tinder in the charcoal of the forge. "There now, Ma'am; that will serve well as an ember."

"A man is just bound he'll be independent, ain't he?" the Widow tittered. "Don't happen you've seed aught of Eph Birdsell?"

"Not today, Ma'am."

It was only after the Widow headed off up the road that Gunsmith remembered that he should have told how Eph had ridden down to Fort Ann yesterday. But there had been so much talk around his ears, women-talk 'twixt Mary and Phebe, of gowns and stitchings and turnings and suchlike. And it seemed Preacher was expected up tomorrow, and that would mean more talk, talk being Preacher's trade. It was a relief to have the workshop empty, the coals in the forge rising to a nice glow to the creak-sigh, creak-sigh of the big bellows. Companionable.

Still and all—his mind swung away from Mary and Phebe—that

56

Viney Post was a good child; going back to the Post place to work as he bade her, and coming over of an evening to trail up with him to Eph's to be learned how to milk. She asked mighty few questions, but took note of all he did, and of all Molly did too, whether 'twas to switch her tail or shuffle her feet. Young'un had milked and stripped the cow mighty clean, and done better than many a man, Molly's hind teats being short for a bigger hand.

A dark conspiracy the two had hatched up betwixt them. That Young'un was to slip over every morning, so long as Eph was away, and do his chores and milking before she turned to her own chores. Her elder sister would be grateful for the four-five quarts of milk, and in the end would be forced to admit that Young'un had earned herself the little bowl she coveted, and which was rightly hers long since. Gunsmith wasn't to tell, unless to Mary. Gunsmith chuckled.

He had a short strip of iron on the anvil and was shaping it out with the light hammer when the doorway darkened again.

"Morning to you, Gamaliel Reed!"

"Morning, Sim!" Gunsmith wanted to get to grips with the day's work. But Simpkin Higgins hadn't been along since the two months back when he'd wanted to go partners and Gunsmith had run him out. No sense to making a year-long quarrel out of next to nothing. "Morning, Sim!" Gunsmith made the welcome sound a trifle warmer. "Don't seem you've been around much of late."

Sim Higgins stepped inside a mite uncertainly. And called back, "Come on in, Ruth." And a pale complected spinster lady followed him in.

"Gam, I want you should meet my sister's husband's darter by his first wife." Sim made careful introduction. "She's been helping out to home, has Ruth. A grand hand to cook and spin she is. Nor you can't judge by her age, Gam, for she bakes better than a married woman."

Gunsmith had a first impression that the bandy-legged little horse-trader would open her jaws and show her teeth, and maybe lunge her round a piece to show her paces.

The woman must have had the same thought. "Don't aim to trade me for one of those greasy old guns, do you, Uncle?" She smiled and the length of her teeth would have dropped her price, if she'd been a horse, all of ten dollars. "But didn't Aunt Miriam say to find Eph Birdsell and then to . . ."

Sim cut her short with a glance which was almost a nudge. "Well, seeing Eph ain't here, me and Ruth had best be getting along."

Not till they were a ways up the road did Gunsmith get to wondering why Sim and his niece were rigged out that way; and the Widow Wilson, too, with her ribbons. It wasn't the Sabbath, nor the time of day for jollification, and if there was a burying, he'd have heard.

Puzzled, he turned back to the forge and things he understood. He swung the strip of red-hot iron to the anvil, and started a set of screw holes. It was Eph's notion to have trigger guard of iron instead of the usual brass. Busied with the punch and hammer, he failed to notice the next footsteps, but when he'd set the iron back again among the coals, there stood a woman in the shop. A woman most as tall as he was, who looked like she could scare the skin clean off'n a bear without so much as drawing skinning-knife. The sort of old settler that must have given the Injuns a heap of trouble to massacre, with the poor metal they had in those days . . .

"Well?" She fired the word so close he could most feel the sting of the powder. "Womenfolk so scarce to these parts that even a man your age gits to staring? When you're done, you can p'int out where I can find Mister Birdsell's place."

Gunsmith found words. "He's dead, ma'am, is Den Birdsell. Died close on twenty year ago." Gunsmith couldn't recall if Den had any sisters. Whoever she was, she'd come mighty late.

"Dead?" She seemed surprised. And angry, as though someone had played a joke on her.

"But Eph . . . he's Den Birdsell's son . . . Eph is making out all right. And if so be you're his aunt . . ."

Something he'd said had riled her still more. He was glad to have the hammer in one hand, and the tongs with the hot iron in the other. She gave him one look, the kind that had drove the Injuns back over the mountains, and stalked out. Before he could say Eph wasn't to home.

58

Disturbed in mind, Gunsmith returned to his work. Then Jehoah! If it weren't more females! The Sherman twins, with their "Morning, Uncle Gam!" the dark twin leading by half a word as usual.

Gunsmith had to smile at them, with their freckled little noses and long plaits, their thin, half-grown legs and arms, and their mortal serious faces.

And they wanted?

One elbowed the other to speak up, but the other nudged back. Whatever had brought them was terribly important. Gunsmith tried to help them out with a "Well?"

"Uncle Gam . . ." It was the dark twin speaking alone. That showed how weighty it was.

"Yes, Sary?"

"You won't tell on us? . . . Eph said only yest'day he aimed to get him a cook. And we told Ma. And Ma shawled her head and ran right across to tell Mis' Higgins. It don't mean Eph's aiming to git himself married, do it, Uncle Gam?"

"Not that he's told me, Sary. Though of course, some day he's apt to." Eph was fond of the twins. They must be feared that if he took himself a wife he'd have less time to whittle them dolls out of broken chair legs, and show them how to weave Injun baskets and suchlike play.

"Uncle Gam!" The twins had joined hands, and were speaking together this time, piecing each other out. "D'you think he meaned it when he told you he'd sooner work a team of colts . . . for all the trouble they'd give . . . than one big horse that would weigh nigh as much as the pair of them?"

Gunsmith scratched his head with the tang of a file. "I do seem to recall the argument."

The two pigtailed heads nodded an 'I told you so' to each other. Two freckled faces brightened perceptibly.

"Uncle Gam, how much d'you think we weigh?"

Gunsmith looked up from filing the trigger guard, and gave the question his serious attention. "Seventy pound apiece. 'Bout right, come fall, for killing and pickling."

"And how much is a growed woman . . . fair hog scale weighing?" Again an anxious puckering of brows.

"Anywheres from a hundred up. Now git along, the two of you. I've work to do."

" 'Bye, Uncle Gam!" from both in unison. "And thank you a whole heap."

He was glad to have eased them of their trouble, whatever it was. They were good young'uns. And teaming up the way they did, they handled tasks heavy enough for a grown man or woman. But—Gunsmith looked up from his filing of the trigger guard—what possessed them to be all dressed up in their Sabbath best this mornin~? Had all the womenfolk gone crazy, from the Old Injun Fighter to young-'uns of ten-'leven years? Seemed as if.

The trigger guard took final shape, ready for burnishing. Gunsmith was still pondering. He'd admire to know what Eph had been up to, saying he aimed to get him a cook. And Jehosh! He had the answer now! Mary had warned him of it only yesterday. The women had started in on Eph.

The twins had told their ma. Mis' Sherman had passed word to Mis' Higgins, and the news had spread from woman to woman. Till it reached the ears of Widow Wilson, and even the Old Injun Killer, who must belong with the new folk ten mile or more up the Hogtown trail.

It didn't accord with women's nature to enquire too closely into what they hoped was true. They'd be off after Eph the way one dog sets another to chasing deer. If the Twins were only five or six years older, he'd favor their chances, for they could close up on Eph before he scented danger and took to his heels. But for a long hunt he'd put his stake on Injun Killer; she'd stay by the trail from thaw-out to freeze-up and back again. Tomorrow there'd be a whole pack of folk's sisters and aunts baying on his scent; and wasn't the day following coach-up day from Fort Ann and the south?

Gunsmith's eyes grew damp with mirth. The spectacles he had put on for the close-up burnishing work slid down to the tip of his nose. When Eph rode up home and dismounted, he'd step plumb into a nest of yellow-jackets!

Taking a piece of sawn lumber from a corner, Gam Reed dusted it off with his hand, picked out a piece of charcoal, and paused for inspiration. Then in large and careful characters lettered a sign: To

60

Eph Birdsell (Bachelor). And added a pointing arrow. With that pegged to the butternut tree next to the road he would have peace to work the rest of the day.

*   *   *

Noontide dinner over, and he was scarce back in the shop, tying on his apron, when the day took a turn for the better. For Dan'l and Viney Post slipped in.

A month or more since Gunsmith's crafty borrowing of the un-needed salt had brought its first reward, and the Posts had felt free to borrow neighborly help in return. Dan'l had brought first a hoe, and then a scythe blade from which the temper had been burned out, and Gunsmith showed the boy how, and let him do most of the work. Even had him lend a hand with some gun repairs, as though in payment for the charcoal burned on his several visits.

Young'un, garbed like her brother and just as silent, came down with Dan'l each time, like she was his 'prentice. Gunsmith would hear a tap on the workshop door and go out to let them in. There'd be twilight outside, but though it was early summer the inside of the shop would be dark. So Gunsmith would return to the kitchen for a candle and for an ember to re-kindle the forge. Then the three would work together, heating and hammering and quenching, till Young'un's eyes screwed up with sleep as she pumped the handle of the bellows, and Gunsmith set himself to keep watch on Dan'l lest in his weariness he grasp a red-hot iron, or mash a finger under the hammer. At the first there'd be no more than two-three words between them, unless Dan'l remembered to caution, "No call to be biting your nails, Young'un. Pa don't hold with it."

This was the first time they had come, the both together, by daylight. That showed they were between seasons with the farming, and that their toil had eased a mite. The girl was smiling and plump as ever, like some horses that condition up when others fall away on the same work and feed. But Dan'l's face was peaked, and when he stripped his shirt, the bones stood out sharply beneath the brown skin wherever there was no muscle to cover them. His broadaxe and handaxe, their edges worn so round they were past filing or whetting, showed where some of his strength had gone.

While he and Gunsmith set to work with forge and hammer to

61

draw out new edges, the old man listened to the proud tale of their labors. Corn, roots and cabbages and most garden truck promised well, but winter feed was the problem. Leaves from the woods would serve for bedding, but Peter and Paul must have fresh hay as well as roots and corn.

Dan'l and Young'un had cleaned the railed-off part of the pasture-land used for haying, Dan'l cutting the berry bushes and seedling trees, Young'un dragging them off to burn. Though how they found time and strength for it was hard to see.

Peter and Paul, being sociable minded, had walked into the hay meadow after them, brushing aside the rotted fencing like cobwebs. Dan'l and Young'un had to set-to and split more rail, and patch. The more they patched, the more there was to patch. Till it seemed they'd have twenty-thirty rod of rail fence to split and build if they purposed to take up hay that year.

"Eldest can't help none, being a woman," Dan'l pointed out. "With her cooking, and hoeing the garden, and soapmaking, and suchlike."

"Women!" said Young'un, in a voice as solemn deep as she could compass. "Women can't swing an axe nor handle oxen. Don't know as I aim to be a woman after all."

"Not aim to be a woman? Pa wouldn't hold with such talk," her brother reproved her. "When our hands gits to be six months ahead of our teeth, we'll see can we spare a swap to git ye learned how." As he explained to Gunsmith, there must be a good and a bad way to being a woman, same as to using an axe. And it wouldn't serve to start off wrong, and have to learn all over.

Gunsmith, silently burying a chuckle in his beard, nodded agreement, drove a wedge into the new axe handle to secure the head, rasped the wood off flush, and handed it to Young'un. She tried its edge with an expert thumb, picked out a stone on the bench and started to whet.

Dan'l was busy fitting part of the old axe handle to the smaller handaxe, in place of the haft they had needed to burn out. Gunsmith reached among the dust and cobwebs of the cross beams which braced the shop against the vibration of the machinery, and drew

62

down a pod-auger. He gave its edge a few careful wipes with a file and then a stone, and set the tool beside the boy.

"If you'd take this in exchange for the salt I borrowed, Dan'l, I'll be right pleased. A man don't want to stay beholden overlong, even to a friend."

Dan'l set down the handaxe to take up the auger and try its point and edge. He reckoned out aloud the gain he'd have from the tool when fall came and he set to roll up a log cabin and lean-to. Boring the roof timbers would take the best part of an hour a hole, using a hot iron. With an auger not half the time, and a better fit to the peg. And some day he'd have a puncheon floor to peg, Eldest having seen Mis' Reed's and set her heart on having one like.

'Twas the first Gunsmith had heard of Eldest coming to see Mary.

"Puncheon floor!" Young'un held the whetstone out at arm's length, and spat unerringly upon it. "Puncheon floors is pernickety!"

"They ain't, so, pernickety!" Dan'l protested. "Nossir, Young'un, they ain't. And when you've a call to spit on the whetstone, just kind of dribble till we get you learned how women ought. I reckon that's right, ain't it, Mist' Reed?" He appealed for confirmation. "Women-folk don't spit like they was pinning flies?"

"Pernickety!" Young'un insisted.

The boy and his sister were almost ready to go, and there was something Gunsmith still wanted to find out.

"I was half minded to ask once more did you need corn or seed in swap for more salt. But it's too late in the season now, and seems you had enough . . ." He let it trail off, half-questioning. And to keep the boy awhile handed him a sliver of glass to smooth down the new axe helve.

It seemed that Dan'l had borrowed seed from Sim Higgins, be-cause Dan'l's Pa had borrowed from Sim the year before, and maybe before that. When Sim had drawn the seed up to the Post place, he had brought out a paper, a quill and an inkhorn, and asked Dan'l to set his mark. Dan'l could do more than draw his mark; proudly he set his name to the paper, *Daniel Post*. He had to pretend to read the writing above it, as he could only spell out print. Dan'l had liked the paper, as it made the deal appear businesslike, and not a favor

63

begged from a neighbor. And whatever the paper said didn't matter, he was sure. For he could pay back all this year's borrowings from this year's harvest, the way crops promised.

But Gunsmith was troubled. And when the children had picked up their tools and trudged off homeward, Gunsmith went in and called Mary to the shop to ask her what was best done.

Setting name to paper meant lawyers and maybe trickery. And Sim Higgins was the kind of man who dursen't put his hands to his own pockets for fear he'd rob himself. Yet 'twas no use to warn Dan'l now, for whatever was done, was done.

Mary agreed. Dan'l would stand by his bond, thinking his pa would have stood to it. Not that Old Man Post ever came within a long gunshot of being all that Dan'l now remembered him to be.

"Kind of wondering if there wasn't some ways we could help. Maybe talk with Sim and show him how he'd lose in the end if he tried to be too smart and lawyerlike," Gunsmith suggested.

Mary shook her head emphatically. "No, Gam! You'd start with words, and end by dipping his head in his own pig trough, like as not. And the Posts no better off."

Still troubled, Gunsmith turned to his work. If Simpkin Higgins ever got to walking barefoot over the golden floor of Zion, the angels would need to keep a close watch on him. And pare his toenails to the quick. They would so.

CHAPTER SEVEN

THE wave of high pitched, feverish sound rolled up from the Post clearing, beat against the dark forest and retreated. Welled up again. 'Twas no more than the shrill chattering of the crickets, raising Cain against the heat of the August evening that wouldn't let them sleep. But Young'un stirred on her bed of hemlock boughs, tossed out a bare thin arm, and sighed.

She opened her eyes. Though it was still light outside, Dan'l slept like the dead, as he mostly did excepting such times as he got to felling trees and drawing stones and stumps in his sleep. Eldest, on the far side of the small pole-and-bough shelter, turned restlessly, the skeeters being mighty bad for the time of year.

That Molly—Young'un raised herself cautiously on one elbow— had she been milked? Gunsmith had said, clear as clear, that Young'un was to take the morning's milking, but naught about who'd tend to it evenings. Suppose now Preacher had rode up and held him in talk, or folks had come clamoring to have their rifles fixed for a coon hunt, because of the way the critters were tearing down the ripening corn. Would Gunsmith be sure to keep Molly in mind? It wasn't as though 'twas his own chore that he'd tend without thinking.

Carefully she raised her legs from the foot of the bed, so as not to waken Cat. Cat woke all the same, but only to stretch and settle himself again. It wasn't his hunting time yet, not till close on morning.

Out into the early starlight, drawing the doeskin shirt over her head. She glanced around. No call to waste good milk by pouring out what was left over from the morning, and besides the pail hadn't been scrubbed and scalded. If need were she could use Eph's.

65

Peter 'n' Paul lay in their favorite place where they'd catch the first breath of cool air to flow down the mountain side. They turned slow ponderous heads in unison but, seeing who it was, fell to chewing again. She swung up the trail and into the woods. Warmer among the trees. Darker too. The cricket chorus died to a murmur. Faint rustlings, and an odor of skunk, or maybe it was a fox. Off to the right she heard scuttlings and crashings, loud enough for a bear, but likely no more than a porcupine. When human folks finished their day's labor, that was the time when all the wild critters felt safe to come awake. "That Young'un Post," the porcupine would be grumbling, "she'd ought to be asleep long since. What's she fixing to do, up here in our woods?" But she wasn't fixing to do aught in the woods save hurry through. For all of her they could go their ways, the wild critters, hunting their night's food. She broke into a run.

And didn't slow to a walk till she was right out to the coach road, with the wheel ruts under foot and a faint breeze drifting down the valley. She turned in at Eph's gate, and couldn't but admire his tidy fence, and the house there, standing so strong and sure against the starlight, between the two twin maples. Some day the Post place would be like that.

Then around to the barn behind, to grope down the pail from its peg, and out into the pasture again. Molly might not know what was purposed, so long past her milking time, but when she saw the pail she'd understand and follow up to the barn.

Not a trace of Molly, nor the heifer either, in the upper pasture. Nor down by the water-fill. Way off in the settlement a dog barked, and another answered from up Hogtown road. The night over the valley was still, compared to over at the Post place, where the heat had set the crickets to chirping so. She could scarce bring herself to break the silence. If it had been Peter 'n' Paul she could have whistled. Likely Eph had a whistle or a call. Young'un tried "Molly! Here, Molly!" But her voice came out no more than a whisper.

It wasn't till she had hunted nigh over the whole place and even looked and listened beside the corn patch that she found where the cow was at. Right up close to the barn, but on the far side. When she saw the pail she didn't so much as stir from where she was lying. "No call to come pestering me this time of night," she said,

66

plain as plain, when Young'un stooped down to feel her bag. It was soft and cool. So Gunsmith hadn't forgotten to milk her.

"Better to be sure than sorry," Young'un told her. And went to hang up the pail.

It was then she heard the wagon wheels and voices. Turning in at Eph's gate, they were. Likely it was the same wagon had set the dog to barking down in the settlement. Groping for the peg in the dark barn she remembered she had seen Eph's wagon out in the yard. And besides he'd ridden down on the colt. But it was Eph's voice, and Gunsmith's. By the time she had run around to the front they had drawn up and hitched.

"Best cook in Fort Ann. Though she's kind of little and dark complected," said Eph in a loud whisper. And set to dragging something heavy to the tailboard of the wagon.

Gunsmith caught ahold and heaved whatever it was safely to the ground. "She's heavy for all she's so puny." Young'un heard him chuckle deeply. "Still and all don't know but there's others I'd sooner have my arms around."

Eph dropped down off the wagon, pulled the string of his door-latch, and, one to each side, they carried the thing in. A heavy box, it was. But that didn't account for the comical talk. Young'un hesitated in the shadow of the laylock, for it didn't serve to pry into other folk's affairs.

She heard them set it heavily on the floor inside; iron, it had looked to be. It was more than human nature could bear, to slip off without discovering the purpose of that box.

"Cal'late I'll stop and help you fix her in place," said Gunsmith's voice. "Go fetch in the light so we can see what we're at."

Young'un was up in the wagon and reaching down the pierced tin lantern to him from where it had been hidden beneath a pile of sacks.

"Land sakes, Young'un Post, where you sprung from?" Eph stepped back as though she'd handed him a rattler, no less.

Before she could explain about the milk and Molly, Gunsmith in the doorway let out a rumbling laugh. "Told ye so, Eph! Told ye they was on your trail! They nigh to have pestered me out of my life, the womenfolks has, with their 'Seed aught of Eph Birdsell?' and their 'Where's Mister Birdsell at?'" His voice took on a comical tone like Widow Wilson's. "I 'low you'll be married before the week's out!"

"Cal'late I'll return the wagon first thing in the morning, and stay clear of here till the womenfolk have stopped actin' up," said Eph. He bade Young'un step inside, then closed the door and even pulled in the latchstring. Opening the lantern he lighted a pair of candles from it and set them on the table.

And still Young'un couldn't make sense of that iron box. It stood there on the scrubbed puncheon floor on its three short legs, and didn't reach much higher than Gunsmith's knee. It had a hole in the back with a kind of metal collar on it and in the front a little door that opened on hinges, neat as anything you could see.

Gunsmith and Eph lifted it again and carried it towards the hearth. And land sakes! whatever had Eph been up to there? He had walled in the whole of the hearth opening with stone and clay, excepting for a foolish kind of little hole in the middle that looked as though it nigh about fitted that collar on the back of the iron box. And now, with a handful of small stones and some clay he had ready to hand, he built in around the collar.

"I see you were all fixed for your cook when you rode down for her," said Gunsmith. "Whyn't you take down your own wagon?"

"Ishmael Jones was all set to throw her out, not being able to make her draw proper. But if I'd taken down the wagon he'd have guessed what for, and riz the price on me." Eph gave Gunsmith a knowing look.

As they prodded the clay into place with their fingertips Young'un gathered from their talk that not even Gunsmith had known Eph's purpose. Until Eph, wanting someone to share his triumph, and maybe help lift the iron box, had halted the wagon outside the forge and tossed pebbles at Gunsmith's window, so he wakened and came down. Some kind of a grown-up joke it was, she could see that plain. This talk about a cook, when it was no more than an iron box. And setting it in place and plugging in the stone and clay at this hour of the night, when most folks were in bed; and all the laughing and suchlike. But still and all she'd got to wait and see for herself, if so be she was let.

Gunsmith, wiping his hands on his trousers, stood looking at the box. "Ain't another such in all these hills. Nor a woman who gets wind of one of these newfangled contraptions who won't give her eye teeth to be the first to get to use it." He burst out laughing again. "Don't know but I'd as lief stay and see how she works. Where's your kindling, Eph?"

Young'un took the lantern and ran out and fetched in a basket full of chips and a smitch of dry hay, though she couldn't see how they were going to build a fire with the chimney all blocked up, the way it was. Eph lifted a lid off one side of the iron box, screwed up a twist of hay, lighted it from a candle, held it till it caught and then thrust it inside the box. He spread the chips over the hay, carefully, then set back the lid.

Of course smoke started to pour out, just wherever there was a crack. It didn't make sense, what Eph was trying to do. A fire couldn't burn without it had air. But after a minute or two the smoke stopped oozing, as Eph shifted a slide down at the bottom of the box. There was a crackling sound inside. And land alive!—there was a nice little fire a-popping and a-crackling away to itself inside the iron box. Magic it was, no less! And Eph and Gunsmith grinned at each other like they were touched in the head, or had found a whole silver dollar in the road.

"Well, she draws all right," said Eph, bragging-like.

"She sure does," said Gunsmith. "Only trouble I can see, you'll have a sight of sawing to do, and splitting too, to get your logs small enough."

"But less wood to cut and draw down," Eph pointed out. "Seeing there's no heat wasted, roaring away up the chimney."

That looked to be the truth, it sure did. Already Eph had to go and throw open the shutters because of the room heating up so. And with no more than a few handfuls of chips at that. He bent and opened up the little door in the front and put in a hand. "Oven's hotted up a'ready," he said.

Gunsmith bent down to peer in. "Don't cal'late you could bake bread or the like in that?" he asked.

Eph grinned. "What say we try her?" He looked around the place. "I've got some early apples there. Won't take long." He put

69

some short lengths of wood in the top of the box, brought the apples, cored them with his knife and put them—three of them, Young'un couldn't help but note—on a tin plate, poured a little water from the bucket on the bench into the plate and set it inside the oven. He shut the door.

They sat down to wait. Nobody had said that Young'un should be home and in bed, though she expected they would any minute now. Still, there was that third apple; three apples for two people didn't divide even. And when Eph asked her would she fancy a sup of cider she knew she'd be let to bide awhile longer.

He came up from the cellar with two mugs, one for himself and one for Gunsmith, Young'un not hankering for any since it was like to be hard this time of year. There was talk of this and that, that didn't rightly concern Young'un; of what sort of wood would be best suited to the "stove," that was the name they gave to the iron box. And whether there'd be means to keep it alight all night in wintertime. And wasn't it going to take a sight of cleaning out of ashes? a big fireplace needing such attention only three-four times a year. Young'un could see that if you were used to cooking on the hearthstone you'd need to learn all over again with a cookstove. But, like Gunsmith said, any woman would hanker to own one.

"And that sets me in mind, Eph. Since Viney here is the first to set eyes on it, seems to me she's got some kind of a right to first refusal. To say 'will she or won't she' marry you."

Eph took a quick pull at the cider jug, set it down and wiped his mouth on his hand.

"Of course Eph's getting up in years," said Gunsmith, addressing Young'un this time, "but he has a good house and barn, some likely livestock, and now the little iron stove."

Eph had. And with another pair of hands to help him he could clear more woodlot, stretch out the ploughland and the grazing, both. And he couldn't be harder taskmaster than Eldest and Dan'l together. Young'un had liked him ever since she could remember, and the more after he had brought that string of fish, way back in the spring. If she had to marry, and most folks came to it sooner or later, Eph would suit as well as any. Though of course it would mean parting with Peter 'n' Paul.

70

But 'twas for Eph to speak. And Young'un waited, watching his face. He was smiling, but he had a nice smile, what she could see of it for his short black beard.

"What say, Elvina Post?" he asked, calling her proper and by her full name as no one ever did. "Will you or won't you?"

Young'un wiped back a drop of sweat that had gathered on her eyebrow. It wasn't everyone that was asked in marriage so young. And by a grown man with a right good home. Next-neighbor too, was Eph Birdsell, which made it special sweet seeing she'd not have to dwell far from Eldest and Dan'l.

Eph would give her a gown, seeing there'd be no time to learn to spin or weave for herself. Not at first. And it wouldn't be fitten to go to Meeting on Eph's arm, wearing the patched buckskins. And folks would call her Elvina, just as Eph had done, and the little'uns would all have to call her 'Ma'am' or she'd make pretence not to hear them. Likely she'd have little'uns of her own, soon as she learned the how of it. Maybe Eph would know, or she could ask around of the other married folks. 'Twas a noble prospect.

Only—only the Post place wasn't fixed yet so Dan'l could handle it alone with Eldest. Eph could plough single-handed, but oxen weren't like horses; they had to be led, to have someone walk ahead to show them. Even Peter 'n' Paul. And that minded her of the saying in the Good Book, about not taking your hand from the plough, and something more about not so much as looking off. Marrying Eph would be more than looking off . . .

"If 'tweren't for the cookstove, and the other women all clamoring on his trail, there'd be no call to decide right off," Gunsmith pointed out. "Eph's liable to stay reasonable spry for another few years."

But she was coming to a decision. "There's a sight to do yet, up on the Post place." She began slowly, hoping Eph wouldn't take it too hard. "There's the corn most ready to get in. And then I don't know but what Eldest ought to get herself married first, and that would leave Dan'l with no one to fend for him. Of course," she added, "we'll still be next-neighbors."

"That's so," said Eph, accepting her refusal, and nodding two-three times. "Yes, we'll still be seeing each other about."

So she had said the right thing, and Eph hadn't been hurted a mite.

It had made her kind of sad to say 'no' to livestock and farm. And to Eph himself. But the apple, when Eph took it from the stove all sputtering hot and filling the room with an odor little short of heaven, went a long way to cure her feeling. Eph even brought up a little cup of cream from the cellar, skimmed from the pan of milk Gunsmith had set down there that evening.

Young'un had never tasted the match of it, nor thought she was like to again, so honey-sweet and fragrant. She ate it slowly, savoring every morsel, licking the last drop of sweetness and cream from the horn spoon, running her tongue around her lips instead of wiping it off on the back of her hand the way Ma had taught her. It was beyond bounds to hope for another.

Then Eph got up and said he'd best stable the horses till tomorrow, and Gunsmith said he'd see her a way along the road.

Which he did. Right past the hemlocks, which was the darkest part of the trail. And Eldest and Dan'l had never missed her, hadn't so much as stirred when she got back. Nor Cat neither.

* * *

It wasn't every day that your hand was asked in marriage. It set you to thinking right solemn thoughts, on your bed in the dark of the shelter. Like, why did men marry women, seeing it set the both to quarreling so? And how was it that children couldn't be born without folks got married? Was it Preacher that wouldn't let? But even if she woke up Eldest, Eldest wouldn't have the answers. All she'd say would be: "You'll know all in good time, Young'un. When you're growed."

Eph wouldn't have asked her unless he had wanted to wed. And it stood to reason that if he wanted a wife he'd a right to have one. Nor it wouldn't do for him to take just the first that came along. Or the second, it would be, counting herself as really the first. Men hadn't a proper understanding of what women were like. He'd be as helpless as a man that was raised with oxen, trying to choose him a horse and not knowing the good from the bad.

Wakeful in the soft hot darkness Young'un's thoughts ran this way and that; but they all came back to the same thing: that, seeing she hadn't taken Eph herself, she had a duty to see that the one he did take was fitten. By the time Cat had stretched, and gone out

72

to get himself a mess of mice for breakfast, Young'un knew what she purposed, clear as clear. She followed Cat out, hoping he hadn't overslept this once and that it was still a good few hours to dawn.

It was darker than before, and so still you could most hear your own thoughts as though you spoke them out loud. Of how the Widow Wilson wouldn't serve for Eph, being she was too old. Nor Albacinda, for she hadn't a morsel of gumption and git-up-and-git. And likely Eph wouldn't hanker after being kin to all the Miller childer. It all boiled down to Phebe Callender, who was nowise puny, little though she was. She would flesh up and grow real strong if Eph cherished her.

Young'un had tiptoed out of the shelter and was half up the trail before she got to thinking would Phebe agree. Could be she would need a talking around. She and Eph had quarreled, more's the pity, so it wouldn't serve to sugar up Eph overmuch. But no harm to telling what a good little cow Molly was with her creamy milk, and freshening with a heifer calf most every spring. Bull calves were only fit for vealing. And Eph's colt that was growing into a noble horse. And the old horse . . . though best not to say anything of Prince as Phebe would know the way he laid back his ears and bit. And the fields and the house and barn—Young'un summoned all her best arguments. It was Providence' own blessing she had seen that little stove and could tell Phebe all about it. And of how tasty the apple had been, and the way the stove could warm up the house in the wintertime; why, there wouldn't be a warmer house than Eph's all the way to Fort Ann.

When she reached it, well before dawn, Gunsmith's house was black as the woods behind. Not a light nor a smell of smoke in the whole settlement, and not a cock had crowed. So likely she was in good time for her purpose.

She tossed a stone onto the roof of Gunsmith's house, Phebe being certain to sleep in the attic, and heard it rattle from shingle to shingle with enough noise to set every dog a-barking. But they didn't, not a one of them. It took two more stones before Phebe put her head out of the little window. Young'un beckoned violently, and made signs for Phebe to dress.

Like an age it was, till Phebe opened the house door and came out, quietly closing it behind her. Still no one else in the settlement had stirred.

"If you're truly minded to have Eph for husband," Young'un whispered, "'tis now or never," and drew her out into the roadway.

Phebe didn't say a word, being busied rubbing the sleep from her eyes. And Young'un had her right out of the settlement and a ways up the road before Phebe stopped to say:

"But, Viney, I can't . . ."

"He's minded now to take the first woman he sets eyes on," Young'un declared. "And Gunsmith says there's a sight of 'em, hunting him a'ready. Don't seem you'd make him a worse wife than Widow Wilson, or . . . or Sim Higgins' wife's brother's darter."

Phebe jerked up her chin. "Eph Birdsell is welcome to Jessie Wilson, for all of me." But she came along without further to-do; and if she had not, Young'un was ready with the arguments.

The wagon was still outside, dark against the still dark sky, just as Eph had left it. As she mounted the doorsteps Young'un heard the horses stamp in the barn. Her groping fingers found the latch-string had been pulled in. But there was the door out back. Phebe would have hung behind, but Young'un hadn't planned it over and over just to be turned back at the last minute. She set a firm hand on Phebe's elbow and kind of steered her around.

True enough, Eph had forgotten the other door. But land sakes, if Phebe didn't go and jib again! Only it was too late now, Young'un had her inside. It took a world of caution to grope to the stove, and find the stick Eph had used to lift the lid. The stove was warm enough to make Young'un hopeful. And sure enough, as she put her hand down into the feathery ashes, a red eye of ember winked up at her.

She whispered to Phebe to stay put, seeing the girl didn't know where stools and table were, and hurried past to bring in a smitch of kindling and hay. Wasn't hardly no time at all before she had the fire blown up and had carried a light on a pine sliver to one of the candles. Swiftly she clapped back the stove lid, for the smell of smoke might waken Eph where sounds would leave him undisturbed. Mighty lucky he'd closed the door to the other room when he went to bed.

74

Phebe stood gawping at the stove, scarce able to believe her eyes. Young'un risked a whisper.

"It's the 'cook' Eph brung back last night from Fort Ann. The one he went down to fetch."

"The cook . . ." Phebe started to say aloud. Then clapped hand over her mouth.

Young'un nodded vigorous agreement and pointed. And it was a wonder how Phebe's whole face seemed to change. Her mouth kind of quirked up at the corners and there was a gleam in her eyes.

"I'm minded to teach Eph Birdsell a lesson he won't forget," she whispered. And by candlelight began to move quickly about the kitchen. Young'un saw her purpose. It would be a laugh on the man when folks heard how Phebe Callender had broke into his house and cooked him his breakfast and maybe done his chores, all before he could open an eyelid. Likely she'd slip out in the barn then and leave him nigh frantic to guess which one of 'em had done it, the Widow Wilson or who.

Young'un would have helped, and glad to, but Phebe said she was to slip off home and do her own chores before she returned for the milk. There was sense to that for the sky was lightening a'ready.

*   *   *

It was full sunlight and already getting to be warm, most too warm to carry back the milk, when Young'un came within sight of Eph's again. But it would be Eldest's fault, not her own, if the milk soured; Eldest wanting this done, and that and the other till you'd think the little shelter was a two-story house, no less, and needing to be scrubbed and scoured from attic to cellar. Pernickety was Eldest, and on this, of all mornings!

From Eph's chimney rose a shimmer of heat, and the borrowed wagon was still in the yard. Young'un chirked up.

There was a kind of buzz about, like from Mist' Ditch's bees, but nary a bee in sight; which made it puzzling. And the nearer she got to Eph's house the more the buzz increased. No, not bees, but human talk, all coming out of Eph's house.

The latchstring was out, but Young'un hesitated to pull it, for the noise within. And when she did, the door wouldn't budge, not more than a crack. It couldn't be aught amiss, for the noise was a good part laughter, women's laughter; and that whetted her curiosity the more.

She sped around the corner towards the back door. But out of the side window hung two pairs of brown, bramble-scratched legs. If the Sherman twins could hang half in and half out of Eph's window, Viney Post could too. Young'un squeezed in betwixt the twins and they shoved over with no more than a grunt, not looking to see who it was, their eyes a sight too busy with what went on within.

Now it was plain at a glance why the door hadn't swung open to her push. It couldn't. Eph's small room was packed from log wall to log wall with womenfolk; women sitting and standing, women eating and talking both to once and laughing with the same breath. Not angered at Phebe nor Eph nor anyone, but happy as though dandling their first-born.

And there was Mis' Reed kneeling before the new iron stove, a big mixing bowl beside her, spooning out a batch of batter cakes onto a flat iron plate and sliding it into the oven. Eph, who had aimed to be well on his way back to Fort Ann by this time of morning, was wedged up against the big, closed-in fireplace. And Phebe in the little chair beside him. He had aholt of Phebe's hand, and by the scairt look he was casting at all those women it was plain he'd have bolted, but for Phebe's gentling of him.

Phebe, being a woman, or inclined that way, was giving the other women as good as she took. "No, ma'am, I cal'late to keep him. And he seems the same minded, seeing he ain't let go my hand for two hours."

Eph dropped her hand and looked hotter in the face even than the room called for. But his hand crept back to hers again almost at once.

Hepziba Ditch, hidden behind a woman in the corner, called something Young'un couldn't catch, for the rattle of talk. Phebe came right back at her, not calling her Mis' Ditch, but plain Hepziba, and saying she hadn't so much as suspicioned there'd be the new-fangled iron stove, before today. But still and all, and Preacher now being on his way up, she'd marry that too, since 'twas Eph's. And Eph squeezed her hand, plain for all to see.

That set off the chatter again till Young'un's ears were fit to crack. Most every woman in the settlement was here, and some from out beyond. Gunsmith had said last night how the womenfolk were all on Eph's trail, and for every one that aimed to wed him and his fine house there must be five or six had come along for company. There was even Widow Wilson, squeezed so close onto the woman in front of her she seemed to be browsing on the other's bonnet.

She twisted her mouth clear of the ribbons to say how she'd been hoping all along that Eph would marry Phebe Callender, and how fortunate it was that she just happened along this way and could be among the first to congratulate the happy pair.

She believed it too, Young'un could see that. And most all the other women clapped a few times, to show they felt likewise, even those who'd been trying to marry him. It didn't seem to Young'un that she would ever get around really to understanding the ways of womenfolk. Maybe she never would, not even when she got to be an old thornback of a spinster of thirty years or more.

Well, Eph was going to marry Phebe, maybe this very day. Young'un breathed a little sigh and dropped from the windowsill. The sight wasn't just relief, for it was hard to be asked in marriage one night and before high noon of the next day know that the same man was wedding another. But it was all as Young'un had planned, and, she told herself, she ought to be content.

She glanced around. There was Molly down in the pasture, and it didn't take half an eye to see that she'd been milked. So the milk would be setting in its pail in the cellar, and two-three women would be standing atop the cellar door right now. Eldest would have to do without the milk today and maybe many a day, and there'd be no call for Young'un to come running across to milk Molly. Not ever again.

Young'un started slowly along the path towards home. But it wasn't far before she hastened her stride. Phebe and Eph and the other folk might afford a morning's idleness, but the Posts hadn't time for such, not with the corn ripening and a score of things to set hand to.

CHAPTER EIGHT

YOUNG'UN's left hand reached up, snapped an ear of corn and cast it forward onto the pile, as her right hand snapped another ear from its stalk. Two more visible tokens added to the scores upon scores that had already gone to the sled and then up to the corncrib, tokens that the Posts were winning their six months' struggle against hunger.

Young'un could have sung for joy; would have sung if only it had been the last row. But that was some ways off yet, and the sun sinking lower and redder. Snap, snap, and if the stalk looked bare to the eye, a shake of the stem to feel if the eye told true. Four stalks to most every hill. Cutworm, crow and squirrel pests had forgone their toll this year.

"Full-loaded," Dan'l called from the sled.

To avoid wasted steps, Young'un filled her arms from the nearest pile to carry back to the sled. Then, of course, her nose had to itch, her arms being 'cumbered, and the silk from the corn tassels set her to itching all down her front and back, but her bare neck most of all. It was a relief to jerk her armful upwards into the small frame Dan'l had fashioned on the sled top, to call to Peter 'n' Paul and walk in front of them, scratching to heart's content. Then it was almost as good to drop the arms and let the ache drain out of them. By that time she and the oxen had drawn uphill and around back of the big crib Dan'l had built.

The oxen stopped of their own accord where they'd been halted so often that day. Young'un unpinned the yoke from the pole, Eldest left her shucking beside the crib to come and help. The two of them set a sapling under the sled and levered it over on one side, pouring most of its contents out onto the dry turf. Between them they pulled out the remainder, and turned the sled back onto its runners.

Dan'l whistled, and Peter 'n' Paul trudged off down for another load.

"Rest yourself a moment, Viney," Eldest counseled.

Young'un jerked her hair back with a swing of the head, and seated herself on the wooden stool that Dan'l had made to try the new auger that Gunsmith gave him. 'Twas easier to do as Eldest said than outright contrary her. And besides, it was lonely for Eldest up here by herself, with no Dan'l or even Peter 'n' Paul. It was a rest too, reaching down instead of up, freeing the golden cob from its rustling shuck, and casting it upward into the crib, instead of flinging it down to the ground.

"If Dan'l would give himself a rest," Eldest said the words just as Young'un opened her mouth to say the same, "he'd have more strength for his tasks. He's eating none too good."

Young'un's hands felt an extra large head of corn, her fingers tore the husk back but not off; her eyes approved its unmarred size and beauty which set it aside as fit for next year's seed. With a flick of the wrist she tossed it onto a separate pile. Pick, husk, cast . . . pick, husk, cast . . . "Dan'l's bound he'll have the last of the corn in before tomorrow. To show Mist' Higgins he's done right to trust us with the loan of seed."

" 'Tis sinful pride, no less," Eldest sounded like Preacher, even favored him in looks as she pointed with a finger. But purtier in the face of course. She'd Ma's smooth brows, straight nose, and the littlest of mouths beneath. And eyes that were nigh as big and sorrowful as Peter's or Paul's. Young'un felt a twinge of envy. But, still and all, purtiness filled no bellies on a farm, and it took more than purtiness to keep pace with Dan'l day in, day out, and try to lighten his burden. 'Twas hurtful to see the thinness of his bare arms and back, and the way he had to set his teeth to the hefting of loads.

A sight of the low red sun dropping into the tall trees and Young'un jumped to her feet and hurried to the shelter for the milk bucket. Cat came in from the woods and made to follow her, so she had to go back with him and ask Eldest to hold him till she was up the trail a ways.

The evening's milk, that Phebe said she and Eph couldn't use, had come right handy the last two-three weeks. At the start of the season there had been meat and fish until they had sickened of it. So that the first wild greenstuff Eldest had found, and the thinnings from the garden rows, had never tasted so good before. Then had come a time when Eldest had pinched herself to have food for the other two. Dried meat and fish spoiling in the damp heat, and corn, squash, beans not yet ripe. They had been forced to dig potatoes before they were fit, and to eke out with other roots. There had been wild strawberries, blackcaps and blackberries for the gathering. But raw or cooked they weren't nowise working food. Latterly had come apples and pears from the trees Pa had planted, and corn and vegetables a plenty. But it seemed that menfolk and Dan'l was doing a man's work—needed meat the way womenfolk didn't. There was no gainsaying that men and women were as different, some ways, as horses and oxen. You could see that from the way Dan'l fell off in flesh when Young'un and Eldest throve on the same food. Nor, come to think of it, he hadn't sickened so on everlasting fish and meat back in the spring.

Young'un quickened her pace to a half-run. For the sun gleaming through the thinning leaves was lower than she had thought. Plump squirrels, busy gathering their winter stores, scolded at her from every other tree, or so it seemed. Already they had the best of the chestnuts, and the hickory nuts. Soon as the farm work eased a mite, she vowed she'd have the nuts back again, digging them out with her hands from the hoards at the foot of the trees. The Posts had a right to a share from their own trees.

Squirrels had never seemed so many. All that good stew meat racing from tree to tree. Powder and lead back there in the shelter, but Pa's rifle somewhere up in the northern woods. Of course Dan'l would set his snares, just as soon as time allowed. But squirrels weren't so easy ketched as that. Nor coons neither. Partridges whirred off down the hill, from the purple bunches of wild grapes on the tree tops. She must remember to tell Dan'l where she had marked them.

A late summer, like it promised to be, would mean they could trap and maybe fish for a week or so, and rest themselves and the oxen before starting on the cabin. Dan'l had promised himself he'd have all the popple felled, drawn down, skun and waiting ahead of time. But there wasn't so much as a single stick waiting, out of all the logs they'd need. For there'd been no getting ahead of the seasons this year, only hurrying, toiling after. Though if it hadn't been for the need to split all those fence rails . . .

Surprise at what lay before her eyes checked Young'un's thoughts and stride. The whole valley to the south was painted by the turning leaves. Scarlet, deep crimson, yellow, green, and green that was nigh to black. As if that wasn't enough, the clouds were red where they were low to the west, and yellow where they were higher to the east, and the sky blue-green like water. Young'un had scarce looked up and off all summer, with her eyes on the ploughland, and on the grazing, on the oxen and the growing things, on what she was carrying or the tool she was using. Last time she had glanced down the valley the leaves were no more than budding out on some of the trees.

She broke into a run past the old oak, scarce turning color yet, but its acorns scattered about the ground. It wasn't all acorns the squirrels fancied, and those they didn't were poison. The good acorns, ground fine, washed and mixed with cornmeal, made good famine bread, but Pa said the only safe way was to rob the squirrels' caches. There would be no hunger this year, not with all that corn and roots.

In Mosquito Hollow the stream was tempting warm for the time of year. 'Twas all Young'un could do to step across the shallows, and not shed her clothes and wash the corn itch from her skin in the deep pool.

* * *

She was late to the Birdsells' as it was. For the cow wasn't to be seen at the pasture bars, calling to be milked. Nor Phebe setting under the laylock in the last of the eventide sun, sorting and readying fruits and vegetables for her drying baskets. As Young'un reached the barn, Phebe stripped the last teat, and picked up pail and milking stool, Eph loosed Molly's head from the stanchion, and they all stood aside for Molly to back out. Molly stood awhile at the door of the barn, as though making up her mind where she'd find a bite of grazing so late in the year. Then decided to take a drink while she considered, and moved off down towards the spring.

Eph looked at Phebe, and the two of them laughed. Young'un laughed too, for comradeship, hoping Molly wouldn't be shamed the way Peter 'n' Paul might.

Phebe took Young'un's pail to tie a cloth over for the straining. And gave Eph another look. Eph cleared his throat.

"Kind of figuring on what to do when she calves again, in"—he counted on his fingers—"early February. There's her and this year's calf, a likely little heifer. And the next calf makes three. And the team besides, and wagon and plough and suchlike. Ain't room for them all in the barn. But there's no sale for a heifer from veal age till she's most old enough to breed. Two years of trouble and no return for it. I'd give her away if I knowed where."

It couldn't be true of course, but it sounded to Young'un that Eph was minded to give away the little heifer. Not trade her, but outright give. And just because of the space she took in his barn.

Phebe untied the wet cloth and threw it back into her empty milking pail. "Don't seem as if I've the heart to have her killed."

If only Dan'l was here, maybe he'd think up some way to take the heifer. For the Posts would never in years be able to buy a grown cow. And a farm without a cow was no more than a stretched out garden. The heifer would cost nothing, and Peter 'n' Paul would never miss the little she'd eat, being there was hay and corn for all three and a plenty summer grazing. But no barn to winter her over. No barn. And nothing in its stead.

It was hard just to say "Thank you" for the milk, and to pick up the pail. 'Twas harder when Eph lifted the bars for Young'un, and the little heifer came cavorting up, graceful as a deer, and wanted to squeeze through too, and had to be slapped to make her keep nose out of the milk. When the bars were safely back, and the heifer on the right side of them, she turned her pink nose to Eph and Phebe to see had they anything in their hands or in the other pail. And stamped on Eph's foot, mighty impatient. Then threw up her tail and cavorted away again. A laughable sweet sight, that spoiled little heifer.

"Your corn most in, I hear," Eph Birdsell called after her.

Young'un called back that Dan'l wanted everything ready for Mist' Higgins on the morrow.

"Sim Higgins!" Young'un heard Eph's voice behind her.

Then Phebe saying, "You'll run right down to Uncle Gam this very moment, and tell him about Sim Higgins." And what sounded to be an argument fading away behind her, as she crossed the rutted

82

road and slithered down the steep slope towards the stream, trying not to spill so much as a drop of the four quarts of milk despite the tricky dusk.

It was dark as night under the hemlocks on the further side of the stream. Bare feet had to remember that here was a stone, and there a fallen tree, and pick out a way the eyes couldn't see. When a bough spread across the way, a hand went out unthinking to set it aside, though the eyes could see neither shape nor color. Seemed almost as though you heard things instead of seeing them. Could be that you did, for just as soon as the afterglow faded, the trees set to whispering to each other.

In daylight there'd be beasts and insects, gabbing away. And the same in full night. The trees doing no more than flicker and flap their leaves, or groan their boughs as the wind made them. But in the after-sunset stillness there'd be first one whisper, then another, too faint to catch, try as you might. You could stop, and strain your ears till they felt to have grown as long as the oxen's; and yet hear nothing. Then you went on again, a twig snapping beneath your feet, and dry doeskin flapping around your ankles, and a rustling between sleeve and coat. And the trees would begin to whisper again. You could feel it, even though you couldn't rightly hear it.

'Twas no use to try to catch them at it. But Young'un tried once again. Making all ready in her mind, that in three paces she'd stop sharp as though she'd run nose against tree trunk. One . . . two . . . THREE. Halted frozen in mid-stride, balancing on one foot, the other still in the air. Over on the far side of the valley, two-three miles away, a tree crashed down. And it sounded not eighty rod distant. That was how still the air was. But the whispering of the trees had stopped. 'Twasn't no manner of use trying to trap their talk, though she'd tried most every way. It seemed as though the trees could tell her thoughts unuttered. If human folks got wiser as they grew older, trees, like the big oak she was passing under, must be mighty wise with all their hundreds of years listening and watching and learning. Stood to reason it would know just how you were telling yourself one . . . two . . . three . . . and how you were planning to stop. And be prepared for you.

"That Post Young'un's making ready to trap us again," the big oak would whisper warning to younger trees around. And just as you told yourself THREE, it would whisper, "Hush!" and the trees would hush, just in time, in the very midst of what they were saying. You could most feel their impatience as they waited for you to stop listening and go on.

But there was still another way she'd thought of, and not tried yet account of how difficult it was. Not even thinking of stopping until you stopped. So the trees wouldn't know what was in your mind.

You looked down over the valley, where all those magic colors had been less than an hour back. Too costly-precious they were to leave out when no one was looking. Like Meeting gowns that some folks wore. Soon as they were off the road they'd carry the shoes, and strip the rest the minute they were home. Some day Young'un would have a real gown like Eldest, and body clothes to go under. And tanned leather shoes, maybe, though only for sitting in Meeting. Not for walking. Even greased moccasins blindfolded the feet till they couldn't know where to tread, and you had to look at the ground and tell them where. You'd have to carry a lantern after dark if you were rich and foolish enough to wear tanned leather shoes.

"Stop!" she shot herself the order.

Maybe she'd been part expecting to say it, for it didn't trick the trees. Not a whisper from them. But she'd try again.

The little heifer calf, now. Once you got to thinking about her blithesome ways, and what she'd mean in milk and butter and cheese in a few years, you'd not think about the trees and their talking. And by the time she was fit to calve, there'd be more than the milk. There would be a new little calf every ten-twelve months. Sol Broadmoor would lend his bull, maybe for nothing. 'Twas Sol's old bull had got Peter 'n' Paul, and if the young bull was as good, there might be twin calves from the little heifer. 'Twas a wonder, loving her so, Eph and Phebe had the heart to part with the sweet little bugger.

That minded her to tell Eldest that Molly was like to calve in early February. For it would mean Eph would have to dry her up, so there'd be no more milk from Christmas on. But Dan'l would be trapping then, and there would be no lack of meat . . .

"Stop!" Young'un stopped so sharply to her own order that she all but slopped the milk out of the bucket. And if she hadn't actually

84

caught the last whispers of the trees, she'd as good as. She was down among the beeches now, close to the edge of the farm clearing. Beeches were always scrubbed clean and gray, and stayed all together, not mixing with hickory that shed its untidy bark, nor the white birch whose smartness put their plain gray to shame. They would misprise the noble pines and hemlocks for being different, and pretend they could not understand their foreign talk from the north. They would say sneaky envious things even about the great oak, you could lay to that. Uppity, the beeches were, setting too great stock in themselves. So there was no call, no call at all, to take heed of what they whispered about you.

'Twasn't true either, what they said. Young'un was no more feared of the dark than they were themselves. She didn't have to huddle close with a lot of others the way they did. She wasn't making play with trying to catch the trees talking, just to put the darkness out of mind. And anyways, there was Eldest's supper fire gleaming ahead.

Nossir! Some day she'd show. Some day she'd walk right over the top of Mount Diameter in pitchy nighttime. And back again. Without so much as a stick in hand. Not now, this instant, because of the milk. Maybe not till summer, when the wolves, which would be on their way down now, had gone north again.

Kind of a pity to have missed the wise talk of the oak, and the laughter of the birches. The mean old uppity beeches . . .

"That you, Viney?" called Eldest. "Land sakes, you've been gone a time!"

CHAPTER NINE

NEXT morning's sun rose clear and hot as though September hadn't come and gone. It didn't rise up from beyond the Lake, of course, as it did in summer, but most over the peak of old Hunchback. Pa had showed how to tell the months that way, but Ma had always set more store on the flowers than the calendar. For her, this would be blue aster month, as it was for Eldest.

But Young'un had more to do than stand and gape down from the hillside. Dan'l had left the last few ears of corn standing on their stalks, and nothing would serve but to have the new corn-crib all ready to show Sim Higgins. He'd been up in the woods with his axe since dawn, had Dan'l, while Young'un and Eldest sat and husked. Now 'twas Young'un's task to draw down the sticks he had cut and trimmed.

Pindling little sticks they were, not more than ten feet long and six inches across. Not like the logs they would cut and draw for the cabin. Working the oxen separately without the yoke, because of the rocks and other obstacles, she drew the sticks, one by one, down a ways to where there was a rough trail to the sugar bush. It took quite a knack to stack them over the chain, and bring the chain around and fasten it. Pa and Dan'l had always done it between them when they had drawn down firewood or the like. Still and all she'd best learn on this light stuff before starting on real timber.

Down below, through the thinning leaves, she could see Eldest sitting by the door of the cabin shelling beans. Not that there was door or cabin, but only the outlines in the turf that Eldest had cut with a spade, with stones to mark door and window and fireplace. Eldest had spoken for a puncheon floor and a cellar below, but wasn't

86

like to have them for a two-three year. Nor the shingle roof, though that would come first. Dan'l's thatching on the shelter hadn't kept out the rain, try as he would, and he planned to start in shingling the cabin as soon as he had it built.

Young'un hooked the chain right at last, and passed a rawhide around the tail of the pile. She swung up the heavy yoke with scarce a struggle, where only a few months before she'd had to strain and heave. Showed how fast you could grow, once you set mind to it. Easy to pass the loose end of the chain through the ring of the yoke and hook it back; but when the oxen moved forward to take up the slack the sticks were still dangerously close to their hind legs. Didn't seem to be ary way out of it. She'd just have to be almighty careful, and not let the sticks get to over-running.

She spoke to Peter and Paul, and held firm to the rawhide tail, ready to snub it around rock or tree bole and so swing the heavy bundle sideways if the taut chain from the yoke showed signs of slackening. If she had sinned, and she was like to've done, don't punish the oxen for it, Lord! 'Twouldn't be nowise fair. It Peter or Paul broke a leg so Dan'l had to bring the axe and kill him, she'd never forgive either herself or the Lord.

Maybe that wasn't a right kind of prayer, but the Lord would understand since he'd been raised with oxen, too. In that picture in the Tavern the infant Jesus was lying in a manger, and two oxen were puzzling out how He'd come to be there. They weren't to compare with Peter and Paul, but that could be the fault of the artist not knowing good beasts.

The bundle of sticks ploughed up a rustling heap of leaves, dug deeper into age-old rotted twigs and leaf-mold beneath, threw out a stone or two and a large rock. But the leaves acted as brake, and the rocks rolled off sideways down the hill, safe from the plodding heels. A slanting descent to the regular trail. A sharp backward turn, and Young'un could stop praying.

But she thanked the Lord, and told how now she was surer than ever He wasn't so bad as Preacher and others made Him out to be. Like Gunsmith in a way, he'd be. Big and bearded and neighborly. Years back, when she was very little, she'd pictured Him over in Vermont because of the words about green hills far away, and of course the sheep and His being a sheep-herd. Vermont was full of sheep. Comical the notions you got when you were right young!

Out in the pasture the bundle of poles drew smoothly and needed no watching. Young'un looked up to see Sim Higgins, and—yes, 'twas Gunsmith, talking to Dan'l beside the crib. She drew the poles up as close as she could, backed the oxen a pace to loosen the chain, unhooked it from the ring, and started to unfasten the rawhide tail-rope. There had been no sound of Sim Higgins' wagon, so likely the two men had walked here cross-lots.

"Didn't get a shot. But she's a good little rifle. Heft her." Gunsmith passed the firearm with its long slender barrel across to Dan'l. "Shoots straight in still air, Mary says. But so small a ball don't travel far, nor hit hard."

As Dan'l lowered the rifle to see the muzzle, Young'un was surprised at the small bore. Couldn't hardly have loaded a ball the size of a chokecherry. Pa's rifle took a ball that would be five-ten times as weighty.

Gunsmith explained that it was no more than a trial barrel. Folks had got to demanding smaller and smaller bores till he thought he'd try just how small they could be. He'd had to forge himself new forming and sizing cores for the welding, new boring tools and even extra small rifling rod and teeth, just for the one barrel. But it was well to try out new ideas once in a while. Mary was too busy to test her out, but if he could find someone else to use her all winter . . .

Sim Higgins spoke up, trying to hide his eagerness, "Glad to do a neighbor a good turn, Gam. Course I'll need powder and ball . . . and patches . . . and oil . . . and spare flints . . . and . . ."

"No, Sim," Gunsmith said quickly, "you ain't like to treat her right, and she's no blundering old Continental musket. Mary says so small a bore needs cleaning after every shot, no matter how you grease the patch. And the charge being so light, the powder needs mighty careful measuring. But I was wondering, seeing Dan'l helped me to repair two-three guns, whether he'd help out by using this one?"

Young'un said a quick "yes" before Dan'l could get the word out.

Dan'l hadn't any need to say, the way he was stroking the silvery barrel, and laying thin cheek to the dark-polished curly maple stock, sighting on treetops. He did manage to tell that Pa had left plenty powder and lead. 'Twas Young'un had to ask Gunsmith for the loan of a bullet mold to fit, and an iron casting ladle. Seemed Gunsmith had brought them both in his bag, which he hung with priming horn and powder horn to the end of the corn-crib.

This was most too much to bear, Young'un felt, the way Providence was aiding them of late.

Sim Higgins wasn't pleased at Dan'l having the rifle, Young'un could see that. But when Mist' Higgins saw how he was going to be repaid for his kindness in loaning the seed, he'd feel better. Dan'l had been boasting the last weeks how he'd pay Sim back all his debt twice over, and pile his wagon full with roots and cabbages and squash. Eldest and Young'un had both said not to, but it was different now, and perhaps it would heal Sim Higgins' disappointment a mite.

Yet Sim Higgins didn't look to be disappointed, but something different. The way he stared at the oxen showed he'd put the rifle out of mind already. And Gunsmith was staring at Sim Higgins as though troubled at some thought he had, not smiling with his eyes at Dan'l fondling the new rifle.

"Well, Dan'l, this talk of the rifle's all mighty nice," said Sim, spitting to one side. "But I come here on business. How about paying what you owe?"

"Yes, Mist' Higgins, I'd be mighty pleased to." Dan'l grinned as he leaned the rifle carefully against the corn-crib. "Come see what we've got for you."

Sim spraddled around, looking over the vegetables still in the garden till the root cellar could be fixed. Dan'l said for Sim Higgins to take his pick. But Sim didn't say a word. And when Dan'l pointed to the haystack in the lower pasture and asked Sim if he could do with a load, Sim just said, "That all ye got?" They came back to where Gunsmith was talking with Eldest, Dan'l looking puzzled. Eldest stood up from her stool, smoothed down her dress, then stooped and picked up a handful of beans. She drifted them out through her fingers so they fell back into the bushel basket below. And showed him the other fine seeds, on skins and in baskets, drying around her.

But Sim Higgins said again, "That all ye got?"

Gunsmith's hand combed down through his white beard as he

said, "Seems like a mighty lot to me, Sim. Don't happen your eyesight's been troubling you of late?"

Sim Higgins didn't answer, and came spraddling back towards the corn-crib, where Young'un was waiting beside the oxen. "No pigs, no hens, no sheep," he grumbled. "Naught but corn and two-three vegetables."

Then he walked up to the oxen, looked over Peter, and fetched him a kick in the ribs. By reason of the yoke Peter wasn't able to so much as swing his head to ask what he'd done wrong. And before Young'un could do anything to stop him, Sim Higgins had gone round and planted his toe in Paul. "Ain't wuth much more'n the corn. Soft, the two on 'em. Ain't been worked enough," he growled.

The insult was almost worse than the kicks, which couldn't have hurt really. Peter and Paul had worked hard as any man or beast all year. Even though in early spring they'd been nigh to starving. To save them further hurt Young'un lifted off their yoke. But 'twas the hand of Providence, she felt, that guided the yoke to fall on Sim Higgins' toe.

Sim cussed. But a hand, not of Providence, fell on Sim's shoulder, and Gunsmith warned him, "Now, Sim, behave yourself!"

Young'un had to tell herself mighty sharp that Sim was a friend, for all his seeming. That it was his seed had grown most everything the Posts would have to live on, and she ought to feel a proper gratitude, and not fling in his face the ear of corn that had somehow gotten into her hand.

Without a turn of their heads, the oxen ambled off side by side down the pasture. It wasn't like them to be away when something was happening, they must have taken a right sharp dislike to Mist' Higgins. Which was troubling, for Peter and Paul were mighty good judges of folk. Reluctantly Young'un let fall the ear of corn.

"Well, Dan'l, how about what's owing to me?" Sim Higgins stopped trying to rub his toe through his shoe, and tried a gap-toothed smile. Maybe it felt like a smile from inside his face, but it wasn't much to look at from outside. "Now I don't aim to be hard on ye, but a debt's a debt."

"That's right, Mist' Higgins." Dan'l took his eyes away from the new rifle. "Would you want I should set it aside for you now, or wait and draw it down? It will be easier after the first snowfall, for the sled runners are nigh wore through with dry-hauling."

But Sim set down his sore foot, and made as though surprised. "Now, Dan'l, ye're just kind of joking, ain't ye? Or have ye forgot what your pa's been owing me these six years past? I didn't say aught when your pa lit out and left ye, but now . . ."

"Hold on, Sim!" Gunsmith raised objection. "A boy ain't accountable. And where's the evidence that it's owed ye in the first place?"

Dan'l looked frightened, but with his obstinate Pa-wouldn't-hold look beside. "It's all right, Mist' Reed. Whatever the debt is, we don't aim to stay beholden. How much d'you reckon to be owed, Mist' Higgins?"

Sim Higgins drew a paper from his pocket, the one Dan'l had signed, and began to read aloud. As the long list drew on Young'un wondered how even Pa could have needed to borrow so much that his own good land should have raised. There were other things too, costly wheaten flour when corn meal would have served, and molasses when maple syrup from their own sugar bush would have been sweetening a plenty. Tasty enough the things had been; Young'un could remember a few of them, but she could have fared well enough without, as she'd done this summer.

Not being a storekeeper, Sim must have bought these things to trade on to Pa for the sake of the profit he'd make. Folks said Sim would turn his hand to most anything that would save him working his farm. 'Twas hard to see why Pa was willing to pay the higher price, unless the traders down to the Falls and places had got so they wouldn't trust him any longer. Could be. Pa had complained each year that trapping was worse and worse.

Dan'l and Gunsmith started figuring on their fingers. Young'un could see them turning costly wheaten flour, and tea, and sugar, and this and that into bushels of corn. But corn being cheap, and the boughten goods dear, they gave up, plumb discouraged as the list droned on. At the very end came the seeds borrowed that year, but those were things the Posts could return in kind two or three times over, and not feel the loss.

What sounded like the creak of a wagon wheel came to Young'un from up the trail, but her eyes were on Dan'l. His shoulders sagging, looking a sight too like his pa in Pa's latter years. Dan'l walked up to the crib, filled more than head high with golden yellow cobs. He had earned the right to be proud of that corn, and of the other corn still in the big heap beside. But he looked like he'd never know pride again. All that was left to him was no more than plain pigheadedness to stand by his written bond, thinking Pa would do the same.

He leaned a hand against the sticks of the crib. Only an hour back he'd been planning to build higher so as to hold all the harvest. But now . . . "I cal'late 'tis all yours, Mist' Higgins," he said at last.

He had no right to give away what wasn't his! It wasn't Dan'l alone, but herself and Peter and Paul had grown that corn, with Eldest taking her share with cooking and the garden. But before Young'un could protest, Sim Higgins set to cackling.

"Hee-hee-hee! Still joking, eh, Dan'l? Corn's so cheap hereabouts it ain't scarce worth the gathering this year. Now if you had a couple of fat pigs, and two-three sheep . . ."

"There's the garden truck beside, Mist' Higgins," Eldest had come to stand betwixt Dan'l and Sim Higgins, just as though to protect him. "And there's baskets of beans and such, and sunflower seeds I was saving against the time we have a hen."

This time Young'un wasn't angered. If Eldest could give up her share, she, Young'un, could do the same. Hunger, and it would be real griping hunger, wouldn't matter. The bitter thought of all that aching toil just to fill Sim Higgins' greedy little belly, that would have to be put aside, too. For Eldest had shown there was something more important still. Dan'l wasn't like a woman, he worried so over every hand's turn they did on the farm, whether the seed was in too early or too late, whether the rain would come in time, and blamed himself for everything that went wrong. He had toiled and suffered when she and Eldest had done no more than toil. If he couldn't meet this debt to Simpkin Higgins, the whole of the seven months' struggle since Pa had left would be no more than one long pitiful failure.

Young'un glanced down over the pasture to the ploughland, and up again to the woodland. There was nothing more, search as she might. But if Sim Higgins would be patient, would be content to wait awhile, she could add something. "There's hickories and chestnuts besides, Mist' Higgins. And just as soon as the lake freezes, I'll get you as much fish as you're minded to have."

But Sim Higgins didn't seem to hear either her or Eldest.

Gunsmith took two strides, and laid a heavy hand on the trader's shoulder.

"Now, Sim! There's more to a deal than trapping a neighbor and then skinning him. In the past you've nigh beggared yourself in beggaring others; for there's none left hereabouts who'll trade with ye." His voice was deep and angry. But still striving to be friendly. "Take what Dan'l can afford to give, and no more, so you leave these folks the run of their teeth until next harvest. Then other folks might be tempted to trust ye again, and trade with ye. Seems like Dan'l aims to pay ye in the end, on account of his pa. Though he's no call to do it, to my way of thinking."

Sim shook off the hand, impatient, and tapped the paper in his hand. "Don't seem like ye understand, Gam. It's written here below the list, 'I acknowledge this debt in full. In case of failure to pay on demand I agree to surrender to Simpkin Higgins all right and title in the yoke of twin oxen known as Peter and Paul, the same being in good working condition and free of known fault or vice. Daniel Post.' Now that's a hog-tight dockyment like I've used the past fifteen years, and I ain't knowed it to fail yet." He stopped to enjoy his triumph, cocking his head on one side.

First off it seemed to Young'un as though she'd choke. The warm autumn sun had gone all chilly, too. Even the brilliant colors had faded from the trees. The rumbling and creaking back of her, coming down the trail, wasn't more unreal than Sim Higgins standing there, grinning his gap-toothed greedy grin, and saying the oxen were his. For that was what it had come to at the last. Dan'l couldn't pay for all Pa's debts, so Sim would take the oxen instead.

"Dan'l's just figuring out whether he'll pay or hand over them oxen. Guess it'll have to be the oxen." Sim relished the way he'd sprung his trap.

Dan'l looked off down the pasture, his eyes so big and hurt-seeming that Young'un ached to run up and comfort him. But he put fingers to mouth, and blew. And she knew then that if he did what he had in mind she'd never forgive him. Never.

Shaky, the whistle was, but the big brown oxen in the lower pasture raised their heads.

Dan'l was muttering over and over, "A man can't break his given word. Nossir! Pa wouldn't hold with it. Pa wouldn't hold with a man breaking his given word . . . Pa wouldn't . . ." Then he set fingers to mouth and blew again.

Slowly, all eyes upon them, the ponderous beasts left their grazing, began to climb the hill.

Young'un ran down to meet them. To hang yoke-fashion, an arm about each neck, pacing between them to their slow plodding. The way she used to do when they were no more than tricksy little calves.

"I'll go with you, Peter. I won't leave you, Paul," she just had to comfort them. "I'll leave Dan'l forever and work for Sim Higgins until I can buy you both back. But we'll never come back here. Never!"

*   *   *

Her eyes were kind of blurry, so she didn't see whose wagon it was came rolling out from under the trees. Didn't know the driver till he spoke.

"Morning, Eldest—morning, Dan'l." It was Eph Birdsell, and mighty cheerful, not knowing what was happening here. "Morning, Uncle Gam—morning, Sim." He dropped off the driving plank, and knotted the reins. "Fine yoke of oxen you got, Young'un. Can't call to mind when I've seed a better match with more weight to their shoulders. If a man was crazy enough to sell, they'd fetch maybe . . ."

"Morning, folks!" Sol Broadmoor in his heavier ox-drawn rig came creaking up behind. He nodded to Gunsmith, stared hard at Sim Higgins and cautioned Dan'l in what only pretended to be a whisper, "Don't let that bandy-legged little feller git too near them oxen, or ye'll find him trying to sneak 'em away in his breeches pocket. Can't nohow trust him within sight of what he kin lift." He nigh rolled off his wagon seat bellowing at his joke.

Young'un found herself smiling, too, and blew her nose to clear her eyes. Other wagons and sleds were drawing down through the woods and out into the sunny pasture, led by a dark complexioned man walking a pack-horse. That rifle of his in the crook of his left

94

arm, she'd know it anywheres after the trouble Dan'l and Gunsmith had taken to rebore it and cut fresh rifling.

Sim wasn't looking so pert now. Must be all of eight men drawing their rigs round in a circle, and not one of the eight but there was talk Sim had tricked him in some wise. The dark trapper had once spoke of cutting Sim's ears off so folks should know him and be warned.

"Now, Dan'l, boy!" Sim stuffed the paper hastily into his breeches pocket. "Just yoke up and lead my oxen down to home for me, there's a good lad."

"I've druv up to do a little business with Dan'l." Eph might have been talking to the oxen for all the heed he took of Sim Higgins. "So if Dan'l's willing, I guess Sim'll have to wait."

"Sim'll wait, all right!" Sol dropped from his wagon. Dropped light for a man who weighed two hundred and thirty on the Tavern hog-scales. His large hand patted Sim violently on the back. "Ye'll wait, won't ye, Sim?"

"Fust come, fust sarved." The trapper hitched leading-rein, and settled himself cross-legged on the ground. The other men closed in around. Then if Cicero Ditch, the Taverner, didn't bob up from under someone's elbow. He and Sim couldn't abide each other, both being little fellers. Taverner walked up to Sim and held out his hand, and Sim put the paper into it, meek as Moses.

Cicero ran a thumbnail down the list, like he was summing the chalked-up drinks on the door of the Tavern ordinary. "Forty-two dollars, near as." He read on, shook his head. "Note ain't nowise legal, signed by a minor. And Sim knows 'tain't wuth so much as the ink, leave alone the paper it's writ on."

Dan'l, mazed with despair, but still mule-stubborn, gulped out, "I got to pay! Mist' Ditch, I got to!"

"Always heard tell there's no fool like an old fool." Cicero looked at him pitying. "But I ain't a-going to believe it no longer, Dan'l."

There was that in Dan'l's eyes that was more than Young'un could bear. He hadn't the hope, just a sprouting seedling of hope that was springing up in her heart. For he'd not heard Phebe last night tell Eph to run down and tell Uncle Gam about Sim Higgins. Eldest couldn't know either. She hadn't so much as sobbed, but just stood there like she was a winter-killed piny, her face white, and her purty little mouth drawn down at the corners and trembling. Young'un would have run to her to hold her tight, but Peter and Paul needed her still more, for it stood to reason they couldn't guess the half of what was going on. She drew their silken ears close together so she could speak to the two at once.

"Young'un will stay with you," she whispered soft. "You won't never be hurt, Young'un won't let it." But oxen were menfolk in a kind of way, though nicer. "You old Peter'n' Paul, if I was your heft, I'd not be afeared of anything less'n maybe a rattler or such. You hear me? I just wouldn't be afeared."

Peter's skin twitched to show there was a fly his tail couldn't reach. Young'un gathered such spittle as there was in her dry mouth and *pfft,* the fly fell damply to the ground where she ground it under her heel. Dan'l hadn't noticed, to say Pa didn't hold with spitting and suchlike. Only the dark complexioned trapper looked surprised. To show him it wasn't just luck she stood off and *pfft,* knocked a fly off the tip of Paul's far horn. Then she felt kind of ashamed, for that was vaunting and being puffed up, as the Good Book said, and 'twasn't no time for such.

Gunsmith and Cicero came back from taking a closer look at the garden patch. "If Dan'l hands over all he's raised this year, corn, hay, roots and all," said Cicero, "he'll still be debted to Sim Higgins nigh on eighteen dollars."

Gunsmith cleared his throat. "Seems like, if I was Dan'l's pa, I wouldn't care to raise and break the best yoke of oxen in the countryside, and have Dan'l hand them over to a man who can't so much as drive oxen, only horses."

Dan'l's head rose a mite. Young'un hoped that courage and maybe horse-sense were coming back to him. But he was still too mazed for that.

Gunsmith looked around him, slow, at each man. And his next words might have been spelled out. "Not—when—Dan'l—can—call—in—what's—owing—to—him—by—his—neighbors."

"Now if that ain't just what I druv up for!" Sol didn't look to be so surprised as he sounded. "Something 'minded me only this morning," he winked at Gunsmith, "to come pay my debt to Dan'l.

Gam here said a whiles back he didn't so much as lay finger to my broken stock. So it's Dan'l I'm beholden to." He swung up on to his wagon and started to tug at the sacks.

"Don't that just beat all!" Eph Birdsell struck in. "I came on the selfsame errand. Dan'l here fixed my sett-trigger so it works the best in years. I brung along two-three things that'll maybe clear the score."

The trapper laid aside his rifle, and sprang to his feet. "Fair's fair, folks, and I reckon I'm next." He started on the knots of his pack-saddle.

Men who had been standing around hurried back to their wagons and sleds, and began hauling and tugging. And one team tried to bolt, scared by the commotion. While Cicero figured out the value of the sacks and baskets that were carried in, Gunsmith called out the price he set on a new trigger guard, or the labor that had gone to cherrying out a bullet mold to fit a rebored rifle—of this and of that.

Folks, even neighbors, didn't get to paying debts before they were asked, and more than they were asked, the way these were trying to do. Then Young'un saw the shape of it. If Dan'l was obstinate in holding to his bond, these menfolk, being menfolk, were just as obstinate. Bound and determined they were to trick Mist' Higgins out of his bond, just as Mist' Higgins aimed to trick Dan'l.

If a load or two was thrown on the pile that wasn't owing to Dan'l, Gunsmith said naught, and Taverner tallied it up with the others. The higher the pile grew, the more Sim Higgins shifted from foot to foot. And as Taverner's tally rose to over twenty dollars, including all Dan'l's own harvest, Sim Higgins looked worried. When it topped thirty, he was outright angry. Then fear began to show in his face.

Eldest was weeping at last, from hope, no less. Young'un hugged Peter and Paul, kissing their soft noses, for now they were safe. Cicero was tearing Sim Higgins' note across and across, and saying, "Ye're paid in full, Sim, and there's ten-twelve witnesses to the last deal ye'll ever make in these here hills."

Dan'l's courage came warming back in to him. "Aim to trap us a living this winter, and there's the sugaring next spring. And the rifle, the little new rifle." He went quickly to pick it up and see that it was still as he remembered it to be, nigh on an hour ago.

But Young'un was beginning to remember, and so, maybe, were the folks who'd brought their wagons and packhorses. The Posts would have to start again, and worse off even than when they started, for it had been spring then, and 'twas fall now. No feed for the oxen, no grazing, of course, no seed and seed corn for next year. And naught but fish and flesh for victuals. And, what hurt Young'un more than anything else, now Peter and Paul were safe, no saucy little heifer calf of Eph's and Phebe's to raise. Being there'd be no feed.

Eph Birdsell had drawn aside a couple of neighbors and whispered with them. Now he came back to say, "Seems like my pa was owing to Old Man Post, and kind of forgot to say when he died."

And another man said quickly, "Of course he did, Eph. Now le's see how much 'twas." And the two started to scratch at their heads pretending to remember. They might have remembered too, trying so hard, only Cicero Ditch suddenly bent double, as though in pain.

But 'twasn't pain, for he slapped his knees, and ho-ho-hoed till he seemed touched in the head. Soon as he could speak, he said, "Now that I recall, Sim, you've got no team—sold your poor starved critters down to the Falls, aiming to have these oxen in their stead," and ho-hoed again fit to burst and take a 'plexy. Though surely it weren't so comical. It made Young'un chill to remember again what might have happened to Peter'n' Paul.

Cicero straightened himself up again. "Take an armful from this pile, Sim Higgins, and start to carry. Take a good armful, for you're like to wear a mighty deep trail before you've got all Dan'l's harvest to cover, in your barn!"

That set the other men to roaring again and slapping their knees like all possessed. Except Gunsmith who looked from Dan'l standing there as though even the ground beneath his feet didn't seem real any more, to Mist' Higgins making believe he hadn't heard Mist' Ditch. When he glanced over at Eldest, then back to Young'un, who still held tight to the oxen, she knew right well what was in his mind. Or thought she did. That the Posts must winter out with their neighbors. Likely he'd offer to take Dan'l and learn him a smitch of gunsmithing. And Cicero Ditch would be glad enough to take Eldest, and Cat, now Phebe Callender was wedded and gone from the Tavern for good. But Young'un wouldn't go anywhere without she took Peter'n' Paul.

"If I was Dan'l I'd let bygones be bygones and make Sim an offer for half of the produce." Gunsmith spoke up plain and clear, and the other men stopped their laughing to listen. But it didn't make sense, for Dan'l had naught to offer.

Mist' Higgins knew that too, for he set up a cackle. "Such as what, Gam?"

"If I was Dan'l I'd offer to draw down the other half of the corn and hay and suchlike, and I'd offer to go work for Sim two days a week until spring. There's a sight to be done on Sim's place, from raising stumps when the weather favors to felling and sawing and splitting firewood."

That set Mist' Ditch to figuring out loud again. By the time he had turned it into dollars and cents, and allowed for a short winter or long, open weather or Dan'l being snowed in, and the value of Sim Higgins' feed that the oxen would eat for two days each week, he had even Mist' Higgins and Gunsmith confused.

Sol Broadmoor slapped a huge fist into a horny palm. "Ain't nobody going to work for you for less, Sim. Nor nobody else going to draw down the stuff before it rots where it lies."

The dark-faced Trapper was playing with his scalping knife the way woodsmen do, throwing it and catching it. He stopped throwing and scratched his ear with the point of the blade. "I cal'late I'd tell Dan'l 'yes,'" he said softly. "I cal'late I'd tell him right quick, Sim."

Mist' Higgins said, "Yes, Dan'l." Meek as Moses.

* * *

The men drove off, joking Sim Higgins on the way they had bested him at last. The worst day of all Young'un's life, except when Ma had burned, wasn't half ended, by the sun. Eldest went back to running the beans through her fingers as though trying to show herself that the half were still there. Peter'n' Paul plodded back to their grazing, and Dan'l went into the shelter with the new little rifle to find powder and suchlike.

Young'un just stood. Ought she to tell Eldest and Dan'l now, or wait till they saw for themselves? The neighbors, their minds set on besting Sim Higgins, hadn't seen either.

Dan'l would have to set-to and draw down Mist' Higgins' sled loads when he had planned to start raising the new house. And with him and the oxen gone for two days of the week, there would be no way to make up lost time. For the oxen would be weary with the labor Mist' Higgins would lay upon them. And half the produce of the farm would leave hungry bellies unless Dan'l had time to trap and hunt.

Could be folks could winter without walls and roofs in the Garden of Eden and suchlike places in the world. But there was no Garden of Eden in winter up in these hills. Only six months of snow, and frost that bit down into the ground deeper even than the deepest dug grave.

*   *   *

The next day Dan'l and Young'un loaded up the sled, as the bargain was, and drew it down to Mist' Higgins. Scairt, Young'un was, and she'd admit as much, and Dan'l had carried the new rifle. From dawn to dark Young'un led the oxen down and up and down again. It went against the grain to be carrying their own hard-earned food to fill Mist' Higgins' barn and belly. Until Eldest pointed out it wasn't their own garden truck they were sledding down, but Mist' Higgins', and she for one would be glad to see the last of it.

But when the last load was in, if Mist' Higgins didn't come out with a mug of his wife's spiced cider. And say that his share of the hay was best left lying up at the Post place until there was space for it in the Higgins barn. And that if Dan'l worked well, likely he would even forgive him the hay, seeing he had more than enough of his own. Which he had, for all to see.

Eldest, who had taken to calling Sim Higgins a Servant of Mammon, couldn't believe when they told her. But now, all that was left on the Post place belonged to the Posts. Every last thing.

That didn't mean they were back to where they had stood before Mist' Higgins had laid claim to the oxen. They had lost a half of all they had toiled for, and would be working over on the Higgins place when they had planned to be trapping, drawing down firewood, and starting on the new house.

There would be no house, that was clear as clear. And no barn either. But what a day back had set Young'un to despairing now set the three of them to scheming, as they lay in their beds in the darkness.

Dan'l had a notion to carry up the hay from the meadow just as soon as the hard frost set in and it wouldn't spoil. He would build it up the sides of the oxen's stall and over the top. By the time the hay was most eaten, and the cold at its worst, he would have it fixed with Mist' Higgins to keep Peter'n' Paul down at the Higgins place, even if it called for extra work to pay for it.

And Eldest—of all people—called to mind Pa's old tale of how he had wintered out up near Canady by digging himself a hole in a hillside, and stretching pelts over the opening. Snug as a bear, he claimed. And what Pa had done they could do, if so be they set their minds to it.

That night, as they talked, there didn't seem a thing in the whole wide world the Posts couldn't make a go of, if the three but set their minds to it. And Eldest said 'twould be fitting to make the next day a Thanksgiving, and free from toil, now their troubles were past and over.

Not knowing what lay ahead.

CHAPTER TEN

YOUNG'UN threw off her covers and sat up. Dan'l was out already, and so was Cat. Eldest stooping over the fire was hurrying along the breakfast of cornmeal mush, though the sun wasn't yet over the horizon. Peter'n' Paul were to be rested today, along with the other Posts.

She dallied awhile, did Young'un, yawning and stretching, reaching her arms up under her deerskin shirt and down into her trousers for a good leisurely scratch. On account of the cold of the last two weeks, all three of the Posts had had to sleep in their clothes, and till you were used to it, it left you itchy of a morning. Even Eldest scratched, though she took a bowl of hot water off into the dark and washed herself all over every night; or said she did.

Young'un stretched again and yawned more loudly, hoping that Eldest would tell her to hurry out and help Dan'l. Then she would remind her that there wasn't a thing in the world she had to do today, without she was so minded.

But long habit was stricter than Eldest could even think to be. It shuffled Young'un's still dusty feet into the patched moccasins, it stood her upright and led her into the brightening light of the doorway; it took her outside, pointed out the still dark pool of the garden and pasture for her task of the day, before she could really make it clear that there was no task. No task a-tall.

A shot banged off, up in the stilly woods. For a moment she thought it might be Pa. But of course it was Dan'l, and the note of the gun was lighter and sharper than from Pa's barrel. She lit out at a run to see how Dan'l had made out, and how the little new rifle handled and fired. But stopped at the fringe of the forest. Dan'l had

102

earned the right to be alone with it, for yesterday and the day before he'd laid it aside without a shot fired.

Dan'l was kind of peculiar with things that he prized, his knife and suchlike. Didn't seem he could reckon a thing really his, nor get pleasure of it without it was in his hand. And if it was something he valued over-much, he had to take it away by himself, like a dog with a bone. But he'd share it after, and even loan it, so it wasn't rightly selfish. Just something in Dan'l, like Peter always needing to be nose-ahead of Paul. Folks were like that.

There was another shot. Eldest called them to come eat, but Young'un still waited. And Dan'l's face as he came leaping down the hill was a memory she'd treasure. He had two fat squirrels, their necks forked between his fingers, and showed how the little ball had pierced through their heads leaving the pelts unharmed. Then if he didn't hand over the polishy new rifle for Young'un to carry in her own hands the rest of the thirty paces to the hemlock shelter. There wasn't a selfish bone in his body. She'd guessed it before, and now she knowed it for sure.

Breakfast was waiting on the narrow split-log table that Dan'l had labored over so. It was mighty heavy and in the way in the small shelter, but Eldest was bound they should eat their food indoors and on a table. Being that Eldest did the cooking, she had the right to say.

But Young'un had to smile when with his third mouthful Dan'l said, "I been studying where I'll have me the new cabin next year." Just as though he hadn't been turning it over and over in his mind all summer.

With his sixth mouthful he wiped the milk off his lips with the back of his hand and said, "Stands to reason the old place is best, where Pa fust built."

Then it was for Eldest to plump down on her stool at the end of the table and say that a house was woman's concern, and she'd marked out plain for all to see just where she'd have her house built, and how.

That set Dan'l to pointing his words with his wooden spoon, and Eldest to pointing back again with hers. Till she caught herself at it. And that made her angry at herself, and of course at Dan'l too for pointing with his spoon the way Ma had said not to.

It seemed to Young'un this argument over the new cabin had started up most every day for six months. It wasn't quarreling, but each trying to do what would be best for all, and not agreeing on what it was. Eldest was right. Pa might have set his cabin in the best spot at the start off, but then he'd cut the trees to the west and north, so the windbreak against the chill of winter was gone. What Eldest planned was to have the new cabin stand further up the hill than the old one, and tight in against the corner of the clearing. There'd be more sun from the east and south, and less wind from the north and west, to make it warmer in winter. And for summer coolness as she worked over the cook fire, she hankered after two windows instead of one, for the cross draught. A door couldn't rightly serve to let in air and keep out livestock, both.

Dan'l just said, "If'd been right, Pa would have done it." As he always did. It just seemed like Pa could never be wrong in Daniel's eyes. Now Pa was the best pa ever was, but look at the way he left his fences, and not having a cow, nor pigs to fatten on the acorns and beechmast in the woods, and getting into debt to Sim Higgins!

Young'un opened her mouth to argue. But closed it again. Dan'l was wilful blind, trying to fit himself to Pa's boots, though Pa's boots weren't so big as Dan'l remembered. He needed the belief to help him do as he'd done with the farm. For he set no stock in himself, judging himself as a full-growed man, and seeing only how far he fell short. Poor Dan'l! She'd best leave him be.

She hurried through the rest of her meal, so she could get to look at the rifle before Dan'l had it again. Some day maybe she'd be a great marksman, like Mis' Reed; better than any of the menfolk hereabouts. Or maybe she'd leave all that to the menfolks, and just learn to be a woman instead. Only nobody seemed to know the how of that. Whichever it was she chose, the choice lay with her here and now, this wonderful idle sunshiny day.

Dan'l came out, still wearing the bag and horn, that he hadn't put off to eat breakfast. She passed him the rifle, and watched him go down the pasture, Cat following after and Dan'l trying to drive Cat back. Till Cat found a field mouse hiding in a tuft of grass and stayed by it.

Whatever Young'un did today, it must be something she had never done before. Like taking a leap and landing plumb on the summit of Old Hunchback opposite. Something downright marvelous like that. So folks would say, "Did you hear about Young'un Post taking a leap clear acrost the whole valley? A three mile leap if 'twas a yard!" And someone who really understood would say, " 'Twas high time, too. Always planning it, she was, and always putting it off. Another year or so and she'd have been woman-grown." For of course you had to do your magicking when you were little. 'Twas past the power of grownups.

Or she'd flap her arms two-three times, and light off and fly. Not the fussy frantic way of partridges whirring off down a hill, but more like the easy flapping of a cunning old crow who just idled along watching everything in sight. Best still, like the hawks that nested over lakeside, where Dan'l was heading right this minute. The deeper they dived, the higher they'd swing up at the end of the dive, and all without a beat of the wings. Must be mighty difficult till you had the trick of it.

"Viney!" Eldest called from the shelter. "Don't you aim to feed Peter'n' Paul today?"

"Dan'l fed them afore 'twas even light." She'd seen that, else she'd have tended them herself.

Having half decided to take that magic leap or flight, Young'un had to find reason now for not doing either. For supposing she tried, and failed? 'Twould be heartbreaking, and it was a day so beautiful you were on the brink of heartbreak anyways. Swimming was most the same as flying, when you came right down to it. It was the way fish flew. Of course the deep pool down in Mosquito Hollow would be cold as ice, but it was always that, even in midsummer. And swimming would clean you and stop the itchy feel the way no flying or leaping could.

Eldest came to the doorway again, to set the scalded milkpail in the sun. "Land sakes, Viney, don't stand there dreaming! Go see how the water's holding up in the oxen's drinking pool."

Well, she'd do that first, and afterwards she might magic Phebe's purty little heifer calf along, and then magic her back to her home before anyone noticed the loss. Or magic the cabin all built and finished and hold it there for minute after minute. Of course not telling Eldest, who thought all magicking was silly, and heathenish besides.

She took spade in hand, for she suspicioned the pool would bear cleaning and deepening. Halfway down the pasture Peter and Paul left their heap of chopped cornstalks to follow and see what she intended. She had to wait till they took a deep drink, not wanting to muddy the water first.

Young'un had shed her clothes, had deepened the spring-fed pool by a good foot, and built up the dam on the lower side when she first heard whip-cracking, and the creak of wagon wheels.

Could that be Sim Higgins back again?

With Dan'l away hunting, she'd best run up and stand by Eldest. She'd need to wash the black clay off legs and arms and most the rest of her. And the water was so stirred and muddied 'twas like washing clay with clay. But it would dry and fall off. She grabbed up her wrinkled deerskin clothes, crammed herself into them as she started to run.

Halfway up the pasture she could hear children's and women's voices coming out of the woods, and there out in the open was a man leaning on an axe, talking to Eldest, in a voice that sounded like he was hog-calling.

"Ain't nothing to beat the rolling up a house for gathering neighbors together, unless maybe a good burying," he roared. "There's folks that ain't so much as called a cuss-word to each other in years that'll be set to haul on the same logs, and will be joking each other afore sundown."

Eldest was smoothing the front of her gown, just like Ma when Ma failed for words.

"I don't say but there's been two-three house raisings of sawed timber the past few years," the man bellowed again. "But that ain't chaff to clover set against a real old-time rolling up. We'd ought to be mighty obliged to you, Mis' . . . Ma'am, all of us had."

The stranger lifted his axe and set off up into the woods. Eldest preened her gown again, likely 'twas the thought of being called Mis' . . . Ma'am made her, and set off after as though to ask what the man meant by his talk of raisings and rolling-ups.

But Young'un knew. She just had to stand and laugh at herself for getting her magicking so twisty. All she'd purposed was to have the cabin there so she could see it, and then to let it go again like morning fog. It took considerable magicking to do just that, so you could really make your eyes believe. But here was something her eyes told her, instead of her having to tell her eyes. Folks in twos and threes and wagonfuls of folks, most everyone for miles around, all chattering and laughing and creaking their wagons and sleds down the trail, and streaming out into the upper corner of the farmland. All set to build a real cabin, of real solid logs.

One axe, then two, began to ring out, up in the woods. Teams and yokes were unhitched, some being led off up the hillside, and some being unyoked or unbitted and tied to wagon wheels till they'd be needed. Women were climbing down from wagons with baskets of food on their arms, and all talking to Eldest at once. Childer were running off all-sides, looking for hickories and chestnuts, being warned by their mas against rattlers up here in the wild woods. One had already cut his foot against the edge of a razor-sharp adze and was sent back howling in a wagon. Howling too lusty for real hurt, Young'un knew.

Came a thunderous crash up on the hillside, and a cheer from all the men. The first tree was down before the first dog had found the trail of the first rabbit. And that showed how soon. Young'un saw Gunsmith and Mary, off-saddling their old Congress pony, and ran up to ask could she help. And to tell how wonderful the loan of the new rifle was, for all the meat it would bring in, and how Dan'l was away with it this very minute.

Behind her she could hear the womenfolk telling Eldest to have the cabin made bigger, and to set her foot down sharp. For if she didn't, the men would raise the finest barn in the countryside, and kind of hitch a lean-to on for folks to live in. 'Twas the way men were, and she'd ought to be warned in time. And to see the men did it right at the start-off, for if they didn't 'twouldn't never be done over, for all their promises. It was now or never with men, and mostly never.

Axes were snick-snicking, trimming the boughs and top off the fallen tree, and smack-smacking into another. And two men were digging out foundation holes at the corners of the cabin, a good four feet wider apart than Eldest had first marked. So she'd taken the women's advice, or the women had told their menfolk themselves. Sol Broadmoor, who was proud of his newly bought heavy-thewed team as he was of his own strength, had hitched a chain around a huge flat boulder and was drawing it down for a foundation. He hauled it to the hole where one of the neighbors was delving, and joked him about how would he like his tombstone? Standing alongside, or lying on top? The man jumped out quick, caught Sol a wham across the pants with his spade, and the two roared with laughter till they could scarce undo the chain.

Far down the hillside toward the brook there was a crack so faint Young'un could scarce hear it. But the childer down in the pasture set up a shout and lit out towards lakeside to see what Dan'l had killed. That drew off the other childer and the dogs, and kind of quieted things, till the first log came sliding and grinding down the hill behind a double team. It was scarce out in the open before Gunsmith bestrode it, and started in with the adze to cut a flat on it. More folks were lamed for life by an adze glancing off a knot than met with ary other mischance; so adzing was the task for an expert, and coveted according.

Cicero Ditch drove up with Mis' Ditch and her feathered bonnet. And Sim Higgins of all people, jouncing around in the back, trying to steady two cider barrels, and cussing that nobody had thought to warn him of the house-rolling till most too late.

Eph Birdsell called back to him that they hadn't been minded to build house and barn and have Sim steal the whole building just as soon as their backs were turned. And that drew a laugh, too, even from the womenfolk. It was that kind of a day, from the sun to the air, to the smiles on folk's faces. There'd never be another the like of it.

Gunsmith's log was flattened on one side, turned over by three men with hooks, and flattened on the other side. There was another log being adzed, and another being drawn down. Two-three trees being dropped, and two-three more being trimmed, by the sound of the axes. Young'un knew she'd ought to help. But how? It was Peter nudging her in the back told how.

She called the oxen over to where the yoke lay, then to where the heavy chain had been cast aside. With Gunsmith's help she set the two oxen to drawing the first log into place. They were notching the end before she could draw the chain clear, and another log was ready for the far side. Soon as she had that in place, lying on the rock foundation, then there were the shorter end logs.

An argument rose up over who was skilled to build a rock and clay fireplace and chimney. Saws grunted and growled, cutting the short logs where door and windows were to set.

That gave time to lay the beginnings of the barn. Eldest had set no marks, and the menfolk, knowing what kind of barn they'd build for themselves, if they ever had to do it over, weren't contenting themselves with a lean-to. What they lined up was aimed to hold Peter and Paul, and the sled, and tools, and the corn from Dan'l's crib, and a cow and her calf and hens and only be half filled then.

Cabin and barn began to rise so Peter'n' Paul had to use a long rope and block, and two long sloping poles to roll the logs up into position. Young'un found it easiest to bestride the wall, and call down orders to them from there.

Teams that were wearied were changed for teams that were rested, and the log walls rose higher and higher. Till Young'un was looking down upon bent heads and shoulders. Eph and Gunsmith were set to hewing and pegging door- and window-frames, and the fireplace of flat rocks and clay was keeping pace with the walls, and drawing in to its throat and chimney. Chips were knee-deep beside the adze men, and had to be scraped aside from time to time. And still trees thundered to a fall up on the hill, still were being trimmed into logs, still with much hollering were drawn down behind steaming teams. Seemed like there'd not be a tree left, except those that were forked, or too big for use, from here to Canady!

A new sound made Young'un look up and off. Twenty or thirty childer were making believe to be a team, and hauling on long lines that must be grapevine. Behind them all came Dan'l with the rifle, walking proud and stiff-legged. It didn't take long to hear the cause, for the little girls that hadn't been let to haul came bouncing up to their mas.

"Dan'l's shot a deer with the little new rifle! He has so! Clean atween the eyes. And it flopped over a cliff. And we had to cut grape-

109

rope and haul it up again." And the same thing was told and retold.
And Dan'l would start a fire and they'd roast the whole deer, the
whole deer all to once!

That set the womenfolk off to kindle a huge fire, and some to running down to see did Dan'l know how to clean the deer, and some to
disputing how the deer would best be cooked.

Young'un would have jumped down, too, only for the awful
thought that came to her. For Dan'l it would seem the day before
yesterday, all over again. But this time it wasn't Sim Higgins who
would break Dan'l's pride, but his own sisters. Only at this morning's
breakfast he'd said again where he aimed to set the cabin, just where
Pa had set his, where the land soured by the burning hadn't yet
grassed over. And just as soon as he looked up, he would see the
cabin, already half built, and the barn beside, laid just in the marks
that Eldest had cut in the grass. He would come in the long run to
see the choice was good, but that wouldn't heal the hurt of thinking
that Eldest and Young'un had gone against him. And behind his
back.

And they hadn't either. It had just happened. Neighbors had found
the marks Eldest had cut in the ground. And even if 'twas Eldest
and not the womenfolk had set the marks wider, she hadn't stopped
to think "Here's where I've always wanted it, so we'll set the cabin
somewheres else." That wasn't in human nature. She hadn't thought
at all, only felt mighty grateful to such kind neighbors. No, it was
Young'un herself was to blame, if any. But it was too late to mend
matters now. All she could do was watch Dan'l, and hope.

Dan'l didn't say, he didn't so much as draw near. When the men
stopped work and the womenfolk spread out the food they brought,
Dan'l was still working on the deer with axe and skinning knife,
way off down by the pool. With the other childer he carried the meat
over to the burned-down coals of the fire the womenfolk had made
for him, but turned aside their offers to help.

Over their noontide meal, the womenfolk got new ideas and the
cabin had to be altered to allow a half floor, like a wide shelf stretching out from the fireplace end of the cabin, so Young'un and Eldest
could have a warm sleeping place in wintertime. And the menfolk
saw that with just a few changes they could set a bigger hayloft in

the barn over the heads of the animals. 'Twould cool the place in summer and keep it warm in winter. Saws had to be filed up sharp, and axes set to the grindstone in someone's wagon, and the work went on again.

But it wasn't the same as the morning. Not to Young'un. When the end logs narrowed in to a point and were crowned with a roof-tree and pegged braces, she hoped it was all over. But there were still the light saplings to be laid on from wall-top to roof tree, and lighter flattened pieces laid lengthwise over these to take the shingles when Dan'l could get around to fashion them.

Then 'twas all over, save the eating of Dan'l's venison. And she had her chance to go to him.

This was a new Dan'l, one she'd not ever seen before; being almighty polite and pressing with his venison, talking the unnatural way that Eldest did at times.

The last bite was eaten, the women back in their wagons, and the children scampering up the trail to see could they beat the growed folks to reaching home. Dan'l and Eldest were saying their "Thank you" all around, and the men saying, "Shucks, 'twas nothing," and for Dan'l to see careful to the chinking, for the green wood would warp every which way. The women were telling Eldest to see she reminded them of the slips and flowers they had promised, specially those for Ma's grave.

'Twas all good as ended, when Dan'l suddenly lit out and ran. Young'un caught him in the new barn, looking around him as best he could for what was in his eyes. Then just as sudden he pushed past her and out. Back to the tail of the wagons.

"You hadn't ought to've done it!" He shouted it at them, up the trail. "You just hadn't ought to've! There ain't no ways I can find to thank you. Nor ever will!"

Then he had to turn back again. And run and hide.

*　　*　　*

Outside the square holes of the cabin, darkness drifted down, filled with stars. Soon those holes would have shutters, and some day far off they'd carry real windows paned with real glass. Above and across the framework of roofing poles that were spaced for Dan'l's shingles, the Milky Way streamed like the breathing trail of an otter diving

deep under the stilly water of a dark shadowed lake. On the square
stone that formed the hearth, a fire burned on a thick layer of ashes,
a tiny fire so as not to dry the clay of the chimney too fast and make
it crack and fall. And the womenfolk had warned not to heat a
green hearthstone till the damp was out of it, or it was like to ex-
plode.

Eldest had drawn her stool up to the hearth, and was sitting, chin
cupped in hand, her eyes on the flicker of flame that bloomed up once
in a while and reddened the log walls. Cat was sitting opposite, washing himself from tail to whiskers to show he was pleased to be back in
a real home again, even if the grass hadn't yet worn off the earth
floor.

To sit still like Eldest was more than Young'un could compass.
And she hadn't a mind for work, like Dan'l over by the door, pounding away in the half-dark with frow and mallet, splitting his first
shingles of the first score of the first score-hundred and more he'd
split and smooth this winter and the next.

For this wasn't a day like any other days. Twice she had run out
to stand in the old shelter, so as to come back to the new home and
savor it. Then she'd had to run out to take a look from the outside,
to know for certain the cabin was as she remembered it from inside,
and to set eye to the chinks between the logs to catch the twinkle
of firelight coming through. And of course it was needful to go visit
with Peter'n' Paul in the grand new barn, and promise them a close-
laid hemlock bough roof and a deep layer of warming hay overhead,
just as soon as she and Dan'l could get around to it. Even so they
seemed contented, most as contented as Dan'l and Eldest.

Young'un was scarce back in when a yellow light gleamed up
from the window on to the rafters and the half floor overhead.
Then a lantern shone in the doorway, and Dan'l stopped banging
away with his mallet to say, "Mist' Jones, Preacher! C'm on in, and
set awhiles."

And there was Preacher, saying thank you he'd be delighted, and
how sorry he was to have missed the rolling up. But he wouldn't take
Eldest's stool. And when Eldest told Young'un to run to the shelter
and bring the other stool, he said please not to trouble, for he'd a mind
to stand.

He looked around him and said how close the logs set and how it showed highly skilful adze work. And Eldest said, "Didn't it, now?" Just as though she knew good adze work from bad.

He said how big the cabin was. Dan'l wanted to show him the barn which was more than twice the size. But Preacher said no, not now, but some other time he'd be delighted.

So Dan'l went back to his shingle-splitting, and Young'un took Eldest's stool, seeing she wouldn't use it as long as Preacher was visiting. Though it wasn't as if Preacher was a stranger, seeing he'd walked over three-four times even after the burying. Eldest had taken more consoling than you'd have thought needful, and it seemed only Preacher could do it, other folk not having the practice he had.

Preacher coughed two-three times, the way he did in Meeting before giving out a hymn or starting on his sermon. But he said nothing. Like as not he had a sore throat, and that was why he wore the woolen comforter, for it wasn't real cold, maybe not freezing even.

Eldest and Preacher stood side by side, not looking at each other, nor speaking. Till Young'un had to pretend to laugh at Cat, Eldest and Preacher looking so like Peter'n' Paul, though not the match the oxen were. It came to her they might almost be talking without sound, the way the oxen did, only of course they hadn't the sense.

Then Eldest said in the tinkly voice she kept for growed folk, "Mist' Jones, you'd ought to see the moon rise up over the hills. 'Tis best seen from the pasture bars."

Of course Preacher didn't know better, that all he had to do was turn and watch it through the new window hole. And he and Eldest were outdoors before Young'un could think whether 'twas right to tell him. Dan'l moved the lantern over so it threw light on his work, and Young'un cupped chin in hand like Eldest, and settled herself to put twigs on the fire and think real growed up thoughts.

Awhiles back, or maybe it was no more than this same day, there had seemed nothing in the whole world that mattered, that really mattered, but the farm. Growing food for themselves and the oxen, fixing to have a roof overhead to keep out rain and cold. But they had that now, or as good as. And now it seemed no more than a stage in a long journey. 'Twas a stage you had to reach, and it was heartening to reach it, and rest awhile, and think what lay beyond.

Cupping chin on hand, watching the flicker of flame bloom up and die down did something to you inside, deep down; the way Meeting did, only different. It set you to thinking how Pa was faring up there in the north woods, getting set to run his winter trap line. And how he'd made out all summer when pelts weren't worth the skinning. Could be he'd suffered. It was Pa's way, she could see that now, to set out without any thought to the future, or so much as spare flints for his gun, or a bag of salt.

If he came back now, he'd be proud as a turkey gobbler at all that had been done, and surprised too. Only there'd be a hurt inside him, belike, and the feel that he'd ought to have done it himself.

When you thought of Pa, you thought of Dan'l; Dan'l aiming to be his spitting image, or leastwise how Dan'l pictured him. You couldn't but hope that Pa would tire of running the woods and come back soon. Leastways until you bethought you what it would do to Dan'l to know Pa again as he really was. Then you didn't know which way to incline your wish.

Young'un stretched, and looked up to see the moonlight bright outside the window and door, and to note that Dan'l had snuffed the lantern, not aiming to waste good candle, his or another's. Eldest and Preacher should have had their bellyful of moon by now.

Dan'l went out to bring in the salt from the shelter, so the porcupines wouldn't get it. Then he shouldered through the doorway with an armful of hemlock twigs for his bed, brought other twigs and cast them up on the half-floor above, and climbed the notched sapling which served for ladder. He came down again and spread the deerskin flap over the doorway to keep out cold, forgetful of the open rafters above. Too tired even to think, was Dan'l, and kind of staggering in his walk. Young'un jumped up to aid him with the rest of the carrying.

It was then that Eldest walked in. She had her head shawled with Preacher's muffler, and hummed to herself as she unwound it, folded it careful and looked around for where she should lay it.

"Where's Preacher?" It was natural for Dan'l to ask. Young'un was minded to ask, herself.

"Mist' Jones? Mist' Jones?" Eldest might have sung the name

outright, and there'd have been little difference. "Oh, he's a-ways up the trail, most on to the road by now."

"But his lantern . . . and ain't that his muffler?" Dan'l knuckled his eyes to open them, and try to understand.

"Mist' Jones loaned me his muffler to shawl my head for fear I'd take a cold in the night air. He was mighty concerned for me." Eldest smiled around the cabin, as though the cabin would understand just how concerned Mist' Jones had been.

Dan'l picked up the lantern, not staying to light it from the fire, and grabbed at the muffler still in Eldest's hand. "I'd best run after him. Must be he forgot."

Eldest snatched her hand with the muffler behind her. "Mist' Jones is mostways to Gunsmith's now, and you're wearied besides. And he told me to keep the muffler till he was up this way again. The lantern's Gunsmith's, so you can return it any day. And . . ."

Then Eldest must have recalled she was womenfolk and older than Dan'l, who was no more than a boy. Eldest's hand, the one without the muffler, pointed at the waste log-ends Dan'l had been splitting, at the rough-shaped shingles leaning against the wall, at the bark and litter lying around. "Land sakes, Dan'l, folks would think you'd been born and raised in a barn! First dawn tomorrow you take that trash right out of here and off my new dirt floor. You hear me?"

"Yes'm. I cal'late to," said Dan'l meekly. "Yes'm." Just like he would to Ma. He stepped over to his bundle of hemlock boughs, lay down and curled up. Likely he was asleep before Young'un and Eldest had climbed the bear-pole to their half-floor.

But Young'un lay wide-eyed watching the stars, faint and creamed over by the moonlight, saw one pass out of sight behind a rafter and come slipping out on the other side, like the bright eye of a squirrel peering round a bole. Only a squirrel never made her feel so small and lonesome.

Eldest rustled her dried bedding, and sighed as she nested her cheek down upon the folded muffler. Young'un didn't need to see to know. And Eldest's sigh was just so much extra happiness which had to leak out, being she had more than she could hold. Which made Young'un more lonesome still.

She was fixing to marry Preacher, plain as plain, was Eldest. Though Dan'l hadn't seen it yet, and wasn't like to, being a boy. If he did, he'd say Pa wouldn't hold with it, thinking of the farm, and how hard it would be to spare her. But hard or not, they'd need to let her go, out of plain justice, and Preacher would take her off to Fort Ann where he lived with his aunt. And they'd not see her again, excepting when Dan'l drove down for spring victualing, for Preacher hadn't a rig to drive her up with him when he came to hold Meeting. 'Twas heartache, even to think of, being parted that way.

A porcupine started gnawing away at a new timber for the taste of the salt sweat that someone's hands had left on it. She'd ought to call to Dan'l so he'd go out and kill it. Or go herself, though she was always feared a porcupine would shoot its quills the way some said it did.

Then a new thought came to her. Maybe Preacher couldn't marry Eldest after all, for how could he jump around being bridegroom and Preacher all to-once? He couldn't, any more than a hog could take knife and stick his own throat at killing time. The thought would have been mighty comforting if Eldest's sad white face hadn't seemed to come opposite her, asking if there wasn't ary way round or over.

And there was. And it was Young'un's bounden duty to tell it, despite herself, if Eldest and Preacher didn't think of it first. They should get themselves another preacher, that was all. Mist' Jones would know how and where. And Mist' Jones would be just Mist' Jones while the other preacher said what was needful. Easy as that. She'd tell Eldest in the morning, and save her worry.

With a load off her conscience, Young'un wriggled down and closed her eyes, and pulled the cover over.

CHAPTER ELEVEN

OF ALL the headstrong little heifers! Young'un leaned harder against the warm flank, to save herself from being crowded off the beaten track into deep snowdrifts. The little heifer leaned in towards her, and, being the heavier, shouldered her off again. Seemed like the playful little critter, never having seen winter before, suspicioned that Young'un had put the cold white stuff there a-purpose, and that being so, held it was for Young'un to plough through.

The gift of Eph's heifer was a secret, and the biggest that Young'un had ever cherished. If the little critter turned out as good as Eph's Molly and met with no mischance like broken leg or rattler bite, she would be worth more through the years than house and barn, and even Peter'n' Paul; for there were her calves, and her calves' calves to be thought of too.

Come to think of it though, there was no call to slight Peter'n' Paul, for without them there'd be no ploughing, nor winter feed laid up for the heifer. And but for Eph there would have been no little heifer; and but for the neighbors there would have been no barn for her. The more you thought, the more you saw the need to give thanks to nigh on all creation. Only there wasn't the chance, not with the little heifer wrestling you for who should keep the trail and who go ploughing knee-deep through the snow drifts.

Dan'l wasn't to see her, not at first. And that was easy, being as he'd lit out hunting soon after dawn and wouldn't be back till near dusk. Meat was hard to come by these days, with the snow so deep. Could be Young'un would tell him, "There's a kind of beast in the barn. Looks a heap like Peter'n' Paul, only smaller . . ." And Dan'l wouldn't wait to hear the end of it, but would take his rifle and run round to see was it a deer or a bear. Or could be Young'un would twist the happening all around to confuse Dan'l, and say "Phebe sent a friend of hers across to live here awhiles. Didn't seem I could tell her 'No.' She's back in the barn looking at Peter'n' Paul." Only that would be likely to fright Dan'l out of his five senses; he being more like Ma or Eldest and not having the understanding Pa had.

No matter which way Young'un turned her thoughts, every so long they swung back to Pa and what he was doing. Folks who claimed he was likely dead just didn't know Pa; there wasn't a thing in all the northern woods that could harm him. And those who said likely he would marry again somewheres and Cold Brook would see him no more, they were wrong too. Pa wouldn't burden himself with womenfolk up in the woods. Nor he nor Dan'l didn't hold with women. Pa would come back when he got good and ready, and he'd have no cause to hang his head, no matter what folks thought.

Her mind half on the wonderful little heifer and half on Old Man Post, Young'un had been walking blindly. Snowshoe tracks swinging in from the right brought her back to the present. They didn't belong to Dan'l, for his left shoe was warped a mite at the toe. Those big ones, sunk deep, would be Hank Broadmoor, who favored an ox, being big, slow moving and kind of gentle. The three round bearpaw shoes belonged to Stumpy of course, one for his crutch. And the track that showed a couple of broken thongs could easily belong to the shiftless Miller boy. If so, then his sister Albacinda would be along, with the whole litter of little'uns.

Anxiously Young'un bent to examine the beaten track while the heifer blew warm breath down her neck. Yessir! The hard beaten snow wouldn't allow separate tracks to be picked out, but there had been a sight of moccasins up this trail, and all headed east towards the Post place. The bigger boys had snowshoed cross-lots, and the girls and the little'uns come round by the trail. Young'un broke into a trot, the heifer cavorting along behind her.

Eldest was down to the settlement, learning herself to spin, against the time when she would be a married woman; and with Dan'l away too, if those childer had left so much as one log of the cabin standing on another 'twould be a mercy! The pleasure they had taken from the house and barn raising had made the young'uns of the

118

settlement lose their dread of the strange Post folk living alone up there in the woods. First a few of the older ones, like Hank, had kind of wandered up to see were the logs settling down nice and even. Then with the first fall of snow, chores being light in wintertime, most every young'un and little'un in the whole of Cold Brook had started to flock up the hill.

At first Eldest had been plain scairt of them. Then she had taken to setting them stints to make them useful and keep them from under foot. It wasn't long before she had taken to telling them, "You pesky childer running the roads again?" And some had even got to pulling off caps and answering, "Yes Ma'am" and "No Ma'am," just like Eldest was already a married woman. Which she was, or good as, in her mind.

When Young'un and the heifer broke out from the bare woods there was no one in sight, only Peter'n' Paul standing outside the barn and lipping a stand of cornstalks, not minded to eat nor yet to let it alone. Young'un ran the heifer up to the barn. But at the very doorway the pesky critter splayed her legs and stopped. It wasn't her own barn and she knowed it. Young'un tugged at the lead rope, then put out a finger for the stubborn critter to suck on. But the heifer would not be drawn or coaxed. And the noise of the settlement childer inside sounded like they were tearing the walls down, if no worse.

The oxen plodded up to look in, only there was the new heifer blocking half the doorway. Peter crowded up beside her. Then the heifer gave a leap that carried her into the barn and most across it. Young'un caught the headrope around a stanchion, and looked back to see what had changed the little critter's mind so sudden. It was Paul, unwilling to be left behind his yoke-fellow Peter, had put head to the young heifer's tail and shoved. And now he was trying to look innocent as a boy who pinched a girl in Meeting.

"You old Paul!" she told him. "Nobody ever learned you that, you thought it up yourself. I'd take shame, I would!"

But the two oxen just put heads together and trudged to where they most usually stood. It was plain they was minded to hold by their rights. Jealous they were.

Viney hurried to pull down fresh hay for all three, and scolded the oxen good. That was no way to act, she told them straight, when a purty little heifer came along to keep them company.

There was a sight more she had to tell them, but it must keep till later. Stumpy came jerking around on his crutch, and yelled "Here's Viney, and a new little heifer. . . . Eph's heifer 'tis . . ." And the other boys came tearing around from the house, each wanting to know afresh how old she was, how much had Dan'l given for her and the like.

Then they found Dan'l's frow and mallet and drawknife and started to gouge chunks off the wall-logs. Eldest and Dan'l being away, it lay with Viney to stop them. Maybe she could do better than just stop them.

"You Fordyce," she told Hebron Miller's first-born, a tall gangling boy, "let me learn you the right way to use a frow." She grabbed it from him, took the mallet from Isa Broadmoor, and up-ended one of the log ends Dan'l had stacked in a corner.

Before she could lay the heavy blade of the frow across the sawn-off end of wood and pound it with the mallet, Fordyce had grabbed it back. "I don't cal'late to need learning the how from a girl, neither you nor Albacinda!" And began to pound away.

Young'un smiled. "Easy enough to split shingles, but it ain't nowise so easy to judge the grain and split them true."

That left Dan'l's broadaxe and saw and the drawknife, and enough boys to do a sight of harm with them, like Stumpy trying to shave hairs from the oxen's tails this very minute.

Viney laughed. "Stumpy don't know what a drawknife's for. Just look at him!"

Stumpy stopped. "I ain't but waiting till that Fordyce splits me a good shingle slab. Then I'll show."

That left the Broadmoor brothers, Hank and Isa, and of course the little girl Consolation who always tagged along with Hank, nobody else being able and willing to father and mother her the way Hank did. Hank was seventeen, and being a Broadmoor was boned and thewed so he could swing a hundred and twenty pound load to his shoulder as easy as he could little Consolation. Folks said he'd drawn his wits from his ma who'd died bearing little Consolation.

He wasn't one to be tricked, nor managed without he saw reason to be.

He grinned, most as though he'd guessed her thought, consarn him! "We got a shingle horse to home we clamp the shingle slabs on for shaving. Too fur to fetch it, I cal'late, but what say we borrow Dan'l's axe, fell us a sapling, split her and make us a horse here?"

Young'un handed him the axe without a word. It wasn't needful to talk with one so understanding. And Isa would do whatever Hank did, and little Consolation tag along with them, and just as well, for the child couldn't be let to play with the other little'uns, account of her jealousy and her scratching and biting. Nor she wasn't fit for the older ones account of the way she would pummel and knee-kick and bawl, "I hates you! I hates you!" And for no mortal reason unless 'twas to call attention, or get Hank into a fight protecting her. Spoiled to a stench, was little Consolation.

Young'un stopped at the door. She had an idea that might keep them to work. "Kinda fun up here in the woods with no growed-ups around to call you offen this chore or on to the other. Once you get yourself a task you can keep on."

Then she hurried off round. For what the boys could damage in Dan'l's barn was naught compared with what the girls might do amiss in Eldest's house. On her way she picked up two pairs of snowshoes left out in the sun on the south side, and carried them around to the shade on the north. Freeze and thaw was the ruination of thongs, however careful you greased or waxed or rosined them; a sight worse than plain use and wear.

Inside the door, land sakes what a clamor! Mostly it was from the late-brood little Millers; and the smell, kind of like a wet hound dog, was theirs too. After Fordyce and Albacinda, Mis' Miller had quit bearing for a whiles. Then, like a lot of puny apples on a late blooming bough, along had come this new brood. You couldn't hardly lift your eyes but Albacinda had another baby sister to dandle, and the last dandled brother to learn to walk, and the sister before that to show how to wipe its own nose, and so on up. Young'un caught the third from smallest and had her outside just in time. They weren't hardly housebroke, the most of the last litter.

She brought it back in, a mite doubtfully, for it hadn't done all that was expected. " 'Llo, Cindy," she greeted Albacinda to show the girl she was welcome, even with the little'uns. " 'Llo, Sary and Samanthy," to the Sherman twins, who had lined up a row of young Millers all squatting on their hunkers, and were teaching them to frog-hop under the table.

At the table, shelling acorns, was a girl who scarce looked up from her task to call, " 'Llo Viney. I'm Amy." And it was Amy Higgins no less, whom she'd scarce ever set eyes on, even in Meeting. Nor when she took Peter'n' Paul down to help Dan'l with Mist' Higgins' hauling; Amy's pa being kind of worthless for all his tricky ways, and her ma so hog-fat and breathless she couldn't do a hand's turn, it all fell to Amy Higgins, to raise garden and hens, cook and tend house and even split and carry firing. Leave alone milk and do the chores when her pa was away trading or visiting around.

"Sary and Samanthy brung me along." Amy must have mistook the cause of Young'un's silence. "But if Dan'l still holds it against Pa, account of the deal they turned . . ."

"Course he don't. You're hearty welcome, Amy Higgins." Young'un closed her eyes on the crowded cabin to make her next words true, in a manner of speaking. "I don't see hardly a soul up here in the woods."

Cinder took up her pounding with the heavy wooden pestle, in the mortar Dan'l had hollowed out of a birch log. That must have been the noise that had made Young'un think the cabin was being pulled apart. She took a look around. Except for Cat, who had climbed up to the half-floor instead of sitting by the fire, there was naught out of place and naught looked to be broken. Yet it wasn't in nature for a dozen boys and girls and little ones to leave the place like this, with no grown-up to watch over them. Nor for Cinder to be pounding when she could be idling, nor for the Sherman twins to be playing with the babies when there were oxen and axes and boys around.

Young'un hitched herself a stool to the table and began to help with the acorn shelling. It looked like it might pay to learn the ways of this Amy Higgins.

"Pa says there ain't nobody bested him in years, but your Dan'l. Don't happen your Dan'l's got cloven hoofs and horns and a tail?

It set me to thinking I'd come see for myself, Pa not holding with my talking to you or him down to home." Amy laughed, and Young'un laughed too at the comical picture she'd made of Dan'l.

Not so much to look at was Amy Higgins, with her little bones. It was hard to see how she could tend her share of a farm, do chores and cook and what-all; except that her hands moved so fast. With her light-brown hair, betwixt beech-leaf brown and deermouse color, in long shiny braids down her back, her little turned-up mouth and the quick squirrel-like peek of her gray eyes, she didn't look to be a Higgins at all. Nor she didn't favor anyone else in looks either. Kind of like the blithesome heifer, or again like a pert chickadee. Though it was hard to see why, except that she was lovable.

"Seeing you had a bushel or more acorns I cal'lated to make myself useful." Amy scooped a pile of shells into her skirt, carried them to the fire, sent Sary off to fill a sap bucket with good fresh water from the unfrozen spring, greased Eldest's baking board and set it in front of the fire to warm, then came back to the shelling. All in one breath it seemed like.

Then it was no time at all till the acorns were all pounded to a paste, the paste mixed with water and pounded again. Until Amy, tasting, found the bitterness was gone. With growing interest Young'un watched the rest of the preparation, the squeezing of the paste to dry it, the mixing with grease and salting, and spreading on the hot board.

She had another interest too, had Young'un. Pa had told how acorns were good food for hunger times, so Young'un had gathered these from the squirrel hoards before the snow grew too deep. Only to find that Eldest couldn't cook them. And here was Amy showing how. There wouldn't be a heap of acorns left by the time Amy was through, but that was cheap enough price for the learning, and Ma had used to say there was nothing to be had free in this world of sin. Just as soon as the snows thinned out Young'un would go scratch out enough acorns to give the Posts acorn bread right on through to spring, she would so.

Albacinda tossed back a curl and started to say "Acorns ain't fit for aught but hogs, and folks that . . ." when the nutty fragrance of the baking cakes made her stop and change her mind. And the little'uns ceased playing and had to be given half a cake apiece, and there were enough from the first batch for the twins and Cinder and Amy and Young'un. The crusts were brown, nigh onto black, that being the nature of acorn cakes. But folks that chose food by eye and not by taste and smell had ought to live on potato blossoms, as Amy said, instead of their roots, and purty looking fur instead of the ugly meat that lay beneath. Or maybe just content themselves with laylocks and icicles, and a few feathers off the bluejays. 'Twas mighty comical to hear Amy tell, but there was sense to it besides, when you came to think.

Cinder carried around the next batch to the boys, warning them that those who left their work and came to clutter up the house would get no more. Batch followed batch, and the cakes were filling too. 'Twas heart-warming to pleasure all these mouths with what the Posts could spare; and there would be no more talk after this of "those wild critters up at the Post place." For even little'uns weren't like to be feared of those that fed them. The boys that had noontide chores came around for their snowshoes, and Cinder led off the young Millers so as to have someone to carry those that wouldn't walk. Soon there was no one but Amy left, scrubbing down the table and sweeping up the hearth. Handy as Eldest, she was, about the house.

Scrubbing and cleaning with her, just to show that she could, Young'un kept wishing that Amy had been a sister. For it wouldn't be long now before Eldest was married and living at Fort Ann; that was plain as plain. And there'd come a day when Young'un herself might set her thoughts towards marrying. And not be able to, account of leaving Dan'l sole alone with none to cook for him or tend him if he fell sick. And no chance that Dan'l would ever take himself a wife. Except to work at Gunsmith's forge he never set foot in the village, and wouldn't so much as go to Meeting without Young'un or Eldest stopped behind to keep an eye on house and oxen. And when folk his own age came visiting, he would make excuse to take axe and go down to the lower pasture, or light out for the hills.

Someone scuffed moccasins against the door log to shed their snow. The door opened quietly on its leather hinges and Dan'l came in. Likely he'd scouted the party of young'uns on the trail, but hadn't counted them. And now the light coming in through the window holes was dim after the snow-glare outside. He walked to the fire-place, to hang rifle and bag on the deer-horn hooks. Just then Amy stood up from tending the fire.

Each looked as surprised as tother. Dan'l with his arms raised up, the rifle and strap to the bag stretched out to go over the horns. And Amy springing up between them and Dan'l, so she was caught, as Dan'l, unthinking, lowered his arms. Likely Dan'l had never been so close to a girl that wasn't his sister, in all his born days. Nor he couldn't have got much closer.

It lay with Amy to duck out the way she'd sprung up, if she wanted to be rid of the bag around her neck, Dan'l's arms about her and the rifle behind her back. It wasn't in nature for Dan'l to let go the rifle with one hand and risk dropping it, not for any girl in the whole countryside. Young'un could see that plain. And Amy seemed to have taken leave of her senses. For all she did was to clutch tight to the crock of saved-over cakes she was holding, squeezed between her and Dan'l.

Young'un didn't so much as let loose a laugh, it all happened so sudden. And besides, 'twas the kind of happening you'd need to remember and take off by yourself to get the full savor of. And it hadn't finished yet.

For Amy said in a small breathless voice, "I'm Amy. Amy Higgins." Which Daniel knowed already. And when Dan'l opened his mouth, she pushed a whole cake into it. Scared of what he might be fixing to say, belike, or maybe just striving to please.

'Twas more than mortal frame could bear. Young'un kind of flopped down on a stool, and laid her head on the wet table. A sound, the like of which she'd never heard before, made her raise her head. Dan'l it was, coughing and choking over the cake, while Amy pressed tighter against him and the crock, striving to reach around and pound him on the back to cure the choking. Young'un's head sank back again on the table, and she was nigh to choking herself.

Next time she looked the two had somehow come untangled and drawn apart, Dan'l still with his rifle and bag, Amy with her crock, and neither thinking to set them down.

Amy said, "I best be going."

Dan'l said, "I killed me a wolf today. The first this year."

Amy said, "A wolf?" like she'd never heard of one.

Dan'l said, "I was fixing to give you . . . to give your pa the pelt. There's a bounty on them."

Amy said, "It's purty, sure." Though she hadn't so much as set eyes on it.

Dan'l said, "It's not purty, just an ol' wolf. Not purty, like . . ."

Amy started to say something more, but Young'un got up from the stool, and took the crock away from her. 'Twas the only crock that size, or thereabouts, and Amy's hands weren't to be trusted, the way they were twisting about.

That seemed to awaken Amy. "I . . . I best be going, Dan'l." She made for the door, and said the name over softly to herself—"Dan'l."

Young'un called a good-night after her. Not that Amy was like to notice. Nor Dan'l. It could be that Dan'l wasn't fit this moment to be told about the new heifer and what it would mean to the farm. He would think you were telling about Amy. And by the time he had come to understand, the juice of the surprise would be all squeezed out and wasted. Best let him happen on the little heifer herself when he went to the barn, and get the full force and pleasure of it.

But Dan'l made no move to go see to the beasts, the way he always did when he'd hung up his rifle. If Amy had grabbed a crock and stunned him, like a calf before sticking, he couldn't have been any more dumbfounded. He stood there, in the middle of the cabin; just stood, holding on to rifle and bag and powder horn, and turning them around as though wondering what to do with them.

Young'un began to set the pots to the fire for supper. That seemed to break Dan'l from his daze.

"Where's Eldest?" he asked.

"Down to the Settlement, maybe at Grandma Truttle's learning to spin."

Dan'l hung up his rifle and the powder horn and bag, and warmed his hands to the fire. "There's good sense in being forehanded. Soon's she's learned good we'll get us two-three sheep for a start off, and . . ."

"Eldest's liable to get herself married first!" Young'un spoke up right smart. But she could have saved her breath. Dan'l was deaf, and blind too, where it served his precious farm. She tried again.

"Time the sheep's raised and clipped Eldest will be living in Fort Ann."

"Nossir, Young'un, there's a heap you ain't old enough to understand yet. Eldest can't nowise walk into Fort Ann and say 'Please ye, I want me a man and a house.'" Dan'l was making things clear as he knew how. "Nor Fort Anners ain't liable to come up into these woods asking for Deborah Post, who they haven't so much as set eyes on. Leave alone marry her."

"Preacher does! Preacher will!" Young'un insisted. "And Eldest would break fence and run to him tomorrow if he said to!"

In the firelight a momentary doubt wrinkled Dan'l's brow. Then it cleared. Against the wall of the cabin his shadow towered, more than man-size. "Eldest knows the farm can't spare her. Pa wouldn't hold with it."

The man of the house had stated the case, made clear his point. He lighted a pine sliver to kindle the lantern.

On the way to the barn he stopped in the doorway to repeat, sternly, "Pa wouldn't hold with it, Young'un."

CHAPTER TWELVE

Up on the Post place there were just three seasons of the year. One that was friendly and neighborlike; one that didn't aim to concern itself with the human folks; and one that was downright hostile. It had seemed that way ever since Young'un could remember.

The first came when the sun started to smile in springtime, and the land looked up from under the melting snows to say, "I'm minded to go partners once again, if so be I'm let. Lend me the loan of a little seed and suchlike and I'll give you back four bushels or more for every one. If the season favors." And the Posts and the Post land would toil together for nigh on six months. And sure enough the land would keep its bargain. If the season favored.

Then the land would say, "I've worked days, and nights too while you Posts slept. I cal'late to've earned my winter's rest." And there was naught that the power of man could do to turn it from its purpose, nor grow so much as a blade of grass. Mostly this was a time of triumph, of measuring up the riches in baskets and sacks, and laid out in a trench, and stored up in the barn. And of haste too, gathering in the last red apple and suchlike before the frost could spoil it. But this year 'twas neither, only an anxious measuring of months and mouths against what Mist' Higgins had left.

The third season was the cold enemy that raided down from the north and over from the west. An enemy that had to be fought, and fought anew each year, with axe and firewood, and victuals and cook-pot, and roofs and walls and moss-chinkings, and downright human stubbornness beside. A good fight was right warming to the blood, and anyways folks that cherished life had ought to be willing to fight for it.

Some years the third season would do no more than scout around, frost an ear in one family, freeze a new-farrowed litter at another place before it could be found in the morning, and set another neighbor to borrowing pails of water and planning to dig him a right deep well the very next summer. Then off would go the cold again, though it didn't hardly seem winter was scarce begun, off to the north and the west with the wolves and the bears.

Some years winter came down like an enemy that pitched its white tents, and laid down to a long siege. Tree trunks burst with the cold and sounded like musket shots in the still night. Fingers didn't hardly straighten out betwixt one task and the next, and each chore was like ten. Nor you couldn't lie still at night, for the chilly fingers reaching in right to your bones. Critters that were puny or ailing were best killed off, and their feed used to keep other critters alive, for they would never see green grass again. The enemy pressed right up against closed doors and shuttered windows. And when the doors stood open again in the next year there would be a stiff-froze body to carry in from the lean-to asher or barn where it had been kept over. For sure enough there would be someone up in years, or with the lung-sickness, who hadn't had the heart to fight through.

Winter this year was nowise out of the ordinary. When Amy and the childer had used up the acorns, neither Eldest nor Young'un had grudged what was easy to replace. Or would have been easy in other years. Nor the Posts hadn't stinted themselves on the first chestnuts, knowing right well there were more to be had buried under a score of trees.

But then things started to turn awry, the way an axe would slip for all the axeman's care and skill. First it was the flint in Dan'l's borrowed rifle getting damp into it and splitting with the frost. That should not have mattered, for it was time he had a new one, flints getting blunt after the first fifty shots, especially if the frizzen steel was tempered over-hard. But Dan'l wouldn't borrow again, even from Gunsmith, so he did a day's work sawing and splitting Gunsmith's firewood to earn him two-three more flints. Time that should have been spared for the Posts' own winter fuel. Next, Heifer chose to wander off late one evening, remembering Eph's summer grazing, belike. And it took Young'un the best part of a night, trailing her through the snow by the light of pinewood torches, to bring her back. Feared she was of wolves, but more for Heifer than herself; wolves scared easy with a torch. Then 'twas Dan'l again, falling through the ice on the lake, trying to set his tip-ups. Dan'l was right enough that the best fishing was where Cold Brook ran in, and right enough to get his claim in before other folks that needed the fish less. But the ice was thinner there than elsewhere, and it cost Dan'l two days indoors to get the chill out of him, and his voice no better than a crow's caw for a week after.

With only five days in the week left over from working down at Mist' Higgins, it seemed like one thing after another came between the Posts and their fueling and their victualing. With trees all around to be had for the cutting; and squirrel, coon, porcupine, chestnuts, butternuts, hickories and what-all besides just waiting to be taken. And never had the Posts stood so badly in need of the things so nearly within their grasp. Cold and hunger were coming mighty close.

And then hard winter set in, and without respite. For a week or more the snow would drift down, slowly, steadily, as though the gray sky held naught but gray flakes and never would be clear again. The deep snow buried Dan'l's traps and snares, safeguarded the squirrels' hoards from Young'un's searching fingers, covered the ice so deep there was no cutting the score of holes needed for fishing. And the two-three fishholes, that had looked deep as wells, filled with snow mush, and froze-in the lines so that the prized fishhooks were lost. Even the Posts' own vegetables, buried deep in a trench and layered with leaves against the frost, were hard to come by.

The oxen must be spared, so they should have strength for the two days' work each week down to Mist' Higgins, and for the heavy labor of breaking trail down and back. So it fell to Viney to drag down the wood that Dan'l felled and cut to length up on the snowy hillside.

Cold it was, even when they could spare the fuel for a good fire. The snow had covered Dan'l's rough roofing of boughs, and that was a mercy. But even after Young'un and Eldest had chinked every crack between the logs and pegged deerhide tight over window and doorway, it seemed to Young'un as though she had never known what it was to feel warm, nor ever would again.

In the same silent steady fashion came real hunger. Not just the gnawing in the belly that made you savor your victuals the more, but a hunger that sat down with you to table, and rose with you again, and followed you out to your toil and even through the chilly night. Day by day there would be naught but a few beans and perhaps a potato or a handful of cornmeal, from the victuals that must be parceled out till spring at least. It wasn't the griping ache of quick starvation, but a day-by-day whittling down of human strength and even human hope. Till Eldest's eyes were big and dark in her thinning face, and Dan'l couldn't spare strength for an unneeded word; and it seemed an age since Young'un had so much as smiled, and her legs began to lag, no matter how she urged them.

Dan'l did his best with the little rifle. But there was nary a deer track anywheres around; even the wolves, that had come down early from the north, had gone. Woodchuck, porcupine and the bears were hidden deep asleep; which was another mercy, for Dan'l in his desperation would have given no thought to how small a bullet the little rifle threw, and how big and dangerous a bear could be.

Then would come a day of bright sunshine, turning the gray world to dazzling gold and blue and white, and the squirrels would be out again so that Dan'l would summon up enough ambition to shoot maybe a brace. The hot meaty stew, eked out with vegetables to last two-three days, would start the warmth and even the strength to well back to Young'un's body. But when the snowy sky clamped down once more the strength and warmth went, faster than they had come.

The worst days were those that followed the weekly toil down to Sim Higgins'. Since oxen were slow-moving critters at the best of times, Young'un and Dan'l had to set out before dawn; and often as not the yoke had to break trail through snow that had part thawed, then frozen again into knife layers of ice, so that it bruised their legs as the critters slipped and plunged. Even so, Mist' Higgins complained of their tardiness, and set Dan'l straight to work, without time to rub down the oxen's swollen legs. When the snow got to be too deep and the ground too hard froze for digging and pulling tree roots, Young'un had hoped that Peter'n' Paul could be rested up. But Mist' Higgins set them to drawing down logs from his woodlot, more than he would be able to burn in the next five winters, seemed as if.

Since there had been naught agreed about food in the bargain 'twixt Dan'l and Sim Higgins, Dan'l and Young'un brought down such food as Eldest could spare, and warmed it over a fire in the smokehouse. It was that or nothing, since Mist' Higgins held that if they once came into the kitchen they'd get to idling there in the warmth.

At first off he didn't allow feed even for Peter'n' Paul, not so much as a smitch of hay. But one day in the barn Young'un set to and pulled down hay for the poor critters right before his eyes. And she even grained them a mite when Mist' Higgins wasn't around. Dan'l was feared that it would break the agreement, but if Sim knew aught of it he said nothing.

Returning to the Post place after the long day's toil, it would be late and full dark. Too dark and too late to gather fuel for themselves; and naught remaining of the morsel of fish or meat they had left with Eldest. It was all to start fresh again on the morrow, if snow didn't stop Dan'l from hunting and Young'un from drawing down firing. They would take a pine knot for light and, while Eldest hotted up the boiled cabbage and suchlike for supper, go out and see to the critters.

If it hadn't been for the little heifer, Young'un and Dan'l too would have been plumb discouraged. But there she'd be, at the tie-up in the barn, and purty as a picture. She'd give a little shuffle to her feet, to bid Peter'n' Paul welcome as they trudged in. Then she'd turn to Young'un and maybe Dan'l and ask, clear as words, where they'd been and how they'd fared. Not sharing the toil of the oxen she was making out mighty good on what little they could spare her. Dan'l would find courage to say: "Don't seem like she's going to be stunted any. More value to the hay than there looked to be when we cut it."

The Posts weren't licked yet, though times they'd come mighty close to it. There hadn't a laugh been heard since goodness knew when, and it was a month or more since the childer had last come up from the settlement. Often as not Preacher didn't appear at Meeting, and when he did come it was more than he could do to struggle

132

through ice and snow on up to the Post place. Seemed like there was naught left in the whole world but snow and cold and hunger.

* * *

In the darkness of early morning, Young'un stirred on the hemlock bed and curled herself into a tighter ball. Trying to think, she was, if there was any way that Eldest had missed, so they could save time, toil or victuals. Yesterday she and Eldest had set together what food they could scrape up, and sent Dan'l and the oxen off alone. For this time there wasn't the food for the two to go. And now, after throwing down hay to the heifer, she had crawled back under the covers with Eldest for the sake of the warmth, until such time as the day lightened, and she could take handaxe and spade and go down to the lakeside to see could she catch a mess of fish. If only they could make shift till Eph's Molly freshened and Eph let them have milk again. But that wouldn't be till late February.

"Folks to home?" called a voice outside. Eph's voice.

Eldest didn't so much as stir. Likely she hoped that Eph would be off if they didn't answer. But Young'un dragged herself from the warmth of the bed; Eph wouldn't have come without there was cause. She unpegged the doorskin so he shouldn't burst it aside; even the slight labor of whittling new pegs was to be avoided.

But he didn't offer to enter, didn't so much as slip his snowshoes. "We've need of Peter'n' Paul. Scotty Fergus is snowed in and either sick or dead. Where's Dan'l at?"

"Down to Mist' Higgins. And Peter'n' Paul too."

It was like plunging into Cold Brook to do it, but Young'un pulled her squirrel skin cap tight over her head, took down her snowshoes from the peg, and went out to join Eph. If the oxen were needed she'd be needed herself; Dan'l hadn't the knack with them that she had, as he'd be the first to admit.

Even last night it had snowed again. But Eph broke trail and Young'un's snowshoes shuffled easily up through the woods and out onto the road.

"Scotty came home from his winter's trapping two-three weeks back," Eph explained. "Snow was too deep, he said; but he looked to be mighty sick. And yesterday and today there wa'n't no smoke from his cabin. Hank Broadmoor and the other boys set off to snowshoe over. If he's alive they'll kindle him a fire. If he's dead there's no need for haste in this cold weather."

Scotty, she recollected, would be that dark-complected trapper that had threatened to cut off Sim Higgins' ears the time Dan'l and Mist' Higgins were striking a bargain.

They were down by the Birdsells' turnoff now, and scarce a need for the snowshoes on the hard packed road. But she hadn't the gumption left to take them off; just slapped along, wearing out the thongs and frames. She saw Eph Birdsell glance off, up the hillside, the way they were going. Worried. And he had cause to be. Every two-three winters, it seemed, a lone man or an old couple fell sick, too sick to light their fire or fend for themselves. And if neighbors didn't catch them in time they froze to death, right there in their own homes.

They'd most reached the Tavern when Eph let out a yell. "Smoke! Look, Young'un! Smoke!"

And she managed to lift her eyes from the ground ahead; sure enough, there was a thin trickle of smoke rising up from among the dark pines and fading into the lowering sky.

Down at the Tavern, in the growing daylight, folks were coming out from the warmth, caps well down over ears, breaths white on the frosty air, comforters well up over their mouths. Some were for starting, straight off in a bee-line, but Mist' Ditch came hurrying out to say that the trail had been broke as far as Sim Higgins', and that would cut off a quarter mile. Some turned back to their stables to get their beasts, some set off down the road and around to Mist' Higgins', others with snowshoes started cross-lots, following after Eph and Young'un.

It seemed to Young'un that the way to Sim Higgins' was weary long, and it was hard to believe it hadn't been growing longer, week by week. Once or twice lately, going down to Mist' Higgins' in the dark of the early morning she'd took to weeping because of the cold and the toil. And now, when she got to the struggle over the stone and root fence she nigh to have done it again. But it wouldn't serve to weep now, not with all these folks around; they'd think something was amiss, and that would start them to questioning. Somehow she hadn't the strength for the answers.

134

It took a long while, it seemed like, for the Higgins place to grow from a dark spot in the surrounding white snow to a house and a barn. Young'un got to hoping Dan'l had left Peter'n' Paul in the barn. And not just for the sake of the oxen, but so that she could get a minute to rest up when she helped Eph swing the yoke to their shoulders. But the oxen and Dan'l were up in the woodlot and up she had to climb behind Eph's hurried pace, not at the steady slow trudge of Peter'n' Paul. Dan'l's axe blows came mighty slow, lately he'd taken to resting between every few strokes. And when she came up with him Young'un noted how blue and cold he looked.

Eph, who was ahead, said a few words to him that Young'un didn't catch; Dan'l drove his axe into a stump and started to lead the oxen. Between them Dan'l and Young'un swung the sled and headed off after Eph. Where the snow had been trampled by the winter's work, Dan'l led, and the oxen followed. Then Dan'l came to the edge of the new snow, a bank four-five feet high, scrambled up onto the crust, took a pace, and then having no snowshoes, cracked through. Young'un swung around, clambered up beside him and called to the oxen.

They kind of hesitated at the bank, then leaned forward, trampling away, using their breastbones as a snow plough. And with the ice layers cracking and crunching beneath them, blundered slowly forward. It wasn't a fitten task to put oxen to, and it hurt to see their struggles. Just one bad slip and in this cold a leg bone would snap beneath their weight, quick as a pipe stem. Young'un would have stopped them then and there but for the thought of the man, dead or maybe dying, up yonder on the hillside.

Someone gave Dan'l a hand and set him back on the bank. Other folk, with snowshoes, had skirted around and were following fast after Eph. But Eph sent the most of them back. And some with snowshoes, some laying theirs on the sled, they set-to with Dan'l's axe and with short lengths of the cut wood, to pound away at the ice layers in front of Peter'n' Paul. It helped, for the oxen hadn't to plunge so deep. And then Gunsmith came up, and while the oxen rested awhile blowing out great jets of steamy breath, he showed Young'un how to fix one of his heavy cowhide aprons in front of Peter and another in front of Paul. It was only then that Young'un saw that the ice had begun to cut into the tender hide of shoulders and neck.

Young'un went on ahead again, and whistled. But for once Peter'n' Paul didn't stir. A man who was behind them would have twisted the oxen's tail, to drive them forward, but Dan'l, seeing the intention just in time, gave a kind of sob and threw himself from the sled clean onto the man's shoulders, bearing him down into the snow. Young'un snatched up a billet and hurried to his aid.

"Ain't *nobody* going to touch Peter'n' Paul!" Dan'l warned, most sobbing with anger and with the cold.

The man, he was some kind of stranger, picked himself up and made for Dan'l. But catching a glimpse of the stick of hickory in Young'un's hand, he thought better of it.

"Shucks, I wa'n't but trying to help!"

But for safety's sake Young'un passed the club to Dan'l. Then bent to feel the oxen's legs and shoulders. There was nothing amiss. Oh, of course, the stiff horsehide aprons had thwarted them. She flapped the leather two-three times.

"See, it's naught to hinder you," she coaxed aloud. "It's to aid. Now, you old Peter'n' Paul, lean into that yoke." And as she went forward the oxen and sled came creeping slowly after. They had the sense to see how the cowhide saved them from the sharp-edged ice, and it put new heart into them.

So they pulled up and up the steep long slope, breaking trail to Scotty's cabin, stumbling, finding foot again, rod after rod. Young'un cast her eyes back to the sled and the laboring oxen; down over the long stretch of unbroken white snow to where people that looked to be no bigger than ants came hurrying up from the settlement; and forward over the wide furrow the men had broken through the layers of snow and ice. Hoping, she was, that the men with snowshoes who had gone on ahead would carry down the sick man. It wasn't nowise fair that the whole labor of breaking trail should lie with Peter'n' Paul. But of course a horse would be useless in these deep drifts.

She had halted the oxen again for a rest, and they stood with thin sides heaving and legs trembling. She went back to help Dan'l rub down their legs, and to set back the leather aprons where they had worked awry. With the cold and the weariness of the past month it was all she could do to see and to understand one thing at a time, or she would have remembered that it wasn't in Broadmoor nature to sell off their oxen just because they had bought the new team of horses. So it seemed more like an answer to prayer than just happenstance when Mist' Broadmoor and Isa came trampling a way around Peter'n' Paul and the sled. And right behind them the Broadmoor oxen.

Heavy they were, and well conditioned, though not to match in size and looks the Post beasts. They crashed through and onto the trail ahead. So, after a rest, Peter'n' Paul had no more than to follow in their hoof tracks. Another twenty rod and the Broadmoor oxen pulled out, leaving Peter'n' Paul to break trail again. Then 'twas for them to draw out and the Broadmoor oxen to pass ahead.

The trail was made right up to the little frozen stream beside the trapper's cabin. The Posts might have gone on, crossing the stream, but Sol Broadmoor warned that the ice bridge would break through. And out from the cabin came a knot of men, struggling with something heavy. Young'un saw the reason why they'd not carried the man down on their snowshoes. The icy crust gave no grip to the shoes, so that the men who were carrying the trapper on his own wooden door were slipping and sliding this way and that, scarce able to stand upright. And a man who took off his snowshoes was no better off, for he cracked belly-deep through the crust.

When the group came to the deep hollow over the stream with only a thin ice-bridge over running water for support, Young'un watching, held her breath. It was Hank Broadmoor, who had his dead Ma's sense, who thought out what to do. A dozen of them slid down onto the thin ice, laying flat on their backs; and, as those from above lowered the door, the men on the ice reached up and passed it along from one to the other, till those on the further bank could reach it.

They had covered the trapper's face against the cold, Young'un noted as he passed, so he must be a mighty sick man. But they hadn't far to carry him to the Broadmoor sled. And down below in the woodlot the horse sleigh had drawn up and had turned and was all fixed with hot bricks and more coverings, to take him down to the settlement.

When Young'un and the oxen reached the woodlot, Mist' Broadmoor was still waiting. He had Dan'l's axe to hand back, and a number of questions he said he wanted to ask. Like how much feed and what kind did Sim Higgins allow the oxen when they were working for him? And what kind of a table did he set?

Young'un told him, best she could for her weariness, about the feed. She couldn't say about Mist' Higgins' table, being they hadn't never been allowed to come inside; he holding that if Dan'l came in where it was warm he'd idle over-long over his vittles. What vittles there was the Posts brought down themselves and hotted-up in the smokehouse.

Sol Broadmoor looked kind of funny, but he allowed they ought to lead down the oxen before they got chilled. And he still had some questions to ask. Like how many days had Sim Higgins used Dan'l alone, and how many days the oxen and Young'un besides?

Dan'l had to return to the woodlot to finish his work, so it fell to Young'un to answer. She hoped that what she told him made sense, but couldn't be sure; by now not even Mist' Higgins' barn, or Mist' Broadmoor himself seemed real. And when he said he guessed he'd best step across and have a word or two with Sim Higgins, Young'un forgot to say "Yessir," and would have lain down beside the oxen and gone straight off to sleep, but for the thought of Eldest, alone up there in the house.

She didn't remember putting on her snowshoes again, nor whether she went cross-lots or round by the road. There was a time she saw the tips of her snowshoes moving ahead of her over the whiteness; another time she heard voices and knew she was passing the Tavern. But it was all as though she were walking inside of an eggshell that made her sole-alone in the world. And that was kind of laughable, seeing she had been born so many years and hadn't ever been a hen-chick even at the start. Yes, she was sure that was a fact.

Hen-chicks were warm too, the mother hen saw to that. Young'un wasn't sure whether she was warm or whether she was cold. Times she was near to froze; times it was somebody else who was cold. And she must have gone a right long way for she'd been walking for days now. And maybe nights too.

And then, land sakes, she recollected Gunsmith's leather aprons.

Gunsmith would need them this very day. She stopped. And that wasn't hard. But when she tried to turn around one snowshoe overlapped the other. So she lay right down in the deep snow because that was the easiest thing to do.

*   *   *

And there Young'un was, crammed so tight in Phebe's little armchair that she couldn't have moved if she'd wanted to. Must have taken leave of her senses, she must, awhile back. For a body couldn't be cold beside Eph's new iron stove. Nor there couldn't be oxen and cracking sheets of ice and snow. The only thing that was real was Mist' Broadmoor. But he hadn't led up his yoke and sled, he was sitting over by the table talking to Eph, just as plain as plain.

"Another sup?" said Phebe, and held a hot pewter mug to Young'un's lips. "'Tis eggs and milk, with a touch of Medford to make it set well."

The same taste was already in Young'un's mouth, so she sipped and swallowed again.

And next it was broth, meat broth, in a steaming bowl. That set Young'un's innards to rumbling where before there had been no more than cold and emptiness. Phebe laughed, and Young'un laughed too, and rumbled again. There'd been a sight more rumbles than laughs the last few months, that being the way with empty bellies.

Then Young'un recollected. "There's Gunsmith's aprons!" she said, and made as though to get up.

Phebe looked at her curiously and frowned. So she had to explain about them.

"Thought you was outen your senses, Viney." Phebe smiled again. "Uncle Gam won't need his aprons yet awhile. And Dan'l will find them on the oxen when he leads up from the settlement."

"Dan'l will be along most any time." Sol Broadmoor's deep voice cut in. "Had a kind of a word with Sim, I did. Might ha' knowed he'd be up to something."

Young'un remembered Eldest, and said she'd best be going now. Which Eph wouldn't let her.

"If you'll set awhiles, Viney," said Phebe, and winked across at Eph, "Eph and me'll walk over with you and Dan'l. I haven't so much as stirred out of the house since land knows when."

So there was naught for Young'un to do but just set and set. And grow warmer and warmer, clear down to the middle of her; which she hadn't been for as long as she could remember. And to eat some of Phebe's dried-apple pie with her own cheese, which Phebe wouldn't be denied.

She must have slept awhiles then, or come close to it, what with the heat and the food; for the voices kept going way off into the distance and coming back near again.

"I made it mighty clear to Sim," once Sol Broadmoor's voice boomed out, "that the bargain is most worked out. Seeing he's used the oxen all the while, and had Young'un to lead them. And what I come up to say is that it lies with you as next-neighbor to make the same clear to Dan'l Post."

Then the voices went way off again to a purry sort of rumble. Young'un had to say something or fall plumb asleep. "Molly freshened again?" she asked Phebe, account of the milk.

"Not for another month or more. But Hebron Miller's letting us have what we need till then."

That set Young'un to thinking again. A month. That was about all that lay between now and the time the Posts would have milk again. Seemed they'd ought to make out someways for only a month. And there was a meaning behind that talk betwixt Mist' Broadmoor and Eph, if only she could get ahold of it. That the Posts had most worked off their debt to Sim Higgins: was that it? And that she and Dan'l and Peter and Paul . . . she had to put names to all of them to make it seem real . . . would now have two days more each week; time to set traps and tend them, time to cut more wood for the fire, time to fish through the ice, time to toil for themselves.

The coldest part of the winter still lay ahead, and there'd still be hunger. Hunger, of a sort, right away on till late spring. But when the vittles ran short again, as they surely would, they could fill their platters with Hope. 'Twas a tastier dish than Despair, and, it might be, more filling.

Young'un smiled at the thought and let the voices fade off into the distance again.

CHAPTER THIRTEEN

A PREACHER in a pulpit is a man in authority, with power to chastise the wilful sinners and rebuke those who stray from the path through ignorance. But a preacher on the driving seat of a wagon, who has forgotten to take a whip, and whose team haven't the sense to know that a coach is coming and has the right of way on a one track trail . . .

Phineas Jones took a shorter grip on the reins and sawed again at those leather-mouthed horses. They shook their heads, and he came near to pitching forward onto their backs. The team stopped, but refused to turn out of the well-worn ruts.

The coach swung into view beyond some trees. The pounding of sixteen hoofs grew nearer, nearer. Someone called warning. Then with a spectacular swerve horses and swaying coach pulled out and round in a swirl of dust.

"A mite o' trouble with your congregation, Preacher?" The coach driver turned back a red and grinning face.

"I'm sorry." That was all Phineas Jones had time to answer before Bloodgood and his coach were out of hearing. And he knew he'd be sorrier yet. Six people aboard the south-bound coach who would tell of the young preacher who hadn't enough gumption to pull off the road. And that Bloodgood man who could hear of a happening, in Ticonderoga, and tell it fifteen different ways, and each more comical, before he reached Fort Edward. He'd have Preacher standing up on the seat and preaching down at the team; and the horses, like Balaam's ass, answering back to him. And likely he'd add deer from the forest, and a bear carrying round the collection plate. Preacher's thin neck and ears reddened with shame, for he was sensitive. He slapped the reins, and called the team by a word no preacher had a right to use. The team, being used to such words, moved off and broke into a trot.

Preacher drew them in to a smart walk. For where the road wasn't rock it was stump, and where it wasn't stump it was bog, although it was past midsummer. And the load lying behind in the straw of the wagon wouldn't stand much jouncing. He'd driven at a walk all the way from Fort Ann, and it would spoil the surprise he aimed to give the good folk of the little settlement of Cold Brook if so much as a pane of glass was busted.

That last handful of cabins had looked to be deserted, for no children ran down to the roadside to call greetings, no woman so much as waved apron from doorway. But this was nigh to the end of the toilsome drive. A slope, black and smooth, led down to the brook. And there across the wooden bridge lay the Tavern to the right, and to the left Gunsmith's shop with its water-wheel.

He had another surprise too, for he had talked Aunt Johanna round at last, so now he'd be able to tell Deborah that they would have a house of their own just as soon as they were married. It was noble of Deborah to say she could not leave Dan'l and Viney until her father returned. But who could say if Ebenezer Post was even alive? The old man had brooded for a while over the ashes of his wife, his home and his hopes. Then he had set off north, but with no provisions for a journey, no money of course, and leaving behind him a pile of debts. One thing only he seemed to have taken, his rifle. The fact that no one had discovered his body meant little; the woods were thick and without settlers. And Ebenezer Post might have traveled ten or twenty miles before committing his sinful act of self-destruction.

Not for anything would Preacher give Deborah or her brother even a hint of his suspicion. He must be patient until they realized the truth for themselves.

Meantime he honored Deborah for her self-sacrifice, and treasured her the more. The most that he could do was to point out that, as a preacher's wife in Fort Ann, she could serve the Lord more effectually than when hidden on the farm. A beautiful flower she was, blooming unseen in the midst of the forest where trod no foot of man . . .

Preacher's imaginings had lifted mind and eyes far from the road, which stretched smooth and black and inviting ahead of him. He failed to note the wheel ruts and hoof marks that turned out, up a bank, and broke trail through a clump of bent and scarred sumach. His riding horse would have made the turnout of his own accord, by long habit. But this was a Fort Ann team. They went straight on.

Phineas Jones would not harshly pluck that rare blossom. With reverent hands he would transplant it, and tend it and cherish it in his new home. Forgetful of the smallness of his yearly income, paid mostly in gifts of farm produce, he had Deborah robed in a rich gown, in a parlor filled with rich furnishings and admiring members of his Fort Ann congregation. Forgetful of the road and his team . . .

His nearside wheels struck hard, lifted high, came down again into deep mud. And stuck.

He slapped the reins and shouted. The team struggled for footing, heaved, seemed only to mire themselves and the wagon deeper. Then, shivering with defeat, came to rest.

Phineas Jones must have shouted good and loud. For a stocky boy in patched deerskins glanced out of Gunsmith's shop, turned back in, and appeared again with what seemed to be an axe and a younger brother. Preacher groaned. Doubtless this was ordained, in chastisement of his overweening pride of a few moments back. But of all the people in the settlement the last he would have chosen to find him in this humiliating position were Deborah's brother and younger sister.

They crossed the bridge, solemn as ever. Not laughing at his misfortune so he had a right to resent it. Not asking, as they'd a right to, why in Tophet he'd driven plumb into the old slough that he'd ridden around a score of times before. They just joined him, wading around the wagon.

"Yessir, Preacher, that's what you've done; straddled your wheels across an almighty boulder." Dan'l gave expert verdict as he sounded the deep mud with his axe-helve. He drew the helve through his hand to scrape off the mud, pushed back the straggling hair from his eyes and turned to Viney. "Guess we'll have to lift the wagon out'n where she lies."

Viney nodded agreement.

You couldn't hurry these folk of the hills and Phineas Jones

143

knew it. But how could they hope to lift the wagon, these two, sturdy though they were? Far better to call out Gunsmith and a few other men to unload, then lay down brush, hitch on an extra team, lever up the body of the wagon, and all push. But the boy wasn't so much as considering the hub-deep wheels. He was looking up, with peaceful brown eyes, at the overhanging tree-tops. Then he said, "Young'un, you best call Peter'n' Paul." And stepping aside into the woods began to chop.

Viney nodded without speaking and picked her way, skilful as a cat, to the dry bank of the turnout. She put two fingers to her mouth and whistled. From round the corner of Gunsmith's shop paced the two large brown oxen, halting at the bridge. Viney whistled again, and they plodded solemnly on to the brink of the slough, where they stopped to stare, it seemed reproachfully, at the unlucky team. The horses fidgeted, and Preacher sympathized; for Viney, freckled and grave-faced, was looking down on him from the bank. Preacher lifted a foot from the mud and set it back again.

"Can't you," he checked his irritation, "can't you go call a few men to help?"

Viney's freckles spread to a grave smile. "Stronger than any men hereabouts." She nodded in the direction of the oxen.

"But oxen can't lift. And if they try to haul out the wagon by main force they'll tear off the wheels!" And that would be the final humiliation, for Phineas Jones had borrowed the wagon with difficulty.

Viney's smile widened. "Menfolk is mostly up the road disputing over the new Meetinghouse. Womenfolk too."

Silence, except for the sound of chopping in the woods. Silent oxen regarded the horses, who twitched ears and skin though perhaps only on account of the flies. A silent girl looked down upon Phineas Jones from the bank, until he wished he were safely in the pulpit at Meeting and Deborah's younger sister below him on the benches.

Her steady gaze made him ill at ease, brought a youthful flush to his cheeks. For it reminded him of his barefoot days, when young Phineas was accounted too absent-minded and fond of book-learning to be trusted with team or wagon. Though young Phineas had tried his best to be like other boys, even to . . . his tongue unconsciously sought the wide gap between his front teeth . . . wasting much time upon the pointless youthful contests of skill. It was nothing to be ashamed of, of course, but he suddenly felt that if he opened his mouth to break the burdensome silence, Deborah's younger sister would surely notice the gap.

Then came Dan'l, dragging a long thin sapling. He hooked the butt end over a high bough, and lashed the thin end with rawhide to the oxen's yoke. Viney set them to pull. When the bough was bent down far enough Dan'l hooked a shorter sapling to it, lashing the other end of the short sapling to the wagon. Then Viney backed up the oxen, Dan'l hooked the long sapling over another tree, and the oxen drew that down, also.

Preacher stood by, helpless to do aught, not knowing what was intended. Without a word between the boy and his sister, just as though this were a simple task of every day, they attached four such ingenious lifts to the wagon, each raising it a mite further from its oozy bed. Then Viney went around to the horses' heads, and spoke to them. At the first heave they hauled out the wagon, half suspended as it was from the trees.

Dan'l cut the saplings. One by one the trees sprang back, hurling the saplings like massive javelins high into the air. And the weight of the wagon settled back on its wheels, on firm ground.

"Don't cal'late she's come to no harm." Dan'l unlashed the cut ends of the saplings, and coiled the rawhide thongs. He contemplated the near-miracle he had performed with satisfaction but no surprise, and offered a word of neighborly advice. "If you're ever in trouble, Preacher, there ain't hardly nothing that two-three trees and a good axe can't cure."

Mud to his knees, Preacher climbed back to the hard seat and took up the reins. Just below him stood Viney with the yoke of oxen. A fly settled on one of their horns. The girl's lips pursed for an instant. The fly vanished. Now, had she been a boy, the feat would have been possible, though difficult—again his tongue sought the gap between his front teeth—but a mere girl! Perhaps the fly had just flown away. Preacher shook the reins, firmly said, "Giddap there!" and rolled on to the bridge, calling a warm thank-you over his shoulder.

As warm a thank-you as he could achieve, but perhaps not as

cordial as he intended. For a new doubt began to assail him. This time a doubt of Deborah, of all people. Not of her unselfishness of course, for no one could doubt her noble self-sacrifice when with downcast eyes she met his proposals for marriage with a murmured, "Be patient a little while, Phineas dear; Dan'l and Viney are so young, so helpless without me."

It might be that her judgment was at fault. That living so close to them she had not been able to realize how they had grown. Surely she was wrong, for surely these were no helpless children who had so casually and skilfully lifted his wagon out of the slough. No, he would summon his arguments, and convince dear Deborah that it was wise to take the little house next to the church while the offer still held. And persuade her of her duty to minister to the needs of a preacher of the Gospel so that he might the more effectually pursue his appointed course, chiding the evil-doers and bringing the comfort of God's grace to those in need of spiritual consolation.

Phineas Jones had no difficulty in finding his congregation. He had scarce turned the top of the steep hill beyond the settlement when he heard them. They were all milling around on the patch of ground between Ephraim Birdsell's sugar bush and the road. Nigh on fifty folks, counting the children; twice as many as had ever come to Meeting at any one time. Babies that were too young for argument lay wailing and unheeded on the dry August grass. Two boys were fighting, out of excitement at so much talk, and the feel of the summer sun. Preacher's eye lighted on Deborah, talking with Mis' Reed, and looking cool and fresh. Then people dropped their disputing long enough to crowd around the wagon, and admire the windows wrapped in their straw rope in the back. And to say how noble the Meetinghouse would look with so much glass, and that there wasn't a Meetinghouse for a day's journey around, barring only the one at Fort Ann, would come up to it. Once 'twas built.

Then the argument began again. There was a site south of Cold Brook would suit two-three families; but all excepting those two-three families agreed at once it was too far south. So Eph Birdsell and his wife Phebe said again that they offered this site beside their sugar bush; but of course that was too far north to suit some.

Mis' Ditch, Taverner's wife, who was always one to oblige, gave the blue feather in her hat a toss, smoothed down her silk bodice, and came out with an offer. The Tavern belonged to Cicero, but folk claimed he wasn't allowed so much as to swallow his own spittle without Hepziba Ditch gave him leave. So it was Hepziba, not Cicero, who made the offer of part of the Tavern yard, which, being plumb in the Settlement, lay convenient, handy for all. That might have suited fine, only Mis' Ditch's feathers and silk bodice had already set some of the wives to claiming she was obliging in more ways than were fitting. One woman spoke up sharp that the Tavern yard was no fit place for a Meetinghouse. And another whispered something not meant for Preacher's ears.

Mis' Ditch flushed up angrily. "I'll thank them that feels that-a-way not to come to Meeting in the Tavern ordinary, like they've done these many years."

It took Preacher all he had to get her talked around again. And by the time that was done he had no gimp left to settle the women-folk on which site they favored the most. Even if he'd been certain in his own mind, which he wasn't. And it was clear there would be one-third of the women for each site, and two-thirds of the women against it, whichever way 'twas.

Seemed too that the menfolk had only been waiting their time to argue. Some favored to roll up a Meetinghouse of logs, like a barn, only better. Others said it would be more fitting to raise a frame building of sawn lumber, especially now they had these glass windows. Those favoring the logs asked who was going to haul the lumber all the way up from the sawmill at Kane's Fall, and haul down logs for the sawyer in return.

Simpkin Higgins, the little bandy-legged horse trader, had what he believed a smarter idea. "Taking it we're all good Christians here, and each willing to do his share, what's to hinder we borrow the loan of a sash-saw, hitch it to Gunsmith's water-wheel, and cut our own lumber right here where it's needed? There's trees a-plenty."

Gunsmith nodded, slow and cautious.

"Course we'll need to knock the south side out of his shop, to feed in the logs." Sim's little close-set eyes glanced around him triumphantly. "But Gam won't begrudge that; nor if it interferes with his work a mite. We all got to do our Christian duty."

Gunsmith, being big, was kind of slow in thought. Preacher could see him combing his white beard with his fingers, weighing up the loss of his trade for a good six months against his duty as a neighbor. Then, surprisingly, he nodded again.

"Seeing 'twill be green lumber, 'twon't serve to lay the new cut planking out to warp and cockle in the summer sun. Yet we won't hardly have barn space for it, account the hay, and the coming harvest." He stopped combing his beard, and his eyes twinkled ever so little. "We'll haul the planks and sawn timbers down to Sim's and stack it up in his kitchen and bedroom to season. He won't begrudge the mite of discomfort climbing around it, nor yet the two-three openings we'll need to cut through his house-sides to quicken the drying."

There was laughter then. And more laughter when Simpkin Higgins declared he warn't sot in his views like some he could name, and was willing to admit when he was wrong. And, come to think of it, them that was minded to roll up logs might have the right of it after all.

That left things much as they were before. Phineas Jones took the opportunity to make the speech he'd been turning over in his mind all the way up.

"A well-wisher, a good Christian of Fort Ann, has presented these windows. And another gave me the loan of his wagon and team to draw them up. I sincerely trust that you will profit by their example of true neighborliness, and lay aside your personal wishes, your private differences, and come to an unanimous decision for the good of the community." Worked up by his own words he had his hat off, his curls blowing this way and that in the breeze off the hills, and his pale face flushing with his own eloquence.

He'd have ended there, but for Deborah. She had come to stand close beside him, and the look on her face tempted him to go on and show how he could sway these folks to do his bidding. "If the folk, the good Christian folk, of this congregation cannot come to agreement as I now advise, there are other congregations who will be glad, yes, only too glad, to have these glass windows."

Scarce time there was to enjoy his triumph. For right away someone spoke up and asked Preacher to decide for them. He had to cool

148

off and think quick. For, young as he was, he knew better than to take on that responsibility.

"Perhaps we could hold some kind of a contest," it was the timeliest inspiration he'd ever had, "and agree beforehand that the winner is to have the say-so."

The idea caught on, folks being mortal wearied of the dispute. A shooting match would serve the menfolk best, and maybe a sewing match for the women.

Phineas Jones was smiling again, when Cicero Ditch spoke up. "Preacher, he'll be judge. To save more argument."

Phineas Jones stopped smiling. With good reason. For if he'd taken upon himself to decide where the meetinghouse was to be built, he'd have had no more than two-thirds of the women against him. But if he had to declare which woman's sewing was the best, there wouldn't be but one woman left on his side, the one he judged the winner. Fetlock-deep he'd been at the start. Now he was belly-down, and sinking deeper.

They were waiting for him to speak. But he couldn't so much as think. Deborah beside him was whispering, but he couldn't listen to her now. She whispered again. "Menfolk sew," she murmured, "womenfolk shoot." She kept saying it over and over. At last he began to understand.

"Perhaps such contests would, after all, lead to yet more dispute when I chose the wrong winner. For who am I to judge of fine sewing?" The words made sense, he hoped, but the next ones were those that mattered, and there was no time now to turn Deborah's suggestion round and see it from all angles. "Instead, I now propose that the women shoot, and the men sew!"

There was a moment's silence while folk weighed it out, and Phineas Jones wondered if he'd said wrong. Then such a spate of talk it sounded like the Buttermilk Falls of Mosquito Hollow when the spring thaw sets in. Husbands joking wives about who they'd go gunning for. And the women coming right back at the menfolk with warning not to stitch their worthless hides to a worth-while piece of calico, or they'd be minded to cut off the finger to save the cloth.

Phineas Jones had the good sense to say no more, except to promise he would ride up next week in time for the contests.

CHAPTER FOURTEEN

Such news as Young'un didn't get to hear from Phebe when she went over with her pail for the daily milk, came breathlessly across country in the mouths of two-three childer. Seemed to Young'un that the settlement folk had the swarming fever, the way Taverner's bees had this time of year, and couldn't bring themselves to workaday tasks till the sewing and the shooting were done with. It even got so that the fever took a hold on Dan'l.

Hilling corn down in the lower patch, Dan'l set down his hoe, tiptoed over to the little rifle propped against an apple tree, and beckoned to Young'un. Quiet as an Injun, feeling each step with her bare toes, Viney crept up beside him. Likely it was that old black groundhog, and Dan'l wanted her to edge in between the critter and his hole, so he wouldn't be able to escape if only light wounded.

'Twas the groundhog all right. Dan'l took her hoe and set the little rifle in her hands. She just held it, not guessing his purpose, and he had to come right out and whisper "Shoot!" before she could believe. Then she thumbed back the flint, set stock to shoulder, bedded the bead nicely into the notch of the sight and set the two about where the groundhog's shoulder lay.

She started to squeeze the trigger, but the sights kept wavering. So she had to draw a deep breath and start all over. When the puff of smoke cleared away she looked to see the groundhog dead. But there he was, a good rod to one side and just diving down his hole. Not a hair of him harmed neither. Still and all she had fired the little rifle at long last, and if Dan'l would but learn her how, the way Pa had learned Dan'l when he didn't stand as high as the muzzle of Pa's rifle . . .

"Cal'lated to spare you enough powder and ball for the Meetinghouse match." But Dan'l shook his head gloomily. "But we can't spare the two-three hornfuls for practising up. There's scarce enough left as 'tis, till harvest-time and we can swap for more."

So it was triumph and disappointment all in one. And surprise too, that Dan'l should have had it in mind for her to go down and shoot for the say-so over the Meetinghouse; it was the first time Dan'l had ever spared glance or thought to aught beyond his own fences. It all showed, plain as plain, how different this year was from last.

Hunger was ended too. First Molly had freshened again. Then the wild greenstuffs Eldest gathered in the spring—skunk cabbage, brake ferns, burdock, lamb's-quarters and such—had hastened it on its way, though for a time it was hard not to eat the beans and seed corn needed for the sowing. After the cold winter and deep snows the wild critters were easy trapped or shot, so each week there was more for Eldest to set on table, and more grazing for Peter 'n' Paul and the blithesome little heifer.

The day came when Dan'l pushed aside an unfinished platter and said, "I've had my fill!" And all three looked up and burst plumb out laughing. Not that 'twas anyways comical, but out of surprise, seemingly, and happiness.

All three, even Eldest, had laughed fit to choke. And the eating done, all three had gone out the door of the house and stood looking out and down over the fields to the woods beyond. From the solid built house and barn at their backs, to the cattle down on the slope in the farthest meadow, it all belonged to the Posts. The sun, low and red over the dark western hills, still dipped the farm in its glow, browning the mowing-meadow as though it was most ready for cutting, tinting the corn that stood a good two foot high. Apples already promising a good crop. Cabbage, squash, beans, potatoes— Young'un stretched out her arms as though mindful to take it all within her grasp and hug it, just from the love that welled within her.

A rabbit ran out of Eldest's garden. Dan'l reached back for his rifle.

And again there was talk in the Post place. Of the coming Meetinghouse, of neighbors and their doings. It was as though a hillcloud had lifted, the cloud that had cut off the Posts from even their next-neighbors and from all but the ground beneath their feet and the next toilsome task that lay before them.

Each time that Young'un returned from the Birdsells' with the milk Eldest had a sight of questions to ask. Even Dan'l listened to what Young'un had to tell, though he made pretense not to.

Of how, if the men took stitching lessons from their wives, it was done in secret. But there wasn't a woman for miles around, and some a sight further, who didn't claim she would win at the shooting. Right away they had started making ready. Though none would let their husbands show them how; husbands being known for a kind of half-wits that women marry out of pity, to protect them. At least that was the size of things if you gave heed to the talk.

Mis' Reed, who tested and sighted all Gunsmith's rifles, didn't stand in need of practice, Young'un could see that. Maybe that was why Gunsmith was slated to get the women all trained and gaited for the day, and, meantime, to save what lives he could. But what with redding up old muskets and straight-cuts and twist rifles, pouring ball to fit all the different kinds of bore, cleaning barrels, setting new flints and shaping up worn frizzen steels, Gunsmith hadn't the time to take all the women down to High Rock where they would be safe to practice. Instead he set them down outside his shop to shoot across his barn into empty woods, and Young'un led his old pack horse across to the Post meadows where the mare would be safe. Or as safe as any one these days. Husbands stayed close to home, and ary wandering stranger had to run his own risk. Sol Broadmoor talked of digging two-three graves just in case, but the womenfolk voted him down.

All that week and most any time of day, it seemed to Young'un, there was some woman spraddled out face down on the ground, letting off her piece. Young'un could hear the shots right over on the farm. Passersby got to asking when Cold Brook militia aimed for to invade Canady; or was they planning to follow Vermont and set up a new State of the Union? The womenfolk didn't mind a smitch, but such menfolk of the settlement as had business down to Fort Ann took to staying home to tend the babies and the cook-pots, rather than face the joking.

On Monday, the fifth day before the contest, Young'un had the best happening to tell Eldest. The southbound coach to Albany reined in opposite the Tavern to watch, and two young officers from Ticonderoga began to shout out the military words of command. Might be they got the womenfolk confused. For when they shouted "Present! Fire!" a musket ball crashed into the coach just under where they sat. Before the smoke had all left the musket, the two officers had thrown themselves off the coach. They were hammering at the bar of the Tavern ordinary before the women could load again. Coach had to wait for the best part of an hour, the officers claiming their legs weren't fit to carry them out, what with trembling so.

Of course folks up and down the road had to ask Mist' Bloodgood how come a bullet had splintered a panel of his coach. And in the next three-four days he'd stretched the happening to where the women of Cold Brook had broken out and were taking scalps. Which wasn't nowise true.

*   *   *

When the day came Young'un put on her tow gown, and set off down the trail with Eldest. At the last moment Dan'l cal'lated to go too, but said he'd cut cross-lots. Down at the settlement 'twas a strange sight to see so many womenfolk with powder horns and bullet bags hung from their shoulders, all leaning on their firearms and telling each other how easy it was to shoot, just like most all those things menfolk set their pride in. Not difficult, like getting a good rise of dough or suchlike.

As soon as Preacher was out of the saddle, Gunsmith led off his horse. And the whole settlement flocked off down to High Rock, with the children racing and calling beside, like 'twas to a nutting. And the dogs that had been hearing gunshots for days gone by, and some of which had been tied up for their own safety, just knowed there was going to be the biggest rabbit hunt, coon hunt, deer hunt and maybe even bear hunt they was ever like to see. They'd called in their friends from all around, black dogs, white dogs, spotted dogs, big and small, and were yapping to one another and to the humanfolk, for land's sake to hurry before the heat of the day drew all the grand exciting scents from the ground. Young'un just had to laugh at their eagerness.

The dogs sniffed at the odd-shapen bundles the men were carrying, and the women teased to know what was in them. And when they all came to the flats under High Rock, and 'twas time to decide which contest should be first, the women claimed they couldn't shoot comfortable until the menfolk was done. Seemed like the wives were all set to have their laugh first.

Preacher lined up the husbands and the two-three bachelors sitting tailor fashion on the short grass. And land sakes if that wasn't Dan'l, his bare feet still wet from crossing the brook, setting himself down amid the others! Young'un looked to Eldest to see did she know what was in Dan'l's mind. But Eldest had eyes for none but Preacher.

Each man began to unroll his bundle. Hebron Miller opened out the biggest, a seven-foot bedspread, saying how long it had took him to make it, and how he welcomed this chance to get it finished. When Mis' Ditch pointed out it wasn't a sewed pattern, but woven, Hebron said it made it all the more wonderful to have sewed it all with needle and thread, and they'd best call off the sewing match and name him winner right away. The laugh that followed brought Mis' Miller running; womenfolk, maybe with reason, being like to mistrust their husbands' jokes. When she caught sight of what lay across his knees, with the needle and thread going in and out, she most broke into tears. She claimed she'd never forgive him for dragging her ma's best Rose of Sharon bedspread out into the fields.

Next to Hebron was Gunsmith, spectacles on his nose, running a fair to middling seam down the side of a canvas bag. But 'twasn't the kind of task, well done or ill, to take the women's votes. Three pairs of britches were getting patched at seat or knee, but as Eldest said it put the men's wives out of countenance, seeming as if they didn't do their mending. So it wasn't like that any britches patcher would win either.

Eph Birdsell, squatting very solemn, was working like he'd no time even to raise his eyes. Preacher leaned down close to see what Eph was busied on. Eph held it up, polite, to show. Phebe Birdsell ran forward and boxed Eph's ears, then grabbed the little garment and hid it in the bosom of her gown. But 'twas no secret that Phebe was expecting.

Next in line was Dan'l. And Young'un came close to holding her breath. There was some talk whether he was to be accounted a man. But seeing he was man enough to run a farm, Preacher gave judgment he was man enough to sew. Dan'l was stitching a pattern of porcupine quills to the last pair of moccasins he'd made. Being Dan'l he was setting his whole heart to it, like he'd never done aught else in his life, nor wanted to.

The other tasks, stitching together the torn browband of a horse's harness, basting together two useless scraps of cloth and the like, didn't amount to much, so the women came back along the line, and told Preacher he'd best name Dan'l winner. So then Preacher called on Dan'l to decide whether Meetinghouse was to be log or frame. He did so!

Dan'l looked around him, and hesitated. But Young'un knew what he would say, knew why he had entered the contest. Dan'l had a debt to pay for the help neighbors had given rolling up house and barn.

"Log. Then we c'n all help." Dan'l left no doubt of his decision. "Them that favors sawed timber c'n shape up benches, and windows and doors."

It was easy seen that Preacher was pleased to have the say-so made for him. And the men slapped Dan'l on the back. Then they all turned back to help load the firearms for the second contest, the women's shooting.

Of course Mis' Reed would win, Young'un knew that for certain. But seeing the other womenfolk still fancied their chances, marks of split pine were set up in row five rod away. Each block had a black X painted on the cleft side, and the woman planting her bullet nearest the mark would be winner. Ties were to be shot off, not judged, as nobody hankered after making lifetime enemies.

As well as Mis' Reed there was Phebe Birdsell, and Mis' Ditch, and ten, twelve more. Old Grandma Truttle handled her heavy piece "Killsure" like it was an old friend. She and another woman from over Welsh Hollow way, who looked to be yet older, both put ball well inside the billet. And got to triumphing over the younger women, and saying how in their day a woman who couldn't stand to a loophole and load and fire beside her man, wa'n't accounted fit to bear his children. But that was in the old days of Injun raids, and women didn't have to any more; and when the firing was over, and the smoke was drifting away it was easy to see that Mis' Reed had outshot them all, planting the ball from her squirrel gun plumb in the middle of the cross.

The women weren't satisfied, and said they'd shoot again, loading their own pieces this time, without bumble-headed husbands starting them off all wrong. It was clear to Young'un that Mis' Reed, who could set the ball most where she'd a mind to, would keep on beating them just as long as she set finger to trigger. Menfolk said the same, but it didn't avail. The womenfolk were fixing to shoot again, and each one mighty sure she'd win.

Young'un looked around her to see where Dan'l was. Might be he'd set off home after winning the sewing. But there wasn't a girl or a boy or a child in sight, barring Eldest, standing close to Preacher, and little ones laid down on the grass. Even the dogs were gone, for the first shot had loosed them off barking and baying, making believe there was a wounded deer. They'd be over the hill and nigh to Hogtown by now, running a real deer.

*   *   *

Leaving the women to their loading and priming, Young'un went off in search of the children. But they'd done no more than drop out of sight into the stream-bed, every one from little Consolation to Hank, who'd have been with the grown-ups but for her. And even Dan'l. Stumpy had lined them all up opposite a bank of sand, and was drawing rings on it with his crutch.

"Got to drop your spittle inside the ring, all on it. Them that can't has got to do the chores for the new Meetinghouse soon as it's built." He hobbled to one end of the line, worked his lips, looked down on his ring, and called, "Ready? Shoot!"

Some shot, some didn't. Hank pointed out that Consolation and other little'uns weren't nowise fit to carry wood and water and the like, and 'twould serve best if them that beat did the chores, being like to be the older and stronger. Young'un had seen that herself, so she hadn't wasted spittle. Still and all there didn't seem much sense to shooting spit if everyone was set to lose so as not to have the chores to do.

"What say we shoot, and the winner gives out the chores for the losers to do?" Soon as she'd said it she saw it was like to be a right

156

smart idea. Hank being oldest had ought to win, and he wouldn't lay too heavy a stint on the little ones. Others thought so too, for everyone took stance again, behind the line Stumpy had drawn. And stopped arguing while they twisted their lips and sucked in their cheeks to load their spittle.

The first round threw out the little ones, and the round later threw out Amy and Hank. Amy, who was next to Young'un, hadn't done more than splutter, and said she'd never shot spittle before. Hank wouldn't have been out but for Consolation tugging at his sleeve and spoiling his aim. Then Stumpy drew a new set of marks further off, and Dan'l, two-three other boys and all the girls missed. Except Young'un.

That wasn't how she'd figured it out. It left only Stumpy, and a stranger, and Isa, who was Hank's brother, and herself. Stumpy and the stranger knelt down at the stream and took a drink of water. That lost them the next round, water not holding together like spittle, as they'd ought to've remembered. No, 'twasn't a mite the way she'd figured.

Children were dancing round and shouting. A woman called a ways off, and another came to the top of the bank and said, "They're down here, the whole boiling of 'em." The rifle match had ended, and grown-ups were crowding to the bank top while Stumpy drew a new ring. Just one, for there weren't but Isa and Young'un left.

"Isa, Isa, Isa wore a plug in his teeth all last year, all last year he did!" The Sherman twins were jumping around and pointing at the gap between Isa's front teeth.

"Till his ma caught him," yelled a boy, "and dusted his britches good, and made him promise . . ."

"Tooth spitters has got to stand back a pace, same's always," the Sherman twins insisted.

"It don't matter." Viney resigned the advantage. All the same it was mighty heartening to have the twins hope she'd beat that Isa. And she'd got to beat, for Isa wasn't nowise fit to portion out hay to cattle, leave alone give out stints to those weaker than himself. He'd kind of a meanness in him, Hank having spoiled him, the way he was cosseting little Consolation now.

"Don't matter, huh?" Isa put hand to pocket, drew out a white

157

bean and threw it on the ground. "Hit that, then! And if you don't I cal'late I'll have you do the sweeping. Girls ain't fit for no better. Nor they ain't fit to spit beans. Watch here . . ."

He opened his lips, put tongue to the gap in his teeth, and . . . pfft! . . . threw a shapely gob of spittle . . . The bean moved.

Young'un tightened her lips, drew spittle, but not much, for the match wasn't ended yet, and pfft! . . . the bean jumped. Isa frowned, and Young'un saw a chance. If she could get Isa kind of worried his mouth would dry. "Likely I'll have Isa do the sweeping, if I've the patience to learn him how."

Stumpy picked up the bean, wiped it on his britches, and set it a good two feet further off, while the grown-ups crowded in closer to watch. There was a kind of waiting, no one speaking, like when an axeman stands watching for the first tremble in a tree-top, before the crack and fall. Instead of a thundering crash, Preacher spoke.

"Now, children! I'm sure you mean well." He put on his pulpit voice, not the kind he used up at the farm. "But the Meetinghouse is God's House; and such spitting . . ."

"Fair's fair, Preacher." Sol Broadmoor tried to sit down on the edge of the bank, but it crumbled under his weight. He picked himself up grinning. "Ain't no more harm to spittin' than there is to shootin'."

Preacher could see that, and of course the children had put on the looks that children do when wrongfully accused. And the menfolk, it was plain, sided with Sol Broadmoor. Preacher looked from one face to another. Eldest was beside him again, but she said nothing.

If Young'un had been there, she knowed right well what she'd have to tell him. Maybe she'd be wrong, but his front teeth had never growed that way natural. Preacher looked like he'd break fences and run. But instead he asked, "The one to win this contest allocates the chores?"

Most everybody told him "Yes." Young'un was trying to tell him something else besides. Peter and Paul could talk together without a sound, and times they understood what Young'un was going to say before she said it. Plenty of folks would hold that Preacher was wise as Peter, maybe wiser than Paul. It did seem he'd ought to know what Young'un was telling him, telling him over and over.

"Then . . ." Preacher looked kind of anxious as he said it. "Then I will enter the contest, if permitted."

There wasn't no doubt he'd be let to! "Good for ye, Preacher!" "Preacher's a-goin' to show how." And grown-ups were pressing in to tell him how best. "Don't lift yer shoulders, Preacher, for it gives a shake to the spittle when ye let go." "Stand square, not edgewise . . ." "Now many a spit-shootin's been lost just because . . ."

Preacher was red, redder even than Eldest, who wasn't one to understand what it meant to be a spit-winner. He was trying to get a word in—"unfair advantage . . . as a boy . . . I must confess . . ."

"Plugged your front teeth. And why not?" asked the Widow Wilson.

"Course he did! Boy can't spit no better'n a girl if he don't!" Old Grandma Truttle took aholt of her old Killsure like she was fixing to fight any that contraried her. "Preacher and Isa stand level, Viney there stands a pace forward."

Young'un shot, scarce troubling to sight, then stepped aside. Isa hit too, as she'd expected. Preacher drew spittle, working lips and tongue, shot once over his shoulder for trial, then—*pfft*—covered the bean mighty pretty. Young'un let out her breath, and folks settled back on to their heels again. 'Twas like to be wonderful shooting, all could see.

Stumpy wiped the bean, and cast it forward, but nearer two feet than a yard. Young'un noticed, and hoped Isa hadn't and would overcast. This time she stepped back level with the others. It wouldn't feel like a fair win, else.

This time she measured the range mighty close, for it was harder for her than if she'd shot level last time, the range changing so. She would use a heavy load of the spittle she'd been saving, cast up well, and not put too much breath behind. And think of the bean as a fly that was trying to lay an egg on Peter's foreleg. . . .

"Hit! Viney's hit!" "Young'un's done it ag'in!" folks were yelling. Kind of lucky though, and it weren't more'n a dampener.

Preacher made ready, and Young'un clinched her fingers, and hoped. And tried to think up a prayer. It couldn't be wrong, when 'twas a Preacher you were asking aid for, and 'twas all about a Meetinghouse. Preacher loosed off good and sharp, but a mite too flat and too fast. There was an argument had he hit or only splashed. But most that could see, and some that couldn't, was for calling it a hit.

Then 'twas Isa's turn. He grinned around, mighty sure of himself. And Young'un tried another prayer. For if 'twas right to pray for Preacher, then 'twas right to pray against Isa. Or it didn't make sense.

Isa leaned back, and Young'un began to hope. For it took judgment to shoot up high and get range that way. Instead, Isa was trying for a fast low cast, and would use head-throw to get him the speed he needed.

'Twas an anxious moment though. Now he'd finished drawing spittle, and was taking in. Taking in too much air, belike. Chances were he'd not have right control, with so much wind and the throw of his head behind.

And he missed! Spitting to each side; as clean a split-spit as was ever seen. And a whoop from all the childer, who didn't cotton to Isa having the say-so about the stints. And Grandma Truttle was calling Preacher a "regular spitting hellion" in just those words, and folks that weren't backing on Preacher to win were telling Young'un not to be scairt, but go ahead and learn him what Cold Brook spitters amounted to.

She could best him, too; she knowed it now. And 'twould be mighty fine for folks to say, "Thar goes Viney Post, the grandest little spit shooter that Cold Brook ever knowed." Only there was more to it than that. There'd be the ordering of chores done, and telling Isa and even Hank what stints they had. 'Twould come better from Preacher. And Preacher hadn't a farm to tend besides.

And then there was Eldest, who was like to git herself married most any time. And not a present to give her, except foodstuffs, to start her off right. Unless . . .

Folks were waiting for Young'un to shoot. But she was looking at Preacher. Course he was mighty learned, and kind of holy, but he didn't measure up to Gunsmith, or Sol Broadmoor, or even Hank. Or in a ways, to Dan'l. Eldest would be hard put to admire him the way she'd ought. But if Eldest could say to other wives in Fort Ann "Mist' Jones is outen away the best spit shooter up to Cold Brook—

160

he bested even my sister Viney, whose been knowed to shoot butter-flies on the wing once-twict," then Eldest could take pride, the way she'd ought. 'Twould be a mighty fine present to give her, and secret-like.

Young'un stepped back from the line, and managed a smile. "Kinda dry. Can't raise the spittle. Guess Preacher wins!"

Between folks pounding Preacher on the back, telling him they'd always suspicioned he was real folks when you come right down to it, and wanting to match him against the spit champion over past Hogtown, Eldest got pushed away. But she was looking real happy, as she'd a right to.

There were plenty folk to tell Young'un how well she'd done, even grown-ups. Old Grandma Truttle was bound she'd leave her rifle, Killsure, to Viney in her will, knowing 'twould be in good hands if the Injuns came back again. Cicero Ditch saying if only Young'un lived nearer he'd give her a half-hour's training a day and they'd win every match right down to Albany. Hadn't ever seen but one the like of her before, and he'd died with the lung sickness. Amy Higgins came up wanting to know how it was done, but before Young'un could show, Dan'l took Amy away to learn her.

Young'un couldn't help but stare after the two of them; for this wasn't happenstance, like when they tangled up in Dan'l's hunting gear and Amy's acorn cakes.

Then someone called: "We're all fixed to draw the logs and do the chores, even. But nobody's said to-where." Seemed they'd all come running from the rifle-shooting without deciding.

Preacher caught Mis' Reed's eye, so she should watch his lips, and asked: "There are three sites offered, which do you choose?"

Folks were quieting down, and Mis' Reed's voice came clear, "Not ary one of them."

"There's no place elst . . ." someone started to object.

Mis' Reed couldn't hear what she didn't see, and went right on: "First we fill in the slough, where you bogged down your wagon, Preacher."

That would be easy done with rock, and there'd been talk of doing it ever since Young'un could remember, to make it easier for coaches and suchlike. And plenty of hog-wallows without. But spang

161

in the middle of the road was no place for Meetinghouse, as folks were starting to murmur.

"That," said Mis' Reed, "leaves the old turnout, and plenty enough room behind for a half-dozen Meetinghouses. And right in the settlement."

It was as simple as that, the answer to what had troubled the settlement so long and brought argument that was nigh to quarreling. Rolling up the Meetinghouse would be easy after. Preacher must be mighty glad. Young'un looked across at him.

Glad he was, and more beside. He had Eldest by the elbow, and Eldest, looking scairt, was whispering to him. Preacher just shook his head and held on. 'Twarn't for nothing he'd won the spitting match, and settled about the Meetinghouse all in one afternoon. The shouting quieted down to talk, and before folks had time to start off home he held up his hand for silence.

"I have an announcement to make." His voice was 'twixt his preaching one, and the one he used for hymns and suchlike. "An announcement I have been hoping to make for some time." He took a firmer grip on Eldest's elbow, and Young'un nigh to have choked for joy. "I am about to marry, just as soon as it can be arranged, your neighbor, Deborah Post. And I ask you to wish us joy."

Young'un was pushing in as fast as good manners and the press of people would allow. She wanted to tell Preacher how glad she was he had won the spitting match and Eldest as well. She was to the fore and wondering whether to take Preacher by the hand and shake it, as others were doing, or just to say how happy she was. When someone grabbed her savagely by the arm and dragged her back.

'Twas Dan'l. He was trying to speak. But at first he hadn't the words, his face twisting all ways like he was crazy. All Young'un could make head or tail of was, "Preacher can't! Eldest can't! They can't nowise do it!"

"There's none to hinder." Young'un tried to make Dan'l understand. "If they're minded to wed."

But Dan'l couldn't get that into his noddle. Even though Young'un had warned him a time back when he had tangled up with Amy Higgins and his rifle and hunting gear. That time he had just said, "Pa wouldn't hold with it," the way another might say, "Water won't run uphill," and put it out of his mind as not worth another thought.

162

And now 'twas as if he saw water running uphill, and he clamored for Young'un to stop it running.

"You got to tell Preacher, Young'un. I ain't nowise fit to."

Dan'l was fit for naught at the moment, unless it was to be tied, till the mood was past and he was back in his senses.

"Eldest's needed by the farm. Preacher can make shift without her, the same as he always has. 'Tis Pa's farm, and we're bound to keep it for him. Pa wouldn't hold with Eldest gallivanting off."

Amy must have followed Dan'l, still waiting for those spitting lessons. She stood there beside him, troubled for what was troubling Dan'l, and her eyes most as big as the heifer's. Not understanding his feeling about the farm and Pa, nor his bitter passions, she put a small hand on his arm, striving to console.

Dan'l cast off the hand as though it had been an ember burning into his flesh. And his fury burst forth again.

"Here's this Amy now! *You* learn her how to spit, I ain't agoin' to, never. I got no hankering for ary womenfolk God ever made. Don't reckon to see nor talk to them long as I live." Dan'l kind of choked. "I . . . I got Pa's farm to tend!"

And he lit out at a stumbling run. 'Twixt tears and anger 'twas a mercy he even headed for the right way home.

Young'un put an arm around Amy to comfort her. No sense in wasting breath telling Preacher he wasn't to marry Eldest. And Eldest was happy as a hog in a slough; it didn't take more than a glance to see that. But if Dan'l had hit Amy he'd have hurt her less.

"If you're minded to spit-shoot I'll learn you to lick the stuffing out of Dan'l, at mark or at long throws." Young'un made the offer.

But it seemed Amy had no proper pride. All she said was, "I don't hardly aim to best him."

Young'un tried again. "Dan'l means no harm. 'Tis just he's out of his mind about Eldest. Being he's so sot about Pa's farm. That's why he's so scairt of womenfolk."

Amy looked up, not understanding, not wanting to. But swallowing, and trying hard not to weep. "I hadn't rightly cal'lated to be womenfolk . . . yet awhiles." She quirked her mouth so it would pass for a smile. "Not unless Dan'l wanted I should be."

CHAPTER FIFTEEN

Next morning Dan'l turned to the haying, and mad enough, he was, to chaw his way right round the meadow if he'd lacked a scythe. But after the first two-three times he'd whetted the blade the short jabbing swing grew longer and smoother, and by the time he'd gone down one side, across the middle and up again, the long curved blade was purring its way through the swathes. But all down the meadow he never so much as straightened up, except to take the stone from the water bucket each time he came up with it, and set a finer edge to the scythe. Young'un, busied at her task of lashing crosspieces to the sled to serve for a hay rack, held her peace. If Dan'l's world was awry, it was his own doing and no one else's.

At noontide Dan'l took a glance at the sun, and stiff-legged, as though he had the rheumatiz in both knees, stalked up to the house, without so much as a word to Young'un. With his mouth tight shut he set himself down to table, and began to eat in silence, then paused in his eating while Eldest asked a Blessing. Which was just as well, as Eldest was mighty particular now she was promised to Preacher. When he had done eating he pushed back his stool without a word, and was off before Eldest could think to give Thanks. Soon as Eldest had, Young'un slipped out after him.

Luck served her, for Dan'l had to go back to the house again for his rifle and bag and powder horn, and that let her get ahead of him. So there was a procession of two, each strutting as pompous as a heron in a swamp. Young'un glanced back, mindful of the stone her brother would throw at her if he were in his right mind. But if he saw her mocking, he gave no heed.

The half meadow that Dan'l had opened out was a picture, if ever there was one. Framed by the uncut lower half, and at the top by the rail and root fence, by the forest on either side, Dan'l's cutting was an inner frame for the square patch of hip-high upstanding grass he had still to cut. His swathes lay straight and smooth with not a tuft of uncut grass to mar them; Pa couldn't have cut a meadow as clean as that, mighty few could. But the same Dan'l as had set his will against Eldest's marrying had done that scything; the same mule-stubborn Dan'l that would spare neither Eldest nor a single blade of grass. Nor himself neither. 'Twas the farm first and last, with Dan'l.

Young'un had two-three hickory teeth to whittle and drive and wedge into the rake heads, hers and Dan'l's. Then a swathe or two to rake out from beneath the shadows of the trees to where the sun would ripen it. And by then Dan'l had most finished his scything.

She took the scythe from him, just as she had done last year, while he went to pick up rifle, horn and bullet bag. She bent a handful of grass over the back of the scythe blade, drew it along to the point, to wipe off, then dipped the coarse grit whetstone in its bucket and gave the blade a few touches. She laid the blade flat to the ground, planted her feet and began to swing. It took a few strokes to get the right curve to the swing, a curve just a mite sharper than the curve of the blade. Soon as you had it you knew from the feel, for the scythe grew contented beneath your hands, like a critter eager to work its best if only 'twas let.

Twice around the half-field she cut her swathe, Dan'l keeping ahead of her and to the far side, hoping an animal would break cover. A slight grating noise as her blade met a stone that the frost had thrown up in the spring. She up-ended the scythe, wiped it off, and there was the shine, right up by the toe of the blade; just as she had thought. You could most always feel where the edge had bruised, or maybe hear, and nine times out of ten it was the toe and not the heel. A few strokes of the stone, and off again.

Cat came down, the way he did each year, judging his time so as to be in on the last cut, and not be kept waiting. A mighty busy critter was Cat, in his own reckoning. He wasn't let to go into the stand of grass for fear he would get his paws cut or be shot for a wild critter. And that made three of them, all circling around, all waiting for the very last swathe to fall. And then maybe three-four little beasts would go bounding out at once.

But nary a critter; scarce even a grasshopper.

In the long shadows of eventide, Dan'l, shouldering his rifle, made off to the woods, hoping maybe to get a squirrel or two for the cookpot, and leaving Young'un to set the whetstone to dry and hang up the scythe. Cat mewed complaints, that there was something wrong with the Post farming if they couldn't raise so much as a field mouse or a strayed chipmunk in half a meadow of mowing. No use to tell Cat that with a bright full moon the critters went foraging at night and stayed in the woods or in their holes by day. For he was used to catching baby rabbits and moles and suchlike in the last cut of hay, and had come to depend upon it.

Like Dan'l, coming to depend on Eldest. Cat was like Dan'l, not a doubt of it.

* * *

The next day Dan'l looked at the dawn. And if ever a red sky warned of rain, this one did. Yet Dan'l said no word, but set off down to the meadow with the scythe, sharpened it, and started mowing the second half.

Of all the crazy downright fools! Dan'l had ought to know better than to risk wetting yesterday's hay, and a new cut on top. New cut hay didn't take so much harm, but once it was dried out rain washed away its goodness till it was fit for no more than winter bedding. And this was like to be the only cut they'd get this year.

At any other time Young'un would have protested against such folly. But Dan'l wasn't speaking, and seemed like his aim was to provoke Young'un into words he wouldn't answer.

Dumb obstinacy being a game two could play, Young'un made for the barn, opened the wide doors, rolled aside the chopping block and the clutter of Dan'l's shingle fashioning, took her hay fork from the wall, and set off down to the meadow. The sun was up and already hot and the slight dew mostly gone before she started to rake and turn. By the time she had the half meadow all raked to long straight windrows, she would have given a sight to be able to ask Dan'l whether it was dry enough to carry. She caught up a wisp and twisted it, the way Pa used to, and sniffed it. Smelt sweet and hay-like, it did. And anyways it lay with Dan'l to break silence and say so, if he thought it wasn't fit.

Forking it up into piles aired it still more. But if it was too damp it would kindle itself in the barn, and burst out into smoke and flames and both house and barn would be lost. And every step up and down the long windrows the picture stayed with Young'un. Of course she could lay the hay in its piles and make pretense that was all she purposed to do. But it wouldn't serve; to break Dan'l's obstinacy she had got to be even more obstinate, if so be she could screw up her courage.

Back to the barn again for the yoke, half thinking to see the roof already in flames. She lifted down the yoke, looking to see if maybe it could do with a new bow, but both bows were good as new. She whistled up Peter 'n' Paul, and they came at first call, with never a suspicion of a limp nor trace of a shoulder gall. So she just had to lift on their yoke, lead down to the meadow, drop the bars, drive off the heifer, and back the oxen in to the sled. But it was misery to walk ahead of the sled and oxen, forking up a pile, casting it up on the frame, calling to the oxen to move in, and forking up another pile. Not knowing but maybe the last forkful was the very one that would set the barn ablaze. Or was it the next forkful, or one still further ahead? If only she could find excuse to lay aside her hay carrying and match Dan'l's obstinacy in some other way, some way that held less risk. If only something would happen to hinder the haying.

But nothing hindered; the fork didn't break, and the oxen came up on each call and halted when they were told. The first two rows, at the top end of the meadow, were dry enough; that was some comfort.

She led up to the barn, the loaded sled creaking under its weight. In through the wide doors, which she had measured yesterday before making the hay frame. The barn was plenty big for the sled to draw inside, with maybe a pace to spare between the noses of the oxen and the far wall; the neighbors had been mighty generous when they rolled it up. And now supposing it was Young'un Post whose obstinacy burned it down again!

Rightly it was Dan'l's task to fork the hay up onto the beam and sapling floor above. And Dan'l should have stood on the sled down in the meadow too, spreading the hay as Young'un pitched to him. She had had to throw the hay on the sled just anyways, and now she came to unload, each forkful was caught beneath the hay to each side, and had to be wrastled with. When the fork load was torn loose it was still all Young'un's strength and reach could compass to cast it up to the beams above. 'Twas a relief to aching shoulders and belly muscles to swing up after, and spread the hay thinly over the close-spaced sapling floor.

If Dan'l had been here to help, the two of them could have set hands to the empty sled and dragged it out, the oxen following. But that was more than Young'un could do alone. She considered setting a breeching strap of rawhide around the oxen's rumps for them to back into, seeing the yoke was only fashioned for pulling. But Peter 'n' Paul weren't just ordinary oxen, and when she gave them the order they set to backing. The yoke slid up on their necks until only their horns and their heads held the bows; the pole lifted up and the sled was like to topple over, until Young'un ran back and dragged on it with all her weight.

"There's not another yoke of oxen could have compassed that," she told them proudly. "Not in Cold Brook, not in Fort Ann, not anywheres in the world!" And kissed their soft noses. Prideful they were, and with good reason. If only humanfolks had the sense of Peter 'n' Paul; Dan'l for instance.

Then back to the meadow again. And up to the barn again. Each load a mite dryer than the one before; and that was a comfort.

At midday Dan'l was still silent. Likely it was to tease him into words that Eldest talked of her plans. Or Preacher's plans.

"Mist' Jones' Aunty is bound and determined we're to be wed in her own house," Eldest told. "And Mist' Jones says it won't serve to thwart her. But for that I'd as lief it was here, or at Aunt Mary's."

Young'un could see that. But there wouldn't be many neighbors able to leave their farms and beasts for the long trip to Fort Ann, even though it was for Eldest's own wedding. "Likely I won't get to be there, not in Fort Ann," she had to admit.

"Nor Dan'l neither." Eldest cast him a glance. "Happen, if Dan'l went, 'twould set tongues to wagging, saying the Posts were wild critters of the woods that hadn't yet learned human speech."

Young'un haw-hawed, and even Eldest smiled. But Dan'l didn't so much as look up from his eating. Mayhap Dan'l was deef as well as dumb.

* * *

It was full sundown before Dan'l spoke. Young'un had carried all but the last row of hay, had loosed Peter 'n' Paul so they could join the heifer and catch a bite of grazing before dark. There wasn't a bone in her but ached from the full day's toil, and mouth and nose dryer than the wood-ash on the hearth. And there was the worry of the hay in the barn beside.

She sat wearily back on the sled, thrusting from her mind the thought of smoke and flames, and watched Dan'l.

He was acting mighty strange. He'd give two-three strokes of the scythe, and he'd reach down to the ground. Then two-three more and he'd do it again. If he hadn't been so plumb obstinate all day, now was the time when Young'un would have taken over the scythe and finished the mowing. But it was for Dan'l to ask, and Dan'l wasn't so minded.

There, he was at it again. And this time she saw it was the little rifle he reached for. He dropped the scythe from his left hand and took aim. And waited. Then set down the rifle and picked up the scythe. Then grabbed up the rifle again.

But he was too late. A big fox, black as night, broke from the tall standing grass and was across the meadow and into the woods before Dan'l could loose a shot. A fox, of all things! If it had been an Injun in full war paint it wouldn't have been more astonishing.

Dan'l broke silence at last. To cuss. Then turned his head toward Young'un with a grin.

Well, he hadn't asked, not outright he hadn't. But Young'un got off the sled and finished the mowing for him.

* * *

Lucky it was that they got the hay in, even the second lot from the lower end of the meadow, for the rain struck as they drew up the last load. Dan'l had been right in his judgment of the weather, but right only by the skin of his teeth; and it must have galled him clean down to his marrow not to be able to tell aloud how right he had been. The best he could do was to stand in the door, look up at the lowering sky, and down in the direction of the meadow, then grin.

169

But the dumb-show triumphing didn't serve him aught, even when he'd done it two-three times, for Young'un didn't spare him so much as a glance.

And it wasn't for Dan'l to know that night after night she slipped out of bed to go to the barn and sniff for smoke. When Dan'l wasn't around to see, she drove stakes down into the hay, and each day lifted them out to see were they getting hot.

It rained and it let up. And then it rained again. It got so the ground wasn't fit to work, not even for hoeing up the corn or weeding in Eldest's garden. But there was plenty to do; Eldest set Young'un to drying blueberries and blackcaps over the fire, an endless task now that the old rain had put a stop to their drying in the sun. But if this rain kept on the Posts would have need, next winter, of every last berry.

Between rains Dan'l made two-three tries to pull roots, but the holes he dug filled with water as soon as he dug them, and for all their spreading hoofs Peter 'n' Paul sunk nigh to belly-deep in the mud before they could get purchase for the pulling. For once in a way Dan'l had pitted himself against something more obstinate than himself.

After a whiles he gave in, and set himself to the day-long chore of shingle-splitting and shingle-shaving in the barn. The sooner the barn roof was shingled the better, for rain dripped in streams through the makeshift thatch and threatened to ruin the hay. But shingle splitting and shaving was a winter task and it was plain that Dan'l grudged time in summer, when so much else called for attention. His scowl came in with him to meals, went back with him to the barn, and likely he took it to bed with him at night.

It could be it was only the lack of sun, but Young'un and Eldest too began to get mighty glum. There wasn't hide nor hair of Preacher to be seen at the Post place for two-three weeks, and word came up by the coach that he was a-bed with the colic and a chill, with his aunty tending him. And that didn't hearten Eldest any neither.

What troubled Young'un most was the thought of the corn, so tall and thriving, but at this season needing the sun. And the cabbages too, starting to split their heads because of too much water. If Dan'l said nothing, it got so the other Posts had nothing to say either, or little beyond Eldest holding that they'd ought to count their blessings and that the Lord chastened them He loved. Which was mighty cold comfort.

One afternoon Young'un was plaiting nigh on the twentieth of her drying trays for berries when someone came cantering down the trail. Dan'l's pounding stilled in the barn as the rider passed and came around the house. Someone hitched his horse. And 'twas Eph Birdsell, as Young'un had knowed right well it would be, who scraped his feet and stepped inside. If he had brought an olive twig in his beak he couldn't have been more welcome.

"Flood's out on the far side of Fort Ann." He swung the water off his hat and grinned. "But you're making out mighty good up here, I see."

And they were too. Young'un could see that now, with firewood and victuals and with work aplenty and a dry roof to work under. But it had taken a neighbor to show them. She chirked up a mite and grinned back; then looked around her again to see if the sun had come out or maybe the house had changed. And it had, someways. Now you were shown you got to noticing how close the logs lay, one on the other, for logs that had been rolled up green. And that half floor above, that was good as an extra room. And how smooth Eldest had pounded the earth floor, and what a right noble table and set of stools Dan'l had fixed last winter, and working with no more than the axe, the auger and a maple trunk. Even her own hanging trays, slung from the roof so the mice couldn't eat the dried berries, were woven good as she knew how. Most anyone in the whole wide world would be grateful to have what the Posts had.

"'Llo, Dan'l!" That was to Dan'l who had just come hurrying in. "Uncle Gam said to tell you . . ." Then Eph broke off and grinned again as though just being alive was joke enough. "But Phebe said to tell Deborah first off, before I forget. Phebe said to say that Preacher is to come by the coach, and stay with Uncle Gam a week or two till he's stopped ailing."

Rain or no rain, Eldest grabbed up her shawl and was for hurrying off to the settlement then and there. Only Eph went on to say that Preacher wasn't expected till the morrow. So she set the shawl

171

back on its peg and thanked Eph for the message, making out that a day the more or less was of no consequence. Which wasn't true, it was plain to see.

Then Eph got down to what had really brung him here. Sitting around at Gunsmith's and in the Tavern, the menfolk, for lack of tasks, had got to talking of the Meetinghouse, and how it would be wise to roll it up between haying which was past, and harvest which was to come. For what harvest there was would be late if this rain kept on, and likely the frost would follow hard on its heels.

So they had passed word down to Preacher. And Preacher, who had been chafing at doing his aunty's bidding and swallowing her yarb teas, had sent back word to start right away, and he'd be up to show just how he was minded to have the Meetinghouse.

And there it was. And was Dan'l minded to lend his aid and the help of the oxen?

"I . . ." said Dan'l. And he stopped.

"I cal'late," he began again. And stopped. And his ears and the back of his neck went a kind of red through the brown. He was looking at Eph and gaping his mouth.

And Eph was looking back as though puzzled about what had come over the boy.

"Of course you'll lend your aid, and the oxen too," Eldest told Dan'l straight out.

And there was Dan'l, not able to say "yea" nor "nay" to that, seeing he wasn't speaking to Eldest, nor Young'un neither. Dan'l, who would give a finger to be let help with the Meetinghouse so he could start to repay for the way neighbors had pitched in and rolled up the Post house and barn; Dan'l, who couldn't promise the oxen without Young'un promised too. This time Dan'l had got to come right out and ask Young'un, in so many words, was she willing.

Young'un hugged it to herself, and tried to suck in the corners of her mouth that were trying to spread out and up.

"Why, Dan'l!" said Eldest, and as though she couldn't find words for such ingratitude she said it again. "Why, *Dan'l!*"

Eph looked at Dan'l as though he couldn't rightly believe either. "It don't signify, Deborah. If Dan'l's not willing, or the oxen need rest . . ."

172

"I'll come. And bring Viney with me." Eldest gave Dan'l another glance, that set him to wriggling his feet. "And Dan'l can stay to mind the house."

'Twas all Young'un could do not to come right out and say she'd bring Peter'n' Paul too. But Dan'l had got to be learned. And learned good this time.

Eph was turning to the door when Dan'l caught him by the sleeve. Most anyone else would have thrown off Dan'l's hand, and maybe told him a thing or two for his own good. But Eph was next neighbor. He stopped.

"I . . ." Dan'l tried again. "I'd be heart-willing, only . . ." And he half turned his head to Young'un.

But Young'un looked off through the window, where the rain was easing a mite. Dan'l had got to be learned!

Then Dan'l took a breath. He was still holding to Eph's wet sleeve, and Eph had begun to understand, for there was a crinkle at the corner of his eyes, and likely a smile under his beard. Dan'l swallowed and tried still another time.

"If so be Young'un is willing to lead the yoke," he said, clear as clear. But it still didn't serve him, for Eldest and Eph and Young'un kept silent.

Dan'l was fit to be tied, but at last he came out with it. "You willing, Young'un?" he asked. Even if it was a growl.

"Why, of course, Dan'l," she told him, sweet as honey. "You had only to ask."

* * *

There was less to rolling up the Meetinghouse than Young'un had pictured. Might be that Preacher calling it the House of God had led her to think there would be gold and marble and cedar of Lebanon and suchlike. Not that there was any gold hereabouts, but there was cedar aplenty even on the Post place, and they talked of marble over in Vermont.

Come right down to it, the Meetinghouse that they drew on the ground wasn't so different from the Post barn, except for the windows that Preacher had hauled up from Fort Ann.

While Dan'l and the axemen were up in Gunsmith's and Mist' Ditch's timber lots felling, trimming and adzing, Peter 'n' Paul

173

worked to fill in the hog wallow. There were horses and oxen, sleds and stone boats, and even a couple of wagons, all taking turn to haul down stone from Gunsmith's and other's boundary walls to the slough. But after the first day the wagons dropped out, since 'twas a sight easier to roll rocks on and off the low flat-topped sleds than to lift them up into a wagon and pitch off again. Women, and children too, joined with the men levering over big boulders, picking up leather apronfuls of smaller stones and setting them aside for a surface to the new road after the bigger stones were in place. And it got so that most everyone at the rock pile, and down at the hog-wallow too, knew Peter 'n' Paul by name.

The first time Mist' Bloodgood swung the coach up the bank and around, he called back were they building a fort? On his return trip he rolled his coach carefully over the new stone road, but said nothing. The third time, when the smaller stones were all spread out smooth on top, he shouted not to stop their road building but to carry it up to Fort Ti, and down to Fort Ann besides, if they'd a mind to. And well he might, for there wasn't a solider road that human kind could build.

With the site of the Meetinghouse already cleared, the best stones saved out and laid for its foundation, the logs trimmed, adzed and even measured up there on the hillside, the raising was all done in one day, and the roofing in another, except for the shingles. Most everyone had shingles laid by against his own needs, so they matched up these for size, and had the lower half of the roof pegged on almost as quick as the glass windows were fitted in place. While others were sawing and adzing benches and doors and suchlike, the roofers went off home and split enough new shingles to finish right up to the ridgepole.

Then Preacher held a meeting to give thanks. And well he might and for another reason too, since time and again he had come close as hide to hair to getting killed or crippled, the way he got himself wedged under logs and came up within the swing of axes. Bobbed up everywhere, he had, till folks got to warning, "Here comes Preacher again!"

That was the longest meeting ever held in Cold Brook, and with the most people, from Old Mist' Simmons over Hogtown way, that

174

had to be carried in, so old he was, to a little'un that bawled every minute he wasn't suckled. Folks that had no more religion than a Green Mountain Boy over the border, stood up and bore witness. Two-three women wept aloud for close on an hour. Even Young'un, smelling the new cut pine logs around and above her, and feeling the coldness of the green wood bench and damp earth beneath her feet, came nigh to tears of pride. Till she gave thought to Peter 'n' Paul and the other beasts who had labored harder than any human folks to build this House of God. And Preacher had clean misremembered them in his talk.

It wasn't till she was out, the meeting ended, and standing among the log ends and chips that Young'un came back to earth again. The ground was drying under a hot sun and a slight breeze. It had set in to be right good corn weather. And it stayed that way.

CHAPTER SIXTEEN

THE tow gown might be only tow, the coarsest ever, but it was a gown for all that. And when you wore the old deerskin again, that was neither cloth nor gown, you hurried cross-lots, and let out a sigh of relief when you reached Gunsmith's shop and found it empty.

Young'un raked ash from the forge, put in a double handful of good hardwood charcoal from the big basket, took the tongs and stepped up into the keeping room to borrow a live coal. Uncle Gam had said to help herself, seeing he and Aunt Mary were driving down to Kane's Falls to draw up sawn lumber that was needful for the Meetinghouse benches.

The new Meetinghouse was mighty fine. Young'un stole a glance at it through the workshop window as she came back to kindle the forge. The sun wasn't right to throw a glint from them, but the glass panes were there, in the new log walls. And the roof shingles lay flatter and closer than those at the farm. 'Twas no fault of Dan'l that these shingles had his bested, for the most had been cut a season or more before, and laid by against the time they'd be wanted in folk's houses. Dan'l had done his share of the rolling up; Peter 'n' Paul too, and even Young'un herself. Could be that as much as a twentieth part of the new House of God, as Preacher called it, was Post handiwork.

But inside the new Meetinghouse the old tow gown didn't look so good any more. It was scarce fitting, among the real homespun and even linen. And like the deerskins it had grown desperate tight across bosom and buttocks, till you couldn't draw a deep breath to sing, nor seat yourself without giving thought to those that were sitting behind.

With the bed of charcoal glowing nicely in the forge from the

176

stroke of the big creaking bellows, it was time to sort out the files she had promised to sharpen. Mostly you could tell by the look, the sharp ones being dull and gray, the blunt ones shiny. A stroke or two on the thumbnail made sure. Taking them from the drawer and rack she spread them on the bench and set a small round rat-tail to heat first. The cold chisel needed a lick or two on the whetstone, and by then the file was fit to pick up in the tongs and lay in the groove of the bench-top. You had to work mighty fast; for if you reheated often you burned off the sharpness of the first cuts you'd raised; and if you didn't reheat you dulled the chisel so you had to resharp it, while the rat-tail cooled. Eldest might think she was mighty patient with her spinning, but she hadn't cut teeth in a pernickety little rat-tail, or she'd know what real patience was.

Still and all, doing a job right, the way Gunsmith would do it himself, or near as, beat all Creation. It didn't need to be cutting the teeth back into a rat-tail; drawing a long perfect furrow did the same to you, or milking Eph's Molly so she swung her head around to see if after all it wasn't Eph himself drawing it out so firm and fast. Dan'l had the same joy of labor. Wasn't anything Dan'l hankered after but to do things as perfect as eye and bone and muscle would allow. He'd stand back from a task, stretch his shoulders and say to himself, "Yessir, that's the best Dan'l Post can do . . . yet." And that "yet" said as plain as plain that he wished he had it to do over, and maybe better next time. Weren't many folks like Dan'l.

Young'un had to pull herself up sharp, and remember that Dan'l and she weren't scarce friends, nor talking to each other, these days. For Dan'l was being obstinate again. Seemed like he was bound he'd show that the Post farm aimed to be the biggest and the best in the whole valley. Or else he cal'lated to make it so big that it would be more than he and Young'un could handle alone, so Eldest would feel she'd ought to stay. And Eldest making out she couldn't be spared yet awhiles, and Preacher saying right out how noble his Deb'rah was, and how of course he'd wait till she was good and ready. Eldest wasn't being noble, she was scairt of going away. And being scairt didn't amount to shucks; most everybody being scairt at one time and another.

Young'un started on the big half-round file, cutting deeper than

177

was called for. And that was mighty aggravating, for as she'd begun on the file, so she'd need to finish; or 'twould bite different at heel and at toe.

There'd been but one thing she could do. Words were wasted on Dan'l, but without Young'un there to help he'd be able to clear less new pasture, turn less old pasture into ploughland, so the farm wouldn't spread till it was right out of hand. And what Dan'l and Eldest could do alone, Young'un and Dan'l could do when Eldest was gone. And that would prove to Preacher that his noble Deborah could stop being noble and get herself married.

* * *

'Twas more than mortal hands could do, to stay idle up at the farm, so a time back Young'un had set off for the settlement. Squirrels, chipmunks in the open spaces, and partridges seemed braver than ever. So she had put a broken bough to her shoulder, gun-fashion, to sight on them and see did that scare them. But they knowed right well that Dan'l was the only one with a real gun, and that his axe was thudding away down below the bottom meadow.

That was when the idea had started to dawn on her. Eldest could take time off to spin and weave a gown for herself. Dan'l could trap and hunt until he'd paid Gunsmith in full for the little rifle. Now it was Young'un's turn, and she'd earn herself a gun too. And learn to shoot the way Aunt Mary did, till she could outshoot Dan'l and most others. Dan'l with his Pa-doesn't-hold-with this, and his Pa-wouldn't-hold-with that, and not wanting Eldest to leave the farm. Needed to be took down a peg did Dan'l, for his own good and everyone else's. And she'd do it too!

Being that she aimed to keep it secret, she'd caught Aunt Mary in her keeping room and told her. Aunt Mary hadn't been eager, but at the long last she'd seen how needful it was, and had opened the door to the workshop and called, "Gam, I got you a 'prentice." And Young'un had gone to work right that very afternoon. Simple as that.

There was the rifle Aunt Mary had picked for her, standing in the rack against the wall. And every two-three days Aunt Mary made a chalk mark on the wall showing how much of it was earned. The

178

butt plate was earned right off with a half-inch of the stock. Took longer for the brass patch box. And when it came to trigger and lock the chalk mark hadn't moved for weeks, though she had worked ever so hard.

Young'un finished cutting a coarse-toothed file, and the next one was too cold to work on. Seeing she had a minute or two to spare and hadn't fondled the little rifle even once this morning, she reached over and took it down. She had it to her cheek, aiming through the doorway, when who should come right across the sights but Hank.

He put up both hands, a grin across his broad face, and said, "I surrender me to General Burgoyne, or the Continental Congress, whichever 'tis!"

"I'll take your parole, Captain Broadmoor, if you'd as lief offer it." Pa's tales of the wars gave Young'un the right words.

Hank looked surprised. "There's a sight more to you, Viney, than most folks reckon."

Young'un smiled. It was good to be called Viney, especially by Hank. It told you that you were grown and most a woman, near as, and had a woman's right to a real name. And it made you look at Hank as you'd had no call to do before. He didn't appear to be as tall as he was, being so broad. Most any time now he could quit razoring the first fuzz off his chin and start growing a real beard. The finest head of livestock ever reared on the Broadmoor place he was; Cicero Ditch had called him that. And it was the truth; from his kind of laughing eyes to the sure way his big hands and feet took grip of tool, or the very earth he stood on. His fingers were so strong they were gentle, the way he was handling the rifle Young'un had passed him.

"Some day," said Hank, "I aim to get me a gun of my own, not just Pa's."

"I'll loan you this very rifle." Young'un made the offer. "Just as soon as it's all mine." And told him how she was earning it, inch by inch from the butt-plate up. She was picturing in her mind how they would go hunting together, just the two of them, if so be she could get rid of Consolation for three-four hours. But she had the sense not to tell her purpose.

And well she hadn't. For Hank just passed the rifle back to her

179

without a word. Likely he didn't aim to be beholden to a girl. Men that could rightly be accounted men were like that.

Hank looked around him. "Gunsmith not to home?" he asked. "Pa said to tell his thanks for the way Prince's off fore shoe stays put, after the last time. But it was you shod him?"

"Uncle Gam showed how, and forged the nails." Young'un paid tribute where tribute was due. "The walls of Prince's hoof are thin, and brittle beside, and the Fort Ann shoesmith hadn't used the proper length nails and clinched them right."

"You can turn your hand to most anything, Viney," said Hank. But he seemed somehow put out. "Well, I got to be going."

Young'un swung the neglected file to the bench and was tapping away before Hank was back on his wagon. Hank was like Dan'l and Eldest, who said 'twas nowise fitten for a girl to bind herself 'prentice to a smith. Dan'l and Eldest had reason, for they wanted her hands on the farm. But that didn't nohow concern Hank Broadmoor. Drat Hank! She would earn the rifle yet, and powder and ball beside, and spite the lot of them.

Someone shadowed the doorway. She hoped it was Hank, back again. But didn't turn nor look up.

"Hi, mister! Seed ought of Gam Reed?" came a squeaky voice. Young'un turned.

And there in the doorway stood a plump, beaming man of middle-height she'd never seen hide nor hair of before. Or had she? Might be the peddler she'd seen four-five years back. Seemed like, from his city clothes, worn and greased as they were. But littler surely, than she'd remembered. Not bigger now than she was.

She dropped a file, hissing, into the quenching tub, and drew another from the forge to cut. It didn't serve to let hot iron grow chilled and spoil the work.

"Gunsmith's away," she told the stranger. "Is there aught I can do?"

"Howlin' Injuns save us!" The man stared. "You'll be Mistress . . . Miss . . . Miss . . ."

"I'm Viney. Viney Post." Young'un helped him out. Hadn't the peddler never set eye on deerskins before in all his life?"

"Yes, Ma'am, Mis' Post." He swung a heavy leather bag onto a

180

clear space of the bench top. "But I hadn't heared that old Zeph had married again after his fust wife burned up. Nor it don't make sense now, his running away. What you might call a surprise to me."

"He ain't, not that we know." Young'un had to bend over her work and face the window, so as to see when the chisel missed a tooth. "Pa ain't married again. Pa ain't never run away. Gone hunting and trapping awhiles. Pelts ain't wuth bait nor ball hereabouts these days." 'Twasn't for a strange peddler to be talking that way about Pa.

She had to swing back the file to heat, and the chisel would do with a few licks on the stone. The peddler stopped rummaging in his bag, and watched her mighty close.

"I dunno what to say, Mis' . . . Ma'am . . . Viney Post." Peddler took off his hat and used it to scratch the back of his round ball head. "First you're a man, but you ain't. Then you're Zeph's new wife, and you ain't. Then you look to be a gal of sixteen, seventeen and you ain't that neither, or you wouldn't be trusted to cut Gam Reed's files he's so careful with. Nor you wouldn't know how."

Young'un just had to laugh, the man was so comical with his eyes screwed up thinking, and his wide mouth turned down so troubled at the corners. And that set the corners to turn up, and the fat of his cheeks to run and close his eyes as his mouth opened to roar with laughter. Only there wasn't a roar, just a string of squeaks, like Cat asking for sup of milk. Till Viney had to laugh again, and Peddler to laugh with her.

After that, they didn't seem strangers, and just set to work. The files were mostly done, those that needed sharpening. Peddler asked the loan of Gunsmith's iron ladle, the big one with the double ears he used for casting bullets, and Young'un laid it on the forge to melt down Peddler's chips of pewter plates, while Peddler set the molds up on the bench, wedging tops and bottoms together with wooden blocks. Seemed Peddler didn't cotton to womenfolk, 'count of their all wanting different shapes of spoon handles, and speaking to him right sharp if he didn't remember over from last year's visit and bring the molds they'd asked for. Yes, Young'un could see how pernickety that was. She said so.

Peddler stopped in the midst of his second pouring to look at

181

Young'un and wrinkle up his eyes again. "Don't cal'late I heared you. Not to understand."

Young'un told him again. "Womenfolk is kind of pernickety."

"That's what it sounded like when you said it afore," he complained. "But it don't seem reasonable that a girl'd have that much sense."

Young'un took the ladle from him and finished pouring the batch, not wanting the pewter to cool; for, like lead, it wasted in dross with each reheating, and she couldn't abide waste. There was Gunsmith's charcoal to think of too.

"There ye go again! 'Tain't in natur' for girls and womenfolk to understand the ways of pewter casting. I dunno." He shook his big round head. "I just dunno."

The spoons fresh from the molds were brighter than silver itself, brighter than the newest coin that had ever come up to the valley. 'Twas like magic, turning those dull chips of metal into these shapely shining forms. Except for a set of buttons Ma had treasured, there had never been any pewter, old or new, at the farm.

Peddler cut off the sprue, just as you did from a bullet, and used first a file, then the back of his knife for finishing the edges.

"With these to show for samples, instead of dulled chips of pewter, womenfolk ain't like to be so right down or'nary about the pattern they favor." Peddler wrapped the spoons in a cloth and began to pack away his stone molds. "Seems like we'd be safe now to slip across to the Tavern and unpack the 'notions' from the wagon."

To catch first glance at the Yankee notions that had come all the way from New England, that would be something to remember all year round. If they were only half as purty as these gleaming precious spoons. Maybe she'd even be let to unload and help around awhiles. The files were all in shape and she'd let the forge die down to save Uncle Gam's charcoal.

Peddler cast an eye up and down the road before crossing, and Young'un knew the feeling. 'Twas those womenfolk Peddler was thinking of, but he wasn't nowise mindful of her, although he'd set her age as old as sixteen and more.

"Now there's my Basil," Peddler confided, "he don't nowise take after his pa. He's kind of catnip to womenfolk, and they sheathe their

182

claws and purr over him when they'd tear the hair from his pa for no more than a spoon-mold. Only, catnip waits for the cats to come to it, and Basil sets off after. Left him to water and feed the team, and then wipe off the wagon, but there ain't no sign of him. Off running the roads. Consarn the boy."

At sight of the wagon in the barn Young'un forgot to wonder what like was this Basil; for the whole of the rig, excepting the tarred cover stretched smooth over the hoops, was a pattern of bright paint, red and blue and yellow, with big brass hooks. Like as not this Basil was another Dan'l who set too much stock on being a boy. But what a boy could do, she could, and she'd show. She took Peddler's bucket and cloth and set to work on the wagon, while he went around to see had this Basil watered and fed the team, which he hadn't. And by the time Peddler had done it, Young'un had the side panels washed and wiped dry, and had started on the wheels. Even the spokes and felloes were striped and lined with red and blue; and one of the panels on the off side of the body had a picture of a big ship with yellow sails on blue water; and one of these on the near side showed a coach, plain as life, with four yellow horses going so fast they were belly-flat to the ground like a fox. That showed how fast.

She just had to tell Peddler, " 'Tis the purtiest wagon ever!"

Peddler had shone up the big brass hooks, and was hanging out span-new pots and pans. He stopped. He didn't say aught at first, only, "Wipe your hands dry, and look inside."

Well it was she wiped her hands, for 'twas more than mortal to look and not touch. Painted drawers with real glass knobs, and everything you could think of inside them. And best of all, wrapped to keep them clean, cotton cloths finer than you'd think could be spun and woven, and some as full of colored flowers as a spring pasture. The one with real roses Peddler carried outside the barn so she could see it better.

"I wrastled up yer first customer Pa. Or ain't she the first?"

A stranger, likely 'twas this Basil, not rightly a growed man, nor yet a boy, spat a yellow squirt of tobacco juice. He wasn't much to look at after those roses, pale complected, and spotted, and couldn't have done a smitch of work in those tight city clothes. The first customer was no more than Widow Wilson, and Basil was whispering to her what sounded like "Who's the squaw Pa's picked up with?"

Couldn't be she'd heard aright, for the Widow whispered back, "'Tis only Viney Post."

Then this Basil, that his pa said was a kind of catnip, stepped up and said: "You and me's got to get acquainted, Viney."

It didn't make sense, but of a sudden Young'un wanted to get away. This Basil must have knowed it almost before she did herself, for he caught her by the elbow.

"I got chores to do." She said it to Peddler, but 'twas his son that answered.

"What's to hinder I see you a ways along? You and me's friends."

She hadn't ought to have done it to a stranger. But his hand on her arm irked her somewise. She jabbed once, hard, with her elbow. He gave a gasp and let go. But right next he was whistling after her, and as she turned out of the Tavern yard she caught glimpse of him, strutting and wagging his little bottom, making believe to walk the way a girl did. She'd have been angered more, only she heard behind her a right good slap, and a whining, "But, Pa! I ain't done nothin' to harm."

*   *   *

The next day Young'un went down to the settlement in her tow gown, for all of Eldest's chidings. Gunsmith took no note and set her some breech plugs to forge. But Aunt Mary looked her over without a word and nodded as though she understood, and loaned her a leather apron and her doeskin shooting sleeves. At that the gown didn't come up to the doeskin shirt and the britches for real work. It was more comfortable after noontide when Aunt Mary took her back into the house, found a length of tow cloth that came close to matching, let it into the gown and eased the seams where it irked; and showed her too how to bind her hair with a hank of red thread and cross the plaits around her head out of the way. Cool and convenient it was. And when she got home that evening Eldest changed her tune, and said how it was a plain scandal that a growed girl was working down at the forge like a boy. Which showed what even a touch of prinking did. But of course Eldest hadn't an inkling of the little rifle Young'un coveted so.

184

The little rifle was there on the rack next day, and Aunt Mary had set the new chalk mark another inch higher on the wall, so now Young'un as good as owned stock and lock and breech plug. She hadn't time to take it down and set it to her shoulder, for Uncle Gam was already at work, but her eye could drop back to it from time to time as she toiled.

Work in the forge was hampered these days account of Peddler's wagonful of notions across at the Tavern. Menfolk pretended they had tasks for Gunsmith so they could idle across, and look at the notions, and come back to say they'd no time for such fancy contraptions and fiddle-diddles. Womenfolk went first to the Tavern, and then to the forge to find their menfolk and take them back to buy. Even Amy Higgins came along with her pa, to show the wire straining spoon she had bargained for, her ma not having the ambition to walk the mile and carry her own fat besides.

It was good to see Amy again after all these weeks, and to know she bore no grudge against the Posts for the way Dan'l had acted. If she hadn't been up to the Post place since the spitting, that was because she had a sight of work of her own in summertime. And the more when her pa had been helping raise the Meetinghouse.

She asked after the farm, did Amy. And when was Eldest fixing to get married. When Young'un told of Dan'l's doings at the Meetinghouse raising, and how set he was against Eldest's marrying, Amy just said, "Dan'l's kind of sot, for his years, ain't he?" And smiled as though she found him likable for all that. Amy Higgins would take a deal of knowing, you could see that plain as plain.

Amy couldn't spare a smitch of interest for the smithying, not even for the silver bead foresight Young'un was setting into a barrel, she was so taken with Peddler's cloth, and specially the rose pattern one.

"When I'm married I'll have the spittin' image of it, see if I don't," she confided. "Mis' Ditch knows what's tasteful, and she's bought the whole length, excepting what Peddler measured off and set aside for another buyer. An officer's wife at Ticonderoga, belike."

It wasn't in Young'un to feel envious, the way Amy claimed that she herself did. And she was glad Mis' Ditch had bought the roses for 'twould mean they'd be there to rest eyes on in Meeting after

185

Meeting. She had scarce said that to Amy when Amy had to run off home to show the straining spoon to her ma.

Young'un took another look at the rifle. Wasn't another girl in the settlement or outside had come so close to owning a firearm all her own.

But by the next day she didn't own as much as another hairsbreadth of it. Or the day after. For Peddler was in with pots and pans to mend, with riveting and tinsmithing. And Basil being no manner of use, and off running the roads or visiting up with the Widow on the Wilson farm, it fell to Young'un to work the forge bellows and hand Peddler his tools as he needed them. If she couldn't earn she could learn, and she picked up what she could of fluxes and soldering against the time such knowledge might serve her.

She picked up news too. "Runned across your pa's trail, up north," Peddler just happened to say. "Meat hunting he was, one summer, for the troops at Fort Ti. Didn't make out so well with his trapping this winter, but ain't like to starve, they say." And he promised to pass word on to Pa not to worry, for all was well at home. And to bring back more news if he heard any.

Peddler would be away again in two-three days, and not back for a year, for he would swing east through Vermont. And after he'd gone, Young'un told herself, the work would come easier in the shop.

Next news was that Basil would stay behind and work the farm for Widow Wilson. Talk was, he aimed to marry her for her farm, which didn't amount to much, and that she aimed to marry him to get his help on the farm. And there was argument which one of them would have the worst of the bargain. Didn't seem that Basil was overly welcomed at the settlement. And no reason why he should be.

* * *

But the way that chalk-line on the wall stayed put was plumb disheartening. It got so that going back and forth to work each day Young'un stopped setting a stick to her shoulder, and sighting on squirrels, and partridges. Womenfolk, dressed in skirted gowns, didn't carry rifles. Excepting Aunt Mary, and she only to test them for Gunsmith.

On Peddler's last day Aunt Mary called her into the house.

"Charcoal and suchlike's all paid for, but Peddler don't hardly know how to reckon up what's owing for the help you loaned him." Aunt Mary's sharp eyes made up for her lack of hearing, and seemed to look right into Young'un's thoughts. " 'Twill serve best for the two of us to go over to the Tavern and price what goods he's got left. You'll get better value in trade than you will in coin, hard money being scarce as ever."

There was sense to that, there most always was to what Aunt Mary said. You could get full value for hogs in trade of sheep or calves, or the other way about; but should you ask money, chances were you'd not be able to sell at all. Peddler seemed pleased when Aunt Mary told him they'd take goods, and showed everything from brass finger rings to thimbles, in the first drawer he came to in the wagon.

A ring or better still a thimble would have done fine, if 'twasn't too dear; but Aunt Mary was bound they should look at the cloth, rings being easy lost, and thimbles as easy borrowed when needed. Didn't seem that Young'un was owed enough to make a kerchief, but Peddler started pulling down the bolts of cloth, and Aunt Mary pricing each and saying "No."

"There's the one with roses on, the one you showed first off when you came," Young'un was saying before she thought. "But of course 'tis all sold." Excepting the length that was set aside for the officer's lady at Ticonderoga, if Amy guessed right.

Amy was likely right, for the cloth was folded and put away right in the front of the wagon. But Peddler reached it down and undid the wrappings. And oh, 'twas heartbreaking lovely. Just as she'd remembered it all along.

"Could you spare a piece long enough for a neckercher, a small neckercher, but big enough so it had maybe two roses on?" She had to ask, though for all she knew it might be the same as asking to buy just one leg of a horse, and no more. Seemed like it was, for though Peddler reached for the big scissors that hung from a string, he didn't start to cut.

"Don't look there's much more than a gown length there." Mary Reed stretched out her hand and tried it between thumb and finger. " 'Tis too good weave to waste that-a-way, in snippets."

Peddler began to measure yard lengths, nose to fingertip, nose to fingertip, and even before he had finished Young'un knew that Aunt Mary was right. Unless the officer's lady was most as little as Aunt Mary herself, and you couldn't depend on it, to cut a neckercher would mean to scant a gown. Of course Peddler wouldn't cut now, he even let the scissors swing back on their string; for a gown length was a gown length, and aught less sold only in snippets, smaller and smaller till the last were fit for no more than patchwork quilts.

Aunt Mary and Peddler looked to be smiling, though it was more than Young'un could do to show good cheer, for there was but one hope left.

"If so be the lady you're saving it for don't call for the whole of it, being thin, or short, and you can save me out a bit till next year, I'd be heart-willing to wait." And she would, so.

Peddler's smile broadened, as he looked Young'un up and down. "Now I wouldn't say she was overly plump, nor yet she isn't lean. I'd judge she was making out to be on the tall side as women go. Last time I set eyes on her she kind of favored Viney Post. And she ain't like to've changed much since."

Then 'twas for Aunt Mary to smile and say, "If I was Viney, I'd not scant a gown for the sake of a neckercher." And before Young'un could let herself believe, Aunt Mary added, "I don't reckon the cost, with thread and needle, would amount to more than the price of a good Gam Reed squirrel rifle."

*   *   *

It took more than a week, even with Aunt Mary showing how and helping, to put the gown together. Each cut with the scissors was most more than Young'un could bear, especially when it parted a rose in two. But when the gown began to shape up it was purtier even than the cloth had been in the piece. If it hadn't been such a secret, Young'un would have asked Eldest for help with the sewing. The way the thread caught on rough fingers made her wish she'd spun instead of working at the forge. Only then there would have been no cloth, and no gown. That was the way things were, seemed like.

When all was done Young'un could scarce believe her eyes—or

the hand mirror. Peddler had told truth, she looked all of sixteen-seventeen, and with two-three petticoats under, if only she'd had them, 'twould be nearer eighteen. Uncle Gam was called in from the forge, and since all had been done in the attic out of sight, and the light was dim from late afternoon, he stood awhiles not knowing who was visiting.

Then Young'un set off home, her tow gown parceled beneath her arm, practising a new walk that would be more seemly with the new gown. A go-to-Meeting walk sort of. 'Twas disappointing that folks were all back home, milking or eating, and no one on the road.

Strange thing was she didn't covet the rifle any longer. Not a smitch. And her anger at Dan'l had left her, for Dan'l was only a boy, and boys and men didn't know so much, come right down to it. Aunt Mary admitted as much. And as for Eldest saying that Young'un was too young to keep house, that set you to laughing, and you couldn't laugh and be angered both.

Cat was pacing along the trail mighty pleased with himself, a baby chipmunk in his mouth. When he heard the rustle of the new gown he turned his head and set down the chipmunk and placed paw upon it. And when the rustle drew closer he made a grab for the chipmunk, missed, and lit out for the woods. Young'un laughed; and Cat, feeling almighty foolish and trying to look specially dignified, came back and mewed to be picked up. Young'un grabbed him to her.

Eldest was washing out the milkpail at the door by the last light of the afterglow when Young'un set down Cat. Eldest said, "Evening, Ma'am," not knowing what name to put to the stranger. "Thank you for bringing back our cat, and won't you step inside awhiles."

Young'un did. And Dan'l rose up from the table the way Ma had taught him, years back, and set a stool.

Young'un seated herself, and wondered could she disguise her voice, and tell Eldest not to light the candle. Only laughter caught her, and as she still laughed kind of deep, Eldest knew who she was, right off. That set Eldest to laughing at Dan'l, who hadn't caught on yet. Then Dan'l was laughing fit to bust himself. And my land, there were the three of them just roaring at the joke of it.

'Twasn't the way Young'un had planned it. But it was good,

better almost than the gown itself, to know that come what might there'd always be the three of them. They'd quarrel again, like they'd done time and again. And Eldest would marry and go away. But there'd still be the three of them, for all that.

* * *

It could be that it was the rose gown that made Eldest see, for the first time, that Young'un was old enough to keep house for Dan'l and herself, and so set Eldest free to be wedded. Or again it might have been the sight of Young'un at Meeting, her hands folded in the lap of the gown and her hair ribboned up the way Aunt Mary had shown. For Preacher came nigh to stopping in his discourse when his eyes first lit on her. Young'un never knew for certain which it was.

But the day came when Phebe sent Eph over with her trunk, to loan Eldest for her things. And trudged over after, to see was there aught lacking that a bride would need. Eldest made a to-do over Phebe walking all that distance, seeing Phebe was kind of heavy. Aiming to have her a baby was Phebe, just as soon as she could get around to it, and you could see Eph thought it was mighty clever of her.

And then another day came, when all three Posts went down to Meeting together, and that hadn't scarce happened before. When the Meeting was over, or nigh to being, Young'un hurried around to Gunsmith's, saddled up Preacher's old gray, and fixed a half-sack of corn husks behind the saddle for pillion pad, and all without so much as getting a spot on the rose gown. And there she was, holding the horse all ready when Preacher came out.

He shook hands all round, and most everyone wished him luck. And when he was fixed in the saddle Mist' Broadmoor hoisted up Eldest, and nigh to have pitched her right over the saddle and down the other side too, not knowing his own strength and Eldest not being ready. Soon as Eldest had fixed herself on the pillion and tied a tape around her skirt, most everyone, from Mis' Ditch to Grandma Truttle had to wish her God-speed. And two-three of them wept besides, which was nice. Young'un couldn't weep, not being inclined that way.

But when the two rode off, Eldest holding to Preacher with one arm and waving Aunt Mary's handkercher with the other, Preacher raising his hat time after time, Young'un got to thinking of Eldest going to live all alone there in Fort Ann, aways from anywhere. It was a troubling thought. Until you got to seeing that folks born and raised in the town of Fort Ann might think the Post place a ways off from anywhere too. They might so. No knowing.

CHAPTER SEVENTEEN

IF THE new gown had maybe done a mite towards getting Eldest wedded, likely it did more to starting the trouble over Cicero and his bees. For Hank and others had got to noticing, just as soon as Young'un wore the roses to Meeting, though Hank had not been in it at the start off. And nothing had looked less like trouble, for Young'un did no more than give help to a neighbor.

It was in the late fall that Young'un led Peter'n' Paul down to Gunsmith's so the Fort Ann shoesmith could give them a glance and see did they need shoes. With their great weight oxen have the sense to set down their little spreading hoofs mighty slow and cautious. But for all that they would get stone bruises, sprains, and cuts between the toes, just the same as humans. Peter had started to favor his nigh fore a mite, and Dan'l wanted to know did he need shoeing. Oxen shoeing came higher than horse shoeing, costing upwards of an acre of good corn each year, some said. So naught was to be done unless sore needed.

Most folks' harvest being in barn by now, and Shoesmith having the news from Fort Ann and beyond, there was a good few men crowding in to the warmth of the forge. Sim Higgins was joking Sol Broadmoor about the Tavern bees, asking him how many gills of rum Mis' Ditch gave him for each butt he brimstoned off. Another asked would he start in today, so they could stand a safe ways off and watch him stung.

Shoesmith spoke up sharp and said if there were any such monkeyshines he'd shut the shop doors tight, and not be held accountable for the six-eight beasts hitched outside. A team of good horses had been stung to death down at Stillwater only the last summer, he said.

And that he'd a sight rather face all Rogers' Rangers, for even a Ranger sometimes missed his mark, but a bee never.

He wasn't soothed till Sim Higgins pointed out that Mis' Ditch was away today and tomorrow, and she wouldn't allow the honey to be taken without she was behind her glass window watching. On account the tricks Cicero was always up to, trying to save his best bees and give her those that had made least honey, instead of the other way about like any sensible folk would do.

With so many men around and no womenfolk, the talk got so it wasn't seemly for Young'un to wait. And Gunsmith said he would see to the oxen when their turn came. With time on her hands, and talk of the bees in her ears, she crossed over to the Tavern, went down the yard and through the gate into the vegetable patch. Late squash and all else was wilted down, and the soil crust-hard with last night's frost. Not a bee was a-wing, not one. But when she drew near to the line of bee-butts Taverner stood up from behind one, where he had crouched in hiding at the sound of her footsteps.

"Not a soul I'd rather see!" It sounded mighty fine as Taverner said it. Only she'd be bound he didn't see any difference 'twixt her and a dead sow, excepting that a sow hadn't a pair of hands. And she guessed right.

"Those butts, the ones I've stuffed the holes of with grass, I just got to set them in the wagon." In his worry he did a shuffle with his feet most like a dance. "But they're too heavy, and there's no one else I can trust, or that ain't afraid."

That was right easy remedied. Young'un found a light fence bar, and cut it in two with the woodshed axe. With Cicero tilting the first butt, she set one rod under one side of the plank-end the butt stood on, the second rod under the other side. That way, Taverner lifting carefully in front, Young'un behind, 'twas easy as Adam to bear the butts one by one and set them down safe on the empty wagon. And scarce a buzz from the bees, chilled with the first touch of winter.

Then naught would suit Taverner but they must set up empty butts in place of those they had taken. Taverner weighted the inside of each with a small rock.

"Too light, and Sol will suspicion they're empty," he explained.

"Too heavy, and Sol will choose them out from the others to set over the brimstone pit. And when he comes to take the honey he'll find the rocks. And that will set Hepziba to asking me where the rest of the butts is gone, which I ·don't aim she should."

Young'un could see that it wouldn't serve Taverner any for Mis' Ditch to get to suspicioning. For she would have the truth out of him quicker than pulling the gizzard out'n a dead hen. Still and all, Young'un was hankering to know the secret herself.

Taverner was looking over the butts in the wagon and grinning his triumph, when, crack! he hit the tail-board with his fist, and his face slipped all ways.

"Horses! Hepziba's took the team." He looked plumb at Young'un as though he had never set eyes on her before. "Can't so much as draw the bees out'n the yard without a team."

If that was all that was amiss 'twas easy remedied. Young'un told Taverner to wait, and hurried across the road to the forge. Peter'n' Paul had brought down their yoke to keep their necks hardened and they were always willing to help.

Gunsmith had set the oxen in the sling, and seen to their hoofs himself, Shoesmith having a sight of work on hand. Uncle Gam had pared down the toes which had overgrown, so now the oxen could stand straighter again. He told Young'un to see that their standings in the barn were level and free from rocks. There was no call for shoeing, but kind of the other way about, seeing they hadn't wore down their toes enough.

What with that good news, and the thought that now she could lend Taverner a neighborly turn, Young'un forgot to ask herself whether 'twas right or wrong to thwart Mis' Ditch. She fixed the iron ring of the yoke to the draw-pole of the wagon with a lashing of rawhide, showed Taverner how to set a stake in the spokes of the wheels to stop the wagon from overrunning the oxen on a downhill, and led out of the yard and up north the way Taverner asked.

Taverner had no plan, except to hide the bees somewhere in the woods where they would be safe. "There's a sight of talk about the fool that killed the goose that laid the golden eggs," he complained, "but it don't seem to've gotten around about the fool that brimstones off the bees that lay the golden honey."

194

It seemed worse folly than that, the way Taverner explained it. Folks didn't kill the hen that laid the best, nor the cow that gave most milk; but year after year those that kept bees picked out the butts that had stored the most honey and poisoned off the honey-gatherers over a burning brimstone pit. It stood to reason that working that-a-ways you bred from your worst bees, year-in and year-out. Until 'twas the world's miracle that, breeding back from the least thrifty, the bees gave any honey at all. Young'un could see that clear as clear, once 'twas shown, for it wouldn't serve with livestock.

Young'un was for turning in at Eph's, and asking him would he set the bees out in his woodlot. For you couldn't go drawing the wagon just anywheres into the woods the way you could a sled. But Taverner said "No" because of Phebe. He didn't cal'late to trust a woman within smell of honey, nor her tongue to hold a secret. He was right bitter, account of Mis' Ditch.

Every year he planned to take his honey without killing ary a bee, but for seven years now Hepziba had thwarted him. Seemed that with tobacco smoke and pounding on the side of an up-turned butt you could make the bees walk right up and out into an empty bushel basket. Then you pried off the rooftop of another butt, shook the bees from the basket among the other bees, and sprinkled them all with wheaten flour to stop them brawling and killing each other. That way you took your honey and you kept your bees. Seemed right smart if true. Taverner took oath 'twas true as he lived, and he would show some day.

The Young'un had to break in on his talk to tell Taverner they had passed all the wagon trails, excepting only the one down to the Post farm. And there would be no space to turn, once they were on it.

"Ain't likely you and Dan'l would leave me set the bees up in your woods?" Taverner's voice was most pleading. "Just for the winter?"

Why, of course he could! And if there were any chores to be done for the little critters Young'un would add them to her others and not know the difference.

And that was how Taverner's bees came to be set in rows in the old shelter Dan'l had first made inside the woods, after the house and Ma were burned. As soon as he got over his scare of the bees, and saw they weren't flying, Dan'l came up with his axe and strength-ened the old hemlock bough beds for the butts to stand on. Dan'l was glad of the chance to do Taverner a turn, on account of the good turn Taverner had done him way back when Sim Higgins had claimed Peter'n' Paul for Pa's debts.

No one would think to look in the old shelter for Taverner's bees. And they would be close at hand so Young'un could see they weren't choked by snowdrift. Dan'l promised Taverner not to tell, which he weren't like to anyways, the way he always stinted his words.

It seemed an easy way to oblige a neighbor, and to harm no one. But if Young'un could have guessed what trouble the bees were fixing to make for her she would never have drawn them up to the Post place; not when there were all the woods from here to Canady to shelter them.

To make more certain sure, Young'un and Dan'l drew up a sledful of spoiled second-cut hay from the lower meadow. They stacked it in the shelter in such way that it would leave the bees free to fly when the weather let, but look to strangers as no more than a pile of bedding for heifer and the oxen. And 'twas well they did.

When Cicero brought his bees not one of the three of them had foreseen what the turn of the season would bring. 'Twasn't skunks, that Cicero said were death on bees. 'Twasn't porcupines, that Dan'l was feared would gnaw their way through the bottom boards. 'Twas childer. And 'tis the nature of childer to be prying.

As soon as the chores lightened up in the fall, the little'uns and young'uns from the Settlement and around started running up to the Post farm. Just like the year before. Only some had shot up, some broadened out, two girls had started to slim down the way Young'un was doing herself, and Isa and the Miller boy had got to borrowing their pas' razors of a Saturday night. And little Consola-tion, being bigger, was a bigger pest than ever. Of course there was another baby down to the Millers', and the one of the season before for Albacinda to carry around.

With so many about it was past hoping to keep each and every one away from the old shelter. But it would have taxed even Amy's wits to make play with a stack of blackened weeds and grass. And Young'un got so she didn't worry any longer.

There were noble times at the Post place. With corn to pop this year, and sunflower seeds to roast and salt and eat, and story-telling besides. Between snows they nigh to've gleaned out the forest of acorns for Amy to turn into cakes. When Amy was there to portion out stints to the older ones, and keep the little ones within bounds, Dan'l came in from barn or woodshed, and even told Pa's old tales of hunting and Injuns and war.

Seemed as though once Eldest was married and gone Dan'l quit wasting his time in fretting over her. Nor he didn't hold it against Young'un and Amy and Albacinda and all other females the way he had been fixing to. Could be he was thankful to Amy for stilling the little'uns rioting when she was along. But Amy's ma being too fat to do aught but eat, and her pa sitting figuring out ways to out-trade his neighbors when he'd ought to be working, Amy wasn't to be spared from home as often as other folk.

Dan'l and Hank were shaping to be close friends; being they had so much in common, from stinting words to wanting to show their strength. Hank could out-wrestle Dan'l, and heft a bigger load. Dan'l could out-shoot Hank, and out-run him too.

But when Dan'l wanted to take Hank to see his trap lines, or if Hank aimed to draw Dan'l out to the barn to be shut of the little'uns, there would be Consolation yawping to go along. Most the first words that Consolation had learned were "I hate you," and she screamed them at anyone who came between her and her Hank. Jealous she was, and hateful, though for all that you could see there was good in her. If you tried right hard.

There was the time that Consolation lit into a little Miller, who was head shorter than she was, Consolation being big-boned and strong like all the Broadmoors. The little Miller cut his head open on a stool, and all for denying Consolation the toasted squash seeds that were rightfully his. Young'un just naturally turned the kicking and screaming Consolation over her knees and started in to spank. It was no more than Consolation had been laying by for herself, and fully called for.

But Hank had gone kind of a gray color in the face, through

anger or fear, and grabbed Young'un's arm before she could get in more than three-four good licks.

"The baby isn't to be made to cry, nor even let to," he said as he took his sister's hand. And little sister gave Young'un a parting kick.

Young'un said nothing. Not even when Hank told he was sorry and led the brat off home. She kept her temper when Isa explained that Consolation was untimely born, and his ma's last dying words were to take care of the baby. Seemed that if the baby were contraried she held her breath till she was blue all over and like to die. There had been a sight of trouble to raising her. Young'un didn't so much as say 'twas trouble wasted.

It was weeks before Hank showed up again, and all because of that Consolation. And when he did, there was that Consolation perched on his shoulder as usual. Young'un took a close look at her. Soft she was from being carried everywhere, and fat from never being denied what she hankered after. But naught amiss that the eye could see. Whatever had ailed the baby, it was plain she had outgrown it by now. But Hank couldn't outgrow his ma's dying words.

Amy was up visiting, and Dan'l to home, as it chanced. Young'un led Amy outside to ask her counsel, under pretence of looking at the hole that Dan'l had started to dig in the frozen ground for some beast he'd heard marauding around in the night. Till snow fell, or the ground softened to leave tracks, Dan'l didn't know what critter he was fixing to trap, nor whether the trap should be pitfall or deadfall or what. Naught but a hole in the ground. The hole gave Amy her idea.

Being there were no little'uns for Consolation to fight with, Hank allowed he would go down with Dan'l to the lake end and lay some tip-ups and fish lines through the ice. Consolation wasn't to be let to go account the cold, even if they built a fire on shore.

Just as soon as the boys were gone Consolation started to act up. Naught would please her but Amy must set right to and make chestnut cakes for her. If Amy didn't, young Consolation threatened to hold her breath and die, so folks would be sorry and blame Amy. And the brat began to scream, out of plain ill-temper at not being heeded.

Amy kept silent. She went and fetched in a stick, and, still silent, set it against the brat and measured her height. Then she measured again to make sure. Consolation, kind of puzzled, let up on her yells.

When Amy went out with the same stick to measure it against the hole Dan'l had dug, Consolation tagged along behind.

Amy came in, closed the door against the cold, and shook her head. "'Tis too short yet, though plenty wide enough. Dan'l don't measure so good just by eye. Or could be," she admitted, looking at Consolation again, "she's growed."

If aught had growed it was Consolation's eyes. They looked to be big as stirring spoons. And she hadn't bethought herself to let out a holler yet. 'Twould come though.

"Kind of a pity she's so set on dying, for she won't be buried among the rest of her folks, nor have a nice stone to her head, if she kills herself." Amy shook her head regretfully. "Holding your breath or yelling so you die of a 'plexy is as sure killing yourself as cutting off your own head with an axe."

'Twas then Young'un caught on and said her piece. "Consolation has less sense than a little'un, even though she's older. Most folks just naturally know, soon as they're born, that each laugh sets you a pace further from your grave. Badly ailing folk don't never laugh, nor those that's so old they ain't long for this world. Which kind of proves it t'other way around."

Consolation found her tongue. "I hates you! And I ain't believing a word!"

Young'un looked at Amy, and Amy looked at Young'un, and they both laughed. Amy's idea was a good one, even if it hadn't turned out the way the two had hoped. Still laughing, kind of, they looked at Consolation. Seemed the brat could trick all Creation, and not be tricked herself. She was standing there, that little'un who wasn't little any longer except in the way she was coddled, her fists doubled, and her face screwed up pretty nigh as tight. Then slowly the face and fists began to loosen up, and she swallowed and took a deep breath and swallowed again as though fixing not to weep. She gave a kind of a tee-hee sound that could have been a sob, but wasn't. Next thing she gave a real tee-hee, and her mouth turned up to show she was laughing. And my land, next thing you knew the three of them were all tee-heeing and laughing together!

When Hank and Dan'l climbed back from the lake a long whiles later, the three were setting to the fire on stools, as sociable as could be, and Consolation being learned to peel potatoes, which she had never been let to do before. Amy finished the man's head she was whittling out of a frosted potato, and passed it over to Consolation. It set Consolation to tee-heeing herself a good ten paces further from an early grave.

Hank heard and saw, and nigh to've let fall his string of fish. 'Twas all he could do to ask what the three had been doing.

"Joking over the grave Dan'l dug outside," said Amy.

Consolation gave another tee-hee. By now, after a half-day's practice, she had got so she could laugh real pretty, copying the way Amy did.

With the new caught fish, and so many potatoes all peeled, the visitors just had to be made to stop and eat. With Consolation laughing all the whiles it was a right merry meal. Dark it was when the three set out for home, and as Amy wouldn't carry the pine torch, pretending the dripping rosin would mar her gown, Hank had to. And Consolation being a sight too heavy for Amy to carry she had to walk the whole way. Which she had been fit to do the last four years, but for Hank's coddling.

Not far up the trail, by Amy's account later, they met up with Cicero Ditch. And that was plain mischance. For 'twas Taverner's trying to hide, which he couldn't for lack of leaves on the trees, that first set Hank off to suspicion him. Though all that Hank said to Amy at the time was,

"Cicero looks like he's fixing to rob a roost!"

* * *

Taverner had his good reasons for coming up, though Hank couldn't know. When Sol brimstoned off the best of the butts that Cicero had left behind back at the Tavern, there had been little enough crop but dead bees and a spate of talk from Mis' Ditch. She claimed that none but Cicero would waste time and trouble on bees that gathered so little honey. Cicero came back at her, saying that if he was let to keep bees the way they'd ought to be kept there'd be honey a-plenty because then there'd be bees a-plenty to gather it in.

Then the trouble between Taverner and Mis' Ditch led to trouble between Taverner and Sol Broadmoor, Hank's pa, who had only done Mis' Ditch's bidding. Taverner swore he wasn't agoing to serve so much as a dreg of drink to the man who poisoned his bees. Mis' Ditch stepped up and drew Sol a full quart of cider, as he'd asked, and laced it free with best Medford rum as thanks for his aid with the bees. It didn't lie in a Broadmoor to hold a grudge, but Taverner talked of dropping poison in Sol's drink just as soon as he saw a chance. And he was nigh mad enough to do it.

Which all went to show why Taverner set so much stock on the best of his bees that he had saved out, and hidden up at the Post farm. Nothing would serve but he must hurry up after dark every so often and carry Dan'l's lantern out to the old shelter, and part the hay and see for himself that the butts were all there in place. Like he had to make sure there had been no forest fire to burn them, nor Noah's flood reaching halfway up the mountains to drown them since last he saw.

Each time he came, he'd stomp back into the house, mighty relieved, and laugh over the trick he'd got to playing on Mis' Ditch. It seemed that whenever Sol came to the Tavern, which he did once in a whiles when the day's work was over, Cicero would fly into a fury and let on he would serve no drinks to anyone while Sol was under his rooftree, not even to coach folks stopping over. That lulled Mis' Ditch's suspicion when Taverner threw on hat and coat and slammed out into the night. And, what was more, tied her down to serving the trade so she couldn't follow him to see where he went. Taverner told it right comical.

But that chance meeting with Hank on the trail brewed a peck of trouble. Taverner couldn't rest easy in his mind with Sol's own son so near the precious bees. And next time he was up Hank asked Dan'l and Young'un what Taverner was seeking so late at night. Not getting a clear answer he vowed, only half joking, he would find out for himself, and right soon. Which he didn't, for all his striving.

Hank was no fool, and he took notice that the nights his pa went to the Tavern were the nights Taverner came up to visit with the Posts. Once he was warmed up to the hunt Hank even got so he would trust Consolation to Isa, and follow on after his pa. He would wait around outside, would Hank, till Taverner lit out from the Tavern, then come up to him, pass him the time of day, and walk up the hill beside him whether Taverner wanted or no.

Of course that set Taverner to suspicioning the more; and Hank suspicioning more than enough already. What made it comical was the way they had to pretend to be friendly so as to keep an eye on each other.

*   *   *

All the way from January to near the end of March, Taverner could get no glance at his bee butts, account of Hank. Till he was fit to be tied. He would sit glowering across the room at Hank, hoping that just for once Hank would set off home by himself, which he never did. Taverner talked with Dan'l about nigh everything under the sun but bees. And trying all the while to slide in a question edgewise to Young'un, so she could answer "Kind of a lot of insects around today," or "Seen nothing of our next neighbors for nigh on two weeks," according as she wanted to tell that the day being warm and sunny the bees had been out flying, or that they hadn't stirred from their sleep for weeks. Dan'l had no gift for that kind of talk.

Hank, aiming to thwart Taverner and keep on thwarting him until the secret was out, would start up a spate of talk to Young'un whenever Taverner's face so much as turned towards her. He spun out the talk about Sim Higgins' broken wagon axle so fine he could have hewed and fixed a new axle in the time, and sweated less by half a pint. The night he told of how Basil, who had married the Widow Wilson and run through all the money she had to give, had sent off to his pa for a loan, Hank kept the talk most of one evening. It was hard to see what the colors of the kittens born in the Widow's barn had to do with Basil's debts. Nor, when Basil and his wife had quarreled over his not drawing down firing from the woodlot, Hank hadn't needed to name all the kinds of trees Basil could have cut and drawn down if he had been so minded. Nor his talk of the farm of the father of the girl down in Welsh Hollow that Basil had had trouble over, didn't seem rightly to concern. Still and all 'twas a bout of talk that even Preacher would have been hard put to equal. Likely Hank couldn't so much as clear his throat the day after.

After that, to save his own breath, Hank took to questioning Young'un whenever Taverner looked to be about to speak to her. If Young'un answered Hank and told what she held about smooth-bores, straight cuts, and twisted rifling she told him a dozen times. And the same with how best to train and work oxen, and most everything else she knowed. She came to think Hank had a colander instead of a memory, or was fixing to train oxen to shoot rifles and was scared to start in wrong so they would never be good marksmen. She did, sure.

'Twas always the same. A holler outside, "Anybody to home?" Which there naturally was. Dan'l would open the door to a draft of chill air and a stomping of feet kicking off snow, and Young'un would set stools to the fire. Cicero and Dan'l would talk awhiles, low and contented at first from the warmth and the smell of food, but both getting kind of jumpy. Then Cicero would turn his head towards Young'un, and out would pop Hank's first question of the evening. And more would follow. Hadn't ever a girl or a woman been heark-ened to and even made to talk the way Young'un was. Times she craved to be a deaf mute, and she could easy see that Dan'l wished she was.

The comicalest happening of all was when Hank's pa asked to know what Hank was doing, running the roads that-a-way after dark. Hank couldn't think what to answer but that he was going courting. If there was any courting done it was betwixt Taverner and Hank on the way up and back. But word got around, the way it does, and Amy told Dan'l about Hank and his courting. So the first time after that Hank came up with Taverner, it was a sight to see him trying to explain he was courting Young'un, and Dan'l and Taverner not believing a word of it. Dan'l dursent so much as look at Hank till Hank got through, not wanting to laugh. And Taverner sitting there hunched up on his stool and glaring at Hank just the same as ever.

Young'un couldn't believe either, though she would have liked to. It did a girl no harm to be courted once in a whiles; nor to take her part in the courting too. For it was like firing at a mark before you were fit to set off hunting. It made you a sight surer you could bring down what you would aim at when the time came. And it would have to be her that Hank courted, whether he wanted or no, seeing there was no other girl up here.

And she would go so far as to tell herself she'd rather Hank than any.

But towards the end of the winter it was harder to see the comical side. With Taverner so concerned for his bees, and feared for the time when they would be flying again, and his secret easy for Hank to guess; and with Hank muttering over and over that old men had ought to stay home and not go gallivanting, Young'un got so she worried over where it was all leading. It was plain there was trouble brewing.

When the bust-up came it wasn't in the shape of anything Young'un could have guessed. Or anyone else either.

But that was after the spring victualing.

CHAPTER EIGHTEEN

YOUNG'UN'S bundle was wrapped and tied overnight, in readiness for the journey. There wasn't so much as a glimmer over the hills when she looked from the door, nothing to show that dawn was on its way except the faint breeze that scarce raised a sigh in the leafless woods. The coming of dawn was like the coming of spring; if you had a wisdom inside of you, then you knowed when they were on their way, though you couldn't rightly tell how you knowed.

Opening out the ashed-over fire and blowing on the embers didn't raise a stir out of Dan'l. Menfolk slept heavier than womenfolk. She ought to rouse him, but hadn't the heart, seeing what she aimed to do this day. 'Twas for his good, what she planned, and likely he would never know. But still and all she would feel a mite better within herself if she was to do his chores as well as her own. She sighed, for it was hard to contrary those you loved, even unbeknownst to them.

It was still dark when Young'un had the fire alive, the bean pot set to heat, and had lighted the lantern with a pine sliver. Still dark, except for the yellow lantern gleam, when she made her way around to the barn and propped open the big doors. Snow still lingered banked against the north side, and enough piled up from Dan'l's shoveling on the east so one door wouldn't open to the full.

Barn was right warm with Eph's team resting there overnight, along with the oxen and the heifer. She pulled down hay for heifer and Peter'n' Paul, and set out corn for Eph's team, seeing they had hauling to do. And stood awhile taking pleasure from the sight of them all. Their coats were winter-rough, not smooth the way they would be come summer. But heifer had built bone through the cold months, and Peter'n' Paul were fit for ploughing and dragging even now, hardened as they were with hauling down wood and sugaring off the maples. Eph's horses were well cared for like all his livestock.

The heifer was trying to reach out to the horses' corn, which she couldn't, by reason of the stanchion. Young'un had to slap her nose. "You, heifer, take lesson from Peter'n' Paul, and eat your hay." Young'un had to turn and look back as she went out the door. Couldn't hardly be anything more comforting than a big barn filled with contented critters all eating, and more'n enough feed laid by for all.

Breakfast didn't take hardly no time at all, neither she nor Dan'l being able to eat much for thinking of what lay before them that day. Then she ashed over the fire again, blew out the lantern and carried her bundle to the wagon, black against the gray dawn. The farm stuff they were drawing down to Eldest was loaded already. Dan'l laid his pelts and rifle on top, and went back for his axe.

Harnessing took time, when you were used to yoke and pole. Fixing all those straps and buckles mostly by feel in the half-darkness, and your fingers cold beside, was kind of aggravating. But at last Dan'l climbed to the seat and took up the reins, and Young'un ran back to the barn to loose Peter'n' Paul and heifer so they could go down and water themselves, and maybe snatch a bite of grazing. Just to make sure, she led the team and wagon up into the woods a ways. Then climbed up alongside the driver, and sat there, kind of like a princess on a throne, right the whole way to Eph's. Though princesses didn't get their faces slapped by old beech branches all the whiles.

Eph came out and helped load more maple syrup and two-three other things on the wagon. Phebe was fixing to have another baby, and, though 'twas a long ways from being born yet, Eph didn't cal'late to leave her, nor yet to take her with him on a spring victualing. Not after what had chanced to the first. Phebe had slipped it, that was what all the talk amounted to, after carrying two full pails of water uphill, though Eph had warned her not to. What with pain and worry over the loss Phebe was like to've died too, but for Eph's care and patience. Poor Phebe, she'd been most out of her mind, and Eph looking a hundred year old if a day.

But that was over, and Phebe was bound she'd have another baby just as soon-as. And she was right, you could depend. And Eph was holding back the most of his victualing till summer, so when he went he could take Phebe with him and show the baby around. So there wasn't much he had to throw in the wagon, just things that might spoil with keeping over till the heat.

"Mighty obliged," he told Dan'l. "And you got Phebe's list? I'll be over to your farm twict a day and see naught takes harm."

And Dan'l thanked him for the wagon and team, for he'd good manners, had Dan'l, when he bethought himself. And you were off again, the wagon wheels grinding on boulders, and tearing loose from the thawed mire, and the round rumps of the horses rising and falling almost under your feet, you were so high up. Mighty different from the old sled jerking slowly along under the tails of Peter'n' Paul. Kind of scaring at first off.

Thaw had loosed the scents that had been frozen into the ground all winter. Back there you could tell, even if you hadn't seen, that Eph had spread his barn litter over his fall ploughing before it thawed out too soft for the team. Always forehanded was Eph. The next scent was just ploughland without the dung. And next was something that had died. Pa would have known whether 'twas fox or coon or rabbit. And then folks' cook-fires. All different from the forest smells of leaves and rotted wood and suchlike.

Looking down on the settlement you could see plain as a pikestaff which family ris' early, and which were slugabeds. Aunt Mary's fire had burned down to embers so there weren't so much smoke as blue vapor rising from the chimney. Across the way the two Tavern chimneys were empty, Tavern folks being late to bed. As the wagon was half down the hill one of the Tavern chimneys oozed a drop of yellow. Other smokes were betwixt and between. Being it was early yet, there were no childer running out to beg to be took along, nor their mas to ask would Viney please to buy twopennorth of this, and kindly to match that, and not to forget to ask after the health of Amos' sister Ivy's nevvy's wife, and such-all; more than a human head could hold.

Dan'l druv up outside, unbitted, filled the drinking trough from the brook outside Gunsmith's shop, and went in. Young'un just sat there, high up on the wooden seat, Phebe's bearskin robe wrapped around her. Holding back her thoughts of what lay ahead, she was, for fear aught might happen and she and Dan'l wouldn't get to go after all.

Cicero came to the door of the Tavern to glance at the sky and size up the day to come. He ducked in again a moment, then came hurrying across with a small bowl and a cloth tied over.

"Basswood and wild grape honeycomb I hid away last year, so 'tis set solid and won't spill." He thrust it into Young'un's hands and looked back towards the Tavern. "For Deborah. Cal'late 'tis none too easy for her being a preacher's wife, and life could do with a little sweetening. But you'll bring back the bowl?"

And before Young'un could so much as thank him he scuttled back home. She hoped Hepziba hadn't seen him. 'Twasn't comical at all, as some folks thought, for him to be so mortal feared of Hepziba's tongue. He'd ought to take an axe handle to her if his hands didn't serve. A man who couldn't hold the mastery in his own house wasn't fit for a woman to marry. And every woman knowed it in her heart. There wasn't no right and wrong to it, it just happened that way.

Dan'l came running out, and nigh to've forgotten to bit up, so eager he was to be up on the seat and driving again. Wasn't nothing Aunt Mary craved she couldn't get for herself when she and Uncle Gam drove down in two-three weeks, Dan'l reported. But Young'un was to remember Dan'l to tell Eldest that Aunt Mary said she'd be right glad of a new patchwork quilt, and would bring down a bag of scraps when she came.

Meetinghouse looked mighty purty as the wagon wheels bounced over the stone filling, where the old slough had set. A short trot, a long slow haul up and over the winding hill, and by golly, they were in a different valley altogether. A valley that widened out till you couldn't so much as call your cow if she'd roamed to the further side. Land flat as water in a pool, and only the hills on each side to show 'twas real, and you couldn't catch sight of them only when you came to a clearing. But for the deep wheel-ruts of the road to guide 'twould have been easy as kiss-your-hand to get lost.

The time Pa had taken Young'un along, she'd been no more than a little one, and little ones don't take notice far beyond their own snub noses. Where the road forked ahead here, she couldn't for the life of her remember whether Pa had taken the north or the south fork. Dan'l half turned his head but wasn't minded to ask outright and admit he didn't know. The team chose the north fork, and seeing it had the deeper ruts 'twas like to be the coach road, and no harm done.

Then there was naught to do but tuck the bear robe closer under, cross the headshawl about her neck, hold on to the seat plank and watch the woods close in tight on the road, open out again to farmland and fencing, close in again, open out. Like a big yawning mouth that couldn't stay shut and wouldn't stay open. Might be that one day the forest would gulp. And there'd be a barn and house the less. And gulp again, and another farm would be gone. If Amy were along you could tell her, and she'd laugh and understand.

But Dan'l would want to know where'd a forest find a belly to swallow into? And when you told him 'twas only makebelieve, he'd look puzzled as a pup that had bit a wooden leg, not knowing what to do since 'twasn't real. Young'un had warned Amy that Dan'l was that way, but Amy had only smiled and said 'twould be time enough to shoe her horse after the horse was hers.

Young'un got no further with her thoughts, for Dan'l half turned his head, and of all things, if he didn't start in to talk! 'Twas a fence he'd fix, at the start off; and he was right, it needed fixing mighty bad. Then 'twas a barn he'd shingle afresh, if 'twas his. Then there was a kind of gate that he said to look at close as they passed by so they could make one like it up on the farm, where they had only cattle bars as yet.

Didn't seem it could be Dan'l, not really, scattering a full year's talk all in one morning. But 'twas Dan'l all right who claimed there wasn't a farm he set eyes on to equal the Post farm. Big they were, almighty big, he'd allow, and the soil of the bottom land dark and rich where it showed from the fall ploughing. But there couldn't hardly be pleasure in turning these everlasting straight furrows, not if you'd the skill to follow the curves of a hillside, keeping one eye on the skyline so's to get each furrow level and lose no good from the soil by washoff. 'Twasn't real farming down here in the flatlands only . . . only . . . But Dan'l couldn't call to mind what-in-all it was.

"Only horse-hoeing." The word slipped out of Young'un's mouth just as it came to her mind.

"Horse-hoeing? Don't seem I've ever heard the name. But that's what 'tis. Horse-hoeing." Then Dan'l grinned. "Times, Young'un, I get to wondering if you ain't maybe right smart."

Could be 'twas only a deep rut in the road, but Young'un came close to dropping off the wagon. What with that surprise, and puzzling out what the men were doing with long poles breaking out the ice at the bottom of the water-wheel pit at Kane's Falls, they'd drawn into Fort Ann before Young'un was real ready.

And here were more ways to setting a roof over your head than you could think up in a month of Sundays. Only two-three log houses; the rest were frame, with sawn timber from Kane's Falls so convenient near. And one of stone, with each stone shaped to square, and two-three others of uncut stone. And two more of brick. They'd last forever, you could depend on it, but they looked to be mighty cold. And scarce a house but had glass to most its windows, and some had paint. But land sakes, with so many folk around you'd think there would be someone with enough gumption not to plant elms to each side the road. Elms weren't fit for fruit nor fuel nor fencing. Someone had ought to tell them. 'Twould be no more than neighborly. But likely they were all so rich they didn't care.

Ahead, there, was the church, big as a barn, painted a gleaming white, with a bell in a kind of a small corn-crib atop.

Young'un shut her eyes tight. She didn't aim to spoil the surprise by letting it creep up on her gradual. Eldest's new home was right beside the church, she'd said so last time she rode over to Meeting, a-pillion behind Preacher. That was two months back. But she wouldn't tell any more, and just teased Young'un and Dan'l to come and see for themselves. Forgetting she was, already, how slow oxen moved, and that a farm didn't tend itself.

The wagon stopped. Dan'l jumped down to hitch. Young'un opened her eyes. There it was, kind of a white painted lean-to against the church, with a real brick chimney above, and steps to the door, and glass in the two little windows that fronted this way. Behind one of the windows a curtain parted.

Young'un nigh to've pitched face down on the plank sidewalk,

210

forgetting the bearskin. But she was up the path, and on the doorstep before Eldest opened the door. And hugging Eldest, though kind of careful, almost before Eldest could bid her welcome and to wipe her feet.

Eldest had fleshed up, even in the face. But she didn't look to be as far along as Phebe, which was kind of disappointing, only you must not let her guess it. She was doing the best she could, you could depend on it.

Dan'l stumped up the path with a sack of corn. There wasn't a place to set it among all the tables and chairs and book-shelf and geraniums and what-all. And the floor so scrubbed, with rugs laid about on it, that you couldn't set the sack down if there had been space. Eldest grabbed Dan'l, sack and all, and kissed him just as warm as she'd kissed Young'un. Wedlock hadn't soured her any.

After that they all went out and led the wagon round back by a track that ran betwixt the two houses, and unloaded what was for Preacher and Eldest. Not forgetting Cicero's honey nor the message from Aunt Mary. Then, joyous still, off to a neighbor to find barn space for the wagon and goods, and stabling for the horses. And the neighbor lady warned them to lock the door after and not loan the key to anybody. Preacher hadn't led all the Fort Anners onto the road to righteousness yet, seemed as if.

Dan'l came back to see the new pump, and Eldest showed him how it worked, and told how it wouldn't freeze, not in the hardest winter. Dan'l allowed as how he'd have one some day for the barn. The way his feet tangled with the hooked rug was more than you'd believe, unless you saw with your own eyes. And he got so he was afraid to sit on one of the chairs, and scared to stand, and allowed he'd go see to the team, just in case, and then go find the shoesmith, the one who came up to the settlement. He'd heard the ring of the anvil, driving in.

Eldest wouldn't talk about the baby; babies in a town being different from those born in the country, kind of secret. But she showed the big Bible and other presents from the congregation. And Preacher's own books, a whole shelf of ten, one written in Latin. Eldest said Preacher could turn the words all back into English. Seemed waste to turn it into Latin and turn it back again so you could understand what was written, like ploughing a pasture under, and then turning the sods right side up again. But Eldest said she'd heard tell the book had been made way back before there was English to make it of. Eldest would believe most anything.

Preacher hurried in with a lady of the congregation, and hurried out to find Dan'l, leaving the lady to talk. Which was what she did. Eldest drew a bag of sewing to her lap, and answered, "Yes, Ma'am. Ain't that so, Ma'am!" But Young'un just had to set and set, and wish she was off with Dan'l; or anyways that she'd brought her best meeting gown, and not the plain tow one. 'Twas a mercy when the lady had to go off and tend her cooking.

Preacher came back with Dan'l, and they had a fine blessing for the meal. Only, the we-thank-thee-Lord came too close on its heels for Dan'l to fill up the way he was used at home.

After that Preacher showed his lot of land out back. A spade-garden, too small to turn a team and plough, but with berry canes, apple and pear trees, and a new grapevine. Dan'l snuck off again, and Preacher was called away. And my land if there wasn't more setting to do. Seemed like Fort Anners would wear out ten-'leven chair bottoms a year. Not telling what 'twould do to their own.

Still and all it was good to be with Eldest again, even if she wouldn't talk about her baby, nor even Phebe's. But talk of Phebe reminded Young'un of the list, and she got Eldest to read it all over to her out loud so she'd see had she forgotten aught. She profited to rub up on her ciphering, so she'd be able to tell if the storekeeper at the Falls set down the right values for Eph's winter pelts. It wouldn't serve to have your next-neighbor cheated by a foreigner.

Preacher slept across the way at his Aunt Johanna's that night so Young'un could bundle in with Eldest, and leave Dan'l the bearskin and a quilt on the living-room floor. With the wagon ready loaded, and only the team to water and feed, they were up and off before there was ary other chimney smoke in the town. Young'un walked a piece, to rest up after all that setting.

There wasn't aught to the journey, after being told. First you headed for Kingsbury, which didn't amount to much, being smaller than Fort Ann by a good six houses, and mighty few folks about. And not much beyond but sand and bog and pine woods. Dan'l reached over his rifle and set it between his knees, ready to jump down and shoot him a mess of meat to carry back to Eldest. A teamster with six horses and a long whip called out not to fire for he warn't no enemy. Which showed he was city-folks, to take account of a little rifle like that.

It wasn't till the Falls itself that you had to take aholt of yourself and work to believe what you saw and heard. The roar and snarl of the gang saws in the mills reached out beyond the first house. The spring thaw in the Hudson River was a ways ahead of Wood Creek, for they hadn't been more than breaking out the water wheel back at Kane's Falls. Folks seemed in the same kind of haste as the thaw, not opening their stride the way they should to make time on a trail, but kind of jiggling along like a horse in hobbles. Most ready to pitch forward on their faces, they seemed, if they didn't reach the doorway they aimed for. And excepting Dan'l, not a soul in sight but was dressed in cloth. And buildings set so tight together 'twas a wonder they knew whose was which.

The roar of the river got deeper, deeper, till 'twas lower than Uncle Gam singing in Meeting, the lowest note ever. Too low to catch in your ears, but you heard it in your backbone and right down to your toes. Roaring, it was, to tell the saws to quit their babble. But the saws kept right on with their snarl-cluck, snarl-cluck, filling the air with the scent of pine lumber, knowing they were safe on shore.

And there, 'twixt two rows of buildings, was the Falls itself. Even Dan'l couldn't help but draw up. Taller than a house, taller than the highest first-growth tree, the water pounding down all lathered with fury and fit to be tied. Only there wasn't nothing under all the sunny heavens had the strength to tie it, nor never would.

"Don't hardly cal'late to find a use for it," said Dan'l, being Dan'l. "Not on the farm." And he slapped the reins and called to the team, to git on.

The store was most under the Falls itself, being first-settler old. You knew it right away by the big shingle nailed across above the door, with a beaver painted on. Young'un was starting to carry in Dan'l's pelts, but Dan'l said Eph's must come first, seeing he'd loaned the wagon. Could be the storekeeper would 'bate the price when he saw how many pelts there were altogether. And Dan'l had the right of it.

There had been a heap of pelts and goods passed across the wide worn counter, and the storeman hardly looked up before he started casting the pelts this way and that, riffling up the fur of the best ones with his thumbnail, and turning them over or raising them to his nose when he misdoubted the curing. Young'un told him to set down the values, and watched while he did it. Then they brought in Eph's other goods.

"Set 'Ephraim Birdsell' atop the paper," Dan'l told the man, and said how Eph would be victualing later, on account of Phebe's expecting.

The man made up a bundle of the things on Phebe's list, then searched around the store and came back with, of all things, a bone teething ring. "Seeing 'tis Eph's first, in a manner of speaking, likely he ain't provided," he explained. Young'un thanked him for the gift and sized him up afresh. Even at second glance he wasn't much to look at. Short and fat, most bare on top, and greased all the way down the front from his trade.

He didn't 'bate the price a jot for Dan'l's pelts and maple syrup and such. And he got right friendly when Dan'l told how he was named.

"Don't happen you're kin to old Zeph Post? Your pelts kind of 'mind me of his'n, but your sugar's cleaner. Zeph's was too all-fired smoky."

Young'un nigh to've yawped for joy, or leaped the counter and hugged him, grease and all. He knew Pa, or used to, and 'twas that she had been hoping. 'Twas for that, and what it might mean, that she had plagued Dan'l to let her come, and not stay back to tend the farm.

"Pa still trade here?" she asked. It wasn't beyond hope, Pa being so sot in his ways.

But Trader hadn't set eyes on Pa for a season or more. Two-three old-timers still traded down here from the north, and he would pass word back to old Zeph that his young'uns were making out good and that one had married her a preacher.

Dan'l thanked him.

Young'un waited. Waited while the man did his figuring. The prices he set on the crocks, and the salt, three bushels of oats, and the skillet in place of the one the fire had cracked, left enough over for other buying. Shirt cloth for Dan'l and Meeting shoes for herself, a loaf of sugar, and a pinch of tea. Powder and lead and flints Dan'l could get from Gunsmith in exchange for charcoal and suchlike. And when they could think of no other thing they coveted it still left money owing.

Young'un waited, saying nothing, while the man set down on paper what was still due to the Posts, so they could give it to Eph to trade for them later. They loaded up, and thanked the trader for the goods. And Dan'l went around the store to the back to draw water for the team. 'Twas the moment for which Young'un had waited.

She ran back into the store. "Please to send word to Pa we're hankering for a sight of him." She brought it out all of a breath. "Tell him to come; but tell him, he don't need to stop unless he's so minded."

And she was back, sitting on the wagon plank, wrapping the bearskin robe about her, when Dan'l came back.

There wasn't so much as a shoe cast or a load harmed all the way back to Fort Ann. Nor any news there, except that Eldest had been given a hen and a setting of eggs, and wouldn't Young'un like them for the farm, seeing the price of feed was so high in Fort Ann? And hens so liable to stray and harm neighbors' gardens?

She'd ought to've told Eldest of her message to Pa, Young'un knowed right well she'd ought. But she gave Eldest the victualing present—'twas another bone teething ring like the one they were carrying up to Phebe—and she bundled in for the night with Eldest, and drove off in the morning still without saying.

Right back to the farm she was, and asking Peter'n' Paul and heifer how they had fared and had they missed her, and Dan'l off driving the empty wagon back to Eph's. And still she couldn't say had she done right or wrong to pass word to Pa to come home. Though once come, he didn't need to stop unless he happened to be so minded.

All she purposed was to let Dan'l see him once again, and know him for what he really was, and not what Dan'l was stretching him out to be. Dan'l with his Pa-this and Pa-t'other, and getting his fancies all warped and cockled.

Poor Dan'l, 'twould be kill or cure! And a long whiles for Young'un to wait and worry over which way it would turn out.

CHAPTER NINETEEN

WHEN Dan'l and Young'un went down on their spring victualing they left the dregs of winter behind. When they reached home again, but three days later, by all signs and smells and the feel in their veins 'twas the forepart of summer. Popple and birch were in bud, and even apple; birds that hadn't been seen for weeks were hip-hopping everywhere; Peter'n' Paul and the heifer took a bite here and there, just sampling to see where this year's grazing would profit most. Taverner's bees were buzzing around, visiting the catkins and bringing in bee-bread just as fast as they could fly.

Dan'l took up a handful of soil and squeezed it to judge whether it was fitten to plough, though knowing right well it could not be. Next he bethought himself he would need a bag for broadcasting the oats, and seeing that Young'un was more easy spared than himself, sent her down to the settlement to beg the loan of Gunsmith's against the time it would be needed. Forehanded was Dan'l.

Young'un danced her way down, filling her moccasins with wet from the wheel-ruts that the frozen ground below wouldn't let to drain away, and not caring. For soon it would be barefoot time when the toes could be loosed from their trammels and take a real grip of stone and twig and earth. Except for the new shoes for Meeting she would be foot-free till fall, just like a little'un. No matter what season of the year you were born, 'twas in springtime you added an extra year to your age. You sloughed the old, and hadn't yet taken on the new. Could be that the last footprint you made and left behind belonged to a girl. And somewheres ahead the foot you set down would be the foot of a growed-up.

"Please you, Mist' Reed," she would say, the way Ma used to talk, "to lend my brother Dan'l the loan of your broadcasting bag."

Only, when she came to the forge she found herself calling Gunsmith "Uncle Gam," same as usual. Which showed she wasn't growed yet, nor like to be for another two-three weeks or more.

Aunt Mary found her the bag, and said to keep it if it would serve, as Uncle Gam didn't use it any more. Young'un was out the door again, turning the leather bag this way and that to see where it would need patching, when she caught sight of Taverner.

Being there was no one in sight she hurried across to give him the good news of his bees. He needed it bad, for he drew her down the garden to his remaining butts, and showed her the empty ones that Sol had robbed for Mis' Ditch, and two that had empty combs and dead bees.

Young'un told him quick about his butts up to the Post place, how the bees were all out flying, and looked to have wintered over in good strength except for the two butts to the west that were kind of puny. To see his little face twist up with happiness, you would think he had news of his firstborn, and not a lot of pesky little bugs.

"What's more, they're to-gathering bee-bread on their legs, yellow and orange and a kind of gray-green." She had put her head right close to the holes the bees went in and out, to make sure, and not been stung once. "Could be they're finding it from the willow catkins, and maybe popple. There's little else so early in the season."

"Bee-bread means they have bee-maggots to feed. And bee-maggots will be flying bees in a month's time." Cicero slapped his knees the way he did when his face wouldn't twist up any further. "Just right for the wild cherry, and to set your apple-blossom to fruit. And time and to spare to breed more bees to gather from the wild grape blossom and the sumach, and . . ."

He'd have gone on more, only Mis' Ditch called from the 'Tavern, "Cicero! Cicero Ditch! Where are ye idling at?" just like he was a bound-boy. And he scuttled away right fast to do her bidding.

Young'un turned, and ran up the garden to the road. For she knew the sound of the Broadmoor wagon most anywhere, and cal'lated to tell, without seeing, if 'twas Hank driving. And he was, and pulled up mighty polite.

He asked: "Wasn't that Cicero Ditch with you?" And sat there black as a storm cloud on Mount Diameter, not stretching down a

218

hand to hoist her up so they could ride together as far as Eph's where he was heading.

"I don't hold with old men pestering around after girls, nor with girls seeking them out." He talked low and slow like his pa, and made his words sound kind of weighty. "Old married men at that."

"Nor I don't hold with nigh-to-growed men tagging around all the whiles with baby sisters. Nor it don't seem they've the right to be jealous." It was out before she could check it.

Hank sat there, fingering the reins, and hoping, she knew right well, that she would give some reason for being with Cicero. Hank had grown first puzzled, then jealous over the little Taverner. 'Twould have been easy to set his doubts at rest, but the bees were Taverner's secret. And if you couldn't stay by a friend's secret you weren't scarce fit for Christian burying.

Hank looked at the sowing bag, as though that might tell; but it didn't. He gave a kind of grunt that you could call a sigh and not be far out. Then he slapped the reins on his team and drove on.

Young'un waited till he was past, and let out her breath. And folks who didn't know better would have called that a sigh, too. When she and Peter 'n' Paul drew up Taverner's bee-butts last fall there hadn't been so much as an inkling in her mind of how things would shape up, and that the bees could ever come betwixt her and Hank.

But if he thought he had a right, so much as a jot or tittle of a right, to be angered . . . Young'un swung the bag over her shoulder, and marched off up the road, as free and as joyous-seeming as her tow skirt and her thoughts would let. She started to whistle a tune as she passed Hank's wagon standing outside the Birdsells', but changed to a song, that being more fitting to a woman-growed. The song barely carried her beyond earshot of house and wagon. Then kind of wilted.

* * *

Back to the farm there was no time for moping like an old broody-hen, what with the borrowed bag to patch where the mice had chawed it, and Dan'l calling for a hand with this and with that which he had to redd up all of a sudden. Spring wasn't so much a season as a boundary fence, and summer would be here swift as a cat's leap, once the frost was out the ground.

And 'twas the weather to bring all the children out of the settlement, and likely the last day they would get to come, now that
their pas, like Daniel, were fixing to plough and drag and sow. And
the children had to be enticed down to the lower meadow, away
from the butts. And at that one of them took note of the bees that
were a-wing, and had to be turned from hunting a bee-tree. Cicero's
secret wasn't like to keep, as the weather warmed.

With the children all gone home, a peace settled in with the
twilight. Dan'l looked as near to contented as Dan'l ever could, eating his supper and mulling over his plans for the coming year.
Young'un tried to count her blessings, the way Ma had taught. A
thriving farm with good stock, food and drink for the belly and
clothes for the back, and naught wrong with her health up to the
time of the quarrel with Hank this morning. Since then she suspicioned she was ailing a mite, and was fixing to lose her taste for
good victuals. There was still food before her when Dan'l said his "We
thank Thee, Lord," and pushed back his stool.

And there, at the open door, stood Hank.

She bade him welcome, with a smile. And Hank smiled back and
said the evening being so warm he had thought to walk over. Then
he reached himself a stool, and sat.

Neither he nor Young'un having a wish to hark back to the
quarrel, they watched Dan'l take the lantern and go out to the barn.
And watched him come back again. Just as though 'twas a new happening, the like of which neither had seen before.

But without Consolation to coddle, or Taverner to out-talk, Hank
was more the way he ought to be, telling Dan'l what his pa planned
to sow in this field and in that, and Dan'l telling his plans in return.
Companionable it was, with Young'un joining in, as she finished her
redding up from supper and blew out the candle. And all three enjoying the silences in between. The fire covered over against morning, the day's work done and everything in place, the three of them
sitting there, elbows on table, and voices getting softer and lower.

It might be the relief at being let to keep silent when she'd
as lief, and talk when she had aught to say; but 'twas the happiest
evening for a sixmonth. It could last but a little longer, Young'un
knew, for Hank would need to light out for home. He said once he'd

best be getting along, and Dan'l said not to, it wasn't that late. 'Twas then all three of them heard what sounded to be steps outside. Dan'l reached down his rifle from over the hearth, and, the best he could by feel, shook in fresh priming. Might be most anything from porcupine to deer, porcupine being mighty noisy for their size.

Before Dan'l had done, the steps, human steps, came running. And there in the doorway was Taverner, dark against the starlight outside.

"Where's the axe?" he was trying not to shout. "Give me the axe!"

Young'un pushed past him to the barn, and set the axe in his hand as he came hurrying after. She'd scarce done it when she wished she hadn't, for Taverner was whispering to himself, most out of his mind.

"You can drive a man just so far, and this time 'tis too far." As luck had it he headed towards the old shelter where the bees were, and not back to the house and Hank. "One poisons my bees, and the other spies on me. I don't care which of you 'tis, but come out from among my butts! I'm a-going to kill you!"

There was a sound inside the old shelter. All Young'un could think to do was to step up close behind Taverner, as he waited at the doorway, hoping to grab the axe before he could turn and see Hank standing behind.

But before she could make the grab, a side of the shelter beside her burst out, boughs, twigs and all, and someone pushed through carrying a whole bee-butt clasped to his stomach. Young'un jumped back a pace, startled. The axe swung up, glinted in the starlight and came down. The thief dropped with a moan. Before Young'un or Dan'l or Hank could run in, Taverner had struck again so hard the axe helve snapped. Something warm, blood by the smell, spurted over Young'un. And the next that happened was bees, hundreds, thousands, from the fallen butt.

The bees drove Hank and Dan'l back. Taverner dropped the useless axe helve to stop the butt from rolling further down the hill. It took all the courage Young'un had left to kneel down beside the dark figure, sprawled out and kicking, to see was it past hope. Its last kick, before it lay still, threw her backward.

But what she had seen was enough. She rolled over and jumped to her feet. She could have sung with joy. 'Twas all she could do not to laugh, out of plain happiness to think what might have been and wasn't. For Taverner was no murderer. Taverner had done what would have him talked about and envied from here to the Falls. Even after he was dead there'd be folks to say, "Ain't heard of Cicero Ditch? Why, he was the feller that took an axe and killed . . ."

"A bear!" 'Twas Hank yelled it. "The goshdangdest old bear I ever heard tell of!"

And Dan'l, forgetful of the bees, which weren't stinging anyway on account the dark and the chill, bent down to see closer. "Pretty nigh chopped his head off, did Taverner!" and there was a hush to his voice which told how 'mazed he was.

Taverner had set the butt upright, and was standing there among his bees, wondering belike what had come over him a few moments back. Or could be he was at a loss what next to do, seeing the axe was broken, and the bear dead. He wiped a hand across his face, and then his mind seemed to catch on to the tag end of what Dan'l had just said.

"Serve him right, coming pestering my bees." It didn't sound like Taverner at all, not angry any more, but almighty sure and determined. "You Young'un, go fetch a light. And we'll set the butt back on the stand."

And as Young'un ran back to the cabin to blow up an ember for a light, she heard him tell Hank and Dan'l and the woods and the stars and any else, "Yessir, I cal'late I'm all through with my bees being pestered. Now on, ain't nobody going to touch my bees without I say so."

When she was back with the blazing stick, not stopping to light the lantern, Taverner stirred the dead beast with his foot and said, "If I'd known 'twas only a dumb critter that knew no better than to rob, I don't know as I'd have had the heart to kill him. I thought 'twas—" He checked himself. "But I cal'late least said's soonest mended."

Dan'l looked at Hank, and Hank at Dan'l. Mighty solemn, the both of them. They said no word, but at Taverner's bidding brought

222

a couple of poles, and another light. And one held the light and another guarded the tinder-dry old hemlock boughs, while Taverner and Young'un carried back the butt and set it up again in its place.

Next day all the men and women and young and old of the neighborhood dropped their work to come and say Ooh! and Aah! at the sight of the bear that Dan'l and Hank were skinning in the cool of the barn. All except two, Mis' Ditch and Taverner.

Folk brought up word that he was busy working on his butts back of the Tavern, taking out the rocks while he boasted of how he'd drawn the wool over Hepziba's eyes and saved his bees last fall. He claimed he wasn't interested in the bear, seeing it was dead and could rob no more hives, and that Dan'l could have it, hide and meat the both, to pay for the axe handle Taverner had broke.

There were folks who said how Cicero's standing up to Hepziba was a sight braver than his standing up to the bear, seeing he wouldn't have to live with the bear after, and had had an axe to help his side of the argument. Mostly the talk gave him a week to a month before Mis' Ditch had him back to where she cal'lated he belonged. Poor Taverner! Young'un was heart-sorry for him.

Hank's pa came around just after Hank and Dan'l and the young'uns had taken the hide down to the stream to wash off the blood. Most of the older folk had set off home again, except for the Widow Wilson and Mis' Miller who had stopped behind to help with the rendering down. Heifer and Peter 'n' Paul, who couldn't abide the smell of bear blood, were down in the far corner of the pasture. So Viney had to leave the womenfolk at the fireside and show Mist' Broadmoor where the carcass lay. It wasn't so big, without its thick fur, but more human looking.

He looked at it a long while, considering; and it wasn't the bear he was considering, for he didn't examine its teeth or its paws, nor give a guess at its age and weight, the way the others had. Hank must have told him there was more to last night's happening than met the eye. And his next words proved it.

"There's times I'd sooner stand than lay." He looked at the dead beast and his large hand rubbed his neck just where Cicero's axe had bitten into the bear. "Nor I don't hanker after being rendered

223

down in Viney Post's kettle, nor have my hide pegged out on the barn door." He grinned, and Young'un grinned back, to show she understood.

"There's folks that's quicker witted than the Broadmoors," he admitted. "But from now on I don't aim to meddle with Cicero's bees. Nor others ain't like to neither. Not whilst there's an axe handy in the valley."

He made for the door. "Well, I got a sight of tasks back home, and that Hank of mine running the roads . . ." He broke off, did Hank's pa, to look Viney Post up and down from the stirring-spoon in her hand to the patch she had let in to her deerskin shirt where it had grown too tight across the bosom; the tow gown had been set to dry after washing out the spots of bear blood. "Hank's got more sense to him than I thought," he said. And strode off up the trail.

There wasn't time for Viney to figure out his meaning, for she had the crocks and kettles to see to, and the receipts for laying down the bear meat to listen to. The beast wasn't like a fall bear, rich in winter fat, but still and all the meat would be welcome. And what couldn't, for lack of fat, be laid down to keep, could be easy exchanged for the two young pigs Dan'l wanted to pasture in the woods on acorns and roots.

But best of all was when Hank came in with a foreleg to strip and cook. "Pa says there ain't nobody but Cicero smart enough to bait a bear with honey, nor crazy enough to lay into it with an axe."

Looked like he had more to say, but couldn't, account of the women milling around the fireplace. Viney went out with him, to show which joint she'd take next. Hank stopped her just outside the door, as she'd kind of thought he might.

"Don't seem I've showed the sense God gave me, last few months," he admitted, "but for one thing."

Young'un asked what that was.

"Lettin' on I was going courting."

CHAPTER TWENTY

The hawk, poised on an air current which rose each blazing August day from the bare cliff front above the lake, caught sight of something below. It slid out of the up-draft towards the Post farm. A long slow glide and its hopes were justified. That white chicken was beyond the protection of the mother hen. The hawk seemed to over-balance forward from an invisible ledge, its wings closed for a dive and it hurtled downward.

As the hawk struck, a few fluffy chicken feathers floated off. Then a rifle cracked. The killer lay beside its victim, both dead. Dan'l picked up the hawk, Young'un ran to see if the chicken could be nursed back to life.

"Knowed right well 'twould be the white chick next." Dan'l boasted his judgment. "But the shooting was chancy; as likely a miss as a hit. Consarn the old hawk! I hope 'tis the one killed the other two chicks."

Young'un considered the chicken. "Don't know but it's too small to cook, but I'll try. No harm to seething the hawk, I cal'late. Hawks being clean feeders."

Dan'l handed over the hawk and looked carefully at his rifle. "Seems the frizzen steel's a mite hollowed with wear, so the flint doesn't spark so good. That's the why of the misfire when I tried to shoot the old hawk as 'twas a-hover before diving. Guess I'll carry the rifle down to Gunsmith's and see can I fix it."

It didn't serve to cry over spilt milk, Young'un knew, nor dead chicks neither. If this second setting had been mischancy, the first setting, those Eldest had given, had been more fortunate. They had hatched all but two, and only one lost. Cat had killed that. And though it went to Young'un's heart to tie the poor little ball of fluff around Cat's neck for two days, it had cured Cat of chicken stealing. Cat did no more than look sideways at the others, after.

For all his shooting the wild ones, Dan'l felt the same as Young'un about tame birds and beasts, holding himself responsible if aught befell them. "Should have built 'em a biddy-coop at the first off, and fixed them a pen with bird-scarers over." He followed Young'un back into the house to pick up two-three things to take down to the settlement. "Pa would have fixed a right good pen, long since."

Young'un kept silent. She tried the water in the kettle hung from the lug pole to see was it hot enough to scald the feathers for plucking. But it was no more than lukewarm, and the fire scarce smoldering. No one in this hot August weather kept more fire than was needful. There had been heat enough and to spare last week, making and carrying that first cut of hay in the west meadow. She set to coaxing up the fire.

Bending down to blow on the fine slivers of kindling, she had most forgotten Dan'l when he paused in the doorway to say aggravatingly: "Yessir, Young'un, you were a sight too little to remember Pa as he really was. Likely he'd have raised every one of those chicks."

He was on his way before Young'un could spare breath from blowing up the fire. Not that she would have known what to say. She drew up a flame, fed more chips and kindling, and still she didn't know. Dan'l and his Pa-worship was different from all the other troubles that rightly went with a farm; different because there was just no sense to the crazy idea he'd hatched about Pa. 'Twas like a maggot in Dan'l's brain. And she hadn't the skill, even if she'd known how, to take it out.

First off, when Pa went away, it had been a help. Not knowing where first to set his hand to all that needed doing, Dan'l had remembered what Pa had done, and set to copying him. It didn't come natural to a boy of Dan'l's age to run a whole farm, so likely he'd taken to thinking of himself as Pa, to work up the courage he'd had need of. It had served him well, for not Hank, nor even most growed men, could have done all that Dan'l had. Or would have if they could. Times both she and Dan'l had been too mortal weary to eat, or hold the food they'd eaten. Once in that first year Dan'l had hoisted her across Peter's back when she couldn't make shift to trudge even the few rod from the lower meadow up to bed. There was the time they'd thought to've finished hoeing the corn, only to find there were three more rows, and she and Dan'l had finished those rows weeping like little'uns, for all they tried not. And that was why Young'un just couldn't go down to Eldest or to Phebe or even to Aunt Mary and tell about Dan'l and ask what to do. Whatever was to be done lay betwixt her and Dan'l, and no other. Unless it might be Pa.

And Pa hadn't come. For all she had sent word to him through the trader at the Falls. Could be he'd met with a mishap, and wouldn't never come.

Young'un stood at the door just for a moment to look out and down, over the land. No comfort in all the world could come up to the feel you got from a good farm. And she needed comfort bad. The garden, with its vegetables standing so strong against the burning heat of the sun, drew growth from the soil and moisture beneath them. Hidden by the dark blue-green of the cabbages, the big greedy leaves of the squash and the tall corn, were the beans, the potatoes, the roots, and all else that would keep her and Dan'l in health and strength right through next winter. There would be enough over to spare a taste to the hens and cattle, if only she could keep the piglets out. Those pigs had cost more time in fencing than they seemed to be worth. But when fall came they would be loosed to rooting and gleaning the woods for mast and acorns. Then would come killing and pickling. And all winter your teeth would give thanks to your hands.

It had got so that Young'un took Dan'l's farm for granted. The oats that had answered all his hopes and better; the corn that was as good as any could be found hereabouts. The pasture and hay were as clean as her and Dan'l's toil could make them. Peter 'n' Paul, always willing to help and do as bid, were as fine farmers as Dan'l himself. Heifer would soon have her calf, and likely 'twould be a good one, seeing it was got from the Broadmoor bull. With milk for themselves and the chicks, and to make butter and cheese, and the little calf . . .

"Why, Phebe!" Young'un hurried out to take the shawled bundle from the other's arms. "To walk all this way, and carrying the baby too! You hadn't ought to've, so soon!"

227

She had Phebe indoors for the coolness, on a stool and her back to the wall to rest, all so fast and anxious that Phebe laughed aloud at her care. Young'un laughed too, just for company. And when Phebe turned back the shawl from the little red wrinkled face, land sakes! but he was trying to join in, seemed like. Then the little critter belched, real as life, and set Young'un to laughing again.

Proud as proud, Phebe set to suckling him. For a light woman she was nobly breasted, as Eph must have told her time and again. And the way the little'un lit into his sucking was a sight to see. Though when he'd all done he'd scarce eased the tightness under Phebe's white skin. If Phebe was kind of slow in covering up again, 'twas easy understood. And she flushed all up her neck for pleasure when Young'un said, "My, Phebe, you'd ought to've had twins, at least!"

"He'll grow to need it all," said Phebe. "I don't aim to wean him too soon. Maybe not till the next is well along."

Phebe Birdsell was like that, talking straight out, knowing Young'un would be married herself some day and needing to understand such things. And that reminded Young'un to tell that there'd been no news of Eldest, though 'twas high time. Preacher when he came up to Meeting was no help at all. He hemmed and hawed, and seemed like he thought the baby would be given him by a well-wisher of the parish, same as he'd been given the big Bible.

"There's wisdom to not counting your chickens afore they're hatched," Young'un declared. "But you'd ought to know how many eggs you set under the hen, and plan according." Meaning of course there'd be need of two sets of everything if it turned out twins.

Could be there was another meaning to her words, for Phebe laughed so that she came near to crying. And wouldn't say why. Seemed like she wanted to get home to tell Eph though, for she set out, right after. Young'un saw her the whole way home, and was let to carry the baby so she wouldn't be angry when Phebe burst out laughing, time and again. For all that, Young'un was kind of riled. Married secrets couldn't be as comical as all that.

Hot it was, and in the woods the birds and insects were still. Outside, on the Birdsell farm, 'twas close and choking with the heat, though the sun glare had gone and the clouds blanketed the sky. Young'un turned and hurried home. For if a storm broke, likely the young chicks wouldn't have the sense to get to cover. Ducklings were worse, it was said, dying of fright even inside a closed barn if the thunder growled. She was most home before the first drops, like falling acorns, began to patter on the leaves.

The mother hen was clucking the last of her brood into the barn, so there had been no call for haste after all. Young'un stopped just inside the barn door, listening to the first drumming of the rain on the hard dry ground. Then hearing the sound ease up and change as the surface softened. The first cut of hay being in the barn, a good steady fall would bring on the second cut. Pasture and roots could do with two-three days of this, and if it didn't help the corn any, it wouldn't harm. A farmer had ought to be grateful if he got more gain than loss, not ask for outright gain all around like the man who prayed, "Lord, make a duckpond of my roots and my pasture, but don't let ary a drop fall on my hay that lies betwixt them."

* * *

Young'un was lingering for a last sniff of the damp earth when who should pelt out, down the trail, but Amy and Dan'l. Not laughing and making play of the rain and pretended fear of the wet, but Dan'l lowering, and Amy kind of wild-eyed.

Dan'l went straight for the oily rag he kept in the hunting bag, and began to wipe down his rifle without even bidding Amy to set. Amy stood at the door, shaking the wet from her clothes. She raised one eyebrow, the way she did, times, kind of pointing back at Dan'l.

"Something's come over your Dan'l, Viney. I dunno what." That was another trick of Amy's, to speak of someone as though he couldn't hear, or weren't under the same roof-tree. "He come up with me on the trail, and I made for him to pass, seeing he was running. He wouldn't pass, and wouldn't answer but yes or no, and seemed almighty glum. Thinking 'twas his precious rifle he was frighted to get wet, I set to running, and him after. With that deef and dumb brother of yours pounding along with his rifle I felt I was like to have my scalp lifted any moment. Land sake, Viney, I was almighty glad to see another paleface standing in your doorway."

Viney chuckled. But Dan'l gave a kind of growl.

Amy shook off a few more drops and went and stood before the fireplace, under pretence of drying. Dan'l had to reach up over her to hook the rifle in its crotches, and walk around her to spread the oil rag to dry, and again to hang up the hunting bag. Amy just went on talking as though he wasn't there.

"If 'twas only the rifle he worrited over, he'll be himself again right away. If not, we've got to find out what ails him. Ain't like to be the rheumatiz? I've heard tell that old folks gets the aches bad before a summer storm."

And from rheumatiz she went on to toothache, and to summer scours from eating too many blackberries. It took Amy no time at all to run through all the ailments Dan'l might have, while Dan'l got redder and angrier, and finally made for the door. Amy's taunt caught him just in time.

"Dan'l's almighty scared of girls, ain't he, Viney? Shouldn't wonder but what the sight of a big growed woman would give him conniption fits."

Dan'l just had to turn and come back. He kind of drove his feet down onto the floor to show he wasn't to be budged, not by any girl, or woman either.

"Since you've got to poke your nose into what don't concern you, Amy Higgins, 'tis this that ails me." He tried to glare from Amy to Viney and back, but seeing they were at opposite ends of the room 'twas hard to do. "There's talk at the forge that Hank's courting our Young'un. Not pretence, like last winter. But courting to marry. And Pa wouldn't hold with such. Not while there's work to be done on the farm."

So that was it. Dan'l was taking Hank's courting serious now. And serious with Dan'l meant life and death serious.

"It ain't right. There's three already to the Broadmoor farm, not counting Consolation. And there's only two here." Dan'l held to the nub of his trouble. "If Young'un is wed, there's four to the Broadmoor farm, and only one left here."

Looked at that way there was sense to Dan'l's worry. Young'un could see that. And Amy had set aside her teasing and looked real sorry for him.

"But nature's nature, Dan'l. And you wouldn't want that Viney here should grow to be an old thorn-back for lack of a man?" Then Amy's eyes wrinkled a little at the corners. "My land, Dan'l, I'd not be beholden to my pa for everything! If I called myself a farmer I'd raise my own stock, human as well as critter. You'll want young'uns of your own before you're old. And soonest bred is soonest growed."

There was a sight of horse-sense to Amy Higgins. But 'twas more than Dan'l could do to see it yet, the state he was in. And then, if that wasn't quarrel enough, Hank had to come pounding in, wet as a drowned rat.

"Word's just come up by the coach, and guess what?" He didn't so much as stop to wring water from his coat. "Eldest's bore a son. And they're thriving fine, the both of 'em!"

Amy and Viney wanted more news. But it seemed Hank had told all there was. Coach driver had said just that, and no more. And Hank had lit out from where he was sheltering at the forge, and, rain or no rain, run all the way.

Dan'l was forgotten till he spoke. "You get out of here, Hank Broadmoor. And don't ever come back!"

Hank grinned, thinking 'twas maybe some kind of a joke.

"There's no bad blood betwixt us, Hank." Dan'l milded down a mite. "But I'll have no one come courting our Viney. Not till Pa gets home and gives his say-so."

"If Hank had done a smidgin of real courting there'd be more sense to your talk, Dan'l." Young'un couldn't help but break in.

Hank and Dan'l didn't seem to hear her. "Don't seem I'd ought to wrestle you, nor fight you, Dan'l." Hank's big hands swung helplessly at his sides. "Don't hardly cal'late to know what-all to do."

So they stood there, like two bumps on a log. And seemed they'd be standing there still, only the rain lifted, and Amy said, "I'd best be getting along." And took Hank with her.

Viney wrenched herself out of the house and set off after. It was that, or lay into Dan'l with the heavy pestle, or break his precious rifle across his head. The way she felt just then she wasn't to be depended on, and she knew it. She would let none harm Dan'l save herself; but short of killing him there wasn't, this minute, a hurt but she'd be glad to give him. Sorry she might be after, but not now.

If she'd a mind never to marry, and to get to be an old thornback, that was for her to say. Not Dan'l. If she was minded to take a man, she'd ask no by-your-leave from any brother. A brother who was as nigh to being tetched in the head about Pa and the farm, as he could come. Fixing to be witless, he was. If not stark staring.

She was breathless, of forthright anger, when she came up with Hank and Amy.

"Dan'l had ought to get his come-uppance," said Amy soothingly.

"Sure had!" Hank was for turning back right then and there, only Amy caught his arm.

"No call to set to fist-fighting." Amy smiled. "There's more ways than one to kill a cat, and I'm minded to see could we train pussy instead."

The thought of Dan'l, stocky of body and sot in mind, as a little tame pussy cat set Hank to haw-hawing, and his fists uncurled. Even Viney cracked a grin. Not that she wasn't mighty mad with Dan'l and like to stay that way.

Amy's plan was easy as Adam, the way she told it. "No girl ever went courting a man, so Dan'l will cal'late to be safe in his own home. But if he starts off to look for Viney I'll tell him I'll go help seek, and that he's to let on he's courting me if we meet up with ary person on the road. And that ought to pin him down to home, the way he's frighted of girls and womenfolk!"

It would too, you could depend upon it. And then the talk turned to Eldest's baby, and how soon she'd be up to show it around at Meeting. And Hank promised to send word down by the coach how Viney hankered to see it.

CHAPTER TWENTY-ONE

So a week later, that being the day Amy had set, Viney went down of an evening for a visit with Phebe Birdsell. And who should drop in for a word with Eph but Hank, grinning from ear to ear. And Consolation tagging along, of course. Hank's grin meant he'd seen Amy a ways up the trail. So by now Amy would be setting with Dan'l, letting on how disappointed she was not to find Viney at home, and drawing now one word and now another out of Dan'l, like long rooted oak stumps out of hard-froze ground. She would torment the life out of him, would Amy, just the way a kitten would tease. And serve Dan'l right.

It was a treat to admire Phebe's iron stove, still the only one in the countryside, and hear her tell how it could do most everything except rock the baby or walk out and plough the fields. And talk of any kind was sweet as an apple in February, for there had hardly been a single word 'twixt Viney and Dan'l all week.

What Dan'l had thought in all that silence could only be guessed. Viney's thoughts had gone back and forth like a water-bug on a pool. That Pa ought to've been down to the Falls for his wintering stores. That 'twasn't nowise fair for Albacinda to have her boy walking all the way from Hogtown, when Hank, who lived not more than a mile away, couldn't be welcomed up at the farm. That it would serve Dan'l right if she was to light out and never come back. That she'd go live with Eldest, she would. But she couldn't leave Dan'l to fend for himself, for it would be like leaving Peter'n' Paul tied up in the barn to starve, Dan'l being nigh as helpless in his way. And it all boiled down to her not knowing what to do. It lay with Pa, and whether he was minded to heed her call.

Being they were menfolk, Hank and Eph had to make pretense they'd seen enough of the baby, and Eph took Hank out to show the lathe he'd fixed up to turn trenails and spindles of chairs and suchlike. For once Consolation forgot to tag after. So she and Viney drew their stools up closer to the cradle that Phebe rocked with her foot as she sewed.

Seemed like Consolation couldn't lift her eyes from the baby. It got so Phebe stilled her chat with Viney to ask the child which did she covet most, a baby, or a slice of pie made in the iron stove only today?

"Isa bakes pies." Consolation didn't shift an eye. "But we ain't got ary a baby, not the littlest one, to home. And Pa says we ain't like to have. Can I smell?"

Cautiously she leaned over the cradle and sniffed. "Like hay, only nicer. Can I hold him if I'm mighty careful?"

Phebe let Consolation hold the baby in her arms awhile, the girl being plenty strong enough, being a Broadmoor and rising seven. When the little punkin-seed gave a gassy grin Consolation laid it back gently in the cradle, and stood watching, her mouth open, to see would it do it again.

It was entertaining to see the child. And if this wasn't courting with Hank it would pass for such when Dan'l came to hear of it. As was intended. 'Twould have been mighty peaceful but for Consolation who now had it fixed in her mind that Phebe had offered her pie or little'un; which she had, only joking. Consolation was bound she'd have the baby to take back home, and never having been thwarted or denied she wouldn't take no.

Phebe and Viney ate pie, and good it was, just to tempt the little girl from her choice of the baby. But it didn't serve. Phebe had to say right out that Eph wouldn't part from the baby.

"Not for a likely little bull calf?"

If Consolation was willing to swap the little calf she'd reared herself, it showed how set she was.

"Babies can't be bought nor traded." Phebe tried to make it plain. "Nor minted gold won't buy one, not even the very littlest."

Viney took up the chore, without an inkling of forethought of where her words would lead. Babies lived in houses, she explained,

234

just the way calves lived in barns and pastures, and you had to have all ready for them against their coming. Since babies didn't grow fur nor feathers like critters did, you had to spin and weave for them, and that took four-five years to learn to do good. Babies didn't graze nor browse, so that meant learning to raise foodstuffs and to cook. And you had to clean house mighty good, far better than you did a stall in a barn, babies being pernickety that way. And, come right down to it, you had to make the menfolks around you comfortable, else a baby wouldn't thrive. Nor God wouldn't give you a baby in the first place, not hide nor hair of one, unless you made one man real heart-happy and felt that way yourself.

And Phebe added, to clinch it, "Little'uns is a heap of care, even after."

Most any other girl rising seven would have said she'd liefer have a kitten, then. But not Consolation. A few months back she'd have bawled, and threatened to hold her breath unless she was given what she coveted. But Amy had cured her of that. This time all she did was to listen close to all Viney's rigamarole, and say, "Still and all I cal'late I'll get me a baby." Nor she wouldn't take stool and set, but stood there all evening at the foot of the cradle, watching the baby and all that Phebe did for it.

Hank and Consolation saw Viney mostways home, and allowed they'd wait for Amy. When Viney walked in, Amy and Dan'l were across from each other, elbows on table.

"My land, Viney, what a time I've had to wait!" Amy gave Viney a wink that Dan'l couldn't see. "What-all have you been up to?"

"Just courting." Viney said the words they had planned. "Hank's waiting for you up the trail. You'd ought to let him show you the stars. Never seed so many before in all my born days."

That drew a growl out of Dan'l, for he didn't know that Consolation was waiting too, or that Hank wouldn't have four-five words to say about a star, not if it was to come down and rest in his hand.

* * *

But if Hank was backward in his courting, there were some who were only too willing to do it for him; and do it worse.

Next Sunday Viney was waiting in the road, after Meeting. She had smoothed down her rose patterned gown, her hair was tidy, and

235

her shoes new greased. Half-minded she was to wait for Preacher and send a message down to Eldest, half-minded to walk up the road with Eph and Phebe. Basil, who'd been leaning on the bridge rails when Meeting came out, crossed the road smoking a seegar and came up to her.

"Guess who I come to see!" He took her by the elbow, like an old friend, which he wasn't. "You and your twin sister."

"Don't call to mind I got a twin." Viney edged off a pace, but he followed.

"You'd ought to have two or three. I'm partial to good-lookers."

Basil's talk wasn't the kind Viney was used to, and it always led where she didn't expect. Could be they used that kind of talk in towns where he was raised, but that didn't better it.

"I'll set you up the road a piece." Again he took her arm. "Suthing important to tell you."

It was part dislike, part fear of his strange ways that made Viney decline. Nor it wasn't for a married man to see a girl home from Meeting. His wife, the Widow Wilson that was, had come out of Meeting among the first, and Basil had made no move to leave the other idlers at the bridge. Seemed like the Widow could have fared further and fared better in choosing her a man.

"Got an errand to the Broadmoors." Viney picked out the Broadmoors since they hadn't been to Meeting, and since they lay out of Basil's path.

"Your ways is my ways." And Basil, pimples and all, fell in beside her, puffing his seegar.

It hurt Viney to see the savings of Basil's wife go up in smoke that way. But to hear Basil tell it he could scarce make shift to live without he had the best of clothes and tobacco and even wines. It come of the way he had been reared in cities, he explained, and his pa unable to deny him anything. And how did Viney's tastes run? Didn't she hanker for silks and velvets and suchlike? And cotillions, now, how did she like cotillions?

Cotillions sounded to be a new-fangled dish of hog's innards. Viney had nothing against hog's innards, but if Basil favored the dish she'd be bound not to. "Can't abide them," she said stoutly.

Seemed that they weren't hog-guts nor any other guts, but a kind of a dance they had at Albany. If you believed a word that Basil said, he'd spent most of his life leading these cotillions, dressed up in silk stockings, a plum-colored velvet coat and as much ruffles and lace as the Mayor of Albany himself. And the Mayor had wanted Basil to marry his only daughter. Which he would have done if he hadn't killed a man in a duel, and had to pass himself off as a peddler's son, and leave the city.

It was like the old riddle: Which way would a cow graze if it had a head and tail at each end? A sight easier to say there wasn't no such animal, and no such Basil, than to plague yourself with such imaginings.

She could have out-walked him easy but for the gown. As it was she had him blowing, and sweating the bear grease out of his slicked down hair, as he pawed at her shoulder, waved the seegar with the other hand, and told how most any day now he aimed to go back to Albany, the duel being like to be forgot by now. He'd leave his wife to manage the farm, same as before, for she wouldn't suit the gay life of Albany. Now Viney was a sight different, and would grace most any cotillion or rout or banquet . . .

Viney just had to laugh. Basil had said all this and more to Amy and Albacinda, and likely to Widow Wilson before that. And to that girl in Welsh Hollow whose pa was mad enough to cut the living lights out of Basil.

"Kind of late getting around to me, ain't you?" she mocked.

"You don't have to believe me, but some day you'll be sorry you missed . . ."

"Don't cal'late to waste time that-a-way." The Broadmoor farm was in sight. "If you've got something to say that makes sense, better say it right now. Hank don't exactly cotton to you."

Basil hesitated. He threw away the seegar and held Viney by both arms. Wasn't scarce a boy in the settlement she hadn't wrestled, from Hank down, and there'd been no harm in it, only the pleasure of finding who could beat. But there was something to Basil's soft white hands, softer than any woman's hereabouts, that was like having a worm dropped down your back at Meeting. 'Twas all Viney could do not to call out.

Basil must have guessed. His soft plump mouth spread to a grin.

237

He held her tighter. "I got a message for you. Pa, leastwise the peddler I call my pa, sent word down but yesterday. What'll you give for it? A kiss?"

Kisses weren't so much. Viney had kissed heifer, and Peter 'n' Paul of course, and others besides when she was little. She freed one arm to give Basil what wouldn't be a kiss by any manner of means, then checked the impulse. He would run yawping to his wife, and the Widow Wilson wasn't one to keep a still tongue. And Hank would hear how Viney had broke this Basil's nose or filled up his eye. And if Hank wasn't good and mad he'd likely laugh, and that would be worse. Anyways Basil had let go the other arm now and stepped back.

" 'Tis about your pa," he persisted.

"I'll swap you level then, for news of your wife. Seems you'd ought to know what everybody's saying." Viney hid her anxiety the best she could. Pa might be hurt, Pa might be in trouble. Could be he was dying even.

Basil was trying to hide something too. Men that went gallivanting around the countryside couldn't help but leave time and chance for their wives to do the same. "I . . . I got a right to know. I ain't never trusted her, not from the first. Is it that feller from Hogtown?"

"You tell first." Viney wanted to get this over with.

" 'Tain't much. Only your pa says to tell you he'll be down in the fall."

"That all? Swear?"

Hastily he swore it was. "If it's that feller from Hogtown . . ." Basil's thoughts turned to his own worry.

" 'Tain't." Viney was curt. "What folks is sayin' is . . . I don't hardly like to say."

"You got to. You promised."

"They're telling that your wife—" Viney stopped to think up a word. She was bound to make it good and strong. "—married the most no-account, spineless, useless, lying, crooked critter that ever laid claim to call himself a man." She picked up a handy piece of fence rail. "Now *get!*"

Viney didn't need to go right up to the Broadmoors, but snuck

238

round by the barn. Seemed the Broadmoors had their own troubles. Hank, Isa and their pa were out front the house waiting to go in, and from inside came the voice of little Consolation telling that Sunday or no Sunday she'd have the keeping room swept out if they didn't eat dinner till sundown. Viney swung around unseen, and headed for home. Consolation had ought to be yoked to a plough to work the devil out of her.

Soon as it was safe to, Viney began to sing. Just a hymn left over from Meeting, and without any words. For the only words that mattered were Pa's message. Pa would be down in the fall. He'd promised, and Pa would hold to his word. He was the best pa that ever was. And nigh to being the worst farmer. As Dan'l would see with his own eyes if Pa trailed in, in time to lend hand with the harvesting.

*　*　*

Amy had to call off the next courting night, account of so much work at the Higgins farm, and it was nigh on two weeks after the first time that Viney set off to visit with Phebe. She met Hank sitting on a rock beside the trail, whittling, with no Consolation in sight. Viney looked for Hank to take her arm, the way Basil had. 'Twould have been easy enough, each taking a wheel-rut to walk in, except that even a Broadmoor couldn't whittle one-handed.

He whittled all the ways down to Eph's place, and when Viney allowed there was no call to pester Eph and Phebe each time, Hank said there sure wasn't. And whittled the faster, seemed like. The two stood there, leaning against the bars waiting for Amy to come along. They set her on her ways towards Dan'l. And then, my land, if they didn't just stand there on the trail, saying naught and Hank still whittling.

Viney could have stamped with impatience, and it was all she could do not to snatch the knife and throw it into the bushes. There was Amy, gone on ahead out of plain friendship to keep Dan'l busy. There'd be Dan'l, getting mad and madder when he saw 'twas Amy and not Viney come back. And there was herself, in her best tow gown, the new one, next best to her Meeting one, standing here in the woods waiting. And all Hank did was whittle.

"Let me go get an axe and fall you a pine or two. You'll need more whittling wood." She'd not meant to speak so sharp, but there it was.

It was too dark in the woods, for all the moon outside, to see Hank's face. But he threw away the sliver of wood, and clicked shut the blade of his knife and put it in his pocket. Viney edged in a mite closer. But Hank, who could lift a hundred pound of corn with one hand easy, wasn't disposed to heft so much as the weight of her finger. 'Twas plain waste of man and maid and mottled moonlight sifting through the leaves, it was so, and Viney couldn't abide waste. Hank would have to be learned, if courting didn't come natural to him the way it should.

"What say we go sit on the fence in the lower pasture?" she asked. "I'm kind of weary."

"Sure," Hank agreed. Then his voice sounded like he was anxious. "You ain't fixing to be ailing?"

Viney tried to say yes, but she couldn't, not to Hank. Even if she'd knowed how to ail, which she didn't.

"Womenfolks ain't so strong as menfolks." That was the talk Eldest had used on Preacher, and what served once might serve again. No harm in trying.

"Can heft nigh as much as Pa, and work as long." Hank's stride grew stiff, and by the spotty moonlight sifting through the leaves Viney saw him tightening the big muscles of his arms and shoulders just for pride in the feel of them.

"Girls can't heft, not the way menfolks can." Viney held to the same furrow she'd started on.

"Ain't no call why they should. Girls ought to have a man to do the hefting and suchlike. There's knack to hefting. Now see here . . ." Hank stopped beside a granite boulder, swept the leaves off it with his big fingers, and groped for a good handhold. He showed how 'twas wise to keep the legs close together so's not to burst the belly, as strong folks did more often than weaker. Then there was the first lift, just to stir the load and get its feel. Then the real lift, throwing the weight out and away from you, and your head and shoulders back. Next you dropped your knees at the same time as you hoisted. A kind of twist, and the load was chest level, and you straightened knees, and pushed up with both arms.

For a moment he staggered with the great rock at arm's length above his head. Then stood from under as it thudded down.

"Easy as that," he panted. "Onc't you know how."

Too late it was then for Viney to take up his words about girls needing men to do the hefting for them. But she would remember some other time to set Hank to showing his strength again, different ways.

Then the talk trailed off to horses, which was better than nothing, though you couldn't nowise call it courting talk.

They came to the pasture fence and Hank swung himself up. Viney waited hopefully, but it seemed Hank had done with hefting, or only hefted rocks. She climbed up beside him, then pretended to a knot that would harm her tow skirt, and squeezed closer beside him. My land, there was a sight to learn about courting. And Viney wished now she'd watched Eldest and listened more.

Hank didn't shift, but he hooked his toes under a lower rail so Viney's weight wouldn't unbalance him. Viney laid a little more weight upon him. This was the way things ought to be, with the moon, no more than a half face, showing the black outlines of the hills and trees and silvering the smooth pastures. Hank couldn't but admire the pasture, without so much as a berry strand or an aster or goldenrod to mar its thick close turf. But Viney was counting on the moon still more.

Moonlight was for courting, everybody knew that. It stirred the heart of a girl with a happy loneliness. And, if there was a man beside her, it just left the two, man and girl, all alone in the whole wide world. So the man meant more than he'd ever done before, and you knew if you didn't take him you'd take no other, for ever and ever. And if 'twas Hank, sitting there silent, you knew right well he was thinking the same thoughts. About how far the moon was away, and why folks were born, and where did you go when you died; and not caring, just as long as the other would be with you for ever and ever.

Nor the love that was surging within you couldn't come to an end, though maybe it happened to other folk. Nor it couldn't grow old nor weak nor change, for nobody else had ever felt this way. The most they'd ever done was kind of get the first savor of love.

That was why there was so much left for just the two of you. And there couldn't be more, or something inside would burst.

"Vine, I wish you'd say something. 'Tis too wondrous, and I don't know how to say . . . Vine dear . . ."

Viney's foot slipped on the rail below, for she hadn't rightly hitched her toe in it. She would have fallen back, but for Hank's arm. Hank set her upright again, but didn't let go. Nor he didn't let go her name, the new name he had given her.

"Vine dear . . . Vine . . ." He drew her closer still, so the words came from inside his chest, and not his mouth.

There was naught Viney could say, even if she had the breath, which she hadn't. Frighted she was, at what she'd brought out of him, not thinking it had been there all the time. And she aiming to learn Hank courting!

Next off, his mouth wouldn't serve him for words. Nor hers either. Not the way he was kissing. And Viney kissed back, and couldn't not have if she'd tried as hard as she could.

"Never knowed, Vine"—he couldn't let go her name—"a girl was so soft . . . Vine."

"Could be, Hank, you ain't tried so many, Hank dear."

"Only you. And I'm feared to hurt, holding you real close, Vine."

"I'd mend, I'll warrant." Viney laughed, just from pure pride and happiness.

It was Viney who first remembered Amy, up there waiting. And Hank bethought him of Consolation, who had bid him come back betimes. Seemed that the child had thought up a new way to plague. She wouldn't scarce leave the house to go play with the other children, and pestered Isa, who cooked well for a boy, to show her how. She'd stitched her pa's torn shirt together so he couldn't get into it without he cut out the thread again, and she'd cleaned house till nothing could be found, and the dirt that had set harmlessly in the corners since Ma's death was spread all over.

"Pa's in a regular taking over her, not knowing the why of it, and Consolation not telling." Hank lifted Viney down from the fence, making it an excuse for the last hug that nigh to've taken her last breath. "Maybe she'd heed you, Vine, the way she often does. And

I'd like fine for Pa to see how purty you've growed. He ain't seed you for two-three weeks, Vine dear."

Viney promised to visit, and had to hurry back to Amy and Dan'l.

Amy didn't ask where she'd been. Could be 'twas the pride and happiness showing on her face, or the way she said "Hank" when she told he was waiting for Amy up the trail.

Dan'l stood a whiles at the door after Amy had gone. When Viney let slip a "dear," calling him "Dan'l dear," he took no note. And when he turned back he sighed, which wasn't like Dan'l. At most any other time Viney would have been troubled for him. But tonight there didn't seem to be aught to trouble over. Not in the whole wide world.

CHAPTER TWENTY-TWO

PUSSLEY was the meanest weed ever. Leave it and it seeded itself all over the vegetable plot; hoe it and every broken bit grew to be another big weed most as soon as your back was turned. Only way was to loosen it with the hoe, and lift it as though 'twas the most precious thing ever and you aimed to transplant it to the herb garden. Then carry it a ways off and burn it; and even that took doing, so tarnation juicy it was.

Viney finished another row, feeling mean as the old pussley itself. She was dripping wet with sweat, hands grimed and stained, and her hair, that she'd let to grow long just this summer, loosening so a plait hung over one ear.

It wasn't once in a season she felt mad like this, and it was a shame to waste the happening. She flung down the hoe and set off to find the nearest victim. That was Dan'l, down in the hollow, delving a pit that must be the well he'd talked of in the days before he went dumb. Hotter than the bad place, it must be down in that hole, without a touch of the faint breeze that wafted past over his head.

The hole wasn't deepening fast. Dan'l had rigged a kind of hoist so Peter'n' Paul could raise each basketful of earth and rocks that he loosened. Only he'd ought to've asked Viney's help, and would have only he was so obstinate. As it was, with each basketful he had to climb out by the toeholds in the well-sides, lead off the oxen to raise the basket, swing the basket to one side, empty it, lead the oxen back again, then climb back down the well. More than doubled his labor.

"Hot enough to boil a frog." Viney stood by the well-mouth and with a bare foot drifted a little earth down to fall in Dan'l's hair. 'Twould have served better down his neck only he wore no shirt.

Dan'l said nothing, much as he'd have liked to've, no doubt.

244

"Wouldn't be no chore to lead the oxen and empty the basket, but Dan'l would have asked if he'd needed me," she told the placid oxen. 'Twas hard not to help, even without his asking. And if it hadn't been for that cussed old pussley she would have.

Dan'l went on filling the basket.

"Well, you old Peter'n' Paul, it's too hot to stand around talking, and I've took a fancy to go swimming." Seemed like that drew a grunt out of Dan'l, but could be it was the rock he was lifting.

"Coolest spot in all the countryside, Mosquito Hollow, with its shade and its moss, and the trickle of water over the ledge into the deep pool. If I don't drink up the pool first—I'm right thirsty."

Even that didn't pull a word from Dan'l, down there in his oven. Though she listened for it as she went.

Viney felt lifted in spirits. Once in a whiles you had to be outright mean to get the poison out of you. Dan'l just didn't know how, so the poison festered inside. She wouldn't care to be that good, like Dan'l, most never striking out with fist or word. Folks as good as Dan'l didn't get what they should out of life.

Not stopping to shift from her old and patched tow gown, she set off, half running, half walking, down the trail. The breeze stirring the late summer leaves sounded like water already. A small tortoise— she hadn't happened on one in years—crossed her path. She had to hurry on because of the way the water called for her in the deep shady pool. But drawing what spittle she could, for her thirst, she spat over her shoulder and landed a splash on the lumbering little critter's shell. 'Twas ages since she'd done that too. Little'uns always spat on a thing they coveted, whether a bird's egg or a stick or an apple, so other little'uns shouldn't take it from them. She could still remember when Dan'l spat on his first knife. Likely the shelly beast didn't know he was hers now, but all the same she'd look for him on the way home.

A woman growed, and courting too, this might be the last time she would remember what 'twas to be a little'un, or even a young'un. Anxiously her lips puckered to whistle. The notes came clear and loud. She tried whistling through her teeth, and found she still had the trick of it. Could be you had to be married, or with little'uns of your own, before you forgot how.

As she turned off the trail and started to scramble down the steep bank Viney half thought she saw someone among the trees. A trick of shadow, or if not whoever it was would go on and give Dan'l a hand with his well. The soft murmur of what was a roaring waterfall in winter and spring, set her to whistling some more as she caught aholt of a tree root and lowered herself down onto the mossy rocks.

Hot it was, even down here, with the tree-tops nigh to meeting overhead, and making a shadowy tunnel. This was Viney's own swimming pool, other folks used Cold Brook for the most part. Each year the snow flood brought down dead branches and even tree trunks; and each year Viney loosed them, floated them down to the far edge of the pool, and pushed them down the next waterfall. From the smooth water-worn ledge of rock, scoured and polished by winter ice, to the cool green banks of moss and fern, it was all hers, ever since she had first found it. So little she was those days she'd been hard put to climb out again after she'd climbed in. Best of all was the water, churned at one end by the green-white fall from above, and at the other deep and brown and so clear you could count the trout lying at the bottom.

Viney unfastened the thong which held together the neck of the much patched gown, hitched up the skirt and took hold of the bottom hem. She'd skin it inside out and leave it to air on a tree, for it wouldn't bear many more washings, however careful.

Only, she stopped, but half-way skinned. Couldn't be a sound that warned her, for the splash of water drowned even the chirp of birds. But she swung around.

And there stood Basil.

'Twasn't fright made her drop her skirt back, but more like anger that he should try to see her. Anger too that he kept her thirsty skin from the cool water. He was grinning and his mouth was opening and closing.

Seeing she couldn't hear a word, he slid down the bank and came closer. "We'd ought to be friends, Viney, close friends. There's none others around that's fitted for us. Nor we ain't fitted for Cold Brook."

That wasn't the talk she'd expected. Lies of course, a whole pack of lies. But it was hard not to be friends when another asked.

246

"So that's what brought you." She was kind of sharp, though.

"That and your whistle when you turned off the trail above. Knowed right well you'd change your mind. Girls don't stay angered with me long." And then he smirked.

"They don't have to stay angered. The sight of you would anger them afresh. Ain't never seen such a strutting, worthless little cockerel." Viney held herself in, with difficulty. "Told you once to git. I'm telling you again. Git!"

He stepped back a pace, but no more. "Guess I got a right here, same as you. Land don't belong to neither." Then he smirked again. "Guess I'll set and watch. If the water ain't too cold could be I'd join you."

'Twas the smirk did it. That and his setting foot on the damp moss at the water's edge. Viney didn't hardly touch him. Seemed like he just tottered backwards four or five paces, arms windmilling to get his balance, and eyes and mouth opened in plain stark terror. Didn't hardly splash, but just walked right in till the water closed over him.

After that there wasn't much to it. He'd swum across before Viney could gather her a skirtful of rocks the right size for throwing and cross in the shallow water above the fall.

As he scrambled, dripping, up the far bank, she didn't get but one stone home on him, but he let out a scream like a stuck pig. Nor she couldn't get good aim as he dodged through the sumach with her on his heels. Taverner's pasture land was close grazed and open, so she didn't miss with one stone in three, keeping the shots low to his buttocks and legs, not aiming to stun or kill. Then the tow skirt burst, and she had to stop and gather up the stones.

So happened there was no call for further pelting. Taverner's old sow came up from nowhere. Could be she thought from Basil's squeals that someone was tormenting her litter. She set off after.

Viney shouted to Basil to climb one of the apple trees, the way Cat had done once. Sows could be mighty dangerous. But Basil didn't hear nor heed. He cast one glance behind him, hollered again, and set his bruised legs to working the faster. They'd go all the ways home together to the Wilson farm, him and the old sow.

She cast down the stones. Hotter than ever she was now. She

247.

hadn't thought for anything till her gown was hung across a sweet-scented prickly elm, till she'd unbraided her hair, and dived right down to the deepest part of the pool to hold onto a rock just as long as her breath would let.

Up to the surface she floated and drank in deep lungfuls of the cool damp air. Basil had gone just as though there had never been a Basil. He'd gone with the heat and her anger. The pool was hers again and she was Viney Post, who harbored no grudge against man or critter. Only thing, she wished she'd thought now to bring tortoise along. Likely he was right parched with the heat, living so close to the hot ground and carrying that load of shell around on his short legs. She'd have showed him how to dive, if he didn't know already, as he was most bound to, being able to swim. And she'd have pointed out the ledge under the waterfall where he could sit like in a throne and cool himself with the spray. But maybe he was standing waiting for her because she'd spit-marked him for hers. If he was, when she went back she'd bring him right down to the pool. 'Twould be only fair.

Only she wouldn't go back yet. She'd just lie here in the water and think of naught. Just watch a fluttering leaf high up in that oak; watch it minute after minute till there was no more in her head than "leaf . . . fluttering leaf . . ."

No bed, not of the best goose-down, could compare with water for restfulness. If you couldn't outright sleep you could dream.

You could dream that there was Hank, standing on a rock and trying to say something above the sound of the water. The sound that was more of a stillness that took away sound, than a real sound.

You put a hand up out of the water and beckoned, and said: "Come on in. 'Tis fine and warm." As you always did when a little'un, however cold.

Of course he couldn't hear, but he saw the beckon. So his mouth opened like a trout's two-three times, and he looked from the gown to where you floated, and back again to the gown before he set to shedding his clothes. 'Twas real as real the way he was frightened because he was a man, and you no more than a maid.

Hank split the water clean as he used to, way back. Scarce anything but what Hank could do it better than most. You wouldn't need aught other man if you had Hank, not ever. 'Twas the real Hank here in the pool beside her. She'd brought him here by plain wishing, just as now she wished him to kiss her, and he did. The wettest kiss ever, and likely the best.

He'd another tale though, of why he'd come. Of Basil running screeching across the road, with nothing following. Basil yelling back to Viney to save him. Seemed that Hank thought if Basil was dangered she might be too, and ran back the way Basil had come. And hunted till he'd found.

Way back, all that had happened, ages and ages ago, and didn't signify.

She laid a hand across his mouth to still him. Basil and talk of Basil had no place here. And being Hank he asked no questions, but was content to trust that what Viney had done was right, whatever it was. 'Twould be prideful hard never to hurt a man that trusted so, never in all the years ahead.

Just her and Hank with an ocean below, and an ocean to each side, and trees and a rift of blue sky above. The water drawing them together, or maybe 'twas the soft paddle of their hands, like the fins of the trout. The littlest trout nibbling at her belly and toes the way they did, and no more scared of her than she was of Hank. No mite of hurt or harm or ill-will in all the world, seemed like.

"Your hair, Vine. 'Tis floating out behind you like the petals of a flower, only dark. And finer than milkweed floss, Vine."

"There's more to me than my hair, Hank dear. Best see what you're aiming to marry. 'Twouldn't serve for a Broadmoor to buy a pig in a poke."

She laughed, rolled lazily under the surface, swam, a pale shimmering form across the bottom of the pool. She swung up on a rock and swept the hair back from her face and beckoned again. Hank pulled up, awed and dripping, beside her.

"You're so white. Vine dear, excepting your hands and feet and head." He discovered a new reason for surprise. "Ain't nothing else so creamy white, unless maybe June milk."

"Wished now I was whiter, Hank, seeing you like me that way." She turned around once. "I'm strong-backed for a woman that ain't scarce got her full growth. So I shan't need to call you up from the fields whenever there's two-three pails of water to be drawn, or a little'un to be carried."

If Hank was kind of wordless for a lover he'd good eyes to his head and was using them. Viney felt a blush spread down from the brown of her neck to the white of her bosom. But stood her ground. If it pleasured him, the way his face showed, he was heart-welcome to see the all of her. Though 'twas hard to know what she had, compared with him. Wasn't an ounce of him but was good hard meat and bone. Brown to the middle, like an Injun he was, with long muscles jumping out when he so much as stirred a finger, and thighs and legs and feet fitted to carry his weight through a long hard day and have gimp left over at eventide. The hair on his head whited with the sun, and a down on his body that showed golden as a new-hatched chick when the light fell on.

"You're breasted noble as Phebe." Hank found a few words.

"Aim they should be bigger when there's a call for it. Big breasts means plenty of little'uns, Phebe says, and wide hips means easy bearing. We'll need a good-sized farm to feed all the Broadmoor little'uns." Could be menfolk didn't think of those things, so 'twas best they should know from the start-off.

"But you're kind of little round the waist."

Viney laughed. "That's so your arm will go around easier and not tire." She took his arm and put it around, to show. And land sakes, Hank was trembling.

"'Tis nothing, Vine dear. Only you're so purty, Vine. And I hadn't never cal'lated to feel the way I do. 'Tis love, I guess."

Might be at that. For now he'd set her to trembling too. "Best the two of us should go set in the sun awhiles, all the same." For men weren't as strong as they thought; and when it came to ailing, spendthrift of their bodies they were, careless of wet and cold, liable to be sorry after, unless a woman cared for them and checked them.

The well-sunned rock was almost griddle-hot. Viney lay down and shook out her hair to dry. Hank lay down close. Then, and it couldn't be the drift of the water this time, their sides touched, and Viney had his head pillowed between her breasts.

"There's only Cat that's half so comforting to handle." Viney was purring inside most like a cat herself, what with the sun, the water, the cool green of the trees, and the murmur of the waterfall. And Hank of course . . . Hadn't been no more than her own swimming pool when Hank came along. Now 'twas a kind of little heaven, and his and hers both, which made it doubly sweet.

"Ain't there aught I can do for you? Like building you a chair, or suchlike? Or . . ." Unwilling, he sat up and searched around him. "Or hauling the big rocks out of your pool? Or just anything?"

That was how she felt herself. It was in her mind to learn to weave real good and make him a homespun that was close threaded almost as broadcloth itself. "Some day you can build me a loom of my very own."

But that would take time, like her learning to weave. Men hadn't the patience women had, and Hank wanted he should do something now, on this very spot, to show his love. Viney sat up and her hair falling back on her shoulders gave her the answer she sought.

She took his hand in hers and examined it. "Fingers are mighty broad and big," she said doubtfully. "Can you plait?"

Wasn't a thing he couldn't plait or braid, he boasted, from a whiplash to a horse's tail.

Viney wriggled round till her head rested comfortably between his knees. "A braid on each side, please, mister, starting over each ear," she ordered. "And pull out a couple hairs first to bind the ends. Don't seem I've a smitch of thread on me."

Nor she hadn't, and proud she was when Hank joined in and helped laugh at her nakedness.

It was dreamlike still, with Hank's big hands moving tenderly about her head. But there was no time like the present to plan out the future. Being Viney, she chewed on the bitter meat first.

"Pa sends word he'll be back. And we can't be wedded till then." Right or wrong, she couldn't leave Dan'l alone with no help on the house and farm. Maybe Pa would see a way out. Maybe Pa could be got to stop, and take himself another wife. Though it wasn't anyways likely.

Any but Hank would have protested. But Hank knew that a farm must have first call, for without a farm there'd be no food, and without food no life.

Once over that fence 'twas easier going. The Broadmoor acres had woodlot and to spare, that could be cleared for more farm. Or they two could take the Wilson place, likely, for there was talk of Basil leaving. Or they could take title of their own and clear and burn and fence. Viney wasn't so sure she'd care to start right in at the beginning, not after the long years of setting the Post place to rights.

"Pa'll be sorry if you don't come home, Vine. He's got a mighty high notion of you. Seems he don't know how plumb foolish you are, Vine dear."

Viney waited, smiling already. Hank couldn't hold a joke and she knew it.

"Pa said about my courting, 'First time I knowed a Broadmoor show so much sense. But it don't follow that Post Young'un is witless enough to wed with you.'" Hank roared his amusement. "Pa didn't know how witless you'd be, Vine dear. Nor I. Best I could do was hope."

Hank recollected just the way Viney's plaits were brought around front and crossed and back again. As she stood up and patted them, she knew she'd be hard put to make herself unbraid it again and comb. And just for the pleasure of aiding each other he fetched her gown. And she nigh to've throwed him back into the pool helping him into his breeches and shirt. Which set them to laughing again.

Then they turned solemn and almost sad, though not sad to hurt. Could be it was the clothes did that for them.

"'Twon't never be like this day again, Vine dear."

"Not till we're wedded, Hank," Viney sighed.

"And that long off." Hank looked so downcast Viney was bound to cheer him with a kiss. But the kiss only served to tell the two of them once more how long off was the wedding, the farm, and the little'uns they coveted.

When Hank let her go there were tears in Viney's eyes. She turned and ran, lifting her skirt to hurry across the shallows above the falls. Ran most of the way home so Hank shouldn't follow. And half hoping that he would.

Maybe 'twas love.

CHAPTER TWENTY-THREE

ZEPHANIAH POST, his stained white beard parting to the breeze, swung south along the hills to the west of Lake Champlain. Most folks would have shuffled through the late fall dust of the coach trail, or skirted the shoreline. But not Zeph Post, who'd fit Injuns and French and British before there had been road or settler hereabouts. Up here there was most always a cool air sighing through the pines, and deer trails for such as knew how to use them. No easier walking than deer trails, if you'd learned how to slide your feet, and not stomp, the way settlers did.

Old Man Post stooped low to run his sixty-pound pack of choice pelts beneath an overhanging bough, swung his leather-covered legs lightly over a fallen tree, his ancient joints and thin stringy muscles as supple as ever from hard use. He'd admire to see the man down in Cold Brook, where he was heading, who could match him, pace for pace, for a day and a night and a day. Eyes hadn't blurred any either, as they might have done if he'd stayed around and never looked off further than the rumps of the two oxen or the ground at his feet. He'd match anyone at shooting, barring Mary Reed, once Gam had cut new rifling to the old barrel.

'Twas the rifle brung him, much as anything. There were gunsmiths aplenty, but only one Gam Reed to these parts. The rifle had started to throw off, till now it shot all round Robin Hood's barn. Thicker patches didn't remedy it, after a while, for the rifling was wore out. A ball that misses is a ball lost, that can't be melted down and recast. Losing a ball a day for a year meant close to an extra five pounds of lead to be bought and cached and carried atop of the flints and traps and powder and salt and meal and suchlike.

A hunter that wasn't fixing to be a packhorse just had to have the rifling freshened when it got that-a-way.

Anyways, he'd been aiming to back-trail ever since he'd had word through another hunter, and then Peddler, who had dropped in at Fort Ticonderoga and left a message. Eldest was wedded to the preacher, the young feller that came up to hold Meeting at Cold Brook, if memory served. No harm to that, for she was always puny. But the other two, Dan'l and the little girl, they were real Posts and fit for something better than settlers and farmers. He'd ought to've took them with him and learned them the woods, he knowed that now. But all he'd been fit for was to take himself off alone with his sorrow. Ma'd used to say, "Zeph, you're no better than a wild critter, taking your hurts off to lick them." Poor Ma, she hadn't ought to've married him, nor him her. That was truth.

Old Man Post swung over a couple of small ridges, and came out atop Mount Diameter. Hadn't a thing changed, not the deer yard in the hollow, nor the runways, nor the drinking holes. He swung down the hillside, the view in front blanketed by leaves. He couldn't look to find the farm the same though; he had the sense to know that. Ploughland would be grassed over, berry bushes spreading about the pasture, sumach and popple would be head-high already, and deer would have come down for the frosted apples. Only cleared spot would be where the ashes of the cabin and barn had salted the ground so naught would grow for four-five years. And it wasn't as long as that, was it? Didn't seem so.

No settler would covet that ridge-land, not when he could huddle with the other hairless mice down in the settlement. And Zeph Post would as soon have it that way: the place abandoned and going back to what it had been when first he'd scouted it with Rogers' Rangers.

He came out through the last belt of tangled wild grape vines, which always flourish on the edge of a clearing, . . . and jerked up his rifle the way a hunter does first off when surprised. And stared.

Smooth grazed grass right to where he stood, and right down over the curve of the land. A well-fenced vegetable patch with beans and roots and squash aplenty. The new feller had built him his house and barn tucked in close to the corner of the clearing, for shelter. Bigger than Zeph's, it was, and likely the feller had two-three growed

254

sons to help him. No smoke from the stone and clay chimney; but sled tracks and corn trash at the barn door, where hens were pecking, coupled with shouts down over the brow of the land, showed corn was being brought in. The open-ended woodshed was half filled with last year's wood, which showed the feller was forehanded to a fault. Didn't anyone down to the settlement answer to that, unless 'twas Eph Birdsell. But Eph had Den's farm, and wasn't so much as married, let alone having growed sons to help. Must be a stranger had took up the abandoned farm.

Old Man Post turned off up the trail, a mite hurried. Hadn't cal'lated to find no changes of that sort, he hadn't. Could be there was others he hadn't reckoned on.

But for the pack of choice pelts pressing on his shoulders he'd have been tempted to slip back into the woods, silent and unsuspected as a wandering wolf. He had held those skins out when he sent the others down country, and held them out with a purpose. That purpose, and the need for freshening the rifling of his firearm, held his feet to the rutted trail they remembered so well. If his stride shortened and lost its loose swing, 'twas easy explained: a woodsman was no more gaited to cleared lands and roads than a porcupine or a squirrel was.

He could see no change in the coach trail when he came upon it. But Eph looked to've cleared a few rod further into the woodlot on Den Birdsell's old farm. And a woman with a baby on her arm came to the open door and peered out under her hand, though the sun was a mite westerly of noontide already. Old Man Post couldn't rightly recall who she might be. Down the hill and into the huddle of houses about Cold Brook he shuffled, his legs doing naught for themselves, but only as they were bid, and that grudgingly. If he let himself turn about, his stride would lengthen of its own accord, and the old-age weariness drop from his shoulders and his loins. He was sore tempted.

A few folks called greetings, and he answered. Little'uns came running out, stopped and backed up; mistrusting they remembered the long thin man with the rifle and the stained white beard.

Could be he would have walked straight through the settlement and out the other side, and so swung off back into the hills, only for the needs of the rifle. And Gam Reed's big doors were open and a tapping of metal showed he was at work. Gam would know where the Post little'uns were at, and while Gam worked on the rifle Zeph Post would go see them. Gam would likely set other tasks aside and see to freshening the rifling, just for old times' sake. Old Man Post turned off past the big maple, and shuffled in through the double doors.

Gam Reed was filing a part under the window. The tapping came from a likely young woman, her back turned toward the door, forging what looked to be a scissors blade. Gam glanced up over his spectacles, set down the file, took two long paces, and grabbed Old Man Post's thin dark fingers in a true smith's grip. Old Man Post welcomed the hurt, and did his best to grip back. His Adam's apple made a good few trips before he could speak.

"Mighty good to see you, Gam."

There was a clatter of dropped tongs and hammer. And the woman had her arms about Old Man Post, pack, rifle, hunting bag, horn and all. And kissing his cheek she was, he could feel it through his beard.

"Pa! Oh, Pa!" 'Twas his own Young'un pressing tight against him.

He'd have knowed her before, but for his eyesight being kind of dimmed from the force of Gam's handshake. Old Man Post freed his hand and wiped the damp from his eyes with a greasy buckskin sleeve.

His Young'un was worth a sight to see. As upstanding a woman as ever a father took pride in, or a young man coveted. Someone had done a fine job in rearing her in the last years. Likely 'twas Gam and Mary Reed. Could have been her own pa, only he hadn't been nowise fitted to rearing young'uns, no more than he was to farming. He'd been better out the way, a sight better.

"Young'un, there's no call . . ."

"To bite my nails, Pa?" She laughed, still holding him close.

He laughed too, the best he remembered how. There wa'n't much laughter up in the north woods, nor use for it. "No call to squeeze the livin' lights out'n your pa. I got the word you sent me, Young'un, and I come as soon as I could." Then he turned to Gam Reed, and high time, for his sight was dimming again. "I brung along the gun to have it freshened. Ain't another barrel but a Gam Reed would have lasted this long."

Gunsmith took the firearm and set it in the big wood vise, while Viney helped the old man slip the shoulder straps of his pack and hang his bag and horn. She had the bullet mold out of the bag before Old Man Post remembered that it would need altering along with the bore of the gun. She found him a seat on an upturned powder keg, and gave him another hug, just to make sure he was real.

" 'Tis the finest thing ever, Pa, your coming." She took another good look at him. "I'd got to fearing maybe you wouldn't."

Lucky he was he didn't have to answer right then. Gunsmith saved him. Gunsmith knocked out the pins that held barrel to stock, unscrewed the tang and breech-plug, and was squinting down the bore.

"Smooth-worn, but naught else amiss." He scraped out the shoulder of fouling that had formed at the bottom of the breech, passed a wad of tow through once or twice, and set eye to the muzzle end.

"Muzzle not belled by the ramrod, no pitting . . ."

"Don't burn but the best canister powder. Pegou Andrews and Wilkes, when I can get it, or Edinburgh . . ." 'Twas a way of telling Gam how he'd prospered, and how well his pelts had sold.

Gunsmith nodded. "It pays in the long run, it do so. Mary's been using King's powder, made in France, but she'll be glad to see the bottom of the keg." He clamped the barrel in the vise again, fitted a thin hickory guard to the long boring tool, tried it in the barrel, and turned it slowly and carefully. Satisfied, he withdrew it, tried the bore at muzzle and breech with a series of short, ball-shaped reamer bits called cherries. And finding the one that suited, handed it without a word to Young'un.

Then began what Old Man Post had dreaded. Neighbors came hurrying in, led by little Cicero from across the way. Some gripped his hand, some clapped him on the back, some welcomed him home, and all wanted to know how he had fared. 'Twas worse than what he'd dreaded, for he'd reckoned on reproaches, not welcome. And even the womenfolk, when they drifted along, hadn't aught to say but how glad they were he was back again.

"Don't reckon to stay over-long," he wanted to say, "account of fixing up my wintering, and setting out my trap lines." But he swallowed two-three times and gave news of the north, and the price of pelts, and answered to questions was the elk gone for good the way folks said, and would the wolves come down bad this winter.

Gam Reed was fitting the barrel to the rifling bench and aligning it with the slide. Then he ran the grooving rod into the bore. Without waiting to be told Young'un held the point of an awl to the hickory rod to mark the twist of the teeth as Gam drew the slide. Then Gam pushed back the slide and set in the cutting teeth. Young'un went back to cherrying out the mold so it would cast the larger ball that would be needed.

She clamped the cherry head inside the mold, the shank coming out at the sprue hole, set a brace to the square end of the cherry and turned awhile. Then tightened up the clamp to press the sides of the mold closer together, and turned again. 'Twas plain she knew her trade, for Gam Reed didn't so much as cast an eye over the work. Kind of strange for a girl to 'prentice herself to a gunsmith, but Old Man Post recognized that Young'un could have done a sight worse. A good living to the trade, and always would be, and folks didn't come any better than Gam and Mary Reed.

Eldest would be all fixed too, married to Preacher. No glut to a preacher's house, but no starvation neither. "Where's Dan'l at?" asked Old Man Post.

"Up to the farm, Pa, I cal'late." Young'un didn't say which farm, and nobody else thought to tell. Seemed a pa was expected to know where his own son hired out.

The Miller boy, whose name Old Man Post misremembered, offered to run and tell Dan'l his pa was back, but Old Man Post said no call to. Likely Dan'l was busy with fall chores, and he'd go find the boy himself, soon as his rifle was fixed.

He'd do just that. Go see Dan'l, acting innocent, like he was fixing to stop. Then walk right out the valley, taking Dan'l with him if Dan'l was willing. An old wolf like Zeph Post wasn't to be trapped that easy. Only danger was Young'un, saying naught in all the babble of talk, but looking up oncet in a whiles from her task, big-eyed as a deer when you held its head up and drew your knife.

258

She knowed, did Young'un, same as the deer. But she'd leave him go, for the words she'd sent were for him to come home but he didn't need to stay. 'Twould be a sight easier though, if she held her eyes to her work.

* * *

There hadn't been anything so joyful as Pa's home-coming since Viney could remember. And 'twasn't only for pa himself she was glad, but for Dan'l and herself too. If Pa would stop but a week 'twould cure Dan'l of his Pa-this and Pa-that. Pa didn't measure up to twelve feet high and six broad, nor the kind that would raise every chick of a setting and every seed corn in a hill, the way Dan'l remembered. And Pa would say, easy as easy, to marry Hank, once he knowed how Hank and Viney needed each other. Hadn't ever been a mean thought to Pa, even years back when he'd used a strap on her for trying to kill Dan'l with the axe, and on Dan'l for tormenting her with a spotted adder, neither knowing better.

Only Pa didn't seem like he was happy.

He was shifting around on the empty keg, looking this way and that, but mostly at Gunsmith who was reaching well forward with his strong arms to make long steady pulls of the rifling slide. Few there were could draw the rifling rod through a forty-eight-inch barrel in one stroke, and smooth, like cutting butter. But that wasn't what caught Pa's notice. All Pa wanted was to lay hands on his rifle again and light out, away from all these folks and their chatter. You couldn't blame him, not being used to such in the woods. Maybe she could help.

She made excuse to cleave a way through the throng and set the lead ladle on the forge. And passing Pa she whispered, "Want we should come back when Uncle Gam's finished the freshening?"

But Pa said, obstinate as Dan'l, "I cal'late to stay put." And sat there, leaning forward, fingers spread on thin knees, raising first one hand and then the other like a horse that's itching to go. Gunsmith made cut after cut till he had all eight scored out, resharped the teeth, set them up a shade with packing, and went to cutting again. And still Pa didn't shift nor speak, except to answer.

Till Simpkin Higgins came in with Amy. Then Pa stood up and reached for his pack of pelts, and said, proud as a turkey, "Sim

259

Higgins, I cal'late to be owing you all these years for seed and such-like. I aim to pay." He carried the pack to a workbench, loosed the fastening, and spread last winter's pelts. Big and prime they were, as folk's faces showed; beaver and marten and suchlike. Pa had a right to pride himself.

But Sim Higgins hadn't much as set hand to them when Cicero Ditch called out, " 'Tis paid in full, Zeph Post." And told how at that first harvest Sim was part paid and part outwitted.

Cicero slapped his knees and shouted with laughter as he recalled the doings, and other folks laughed too. Even Sim Higgins grinned and showed his yellowed teeth, bearing no ill-will. But Pa just kind of shrunk in on himself. And when they got to telling what a great little farm the Post place had become, hoping to pleasure him, Pa slunk back to his perch on the empty keg. Like he'd fought and been licked. Maybe others didn't see him that way, but a daughter could.

He tried again, did Pa, when Aunt Mary came in from testing a couple of pieces, set them in the rack, hung up horn and bag, and stripped off apron and leather sleeves. Pa didn't so much as wait for her greeting, but said, "I cal'late to be owing you and Gam for this very rifle, and the freshening he's doing now, and other things besides. I've pelts here to pay."

Aunt Mary made show of not knowing what Pa asked. And told him to come out from behind those north woods, or was it a beard? so she could see what he said. When he got obstinate and appealed to Uncle Gam, it seemed Aunt Mary knowed all right what he said, for she claimed there was too much owing 'twixt the Posts and the Reeds, on both sides, to strike a balance, then or ever. Aunt Mary could be right sharp when she chose, and she chose now. Poor Pa sat back on the keg, like he'd put up the best fight he knowed how, but been bested again.

Pa was acting the spitting image of Dan'l, different as they were to look at. And Viney wondered if it could be . . . and then she knew it was . . . knew what Pa was fighting.

She called Amy with a beckon, and under pretence of showing the new-cast ball, its lead shining like polished pewter, told her to run and hold Dan'l, and not to breathe a word of Pa's coming. Amy slipped out, without stopping to ask so much as a question. The best friend ever, was Amy.

The test ball fitted the new bore with just the right slack, and Viney's work was done. She went to stand by Pa while Gunsmith finished the last pulls of the rifler. Likely Pa had need of her. He had, right off.

Hepziba Ditch was joking Pa, did he aim to take him a new wife, now he was back.

"Pa don't aim to stop long enough this fall." Viney told it so certain sure that none asked how she come to know Pa's plans. Pa straightened up a mite, or seemed to.

"There's naught to do on the farm from now till spring, and Pa's done so good he cal'lates to be gone another winter." Viney held to the same trail. "And there's his traps and his canoe, and his credit at Ticonderoga, and stores and all. And his partner too." Could be he had a partner, though 'twasn't like, Pa being that independent.

Folks drifted off, saying they would see Zeph Post before he lit out again. And Gunsmith screwed in the breech-plug, and fixed barrel to stock. Old Man Post left a beaver skin for payment—he wouldn't be denied—packed up the other pelts, and set off with Viney, up the road.

A few little'uns sought to follow. Viney scatted them, and they scat. Viney fell into step beside her pa and caught his arm close against her. Thin the arm was, from his eating little but meat. Once she had him home she'd start to corn-fatten him and store a layer of winter grease inside his ribs against the coming cold. It lay with womenfolk to keep their menfolk in good fettle.

Only . . . only Pa wasn't to be let come home, that was the size of it. Not this fall, anyways. Pa was like Dan'l, he'd no dependence on himself. He'd done mighty good hunting and trapping, and that had given him the heart to come down and pay his debts and see his young'uns, thinking 'twould set him free. But it hadn't, for he'd found his debts had been paid for him. And now 'twas as though that put him to owing Dan'l and herself; and Eldest, too, though you couldn't always call her to mind now she was married and gone.

Pa had come, not aiming to stop. But the debts had bested him, and the talk of how Dan'l and Viney had labored without any help to set the farm to rights, had bested him again. And the way folks were counting on him to stay had bested him once more. Just the way the farm had licked him, years back. Viney could see it all, plain as plain.

So, left to himself, Pa would stop awhiles. And likely there'd never be another happening like Ma's death and the house burning, to set him free again. Not ever. Poor Pa.

Poor Dan'l too. With his dependence on a pa who never was, and couldn't be. If Dan'l saw Pa now, and saw what he really was, he'd be like a wild grapevine that'd grown up around a dead tree, only to find the tree crumble under him. Dan'l had got to grow to be something stouter than a grapevine, more like an old hickory, and learn a pride in himself, before his pride in pa could rightly be taken from him.

Two bested menfolk in one house, working one farm. It couldn't be let to be. But it lay with Viney, and none else, to stop it.

"Seems like I could carry that pack a ways," Viney suggested. "Till you turn off north."

That stopped Pa in his tracks. "I hadn't thought to . . ." He said no more, but slid out from under the shoulder straps and Viney took the pelts.

Even now she didn't need to let Pa go. A word of how he was needed would make him stay, just as a word had set him to thinking of going. They came opposite the Birdsell place.

"Likely you remember Eph, Pa. He wedded Phebe Callender that helped out at the Tavern, and they've a little'un and hoping for another. Making out mighty good, is Eph, having a trade atop of his farming. He reckons chairs and furniture is a sight easier sold than corn and suchlike."

And talk of Eph's trade gave her a right smart idea. "Could be, Pa, you'll take Dan'l north some winter so he can make more profit on his pelts. Trapping and shooting ain't so good in these parts. Take him as a partner, belike, and show him the how of it."

Viney clinched the plan. 'Twould be mighty thrifty, she said. Better than all-year farming, with the farm idle half the year on account of the cold.

Old Man Post had to stop and look his daughter over from head to toe. "Cal'late to handle a sixmonth's chores and fend for yourself while Dan'l's away?"

No more to it than to say sure she could, to set Pa a ways further along the trail. But closer he reached to the farm, the shorter his stride, and the more he glanced off to the north. Most within sight of the house through the leaves, Pa halted again.

"No call to go pestering Dan'l now, seeing I'll be back next fall . . . and I got a long ways to trail afore nightfall . . . and the pelts are for you and for Dan'l and Eldest, share and share alike . . ." Pa was pattering off his words like there wasn't a breath to spare afore the Injuns charged down. "An' . . . an' I'm more thankful than a pa had ought to be to his own young'un."

A last hug with all Viney's young warmth. Then Old Man Post was swinging, free as a deer, up the hillside. A last moment when Viney could still have brought him back with call or whistle. Then that chance was gone. And not till then did Viney dare let herself think what she had done.

'Twas Hank, not Pa, that the leaves closed over and hid from sight. 'Twas Hank and not Pa she'd let leave her, most driven away. And Pa would come back next fall, but like as not Hank was gone forever.

If Pa had been let to stop, he and Dan'l could have made out someways, and left her free to marry Hank. Pa could have taken himself a wife, and easy. For there were plenty of widows to marry a good farm. And she couldn't ask Hank to wait a whole year and maybe more. Not when the delay was of her own making. Fair's fair; she'd have to set him on to marry Amy, for they'd always been good friends, and he could do a sight worse. Amy wouldn't be fool enough to stay home just to tend an old farm. Besides, her pa, Simpkin Higgins, made a fair living from trading.

Viney's knees had gone soft as summer candles. Could be 'twas the weight of the pelts; she cast them down. At that she had to sit down on a rock, though the rock minded her of Hank and the way he'd shown her how to heft.

Cat came up out of nowheres and climbed up on her lap. Just to tell her what all kinds of a fool she'd been; for Cat took all that claws and teeth could get him.

Viney couldn't weep; there was no more than an emptiness where her heart had been. And there'd always be an emptiness without Hank. Only one thing she coveted now, and that was darkness, so Dan'l and Amy should not see her face. She would bide here till then, and think of what 'twould be to stay an old thornback all her life.

CHAPTER TWENTY-FOUR

AMY HIGGINS patted her curls in place, gave her hot face a wipe around with the new apron, and called in her nicest voice, "Dan'l! Dan'l Post!"

Dan'l straightened his back and looked up from under his cornshuck hat. He laid down the big corn knife and started towards her. Then he turned back. But only to drop the yoke from the oxen, drive them from the corn patch and put up the bars behind them. Dan'l leaving his work in midafternoon! 'Twas scarce to be credited.

"You sure despise me, don't you, Dan'l? Everlasting pestering after Viney, when you've work to do." Amy smiled her best, and let Dan'l get the full of it.

"Ain't saying, but could be I don't. Could be I . . . But I aint saying." He took his eyes off her. "Seeing you're here you'd best come up and set awhile."

Dan'l followed up to the house, not speaking; and carried out a puncheon stool, when she allowed she'd take the breeze in the shade of the east side, instead of waiting indoors. And when she said how dry it was, Dan'l was bound he must fetch her a dipper of water; and when he found the water in the piggen was warm he set out and drew fresh for her from the pool in the woods.

"You're little, Amy," he excused himself. "And you ain't got the strength you ought."

If that was the kind of girl he fancied, she was glad she was little. And she'd not let him see how easy she carried two big pails of water. If 'twas helplessness he craved, 'twas easy learned from her ma, for there wasn't an ounce of Ma's two hundred and eighty pound that stirred, if it could rest.

Dan'l sprawled out his legs on the close-cropped grass beside her, his back against the house logs. He took off his hat, not needing it in the shade, and made to skim it away. Amy stretched out her hand and he reached the hat to her.

Close plaited it was, each corn husk shredded to no wider than a grass blade. Amy admired it. "Can set your hand to most anything, can't you, Dan'l?"

"C'n make shift," he admitted.

" 'Twould suit me purty." Amy placed it on her head, carefully setting a curl to show on each side her forehead. "You'll have to be my mirror, Dan'l, and tell me how 'tis." She cocked her head this way and that like a robin listening for worms.

" 'Tis only an old hat," Dan'l gulped. "Cal'late to make you a better after freeze-up."

Amy lifted the hat and set it on her knees, shook out her curls again, and watched Dan'l from the corner of her eyes. If he favored curls there'd be more for him next time, though she had to tear curl rags from Pa's old shirt. And it looked like Pa's old shirt was as good as gone already, for Dan'l hadn't the art to hide his thoughts, no matter how tight he buttoned his mouth.

She sat there, and sat, Dan'l's hat on her knees, as still as a cold corn pudding. Bound she was she'd make Dan'l break silence, and not just answer her words.

"Viney, she ain't never to home these days, not when you come. I dunno why." Her silence drew it from him.

Amy spared him a glance before looking off again at the hills, their eastern slopes beginning to darken with long shadows. But there was no guile to Dan'l's words, nor suspicion in his head. Amy saw how it might serve her to plant a suspicion there.

"Don't seem I'd ought to come here no more, unless Viney's to come with me. Tongues are beginning to wag, and Pa threatened to strip and strap me; only he dursn't, now I'm growed." She slewed her head a mite to see Dan'l's face. "Pa says I'm running around courting."

"Kinda comical." Dan'l came close to a laugh. "Your pa don't know that it's here you visit, and that there's none but me and Viney, and sometimes no Viney neither."

"Maybe"—Amy chose her words right careful—"'tis Hank he suspicions."

Dan'l sat bolt upright. "Hank? Hank! Then Hank ain't courting our Viney?"

"Maybe he is, maybe he isn't." Amy kept her eyes fixed on the bare dead pine atop Cobble Hill. "Don't seem he'd be fixing to marry the two of us."

"Hank ain't that bad!" Dan'l scrambled to his feet and paced around like a calf on a tether. "No, Hank ain't that bad," he insisted.

Amy dropped her glance from the summit of Old Cobble, but lifted it back there each time Dan'l turned face towards her. She had kindled the straw under Dan'l's belly and got him to his feet, and now she'd best give him a prod to keep him stirring.

"If so be we've angered you, me and Hank, we didn't aim to. And of course we can go visiting some place else." She looked down over the well-tended farm, and an honest longing crept into her voice. "Only 'tis so purty up here, with the fields and the fences all fixed the way they ought. Not like to home, all weeds and wilderness. And the oxen and the cow and calf nigh to busting outen their hides with contentment. It ain't just Hank, nor Viney neither, I come to visit with. If they'd never been born, I'd still hanker to come. If so be I was let."

If that wasn't clear as clear! Any woman would have caught her meaning. But all Dan'l could do was mutter, "If only 'twasn't Hank. If only 'twasn't Hank!"

Amy summoned a laugh and said, "Ain't nobody so set agin marriage as Dan'l Post. First it's Hank ain't to court his Viney. Next it's Hank ain't to court Amy Higgins, who's no kin to Dan'l Post, and no more than a neighbor. Kind of a dog in the manger, ain't you, Dan'l? Not aiming to marry and not willing others should. Seems Viney and me had best get you a girl of your own, so you'll let us be."

Amy had a head on her shoulders, as even her pa allowed. Dan'l was scairt, she saw plain, and in a minute his eye would light on some task that called to be finished before sundown. "Something's keeping Viney," she said. "Cal'late to go indoors and redd up for her a mite."

And Dan'l, eased of his immediate fears, picked up the stool and followed her in, just as she'd intended.

Indoors it was eventide already and the fire had ought to be drawn up and the supper set to cook. But, for all of Amy Higgins, Dan'l should eat no crumb till he had come to an accounting. For 'twas one thing to know his thoughts, and another to make him set words to them. She'd have him say them though, if she had to set them in his mouth and draw them out after. She would so. And before Old Man Post, his pa, came traipsin' along to spoil all.

She set down slap at the table and planted her elbows. And Dan'l, just as she willed he should, drew a stool to the opposite side. Dan'l couldn't set without leaning, and that brought his face so nigh hers she could most feel his sigh on her cheek. That sigh was worth the best of her laying hens, for it told once more what she'd suspicioned for months, and knowed right well today. 'Twas two to one, Dan'l and her against Dan'l alone.

Far away she started her talk, so Dan'l shouldn't shy off. "Pa still claims there ain't nobody to these parts ever out-traded him but Dan'l Post. So seems like if you was to trade with Hank you'd come out best."

Then she started way off again, but leading in to the same spot. "Womenfolk will take what they're minded to have and ask no by-your-leave. But menfolk are more law-abiding. Could be they set too much stock on their honesty." She hadn't reckoned on Dan'l's friendship with Hank to be such a sight of trouble.

"First off, if I was Dan'l Post, I'd let on I knowed Hank was seeking a wife. Next, I'd draw the talk around to Viney and tell she was sound in wind and limb, and a good worker on flat and hill. Then I'd tell truth, but belittling, of what I aimed to trade for. I'd say the one I coveted was knowed to bite and kick, and didn't nowise come up to Viney in size and weight. If I was Dan'l Post I'd have Hank promise to throw in a calf for good measure, afore I clasped hands on the bargain and led my critter off."

If Amy's face had flushed up, Dan'l couldn't see it in the failing light. And anyways he nigh to have fallen off his stool when he caught her meaning.

"You're not courting with Hank?" Like a prayer he made it

sound. Amy hadn't even to shake her head, for Dan'l knowed now, without her telling.

His breath came nearer her cheek. She sat waiting. "I ain't never kissed a girl, Amy . . ."

"Best try then. I've kissed Viney scores of times, and a Post ain't poisoned me yet. Nor me a Post."

" 'Twould be a way to start in courting." Dan'l sounded hopeful.

"And a right smart way to keep on," Amy encouraged.

Dan'l grabbed for her over the table, and she didn't back up any. If it wasn't the best kiss ever, it served well for a start-off, and Dan'l could set his hand to most anything, once he had the hang of it.

"If I ain't doing right, Amy, you got to say."

Amy took another grip on him. "Cal'late to say a heap in the years to come," she warned him. "I'm a right managing woman." And she started in right then and there, telling Dan'l to light the candle. She'd admire to see Dan'l's new happiness show in his face, since he hadn't the words to tell it.

Even if Dan'l did blow woodash right out the fireplace, he had a splinter kindled, and the candle alight, and was back at the table faster than he'd ever done a bidding before. He looked right into Amy's face, grinning proud as Punch.

"Don't aim to swap Hank for what I got already," he boasted. "Hank's welcome to Viney, and if he only knowed it I'd throw in the farm and everything, and start afresh, just so I got you."

Amy pressed her hands to her hot face. "Wait till I tell Pa the way a Higgins has out-traded a Post," she boasted in turn. "He'll reckon the old score well evened."

* * *

That was Hank's footfall on the darkening trail. Viney picked up the pelts and lit out for home; Hank wouldn't come inside, that was a blessing. He would wait on the trail. 'Twould be the last time he'd wait for Viney Post. After this 'twould be for Amy Higgins.

She ought to put a face on it, to go in whistling and singing, seeing she brought news of Pa, and a fine bundle of pelts. But she couldn't compass a note. Likely it wouldn't be needed, for Dan'l would be down in the fields, and Amy with him.

But when she came out of the woods there was candlelight show-ing. And inside were Dan'l and Amy. Viney dumped the pelts on the table and turned her face away. "Pa's been down to Uncle Gam's, and says he'll be back next fall. Pelts are for Eldest and us."

She told it short as she could and bent down to the fire, which needed tending. Amy hadn't done a hand's turn all this time, which wasn't like her.

Dan'l pushed the pelts to one side, not even loosing the rawhide ties. "If Pa says he'll be back, he's like to. Ain't he, Amy?"

Teasing up a few small embers from deep under the ash, laying whittlings across them, Viney knew she'd got so she wasn't even hearing aright, but only imagining. Dan'l wouldn't ask Amy if Pa was like to keep his promise, he'd come right out with "Pa ain't like to break his word," or suchlike.

Then Hank burst in. Not Dan'l, nor any other, he shouted, was going to keep Viney from him. Dan'l or no Dan'l, he was bound he'd have word with Viney herself, and find out what'd been amiss so long. Viney heard him shout it, but she only reached for the meat kettle that Amy'd ought to have set to heat long since.

Amy chirped up with, "Dan'l don't hold with courting."

"Don't aim to stop Hank courting." Dan'l stayed put, at the table, and was looking at Amy, not Hank. "That's for Viney to say, will she or won't she."

And Dan'l was right, though how he'd come to know passed understanding. It lay with Viney to say "No" to Hank as soon as she had the power to. Which she hadn't yet. But she had got so she could take notice again, and Dan'l was acting mighty queer. Grinning from ear to ear he was, like he'd said something mighty comical.

"Amy here has drove a little horse-sense into me." That was Dan'l again, fair bursting with talk tonight. "No knowing why, excepting she covets the farm, and has started right in to train the livestock."

Amy give him a look. "A farm don't prosper with two masters. Nor two mistresses neither." Seemed like that last was aimed at Viney. "Not but what Dan'l and me won't be glad to see Young'un. Hank and her'll always be heart-welcome."

Viney hadn't thought she could suffer any more, for there hadn't seemed aught left in her that words could tear. But it seemed Amy, her best friend, had the power to take the last happiness from her. The farm, and Dan'l, for which she had sacrificed herself, were to be taken from her now. Viney had let Pa go for the sake of Dan'l and the farm. She had let Hank go . . .

But Hank hadn't gone yet. She looked across to where he stood.

And for all she tried, her feet followed her glance till she stood beside him. He was still here, he was still Hank, and still needing her, if ever man needed woman.

Hank took her hand, seemingly without knowing it, which he might, his hands being so big. "But Dan'l said he don't hold with courting?" Puzzled he was, and with reason.

Dan'l shook his head, still grinning from ear to ear. "Nor me nor Amy don't. But as Amy said, just before you two came in, there ain't but one sure way to stop courting, and that's wedding. Amy and me cal'late to wed right soon."

Of a sudden Viney knew she must get outside. The room wasn't big enough for all she felt, with the joy yeasting up inside her. And there was the moon shining through the window, dimming the little beam of the candle. She'd ought to stop and see to Dan'l's food, but if he felt toward Amy the way she felt toward Hank likely he wouldn't notice the lack of supper. And from now on Dan'l was Amy's care.

Could be she went out and Hank following, or the other way round; it didn't concern so long as they were together, and never would from now on. And they were fixed for real courting, and the talk of the little'uns they aimed to raise and the new farm and . . .

Then she remembered and turned back in, just for a moment. Amy was the best friend ever, and but for Amy she wouldn't have Hank. Amy would want courting same as any other woman. And if Dan'l thought he'd be let to sit across the table and tell Amy about his crops and critters, and the new well and suchlike till they were wedded, he'd ought to be learned better.

They hadn't shifted, Amy and Dan'l, except to join hands. Viney gathered up a smitch of spittle and took breath. She sighted on the candle flame. Then, *pfft!*

"Moonlight's for courting," she told the moon-flooded room. She couldn't abide waste, could Viney. Not of candle *nor* moonlight.